Michelle Douglas has been writing for Mills & Boon since 2007, and believes she has the best job in the world. She lives in a leafy suburb of Newcastle, on Australia's east coast, with her own romantic hero, a house full of dust and books and an eclectic collection of sixties and seventies vinyl. She loves to hear from readers and can be contacted via her website: michelle-douglas.com.

Faye Acheampong's journey as a romance author began in 2015, when she shared her creative writing online out of boredom. She has also experimented with playwriting, screenwriting and written roleplay, and is always searching for ways to expand her love of storytelling. In 2022 she was announced as the winner of Mills & Boon's Love To Write Competition, hosted in partnership with Amber Rose Gill. Faye lives in London, but regularly daydreams about moving elsewhere. Visit fayeacheampong.com to find out more. You can also follow Faye on Instagram @fayeacheampong and X @fayeursoquiet.

T0364466

SECRET FLING WITH THE BILLIONAIRE

MICHELLE DOUGLAS

PRINCE'S REUNION IN PARADISE

FAYE ACHEAMPONG

MILLS & BOON

First published in Great Britain 2024
by Mills & Boon, an imprint of HarperCollins*Publishers* Ltd,
1 London Bridge Street, London, SE1 9GF

www.harpercollins.co.uk

HarperCollins*Publishers*, Macken House, 39/40 Mayor Street Upper,
Dublin 1, D01 C9W8, Ireland

Secret Fling with the Billionaire © 2024 Michelle Douglas

Prince's Reunion in Paradise © 2024 Faye Acheampong

ISBN: 978-0-263-32144-9

12/24

This book contains FSC™ certified paper and other controlled sources to ensure responsible forest management.

For more information visit www.harpercollins.co.uk/green.

Printed and Bound in the UK using 100% Renewable Electricity at CPI Group (UK) Ltd, Croydon, CR0 4YY

SECRET FLING WITH THE BILLIONAIRE

MICHELLE DOUGLAS

MILLS & BOON

To all of my wonderful readers.

To those who leave reviews,
who write to tell me they love my books,
and to those who push my books into the hands of
their family and friends and order them to read them.

From the bottom of my heart, thank you!

CHAPTER ONE

CLEO DUCKED DOWN an alley, her heart pounding and her breath fogging the early-morning January air. How had they tracked her down so quickly?

Because they knew you'd go to Fairfield House.

Seeking shelter in the family home in Maida Vale hadn't worked out the way she'd hoped. Her father had woken her precisely thirty-seven minutes after she'd finally fallen asleep to tell her he was tired of her 'attention-seeking behaviour' and that she'd need to find an alternative hiding place.

Apparently an upcoming election was more important than a daughter in need. Especially one as troublesome as her.

Happy New Year to you too, Dad. Her eyes stung. She told herself it was from the cold.

Footsteps sounded in the chill air and she flattened herself in the alcove of a doorway, holding her breath when they halted at the top of the alley. They moved on and she instantly sped down the alley on silent feet, grateful to be wearing soft-soled ballet flats. Her feet might be freezing, but at least her footsteps were silent.

The alley led down to the canal path in Little Venice. Pulling the brim of her hat down low, she turned left and prayed it was the right choice. Seizing her phone, she started to dial a number...

Thumbs and feet both faltered. Margot wouldn't come to

her aid, not this time. In fact, if Cleo messed this up, her sister might never speak to her again.

A lump the size of Fairfield House lodged in her throat. Why hadn't she controlled her temper, why hadn't she...?

Enough.

There'd be time for regrets later. She could whip herself with them then. In the here and now, she needed to focus on not landing on the front pages of the tabloids *again*.

On the path up ahead, another photographer appeared. His back was to her, but he'd turn around any moment. Behind her, she heard the approaching footsteps of the first photographer. Once they reached the path, she'd be cornered. Twisting her hands together, she scoured her surroundings. A wall at least eight feet high towered to her left. She had no hope of scaling it. To her right was the canal. She could swim it. It'd be freezing, but...

Oh, and pictures of you splashed across the front pages of the dailies swimming in the canal in January will make Margot's day, huh?

That'd be worse than today's front page!

Nothing is worse than today's front page.

Her heart pounded in her ears. She needed an escape hatch if she didn't want to ruin her relationship with her sister forever...

She couldn't go forward.

She couldn't go back the way she'd come.

There was an un-scalable fence one way, the canal the other, with canal boats...

She blinked. An open door on a canal boat named *Camelot* beckoned like a bright star.

Not giving herself time to think, Cleo shot across the path and leapt onto its rear deck, the thin soles of her ballet flats slipping on the slick, dew-laden surface, her arms windmilling wildly and her phone flying from her hand to land in the canal with a soft splash.

Don't fall in the water! Don't fall in the water!

Launching herself through the door, she half-slipped down a set of stairs on her backside—not elegant, but certainly efficient.

A lone man glanced up from reading the paper at a dinette. Her picture glared back at her from its front page in silent accusation. Still on her backside, she shuffled to the side behind an arm chair—out of view of anyone who might peer through the door. Lifting a finger, she held it to her lips, then pressed her hands together in a silent plea that he not give her away.

Leaning back, he closed the paper, his gaze briefly resting on the front page. Glancing back, he gestured for her to remove her sunglasses. She did. She had no control over the way her eyes filled, though. Blinking hard, she gritted her teeth, determined to not let a single stupid tear fall. He looked as if he wanted to swear. She wholly sympathised.

Grinding back what sounded like a muttered curse, he eased out from behind the table with remarkable grace for such a large man—not that he was brawny, just tall and rangy. Something inside her give a soft sigh of appreciation. She slapped it hard.

'Hello?' someone called from outside.

Mr Tall, Dark and Scowling started for the door. Praying he wouldn't pick her up on the way and dump her at the waiting journalist's feet, she seized a beanie resting on the arm chair and held it out to him with an apologetic grimace. It was cold out.

He pulled it on over thick dark hair that looked incredibly soft and...

'Hello?' the journalist called out again.

Blue eyes turned winter-frigid. Swallowing, she handed

him her sunglasses before he could turn her to ice. He shoved them on his nose and stomped up the steps.

''Scuse me, mate, have you seen a woman come past?'

Her stomach shrivelled to the size of a small, hard walnut. *Please don't let him give me away.* She closed her eyes and crossed everything.

'Look, *mate*, only thing I've seen...'

Her eyes flew open at the thick Geordie accent that emerged from her reluctant rescuer's mouth. Had he travelled by canal boat all the way from Newcastle? Was that even possible? If so, he was a long way from home.

She shook herself. What did any of that matter?

Focus, Cleo.

'What did you see?'

'A lad scaling that wall there.'

'Could it have been a woman?' The hungry greed in the journalist's voice nauseated her.

'Hard to tell. I called the authorities. Seemed dodgy. And, speaking of dodgy, who the hell are you, and what are you doing chasing some woman? Think it's time I called the authorities again.'

Her tensed muscles released and she rested her forehead on her knees. He wasn't going to blow her cover.

Thank you. Thank you. Thank you.

'No, no, I'm just leaving. Not causing any harm. Just an interested bystander.'

Footsteps moved away at a fast clip. Lifting her head, Cleo buried her face in her hands and let out a shaky breath.

Her rescuer closed the door and strode past her to drop the beanie and sunnies onto the table, before filling a kettle and setting it on the hob. Only then did he turn to her, hands on hips, and she had to crane her neck up, up, up to meet his gaze. He gestured to the dinette and she scrambled to her feet, taking a seat.

'You're going to have to wait an hour if you want to give them the slip.'

And then what? They'd be waiting for her at her flat. Her girlfriends' places would all be staked out. 'Thank you for not giving me away.'

He made tea and slid a mug across to her. He didn't ask her how she took it. And he remained standing, leaning against a kitchen bench, one ankle crossed over the other as he blew on his tea.

She took a sip of her tea, welcoming the warmth even if it was strong, black, unsweetened and not what she was used to. The newspaper he'd been reading rested on the table in front of her, a reminder that she'd once again shamed her family. Those days were supposed to be in the past!

Except apparently they weren't. Tears scalded her eyes. She gulped tea and welcomed the burn on her tongue. 'You recognised me.'

He shrugged.

She gestured down at herself. Ditching her usual uniform of jeans and blazer, she'd raided Margot's wardrobe for a pair of sensible black trousers and a caramel-coloured sweater, before piling her hair up beneath a cloche hat. 'I was hoping this would be enough of a disguise to pass unnoticed until I'd reached…safety.'

Except nowhere was safe, not from the press. If the last eight years had taught her anything, it was that.

'Maybe if you hadn't appeared in the morning paper…'
If.

Guilt, regret and remorse all pressed down on her.

She straightened, registering that his accent had disappeared. Had he assumed it? What an excellent idea!

Glancing up, she caught his scowl, and her shoulders inched towards her ears. 'I'm really sorry I crashed onto your boat like I did. I was cornered…desperate.' She fought the urge to rest her head on her arms. Without meaning to, she spread mayhem and annoyance wherever she went.

'Forget it.'

If anything, his scowl deepened, but the unexpected largesse—gruff though it might be—slipped beneath her guard. She had to blink hard again. She gulped tea as if it might save her.

'Was he worth it?'

'Who?'

Reaching across, he turned the paper over and pointed to her photo. The gesture lifted his rolled-up shirtsleeve to expose a forearm roped with muscle. A tic started up inside her, but she squashed it flat. She'd learned her lesson, thank you very much—men were *off* the agenda.

Turning the paper to face her, she gave a startled laugh. 'Wow, I really did land a good punch, didn't I?'

'I'd have been proud of it.'

For the briefest of moments one corner of his mouth twitched and she held her breath, but it came to nothing, his face settling back into stern lines.

She sobered too. 'He'd just told me he'd been fooling around with someone *close to me*.'

She drained her tea. He filled it again from the teapot.

'I was as angry with myself as I was with him, though. I'd tried breaking up with him a month ago, but he convinced me not to. Told me he loved me.' Something he'd never done before. 'I was trying to be mature—relationships aren't all rainbows and unicorns, blah blah blah—compromise, put the work in...'

'You sound like a self-help manual.'

Her back straightened. 'I've read them all.' She'd done her homework and had put in the hours. She was on Road Straight and Narrow now. 'For all the good it's done me.' She scowled at her tea. 'Men suck.'

'That one does. Though for the next week it'll probably be through a straw.'

She barked out another laugh, immediately clapping a hand over her mouth. Pulling it away, she shook her head. 'I'm through with all of it. Romance is dead.' The sooner she faced that fact, the better.

'Good for you.'

She eyed him over the rim of her mug. 'Are you laughing at me?'

'Nope.' Pushing away from the kitchen bench, he slid onto the seat he'd been occupying earlier. 'I just agree that romance and relationships aren't the be all and end all. Too many people define their worth through them rather than in more stable things. So when things go belly up...' he shrugged '...they don't have the resources to deal with it.'

She didn't know if he meant the comment to be pointed or not but, given her past romantic mistakes, she'd deserve it if he did. And she'd take it on the chin.

She'd thought that she'd drop out of the public eye when she'd stopped acting two and a half years ago. The men she'd dated since, however, had ensured that had never happened. It meant a lot of people who'd never met her and didn't know her made assumptions about her. And she'd take that on the chin too because, in shielding her from those journalists, this man had saved her butt.

She shivered. She really needed to start making better decisions. Whatever she was searching for, it wasn't to be found in any of the places she'd been looking. She'd thought walking away from acting would change everything. It had changed some things, but not all. Her stomach churned: because *she* was the problem. She kept making the same mistakes. How stupid and self-delusional could one person be? She'd honestly thought Clay had been the one.

Don't think about that now.

'In my experience, love is an exercise in deception, disillusion and despair. We'd all be better off without it.'

Whoa. Talk about cynical.

He shrugged at whatever he saw in her face and she shook herself.

Focus on the practicalities.

'So…a quick question.'

He tensed.

'An easy one, I think. If I dropped my phone in the canal…?'

'Gone for good.'

She'd guessed as much.

'Need to ring someone?'

She nodded.

Reaching behind him, he stretched one long arm across the kitchen bench to open a drawer and fish out a mobile phone. He set it in front of her.

Picking it up, she dialled Margot's number and left a message. 'My sister,' she explained, her heart giving a sick kick. 'She won't answer a call from an unknown number. But she'll listen to the message and call me back in under sixty seconds.'

She set the phone on the table and started counting back from sixty. The phone rang when she reached forty-four. She glanced at the man and he gestured for her to answer it.

'Cleo?'

'Hi, Margot.'

'You lost your phone?'

'Afraid so. I was—'

'I don't want to hear about it! Just tell me the press don't have it?'

'The press don't have it.'

'That's something, I suppose. Now listen to me, Cleo, and listen hard, because I'm only going to say this once. If you appear in the papers one more time between now and my wedding, I never want to see you again.'

Cleo would've laughed, except she'd never heard her sister sound so serious. And her sister was the *queen* of serious. Her stomach gave a nauseating roll. 'Margot, listen—'

'No, *you* listen! If you ruin this for me, I will never forgive you. I don't want to see you for the next two and a half weeks. The next time I want to clap eyes on you is the morning of the wedding.'

'But…there are the final dress fittings.' Cleo was Margot's bridesmaid—her *only* bridesmaid.

'We'll make do with your last lot of measurements. Just don't go gorging yourself on cheesecake and crisps for the next seventeen days.'

Cleo held the phone away from her ear to stare at it. She pressed it back again. 'What about your hen night?'

'I don't want you there.'

She sucked in a sharp breath.

'In your current form, you'll ruin it.'

Margot's unspoken 'again' sounded in the spaces between them.

'You will lay low for the next two and a half weeks. I don't want to hear a peep about you, I don't want to see any photos of you, I don't want anything you do ruining my wedding. Do you hear me?'

She tried to swallow the lump in her throat. 'Loud and clear. And, Margot, I swear I won't. I'm sorry…'

But Margot had already hung up.

The expression on Cleo's face had Jude wanting to swear.

'No.' She lifted the newspaper and shook it. 'He wasn't worth it.'

All of the vitality drained from those extraordinary olive-green eyes, and his chest squeezed tight, and then tighter still, as if to make sure he couldn't ignore it. He swore and raged silently, and did what he could to pound it into oblivion.

It didn't work. Cleo's downturned lips, the defeated slope of her shoulders, the way tears had sheened her eyes three times now but hadn't been allowed to fall all caught at him, doing its best to drag him out of his self-imposed exile, his hard-nosed detachment.

Not going to happen. In an hour, after he'd said farewell to Cleo, he and *Camelot* were heading north. He'd settled his grandmother's estate. There was nothing to keep him here now.

'Promise me, you'll do one good thing every day.'

The memory of the promise his grandmother had extracted from him, given reluctantly, plagued him. It'd plagued him for the last week. *Damn it!* If the last nine months had proven anything, it was damsels in distress weren't his forte.

He wrinkled his nose. 'Margot didn't sound best pleased.'

'Understatement much?' She even managed a weak smile.

He stared at it and swallowed.

Slim shoulders lifted. 'It's her wedding in two and a half weeks.'

'She's turned into Bridezilla?'

'No!' Another faint smile appeared. 'Well, maybe a little, but she just wants the day to be perfect.'

As far as he was concerned, anyone who wanted to take the matrimonial plunge needed their head read. 'Perfection is a lot of pressure.'

Cleo blinked and then smiled—really smiled. She had a wide mouth. Her eyes danced, and it was like a sucker punch.

'I don't mean "perfection" in that the sun must shine like it's never shone before, and that there can be no crying babies in the church to break the reverent hush, or that all hell will break loose if the canapés aren't up to scratch—not *that* kind of perfection.'

Okay, she'd lost him.

'Her idea of perfection is that she and Brett will get to stare deep into each other's eyes while they make their vows, that all in attendance will be happy for them and that there's genuine joy at the reception.' She hesitated. 'That all who witness their marriage and celebrate with them will remember the day with fondness—that it'll be a happy memory.'

He ordered his lip not to curl.

'What she doesn't want is for her mess of a sister, who also happens to be her bridesmaid, trailing tabloid photographers in her wake and turning the day into a circus.'

'Are you a mess?'

She held the newspaper beneath her chin. 'I give you Exhibit A.'

Point taken. Cleo Milne was a *total* mess. She might look all sweetness and light, but the media had dubbed her Wild Child for a reason. She'd been an actress on a well-known British sitcom and the kind of woman he avoided like the plague: the kind of woman he'd sworn never to get involved with.

For some reason the front-page spread of Cleo punching her boyfriend—the lead singer of some boy band—reminded him of the look in her eyes when she'd said he'd been cheating on her. His chest drew tight. It didn't matter how famous you were, betrayal hurt.

Reaching across, he plucked the paper from her fingers and threw it face-down on the kitchen bench behind him so she'd stop beating herself up about it. While Cleo might be a mess, her sister wasn't supposed to think that. 'Okay, the timing of that might not have been great, but the berk clearly deserved it.'

'Do one good thing a day. Promise me.'

Pulling in a breath, he nodded. 'Right.'

Cleo glanced up expectantly.

'Margot wants you to lie low until the wedding, correct?'

She nodded.

He could help her come up with a plan, and then they could both be on their way. He wouldn't feel like an unsympathetic jerk, she'd have a direction *and* he'd have kept his promise to Gran: win-win.

'Anyway, just wait. This'll all die down in a few days. Once Margot calms down she'll see she's overreacting. She'll want you at the final dress fitting. She'll want you at her hen night.'

Cleo brightened. 'You really think so?'

What the actual hell...?

He didn't know Margot from Adam. Resisting the urge to run a finger beneath the collar of his jumper, he soldiered on. 'Until then, you need to avoid the press. Is there somewhere you can go?'

She chewed at her bottom lip. He stared at the way those small teeth made the lip plumper, deepening the colour to a raspberry blush. A hard hunger flared in his gut. Gritting his teeth, he ignored it. 'Your father?'

She flinched and shook her head.

'Other relatives?'

'It's just Dad, Margot and me.'

Why couldn't her father help her out? He bit back the question. Families could be complicated. He knew that. 'Friends?'

'That's where the press will expect me to go. They'll leap out at me from some shady doorway or corner, frightening the bejeebies out of me and snapping a picture of me looking appalled and terrified.'

And Margot would throw another fit.

'Margot deserves better from me,' she whispered.

'Cleo...' It was the first time he'd said her name. It rolled off his tongue like music and mead.

What the actual hell...? He was a thriller writer, not a poet! It was all he could do not to curl his lip at himself. *You're not a writer any more.* The unwelcome reminder had him clenching his jaw so hard it started to ache.

'Is everything okay?'

He shook himself. 'How's this for a plan? I'm about to head north. I can drop you on the outskirts of London somewhere and you can hole up in some country inn or rental for a fortnight.'

Her face brightened. The hard things inside him unclenched a fraction.

That's two good things, Gran.

He'd chased the journalist away *and* he was helping Cleo come up with a plan for her immediate future.

His lips twisted. *Go him.*

'Or?'

The excited buzz in Cleo's voice had his eyes narrowing. Behind the olive-green of her eyes, her mind was clearly racing. Foreboding gathered behind his breast bone.

'Or I could hide out on a conveniently passing narrow boat for a fortnight. I'd pay you,' she rushed on, as if seeing the refusal in his face.

'No.'

She eased back, chewing on her bottom lip again. His skin drew tight. He resolutely refused to notice that lip.

'I'll be quiet and not make a nuisance of myself, I swear. You'll hardly know I'm here.'

That would be impossible. 'No.'

'Why not?'

'The reason I took to the canals in the first place is because I want peace and quiet.'

'You've been travelling around a while?'

'Seven months.'

Her jaw dropped. 'Surely that's enough peace and quiet for anyone?'

He begged to differ.

Her lips pursed—not in any kind of mean or calculating way, but as if she was joining dots he didn't want her joining. Except she didn't know him, so she couldn't be joining dots.

'I know I'm in complete ignorance of your circumstances, but surely a bit of extra income would come in handy?'

He had to stifle an astonished crack of laughter. Yep, she was in complete and utter ignorance. And that was how he wanted it to stay.

She huffed out a sigh, as she read continued refusal on his face. His grandmother wouldn't be proud of him, but he refused to modify his expression and didn't soften it one iota.

'A week, then. Let me stay for a week and I'll pay you twenty-five thousand pounds.'

He had no hope of hiding his shock. He shot to his feet, whacking his thigh on the edge of the table as he did so. He swore, out loud this time.

She winced and mouthed a silent, 'Ouch.'

He glared his outrage.

She shrugged. 'I'd pay ten times that to save my relationship with my sister.'

Damn it.

'If I had it.' Her lips twisted. 'But I don't.'

He folded his arms. 'Do you actually have twenty-five thousand pounds?' He doubted it. She might've been an actress on a successful sitcom for seven years, but Cleo Milne was the kind of person who'd have long since frittered that money away.

She seized his phone and accessed the Internet, eventually turning it towards him to show him a bank account that bore her name. The balance showed just over twenty-five thousand pounds.

'It's my rainy-day fund.' She paused. 'It's the money my mother left me.'

Her *dead* mother. He dragged a hand down his face.

'And at the moment it's not just raining, it's bucketing down so hard that I'm going to drown unless I do something big. The money is all yours if you let me stay.'

He couldn't utter a single damn word.

'I know everyone thinks I'm rolling in cash. And maybe I will be one day if I ever gain access to my funds.'

What was she talking about now?

'But when I started acting I was a minor. My father signed my contracts. When I came of age, he convinced me to have the majority of my acting income put "in trust" for the future.'

Was he withholding it? 'So this...' He gestured to his phone.

'Like I said, it's my rainy-day fund.'

'What do you live off?'

'The fruits of my current labours.'

Which were...? *None of your business.*

'Fine.' He had no intention of taking her money but he had every intention of calling her bluff. 'One week on board the narrow boat *Camelot* at a cost of twenty-five thousand pounds.' He thrust out a hand. 'It's a deal.'

Squealing, she seized it and pumped it up and down. 'Thank you, thank you! You're a lifesaver.' Her entire body vibrated with relief. 'Give me your bank account details and I'll transfer the money now.'

Hell, she wasn't joking! And he'd just agreed...

'What?' she said when he remained silent.

'No.'

Her whole being fell. 'But I don't have anything else to barter with.'

Her eyes sheened with tears again. *Damn it!*

'The only way to ensure I don't get photographed is to not leave this boat.'

He couldn't kick her off *Camelot*, no matter how much he

might want to. He pointed to the phone. 'Check how much it costs to hire a narrow boat for a week.'

She searched the Internet. He made more tea, for himself this time. What the hell was he doing?

His grandmother's voice sounded through him. *'You're doing your one good thing for the day.'*

This had to count for entire week of good deeds! Except he knew Gran wouldn't have seen it like that.

'Okay, here we go.'

She handed him the phone and he handed her another mug of tea before sliding back into his spot at the table to view the information. 'This is for a luxury barge. *Camelot* isn't luxury and it's nowhere near as big.' He fixed her with what he hoped was the steeliest of glares. 'Tell me exactly where you think you're going to sleep.'

'I'm guessing that this—' she tapped the table '—folds down to a bed. Which will do me nicely.' She pointed behind him. 'I can see one corner of your bed from here. I'm not expecting you to give it up for me.'

The narrow boat had a single long corridor, with no internal doors except for the bathroom and toilet.

'There are bunk beds further along.'

She brightened.

'*Not* luxury,' he repeated. The amount showing on her phone was an obscene amount of money. He wouldn't charge that for a month's worth of accommodation. Not that he had any intention of offering anyone a month's worth of accommodation, no matter how much he might sympathise with their plight or how beguiling he found their eyes. He'd charge her a reasonable amount, though. It'd keep things business-like and professional.

'You haven't factored in that I get my own personal narrow-boat captain, though.'

He raised an eyebrow and tried to look as severe as possible.

She grimaced. 'And I'm going to need a few things...'

He rubbed a hand over his face when he realised what she was getting at—he'd have to be the one to get them for her. 'You're going to make me go into a ladies' underwear department, aren't you?'

He'd know what underwear she was wearing. That would be wrong on too many levels.

She winced. 'Sorry, yes. I'm also going to need a toothbrush, some clothes...and a phone. I'll give you my credit card.'

This woman was too trusting. 'Hasn't it occurred to you that I'm a strange man you don't know from Adam?'

'I know your name is Jude Blackwood.' She picked up some mail on the table to display his personal information.

His hands clenched. She had recognised the name. Did she know...?

She stared back, not a single suspicion lurking in her eyes. He released his breath slowly.

'And I know I can trust you.'

'How?'

'You could've made yourself a pretty penny if you'd made a deal with those journalists and escorted me off your boat. But you didn't.'

She might be a spoiled starlet, but nobody deserved to be hounded like she'd been.

'And I know people. I'm a good judge of character.'

Seizing the newspaper, he slapped a hand on the front page. 'I beg to differ.'

Her eyes dimmed and he felt like an unsympathetic

'Also, I'm not an idiot.' She thrust out her jaw. ''
knows who I'm with and now has your numbe

with me, but that doesn't mean she's not going to keep an eye on me.'

Okay, she had him there.

'And, besides the fact that you're all grumpy and growly on the outside, the name of your narrow boat suits you: *Camelot*. I suspect you're more gallant Galahad than misanthrope.'

'You call me that again, and I'll throw you in the canal myself.'

His scowl clearly didn't intimidate her because she bit her lip, as if trying not to laugh. She gestured to the phone. 'Do we have a deal?'

He knocked two grand off the price.

'Oh, but—'

'And I want your sunglasses.'

He added the last because he knew she wanted to feel as if she was paying a fair price. Those sunglasses might be ugly, but they'd provide an excellent disguise. They'd come in handy when he had to return to the real world.

Cleo froze like a deer in the headlights; like a statue; like a lamb to slaughter.

For a brief moment he thought she might hug the stupid ugly things and burst into tears. Instead, she wordlessly pushed them across the table to him. He couldn't say how he knew, but in that moment he knew she'd rather pay twenty-five thousand pounds and keep her sunglasses. He also knew retracting his demand would offend her deeply. He wanted to swear and swear.

Maybe, despite all appearances to contrary, like Cleo he still knew people too.

CHAPTER TWO

CLEO REMAINED HIDDEN below while Jude fired *Camelot*'s motor to life, untied the moorings and started along the canal. He seemed ridiculously capable, single-handedly managing the narrow boat with an ease she envied.

And found ridiculously attractive. *Oh no you don't!* She was making some serious changes to her life. Starting today. *No men. No romance. No making headlines.*

Her days of lurching from one mistake to the next, one disaster to another, had to stop. And all the mistakes that had landed her in the papers over the last three years had involved men. The incident with Clay last night had simply been the last in a long line.

A hard burn stretched through her chest. She should've walked away. She'd planned to walk away. But then he said that awful...*thing*...and her 'sensible and dignified' had fled.

She scrubbed her hands over her face. That *didn't* mean she would fall back into old patterns. She *hadn't* been drinking. She *hadn't* been seeking distraction or diversion. Not that her father would believe her, or Margot. And she had no one to blame but herself. It was what happened when you let people down too many times—they lost trust in you.

A weight slammed down on her shoulders. The room blurred, but she blinked back the tears. She'd honestly thought she and Clay would go the distance. Sure, she'd had the odd wobble, but she'd thought that if she worked hard enough, if she didn't give up, they could create the same sense of security she'd cherished when her mother had been alive. Security she'd been searching for ever since. But obviously she'd been looking for it in all the wrong places.

A lump stretched her throat into a painful ache. How could she have been so wrong? How could she have deluded herself so completely? Was she really so needy? Was she so incomplete—so *emotionally impoverished*—that she needed a man to make her feel fulfilled?

This had to stop. She didn't want to be *that* person.

No men. No romance. No making headlines.

Ewan had dated her to boost his credentials and land a role in drama series. Davide had used her so he could play the victim and gain public sympathy by staging an awful break-up. Austin hadn't cared for anything beyond her looks. He'd been appalled when she'd spent a weekend in her PJs watching old movies and eating popcorn. He'd wanted a trophy to parade in front of his friends.

None of those men had truly known her. None of them had truly cared for her.

And now Clay…

Here was a sobering fact—she was gutted to have been wrong about him, but she wasn't gutted to have lost him. So what on earth had she been doing thinking he was The One?

Pulling in a breath, she let it out slowly.

No men. No romance. No making headlines.

So the one thing she *wasn't* going to do now was develop a thing for her unlikely rescuer. Instead, she'd learn to manage her life with the same ease Jude Blackwood managed his narrow boat.

She glanced around. The life he led was pretty…spartan. The money she was paying him would probably be welcome, though it didn't change the fact that he was as happy about her being on his narrow boat as he would be finding dog dirt on his shoe.

But he *had* let her stay. And he hadn't taken her for a ride, as he could've done; he hadn't cleaned out her bank account. So she'd do all she could to be a model passenger. Maybe then she'd be able to convince him to let her stay for longer.

She glanced around again, taking in the dimensions of the boat. Dear God, how was she going to last even a week hiding out in such a tiny space? She'd go mad!

You'll do whatever you have to, to save your relationship with Margot.

Her hands clenched. Margot had always deserved better from her. She couldn't wreck her sister's big day. Margot had already forgiven her enough unforgivable things. She couldn't cast even the tiniest of dark clouds over her wedding—that *would* be unforgivable.

If that meant Cleo was to be confined to a floating prison for a week or two, so be it.

'Hey, Goldilocks...'

Cleo glanced in the direction of the door and Jude's voice. 'Are you talking to me?'

'Yep.'

'I'm brunette.'

'And yet, just like Goldilocks, you stole into my house.'

'I didn't touch your porridge or sit in your easy chair.'

'But you plan on sleeping in my bed.'

She spluttered and coughed. He didn't mean in the actual bed *he* slept in *with him*. He meant his spare bed.

His head briefly appeared, all dark shaggy hair, piercing blue eyes and a scowl. She wanted to tell him to be careful, that the wind might change, but bit the words back. *Model passenger, remember?*

Part of her wondered, though, if teasing him a little might make her the ideal passenger. Jude Blackwood seemed to carry the weight of the world on his shoulders. It'd be nice to lighten his load, if only for a moment.

'Have you had breakfast?'

'Yes,' she lied. She was already enough of a bother.

Those startling eyes narrowed. She tried not to fidget. He pointed to the kitchen bench. 'Make yourself some toast. That's non-negotiable,' he added, when she opened her mouth. 'I'm not having you faint on me from lack of food. You faint, and the entire deal is off.'

She'd hardly faint from skipping breakfast but nodded, model-passenger-style.

'And, while you're eating, make me a list of what you need. Some time this afternoon, I'll stop and get supplies.'

'Is it okay if I have a look around?'

His voice floated back down to her. 'Surprised you haven't already.'

The kitchen was small and compact. There was an oven, a two-burner hob and a small fridge. A microwave was securely wedged into a corner of the bench, and an electric toaster sat beside it. The contents of the kitchen cupboards told her he lived on tinned soup and toast.

She could do that too, but…

Glancing back towards the door, she tapped a finger against her lips. Everyone enjoyed a home-cooked meal. Wasn't there some saying about the way to a man's heart being through his stomach? She might not want to win his heart, but she did want to win his cooperation. And she'd become rather adept in the kitchen during the last three years.

She found strawberry jam in a cupboard, and a notepad under the newspaper, so she ate toast with jam and set about making two lists: one for the essentials she'd need and the other a grocery list. She checked the pots, pans and utensils. *Camelot* had everything she needed, all in pristine condition, which told a story of its own.

That done, she washed the few dishes, dried and put them away. She made more tea and handed Jude a mug, her arm emerging up the steps and through the door while she managed to keep the rest of herself hidden.

'Thanks.'

She might not be able to see his face, but she heard the surprise in his voice. Well, there had to be a couple of perks to having another person on board. When he was driving the boat he couldn't very well duck down to make tea whenever he wanted. She'd be more than happy to play tea lady.

With mug in hand, she moved along the corridor that opened onto Jude's bedroom with its neat double bed covered with a navy duvet. The room smelled of leather and the sea, like Jude himself.

The corridor narrowed again with two doors opening to her left. The first revealed a tiny toilet, the next a compact shower room. And then the corridor opened into another bedroom with bunk beds. One of the beds was made up with a sky-blue duvet. Cleverly constructed cupboards had been created in the rest of the available space, and several boxes rested along the wall—canned food, toilet paper, long-life milk and a box of yellow legal pads. There was a box of books too. Finally, a set of steps led up to the door leading out to the small deck at the front of the boat.

She mentally measured the space between bed, door and wall. If she moved a couple of boxes, she'd have enough room to do some yoga and other bits and pieces. It'd help keep her sane while confined on board. That was something. She *could* do this.

Back in the living area, she surveyed the space where she'd initially fallen through the door. The sweetest cast-iron wood burner rested in the far corner; the chimney disappearing through the roof was shiny, as if it was regularly scrubbed. A neat stack of wood rested in a box beside it.

Opposite the wood burner was that single arm chair, a foot rest and a small table—a space for one lone traveller. And, of course, more of those cleverly constructed cupboards and shelves. She slid back onto a bench at the dinette, refusing to invade what was clearly *his* space.

The light momentarily dimmed, as if they were travelling under a bridge or through an aqueduct. It would've been insanely interesting to go up and see, except she was currently too scared even to twitch a curtain at the windows. Going up on deck was out of the question. Maybe in a few days' time, when London was far behind. But, then again, maybe not.

She checked over the lists she'd made. She read the paper from cover to cover. She turned to the puzzle page to do the crossword and the sudoku.

Except…what if Jude did the puzzles? She'd stolen onto his boat. She wasn't going to steal his puzzles too. For all she knew, they might be the highlight of his day.

A pile of papers sat on the bench beside her. She seized yesterday's paper and turned to the puzzle page. He *did* do the puzzles—all of them. Of course he did; what else was there to do on a narrow boat?

When lunchtime finally rolled round, she made him thick roast-beef sandwiches and handed them up the steps. Again, she heard surprise in his 'Thanks.'

She ate her sandwich in silence. She resisted the urge to try and make conversation with him, though it settled in her bones like an ache. Jude didn't strike her as the chatty sort, and she'd be a model passenger if it killed her. Dropping her head to the table, she mumbled, 'It's going to kill me.'

She tidied the kitchen again.

An hour later she called up the stairs, 'Would it be okay if I read one of the books in the box in the—' she settled on '—spare bedroom?'

He didn't answer immediately. She swallowed. What was she going to do if he said no? Yoga; she'd do yoga. A lot of yoga.

'Sure.'

'Thank you.'

Racing down to her bedroom before he could change his mind, she carefully prised open one flap and then the other, discovering an almost entire set of 'Jason Diamond' books by Jasper Ballimore—a famously reclusive author who shunned live appearances, television interviews and the public eye. She stared at the books and grinned. A bit of Jason Diamond's kick-ass attitude was exactly what she needed.

Seizing the book on top, she dislodged the receipt and it fluttered to the floor. Reaching to place it back in the box, she glanced at the brief scrawl scratched across the bottom of it in big dark letters.

If you're going to continue in this ridiculous seclusion, Jude, at least drop signed copies into bookshops along your route. Randomly signed Jasper Ballimore books are treasured by fans and will keep interest alive.

There was a PS.

When can I expect the next book? It was due three months ago!!! Give me something to work with here, Jude.

She dropped the note back into the box as if it had burned her. *Jude* was Jasper Ballimore? Oh, my God, that wasn't a secret he'd want her knowing! Her heart thundered. *Okay, all right, get a grip.* She was an actress, wasn't she?

Except she hadn't trained as an actress. Playing a part in front of a camera was very different from pretending to be something she wasn't in front of real people about real things in real life.

Fine! Hauling in a breath, she closed her eyes. She'd simply wipe this moment from her mind, never think about it again.

Folding the note, she tucked it down the side of the box before settling on the surprisingly comfortable bunk bed and cracking open the cover. She lost herself to the story for a happy hour, before once again chafing at the enforced inactivity. She wasn't used to being so *still* and it meant the same ugly thoughts kept circling her mind like sharks. Had she tested Margot's patience too far? Did Margot now hate her? Could she fix this?

She always came back to the same conclusion: lie low for the next two and a half weeks and allow the media speculation to die down. That way, Margot's big day wouldn't be marred by the paparazzi wanting to snap pictures of Cleo. They'd want to snap pictures of the bride instead, and the proud father of the bride, prominent politician Michael Milne. The bridesmaid would remain firmly in the background. Cleo crossed her fingers.

Mid-afternoon, Jude moored *Camelot*. She heard him tying off and, well, whatever else one did when mooring in a canal. She pulled herself into immediate straight lines.

Don't talk his ear off. Don't ask him for anything unnecessary. Don't be a pain. And definitely don't remember that he's Jasper Ballimore!

When he appeared, she sent him the smallest of smiles and slid out from behind the table. Rookie mistake, because space on the narrow boat was at a premium, and it shrank alarmingly when she and Jude were both standing in the galley.

She moistened her lips. 'Is there anything I can do?'

'Nope.'

'More tea or...?'

She broke off eyeing the flask he had tucked under one

arm and the lunch box he held in his hand. As if in a dream, she reached for them. The lunch box held untouched sandwiches and a couple of biscuits. The flask was full of tea.

'It doesn't matter, Cleo.'

Oh, God, had her face fallen? She wrinkled her nose. 'And here I was congratulating myself on being helpful.'

He took the lunch box, removed the biscuits and set the sandwiches in the fridge. 'No harm done. They'll keep till tomorrow.'

Clutching the flask, she slid back behind the table. 'This won't.' She poured herself a mug. It was still steaming hot. He slid his mug across and she filled it too.

He didn't sit. 'If it's any consolation, your sandwiches taste better than mine.'

She stared down her nose at him.

'You put hot English mustard on them.'

She'd found some in the cupboard.

'I forgot what a good combination that was. Who knew hot English mustard could make such a difference?'

Her heart gave a funny little twist. What else had he forgotten during his *ridiculous seclusion*?

None of your business.

She gestured to the door. 'Where are we?'

'Uxbridge.'

Uxbridge? *Uxbridge?* She could get from Maida Vale to Uxbridge in an hour on the tube; she could probably cycle it in under two hours. She made herself smile. 'Great.'

He leaned back against the bench, crossing his legs at the ankles. 'You're a terrible liar.'

She grimaced. 'I had no idea cruising the canal was so leisurely. I thought we'd at least be in Oxford by now.'

His lips twitched. She thought it'd be kind of nice to see them break into a full-blown smile.

'There's been a bit of traffic in the canal.'

On New Year's Day?

'Slows things up.' He sipped his tea. 'You were hoping to be out of London by now.'

It was a statement, not a question. She shrugged. 'I suppose so, in an ideal world. But, as long as I stay below and out of sight, it doesn't really matter where I am, does it?'

Jude eyed Cleo over his mug, trying to work her out. She was doing her best to be low maintenance—not to make a fuss or be a bother—but she was keyed up tighter than an anchor winch.

Think it might have something to do with the fact her picture appeared on the front page of the newspaper today? Or that her lying scumbag of a boyfriend cheated on her? Or that her Bridezilla of a sister was throwing hissy fits?

Even he had to admit the woman had a lot going on. And, in spite of it all, she was holding up pretty well. *And* she'd gone to the trouble of putting hot English mustard on his sandwich. He didn't know why that caught at him, only that it did.

'If it's any consolation—' he shrugged '—I hate London too.'

She waved both arms towards the door. 'What on earth are you doing here, then, when you've a whole network of canals at your fingertips.'

He tried not to scowl. 'My grandmother's funeral.'

She froze, a stricken expression in her eyes, and he immediately wished the stark words unsaid. Cleo might be a total mess, but she didn't deserve his bitterness. 'Don't look like that. You weren't to know.' He tried to shrug, but the movement was jerky. 'As executor of her will, I've had to remain and settle her estate.'

Her eyes filled. 'Oh, Jude, I'm so very sorry.'

Her sincerity almost undid him. He needed a change of topic…fast.

'You check out your sleeping quarters yet?' The boat was a reverse configuration, with the sleeping quarters in the bow rather than the stern.

She nodded. 'Your boat is amazing.'

His cup halted halfway to his mouth.

'I mean, it's not very wide.'

He lowered his mug. 'Less than seven feet.' Six feet ten inches, to be precise. Reaching up, he touched the ceiling. 'Six feet six inches high.'

For a moment her gaze rested on him, weighted with something that had an invisible hand reaching out to squeeze the air from his body. Shaking herself, she glanced away. Air rushed back into his lungs.

'The design is clever, each nook and cranny designed for maximum storage. Like I said—amazing.'

'And your bed?'

'Comfortable.'

She really wasn't going to be a prima donna about this? 'It's tiny and cramped.'

'I might not manage a full yoga routine in there but, as you promised me a bed and not a yoga studio…'

Her eyes danced. He resisted the urge to smile back and wondered how long her good behaviour would last. 'You'll have more privacy down there. I'll pin a sheet up in the doorway of your bedroom later.'

'I don't want you going to any trouble.'

'No trouble.' It was as much for his peace of mind as hers. He didn't want to catch a glimpse of a naked leg or…

He shook away the images that flicked through his mind, but not fast enough. His skin tightened as if it had grown too small for him. A throb started up deep inside. *This* was why he didn't want her—or anyone—on board *Camelot*. He wanted peace and quiet…

'You're hiding from life.'

He straightened as his grandmother's words sounded through him, glaring at his feet. 'Did you make a list of the things I need to get you?'

She wordlessly handed him a sheet of paper. His brows shot up at the first item on her list. 'A tape measure?'

'If I'm not going to my final bridesmaid fitting, then I need to make sure my measurements don't change too much. If they do, I can send the dress maker the new measurements.'

He stared.

She rolled her shoulders. 'A bridesmaid has certain responsibilities. I've let Margot down enough. From now on, nothing but perfection will do.'

He opened his mouth. He closed it again.

'I'm not going to starve myself, if that's what you're worried about, but nor am I going to gorge myself on doughnuts.'

She liked doughnuts?

He went back to her list: toothbrush, yoga pants, T-shirts... underwear. His nose curled.

'What? It's the phone, isn't it? I know it's a hassle, but I put all the details there and—'

'The phone is a piece of cake.' He pointed to the offending item. 'I've never bought ladies' underwear in my life. How am I going to find the...?'

She gazed at him blankly.

'The right kind?' He'd walked past the women's lingerie section in department stores. It was bigger than the entire men's clothing section!

She pressed her lips together, as if trying not to laugh. 'It's easy-peasy. I only wear silk and lace.'

What the hell...?

'They're about this big.' She held her finger and thumb about two inches apart. 'And they come in a colour called rose blush—'

He choked and she broke off, laughing. 'I'm pulling your

leg, Jude. I didn't think you'd take me seriously.' Her grin widened. 'You should've seen your face.'

I'd rather not, thanks all the same. Joke or no joke, he now couldn't get the image of Cleo wearing nothing more than a scrap of silk and lace the same colour as her lips out of his mind. He shouldn't be imagining Cleo practically naked. And he sure as hell shouldn't be thinking about her lips.

Intellectually, he'd known that Cleo was attractive—he'd seen a few episodes of the show she'd starred in and had seen the headlines of her many scandals. But in the flesh Cleo was more beguiling than he'd have credited. She vibrated with life. *She sparkled.*

None of it changed the fact that she was the last person he'd ever get involved with. He didn't court scandal. He preferred to live his life out of the limelight, thank you very much.

'You can get all the things on my list at a department store, or even a supermarket.'

He glanced back at her list.

'You don't need to go anywhere fancy. The underwear will come in a pack of five.' She reached across and pointed. The scent of pears filled his nostrils—fresh, sweet and oddly innocent.

'I've written the details here—bikini briefs, a hundred percent cotton. But full brief, boy leg, trunks will all do too.'

She'd written all of that down, as if aware the ladies' underwear department might bamboozle him. He needed to stop making mountains out of molehills. 'Colour preferences?'

'Don't care two jots.'

Obviously she was determined to keep up the low-maintenance masquerade.

He tapped the final item on her list. 'Puzzle book?'

'It's important to keep the mind active.'

His gaze slid to the paper.

'I didn't do your puzzles. I checked the papers from earlier in the week and saw that you did them.'

Her thoughtfulness slid under his guard. 'You could've done the puzzles, Cleo. I wouldn't have minded.'

'Seemed presumptuous—not my paper. And puzzles can be a routine thing. You might settle in after dinner with a nice cup of cocoa and unwind by doing the puzzles.'

She had him nailed.

I know people.

Maybe she did. 'Substitute that mug of cocoa for a dram of whisky, and you just about hit the nail on the head.'

She bit her lip. 'I made another list. I hope it's not presumptuous but, Jude, I love to cook.'

She handed him another sheet of paper—a shopping list!

'I thought I'd make a lasagne for dinner tonight, if that's okay with you.'

'Lasagne?' he parroted stupidly. The papers always made out that Cleo was a high-maintenance, spoiled starlet. And, while he appreciated the lack of foot-stomping about the size of her bedroom, he found it a stretch too far that she was now offering to cook. Next she'd be offering to knit him a scarf!

She's an actress. She's probably buttering you up so you'll let her stay for another week.

'I know it's not diet food, but it'll only be a small one. You can have the leftovers for lunch tomorrow, if you want.' She wrinkled her nose. 'I'm in the mood for comfort food.'

Her expression had his chest clenching.

Actress, remember?

'And I've made a list of ingredients for a stir fry for tomorrow night. I checked the size of your fridge and we should be able to fit that lot in.'

'You don't need to cook, Cleo.'

'I want to, honestly.'

More likely a case of seeing his cupboards were stacked

with nothing but tinned food. He rolled his shoulders. There was nothing wrong with tinned food. And yet the thought of home-cooked lasagne had his mouth watering. *If* she could cook...

'Besides, it'll give me something to do.'

She held her credit card out to him, but he raised both hands, warding her off.

'But—'

'Getting caught with your credit card and going down for credit card fraud?' He shook his head. 'No thanks. Besides, that could blow your cover.'

She swore. 'Then I want an itemised account. You need to bring all the receipts back with you.' She pointed a surprisingly fierce finger at him. 'I want to see *all* the receipts.'

It was novel not to be expected to pick up the bill—a fact that would undoubtedly change if she found out who he was. 'Deal,' he said, seizing his phone and keys.

Her hands twisted together and she suddenly looked young and vulnerable, as if he were her only friend in the world and she was about to lose him. He bit back something short and succinct. At the moment, he *was* the only person who knew where she was; the only person who seemed to care about the plight she was in. She might be a celebrity, but that didn't make her invulnerable. It didn't shield her from grief or heartache.

'Will you be okay while I'm gone?'

She pasted on a too-bright smile that made his eyes ache. 'Absolutely! Is there anything I need to know, or do?'

He shook his head. 'We're tied up safe and sound, but there are narrow boats moored either end of us. Don't answer if anyone knocks. And keep the noise down.'

'Roger.'

It took him off-guard, how much he hated leaving her on

her own. *Crazy.* She'd be as safe as houses, provided she stayed put and out of sight.

'Look, provided I can negotiate the ladies' underwear department without too many hassles, I shouldn't be gone longer than an hour.'

Her eyes danced then. 'Good luck with that. And don't worry about me; I'll be fine.'

Of course she would. He nodded at the paper. 'Do the puzzles. I'll grab another paper while I'm out.'

It took Jude two hours. When he clattered back on board, Cleo jumped up and rushed across to take bags from him.

'What on earth...? Did you leave anything in the shops for the rest of the people?'

'Very funny.' He shoved a bag of fresh doughnuts at her.

She stared at them, then back at him. Her eyes grew suspiciously bright. 'You bought me doughnuts?'

'Comfort food. Won't happen again. Dieting again after today,' he muttered, easing past to set the shopping on the kitchen bench.

She slid into the bench seat, facing him. She stared at the doughnuts as if they were diamonds. He rolled his shoulders. They were just doughnuts. Didn't the people in her life do nice things for her?

Her boyfriend cheated on her. Her sister is making ridiculous demands of her. And her father...? Who knew what the deal was with her father?

'Why are you scowling?'

He jumped, making the scowl comical. 'I have three words for you, Cleo: ladies'...underwear...department.'

She laughed. In this light, her eyes were the colour of sea mist—*really* pretty. And when they danced they could steal a man's breath.

'Was it dire?'

'The sales lady thought me a pervert. She didn't believe me when I said the underwear was for my little sister.'

'Do you have a little sister?'

'Well…no.'

'If you had the same expression on your face then as you do now, then she'd have known you were lying.'

'See?' He lifted his hands. 'I told you she thought me a pervert!'

Another laugh gurgled out of her. It made him feel good, as if he'd done a good thing. He nodded at the bags in front of her. 'Phone, yoga pants, T-shirts, hoody, PJs. Check and make sure they're all okay.'

He upended a bag of pears he'd bought into a bowl. Lifting one to his nose, he inhaled its scent. *Heaven*.

'What's this?'

Damn. He dropped the pear to reach across and pluck the boutique bag from her fingers. 'I…uh…it was supposed to be a joke—make you laugh.' He rolled his shoulders. 'But now it feels pervy.'

Her brows shot up. She eased out from behind the table to stand in front of him. 'Intrigued now.'

With a curse, he shoved the bag into her hands, scowling. 'Joke, remember?'

She pulled out a package wrapped in tissue paper and unfolded it. He winced at the tiny rose silk-and-cream lace panties that dangled from her fingers.

God, what would she think of him…?

Clutching them to her chest, Cleo roared. She bent at the waist as if unable to contain her mirth and literally *roared* with laughter. Tears poured down her face. Straightening, she tried to speak, but one glance at him sent her into fresh gales. She had to hold onto the table to stop from falling to the floor. Collapsing on her back on the bench seat of the dinette, her feet kicked the air, her entire body convulsing and her face crinkling.

With laughter. Something in his chest wrenched free and he found himself grinning.

'You braved a Victoria's Secret store?' Pushing upright, she stood again, mopping at her eyes. 'I can't believe you did that. I wish I could've seen your face.'

'I should've gone there in the first place. The staff just took it in their stride—proper professionals.'

She hiccupped another laugh. 'I didn't think anything would be able to make me laugh today.'

His heart pounded against his ribs too hard.

'Best joke present ever, Jude.'

Really?

'You're a gem. Thank you.'

Reaching across, she hugged him. She was all soft, warm woman, and she hugged him as if she really meant it. He couldn't remember the last time... Everything inside him started to ache.

Letting him go, she slid back into her seat and pulled the doughnuts towards her. 'Doughnut?'

He dragged air into cramped lungs. 'No thanks; I'm having a pear.'

CHAPTER THREE

Cleo watched Jude fork the tiniest amount of lasagne into his mouth, as if he didn't trust that she could actually cook. One bite, and his face cleared, and then he tucked in as if he hadn't eaten in a week.

Something stupid caught low in her belly. He looked as if he hadn't had a home-cooked meal in *forever*. She was suddenly and fiercely glad she'd offered to cook, and beyond the fact that it had given her something to do.

He glanced up, his gaze pinning her to her seat. 'Everything okay?'

'No.' The word blurted out before she could stop it. The joke panties were to blame, and the doughnuts. They'd changed everything. She didn't want to lie to him. He deserved better.

'I know you're Jasper Ballimore.'

He froze.

'There was a note from your publisher in the box of books.'

He set his cutlery down with one succinct and very rude word.

'Your secret is safe with me—I promise. But it's a big secret, and you'll want to protect yourself. Have your lawyer send me something—a non-disclosure or confidentiality agreement—and I'll sign it. I won't tell a soul.' *Please don't throw me off your narrow boat.* 'It's just—'

'What?'

The word was barked from him and she could feel herself shrivel. 'It just seemed wrong to feign ignorance.'

His glare didn't ease.

She closed her eyes. 'Do you want me to leave?'

'So you can run off to the press?'

Her eyes snapped open. 'You think that's what I'd do?'

He remained silent.

Her sinuses burned. 'Oh, that's right—I'm *that* girl. The train wreck, the car crash, the wild child who'll do *anything* for attention. The kind of person who takes delight in wrecking lives for the fun of it.'

Their gazes clashed. He grimaced. 'That's not what I meant.'

'That's exactly what you meant!' Her hand clenched, but she didn't slam it on the table as she wanted to. 'I thought you of all people would understand.'

'Me?'

'Yes, *you*!' She lowered her voice and spoke in a whisper. 'As Jasper B you guard your identity jealously, do everything you can to avoid publicity. I thought that meant you understood the half-truths and lies the media feed on—the twisted version of reality they peddle. I thought you were safeguarding yourself against it so you could focus on the writing rather than the celebrity. And I thought that meant you'd be able to see beneath the lies they printed about people like me.'

All the good things inside her—the things that had kept her going for the day, the tiny threads of hope and optimism—all dissolved.

'You're a writer. I thought you'd have more *imagination*.' Seizing her fork, she stabbed a piece of rocket. 'But you're just like everyone else.'

'Cleo…'

She sent him a tight smile. 'Silly me.'

Jude's hands clenched and unclenched on either side of his plate. 'Everything you just said is true. I'm sorry.'

She stared back stonily.

'*Really* sorry.'

She swallowed and glanced away.

'I've been operating under too many mistaken assumptions where you're concerned, which isn't only unfair but stupid,' he said. 'I should never have made that crack about you going to the press. If that had been your plan, you wouldn't have told me about your discovery in the first place.'

He looked haggard, as if he loathed himself. It was a hundred times worse than his previous scowl.

'I've no defence other than the fact you caught me off-guard. I panicked. My unmasking was the last thing I expected today.'

She suspected *she* was the last thing he'd expected today. He'd made an error of judgement, but he wasn't the only one. He didn't deserve to go to the gallows over it. 'Forget about it,' she mumbled. 'I can get on a bit of a soapbox about it.'

'With some cause.'

She shook her head. 'I've not always made good decisions. I can't blame the press for that. Besides, you don't know me. For all you knew, I could've been about to try and extort money from you.'

He stared.

'It happened to me once.'

'How? Who?'

'An ex-boyfriend. He'd taken photos of me without my permission.' Naked photos.

His Adam's apple bobbed. 'And those photos were published, weren't they?'

'Well, I refused to be blackmailed.' It was also the moment she'd decided she was done with the whole celebrity scene. 'I did sue, however.' And the money she'd been awarded had paid for her website development training. She rolled her eyes; and more therapy.

'Cleo...'

'Apology accepted, Jude.'

He opened his mouth and then closed it; nodded.

'So...' Picking up her cutlery again, she tried for light-hearted and breezy. 'Jason Diamond is your creation, huh? That's pretty amazing.'

Jason Diamond was one of the most beloved fictional characters of modern times. One of the good guys—ex-law enforcement and reluctant hero, he stood on the side of the weak and underprivileged, fighting for those who couldn't fight for themselves. Justice could be his middle name.

He glanced up and shook his head. 'Don't make that particular mistake. I'm nothing like JD.'

She went back to her lasagne and salad. 'JD is always helping damsels and dudes in distress—just like you helped me.'

'I didn't jump in front of a bullet for you.'

He shrugged, as if saving her from the press hadn't been particularly noteworthy. She stopped eating and frowned. Had his shoulders been that broad earlier? Dragging her gaze away, she focussed on cutting her food, lifting it to her mouth and chewing.

Keep things light.

'You might be asked to take that bullet if I screw up again and ruin Margot's wedding.'

A corner of his mouth twitched. 'You're not going to ruin Margot's wedding. She's just stressed. Brides get stressed. It's a thing.'

'A...*thing*?' She raised an eyebrow. 'You have experience?'

'I'm a writer.'

He shrugged again and she could've groaned. Every time he did that it drew her attention to the breadth of those annoyingly *broad* shoulders. Her fingers tightened around her cutlery.

'I do my due diligence; squirrel odd snippets of information away. Believe me, stressed brides are a thing.'

She leaned towards him. 'Are you going to have a stressed bride in your next book? That could...'

She gulped back the rest of her words, recalling his publisher's note. He obviously wasn't writing. And reminding him of that wasn't in the spirit of model-passenger behaviour.

'Thank you for letting me cook tonight.'

He frowned. 'Why are you thanking me? I should be thanking you.'

She sliced a cherry tomato in half. 'I really do like to cook.' It was one of the two things that kept her on the straight and narrow—exercise and cooking. 'And cooking dinner made me feel as if...'

'What?'

'As if I was pulling my weight a bit. Making up in a small way for thrusting my presence on you.'

He pointed his knife at her. 'You're paying me, remember? *And* you traded your sunnies.'

She tried to look casual, or at least not stricken. 'Oh, in that case, you got a bargain.'

'Did you see I grabbed you another pair while I was out?'

Had he? Abandoning her food, she rifled through the bags still sitting on the bench, her hand eventually emerging with the sunglasses. She put them on. They felt wrong, but they covered her eyes at the front and sides—great disguise sunglasses. 'How do they look?'

'Very chic.'

Smiling, she took them off and set them on the table. 'Thank you.'

'You want to tell me why you're so attached to those ugly things you were wearing earlier?'

'You want to talk about the next JD book?'

He pursed his lips. *'Touché.'* Then he pinned her to her seat with a ferocious glare. 'Is Margot worth it—all the sacrifices you're making?'

She went hot all over and then cold. When she realised she clutched her cutlery as if it was a weapon, she forced herself to loosen her grip. 'Yes.'

They ate in silence after that.

A short while later, Jude shook himself. 'I bought a bottle of wine. Would you like a glass?'

'No, thank you.' She eyed him carefully, moistening her lips. 'I don't drink.'

He held her gaze. 'Alcoholic?'

'No. At least, I don't think so. It's just, when I drink, my guard lowers and I'm more likely to do something impulsive.'

'Something you'll regret?'

'Usually something that will cause my family pain and, or, maximum embarrassment.' Such as appearing on the front page of the newspaper having an altercation with her jerk of a boyfriend. *Ex-boyfriend.*

'And, before you ask, I wasn't drinking last night. Clayton just...'

'Got under your skin?'

She should've walked away. But then he'd said that dreadful thing and she'd seen red.

'Stop beating yourself up about it, Cleo.'

Easier said than done.

Jude finished his lasagne. She stood and reached for his plate. 'You want more?'

'Is there more?' He eyed the leftovers, watching as she cut him another generous slice. 'There's enough left for dinner tomorrow night.'

'I don't like having the same thing two nights running,' she informed him. If his expression was anything to go by, that wasn't an issue for him. 'Breakfast and lunch, I don't care. Dinner, I like to mix up. Which means there's enough here for you to have seconds now and for lunch tomorrow too if you want.'

'I want,' he said as she slid the plate in front of him. 'It's great.'

'May I?' She held up a pear.

'Knock yourself out. Help yourself to anything you want. It's part of the deal.'

She sat again, sliced and cored the pear, her mind going over the question Jude had asked—was Margot worth the sacrifices she was making? She suspected he was more like his fictional creation than he cared to admit. He saw her as a damsel in distress and Margot as a villain. That couldn't be further from the truth and she needed to disabuse him of the notion. She didn't want him concocting some Jason Diamond scheme to win her justice. He'd be fighting for the wrong side.

'You think Margot is the bad guy in all of this, but you couldn't be more mistaken if you tried.'

He stopped mid-chew.

'Margot is worth ten of me. And I owe her.'

He finished his mouthful slowly. 'You sure you don't want that glass of wine?'

'Positive, but don't let that stop you.'

He rose and poured himself a glass of red. 'Look…' He slid back into his seat. 'Just because you were a little wild when you were younger…'

'I was charged with being drunk and disorderly twice. I was photographed dancing half-naked in the fountain in Trafalgar Square!'

'Not your finest hour.' He pointed his fork at her. 'But it doesn't make you a bad person.'

'And that's before we throw in the series of disastrous relationships I've had with high-profile men.' With last night's fiasco being her crowning glory.

'Again, it doesn't make you a bad person.'

But it did make her a delusional one—or maybe she was just a slow learner. She dreamed of creating the warm, family environment her mother had. To date, though, she could never have made that dream a reality with the men she'd sought to find it with. She'd just been too blind to see it.

Swearing off men for the foreseeable future wasn't only her wisest course of action, it was the *only* course of action that made sense. Until she could make better decisions where men were concerned, she was avoiding all romance, full-stop.

No men. No romance. No making headlines.

She took her time eating a slice of pear. 'Do you know what Margot's dream was, before she decided to follow my father into politics?'

He rolled his shoulders. 'This isn't any of my business, Cleo.'

'She wanted to work for the United Nations. She made it through the first and second rounds of testing, and the first lot of interviews. The next hurdle was another interview. The powers that be decided at six p.m. the night before that it'd take place in the family home at seven-thirty a.m.—apparently they like to take you off-guard and make things stressful to see how you perform under pressure.'

Jude rubbed a hand over his face, as if sensing this story didn't have a happy ending.

'I stumbled in at seven forty-five after a night out, still drunk.' For God's sake, who stumbled home drunk at practically eight in the morning? 'And I proceeded to tell all assembled that Margot was a saint, and that perhaps she'd missed her calling as a nun.' Acid burned her throat. She'd been so angry at the world. 'I said her perfection was annoying and called them all a bunch of smug do-gooders who deserved each other.'

Jude swirled the wine in his glass. 'I'm guessing she didn't get the job.'

'No.' She couldn't look at him. 'It's the worst thing I've ever done.' She'd *never* forgive herself for it, not for as long as she lived. 'I was so bitter. So lost after our mother died.'

Their mother had been the machine that had kept the family running. Cleo had only been seventeen when she'd died. Margot had been twenty-two. Cleo had been twenty-two when she'd ruined Margot's dream.

'Apparently, I wanted to make everyone as miserable as I was.' And in that instance she'd succeeded. 'I resented Margot for being so seemingly perfect and doing no wrong, even while all the time she was hauling me out of trouble time after time.' She forced herself to meet his gaze. 'She didn't deserve that.'

'And yet she forgave you.'

For which she'd always be grateful. 'When I sobered up, I was appalled at what I'd done. I grovelled for days, begged her to forgive me.'

She'd been so ashamed. She still was.

'Margot laid down the law—said I had to go to rehab. I agreed. I wasn't doing drugs, but nobody believed that at the time, and I *was* drinking too much. So off to rehab I went. She also said I had to get counselling. I did, and it helped. That's the point when I started turning my life around.'

'And maybe she thinks losing that job is a small sacrifice to pay to have her sister well and healthy.'

'She probably does. She's a good soul. But you have to see, after all of that, I can't ruin her wedding too. I can't cast *any* shadow over it. All eyes should be on her, not me. Her focus should be on marrying the man of her dreams, not getting me out of another mess.'

Was Brett the man of Margot's dreams, though? As Margot's bridesmaid, not to mention her sister, it was her duty to make sure of that, wasn't it? And how could she do that when she was stuck on a narrow boat in the middle of nowhere? Her lips twisted. Unlike her, though, Margot was smart.

Be more like Margot.

'It's not too much for her to ask me to keep a low profile for the next two and a half weeks.'

He blew out a breath and nodded. 'I guess not.'

'You asked me if she's worth it—she's worth my every best effort.'

He leaned back, his shoulders sagging as if he'd just lost a fight. Except they hadn't been fighting, had they?

He tapped a fist to his mouth. He had firm, lean lips and she found her gaze riveted to them. A woman could weave fantasies around a mouth like that...

She tore her gaze away. *For God's sake!* She had to stop this. She had to stop making such terrible mistakes. She would *not* start fantasising about a man she barely knew.

'If we're going to successfully hide you for a fortnight...'

She blinked, and then her every muscle electrified. 'A fortnight? Did you just say...?'

His lips twisted, as if he were mocking himself. 'I think we both know I'm going to let you stay for as long as you need to.'

She could hug him! Except, she'd already done that and it had been a huge mistake. Plus, she was only making *good* decisions from hereon in. 'I'll pay you.'

He was a successful writer—*really* successful—but she'd read somewhere that writers didn't actually make all that much money.

'You'll pay me what we've already agreed and take over the cooking for the duration of the trip.'

She opened her mouth to argue.

'That's the deal—take it or leave it.'

Snapping her mouth shut, she dragged in a breath. She'd have to find some other way to repay him. 'I'll take it. And, Jude, thank you.'

He scowled and shrugged.

'I mean it. You're a lifesaver.'

'I'm a moron,' he muttered, making her laugh.

'Why?' Cleo fixed Jude with a gaze he couldn't read. 'Why are you helping me? I know you're a decent guy and all, but I also know you wish me a million miles away.'

She looked so alone and his heart gave a sick kick. She was used to everyone expecting something from her, wanting a piece of her. He suspected Cleo didn't get favours for free; they'd always come with a price tag attached. Was it any wonder she wanted to know what price she'd be asked to pay for the privilege of remaining aboard *Camelot*?

Exhaustion pounded at him. He uttered words he'd have not expected to say to her in a million years. 'Nine months ago, I lost my brother—car accident.'

Her quick intake of breath speared into his chest. 'Oh, God… Jude.'

'If I could do anything to bring him back, I would.'

She scrubbed both hands over her face.

'If you cry, I'm kicking you off *Camelot*.'

It was an idle threat, but she buried her head in her hands and took a ragged breath before pulling them away again, her eyes dry. 'You know how important Margot is to me because that's how important your brother was to you.'

Something like that. His nostrils flared as the familiar grief rose through him. He glared. 'We're not talking about this any more.'

'Okay.'

There'd just been too much loss. He didn't want to face any more, not even as a bystander.

* * *

Jude rose early the next day. He'd not slept well, too aware of another person occupying space on his boat, finding sanctuary on *Camelot*, just as he had. And he was still reeling from the fact that he'd allowed it to happen at all. He might not have been hard-nosed enough to escort Cleo off *Camelot* into the waiting arms of the journalists, but to let her stay for longer than an hour...

His hands fisted. Coming face to face with Elodie, his late brother's wife, at his grandmother's funeral had opened wounds that had barely had the chance to heal. God only knew why, but it had thrown him and left him feeling bruised. When Cleo had crashed onto his boat, his defences had been down.

He cast off at first light. Peering into the mild early-morning light, he could admit to himself that he didn't regret letting her stay, not really. What he'd started to doubt were his motives. Helping Cleo wouldn't erase the events of the past. It wouldn't give him absolution. It would, however, provide him with distraction.

And yesterday morning, sitting at the table, trying to read the paper, distraction was exactly what he'd craved. He'd wanted to drive Elodie's bitter words from his mind, if only for an hour.

And now Cleo was here, all warm, lovely woman, trying her best not to be a nuisance, and that had slid beneath his guard in ways he hadn't expected. Her sparkly chatter, her easy frankness and irrepressible humour were balm to a starving soul.

Which was stupid, and wrong. Because, first, he didn't deserve balm; and, second, unlike his fictional creation Jason Diamond—who in Jude's more optimistic moments he'd once considered his shadow soul—his motives weren't pure. In searching for distraction, he was in danger of using Cleo.

When he added his growing attraction to her—because, damn, Cleo was pretty with her dark hair, that classic English rose complexion and those extraordinary green eyes—it had the potential to lead him to places he had no right to go to.

She was a woman in need. She was vulnerable. His hand tightened on the tiller. He would *not* take advantage of her.

'Good morning.'

Cleo peered up at him blearily from the bottom of the steps, blinking sleep from her eyes.

'Do you know what time it is?'

'Sorry, I wanted to get an early start. I want to put some distance between us and London today.'

She smothered a yawn. 'Good idea. Do you have your flask with you or would you like a coffee?'

'No flask. I was hoping to rely on your good nature. I'd kill for a coffee.'

A few minutes later, she handed him up a steaming mug and sat in his easy chair to sip her own. From there, if she ducked down a little she could peer up at him, and if he ducked a little he could glance down at her. She looked ridiculously cute in her flannel pyjamas—deliberately chosen by him to cover her from head to toe. She wasn't supposed to look sexy in them.

He ground his teeth together. She *didn't* look sexy in them. 'Sleep well?' He didn't glance down. He didn't want to see those generous lips curve into a smile if she answered in the affirmative or that cute nose crinkle in a grimace if she answered in the negative.

'I never sleep well the first night in a new place.'

Had her nose crinkled? He glanced down. Nope, her face was smooth. She'd drawn her feet up onto the chair, a pair of his socks on her feet, because he'd realised last night that she'd forgotten to put socks on her list of things for him to buy. He'd hunted her out a pair of his own. They looked better on her than they did on him.

They're just socks.

'What can you see?'

Her words dragged him from his thoughts. He glanced around. 'There aren't many people around. Why don't you pull on my mac and a beanie and come up to see for yourself?' Nobody would recognise her in that get-up.

She shuddered and shook her head. 'Too risky.'

The story she'd confided to him last night—her guilt over ruining her sister's chance at a dream job—still chafed at him. He understood guilt. He understood wanting to make amends. He might never find redemption for himself, but he'd help Cleo keep her promise to Margot. Family meant everything—a fact he'd only discovered after losing his own.

He shook the sombre reflection away to focus on painting a picture for her with words. 'It's still and pretty. There's a fine mist rising from the water and the canal looks like a mirror. It's the colour of mercury tinged with a rosy glow at the edges.'

He fancied he heard her sigh.

'In summer, the plane trees are a bright green, but at the moment the branches are bare. And, while the sun is mild, it's sparkling off the dew, which makes the city look gilded... washed clean.'

'How pretty you make it sound.'

Speaking of sound... 'The morning is meeting with the birds' approval.'

'Oh, yes! They're singing their hearts out.'

Her smile... He forced his gaze back to the canal. 'There are a few narrow boats moored to our left, which is port. Starboard is to the right.'

She repeated that as it fixing it in her mind.

'Bow refers to the front, and the back—' he patted the railing behind him '—is the stern.'

She repeated that too.

'There's a canal path that runs both sides. To the left there's a brick wall, probably houses and shops behind it.'

He continued describing what he could see. She listened as if mesmerised. But he suspected that was a symptom of a lack of sleep and not enough caffeine in her system yet. He hadn't spoken for this length of time, uninterrupted, in an age. He found he didn't hate it.

'That was perfect!'

He blinked to find her beaming up at him. His pulse stuttered.

'You ought to be a writer.'

He knew she'd said it to make him laugh, but a black cloud threatened to descend.

'Also, I wasn't dissing your boat when I said I didn't sleep well. I'll sleep like a log tonight. I'll probably snore and keep you awake.'

He couldn't resist teasing her. 'You did that last night.'

'I did not!'

He bit back a grin. 'How'd you know?'

'Because, if I had, I'd have a sore throat now.'

'When *do* you snore?'

'When I have a cold, have had too much to drink or am over-tired.'

'Forewarned is forearmed. I have earplugs.'

She laughed and it blew away the threads of that black cloud. He wasn't entirely sure that was a good thing.

She made scrambled eggs for breakfast. He told her she didn't have to cook his breakfast. She said she was making it for herself and it was just as easy to make enough for two, which was hard to argue with. He ate it standing at the tiller.

Afterwards she disappeared for a while. He heard the

shower running. He heard her wash the dishes, and then moving about, as if tidying up. She made tea—which he declined—and sat at the dinette doing things on her phone, probably sending texts and reading emails. And checking the newspaper sites to make sure she'd not appeared in any of them.

She did some stretches in the space beside the dinette, a few yoga poses and sit-ups. She walked the length of the narrow boat a few times. More than a few times… A lot of times…

After lunch—*damn that lasagne was good*—she sat in his chair with the crossword book he'd bought for her.

'Jude,' she called up, 'I'm looking for a five-letter word that means "to push forward". It ends in an L.'

'Impel?'

'Yes!'

They did three crosswords. At this rate, he'd need to stop somewhere and buy her another puzzle book. She disappeared again for a while; he thought she was taking a nap, but thumping vibrated from the front of the boat—something unfamiliar. 'Are you okay?' he called down the stairs.

No answer. Damn it! Was Cleo okay?

Easing into the bank, he threw the middle mooring rope over a bollard and tied off, before racing through the boat's very narrow corridor. The thumping hadn't stopped. He halted in the doorway to her bedroom and then rested his hands on his knees, relief pouring through him.

Cleo had her back to him, her phone in one hand, earbuds in her ears, dancing—in a head-banging style—to some playlist or other. Easing upright, he grinned. She gave a silly little shimmy before jumping and turning on the spot. She still didn't see him, though, as she had her eyes closed, her mouth moving silently to the words of the song. Then she froze and opened one eye, as if sensing him there.

Scrunching both eyes shut on a groan, she covered her face with her hands. Straightening, she pulled the earbuds from her ears and glared. 'I know this is your boat, but you're not allowed to sneak up on me.' She gestured around. 'Privacy, remember?'

'I called out but you didn't answer. I felt thumping. I was worried.'

Her cheeks went bright-pink.

'I thought you were stuck somewhere or had fallen or something.'

She groaned again, even louder.

His grin widened. 'It was quite a dance.'

'Hey!' She thumped his arm. 'I didn't know I had an audience. And I'm sorry if I worried you…made you pull over…'

'No probs.' It was time for a toilet break anyway. There were a lot of pros to his solitary cruising, but tying up whenever he needed to pee was not one of them.

'How do you do this?' She thumped down onto her bunk bed. 'How do you not go stir crazy?' She gestured. 'How do you keep so *fit*?'

'I go running, first thing in the morning and then again in the evening.'

'You didn't go running last night.'

'I had unexpected company.'

She blew out a breath and nodded.

She was bored and it was only day two. She'd be climbing walls by the end of two weeks. 'What do you do, Cleo?'

She stared at him blankly.

'During the day, when you're at home—what do you do?'

Her face cleared. 'I'm a freelance website designer. I've several jobs on the go at the moment. If I were at home, I'd be working on those.'

'What equipment do you need to do your work?'

'Just my laptop. It's got everything on it: the software I

use, all of my clients' details, all the work I've done on the projects so far…'

'Is there someone who could have your laptop couriered somewhere for you?'

'My flatmate Jenna. We've been friends since… well… rehab days.'

'Do you trust her?'

'With my life.'

Cleo, he suspected, was far too trusting.

'Right, have her courier it to this address.'

Turning, he walked back to the galley, jotted an address down on a scrap of paper and handed it to her.

She stared at it and then at him. 'You're a life saver, you know that?'

His lips twisted. Yeah, he was a real knight in shining armour.

CHAPTER FOUR

CLEO ARRANGED FOR her laptop to be sent to the address Jude had provided.

'All done,' she called up the steps.

'Excellent.'

That was it. He said nothing more. Of course he said nothing more—the man was a recluse. He enjoyed his solitude, solitude she'd so rudely disturbed. Her stomach churned.

Don't bug him. Don't pester him with a thousand questions. Don't give him a reason to retract his offer.

Nobody would think to look for her on Jude's narrow boat. *Camelot* was the perfect place to hide. She couldn't give him any reason to abandon her on the side of the canal.

Zipping her mouth very firmly closed, she reached for her Jason Diamond book and lost herself in its pages. She came to with a little bump a couple of hours later when they moored. Voices carried over the water, along with the low hum of traffic. Water lapped against the hull and somewhere nearby a lark sang. The lapping water and bird song was soothing. The sounds of traffic and people not so much.

'Where are we?' she asked when Jude descended inside.

'About quarter of a mile from Hemel Hempstead's town centre. Normally I'd moor at Apsley, but we made good time today.'

No doubt due to the early hour they'd set off this morning, and the cracking pace he'd kept up all day.

Those broad shoulders lifted. 'It's not far for me to duck out and grab a few things.'

She bit her tongue to stop from asking what *things*—none of her business.

'Need anything?'

She shook her head. He stared at her for a long moment and it made her fidget.

Don't frown at the poor man. Instead, she pasted on a bright smile that made him blink. Too much? Ugh. Why could she never get that balance right?

'Thanks for checking, but I've everything I need. We've all the ingredients for dinner. And, if we're stopping in Berkhamsted tomorrow, I'm guessing I can grab a few additional things then if I need to.'

'What shoe size are you?'

She frowned, even though she wasn't supposed to frown. *'Why?'*

He merely raised an eyebrow and she threw up her hands. 'A four, but—'

'Can I get you to do me a favour while I'm gone?'

'Absolutely. Anything,' she replied, shoe sizes promptly forgotten. She'd do anything she could to repay his kindness and make sure he didn't kick her off his boat. 'What do you need done?'

'I want the names of five charities to donate a thousand pounds to.'

Five thousand pounds was how much she was paying him to keep her hidden onboard *Camelot*. She swallowed. 'You're donating five thousand pounds to charity?'

He remained silent.

She forced herself to ask a different question. 'The search parameters...?'

He shrugged and her mouth went dry. His shoulders were *the best*. She could imagine dancing her hands across them, glorying in their breadth, testing their strength…watching his eyes darken with desire as she did so. A bit like they were doing now…

Fingers clicking under her nose had her blinking. 'Earth to Cleo!'

She jerked and blinked. 'Sorry! Off with the fairies.' Heat flooded her cheeks. 'Parameters…?' she croaked.

'Local would be preferable, and I'd like some proof of efficacy.'

'Consider it done.'

He turned and started up the steps. 'Same rules as before—keep the door locked, don't answer if anyone knocks and…' He held a finger to his lips.

'I'll be as quiet as a church mouse,' she promised.

'No dancing,' he said with a grin, closing the door behind him.

She stared at that closed door, feeling oddly bereft. Jude might not be chatty, but his presence was oddly reassuring. Shaking herself, she pulled out her phone and started researching local charities. What on earth would he be into, though? What would he like to support—be *proud* to support? Where on earth should she start?

Abandoning her phone, she reached for pen and paper and jotted down all the things she knew about Jude. He was a writer. He lived on a narrow boat. She tapped the pen against her chin. He'd been in London to attend his grandmother's funeral. He'd lost his brother in a car accident nine months ago. No wonder he rarely smiled. She couldn't begin to imagine how awful it would be to lose Margot like that, so suddenly.

What on earth…? Losing Margot in *any* fashion would completely and utterly gut her. Her chest clenched and her breathing grew rapid. If she didn't succeed in lying low for the next fortnight…

'Stop it!' she hissed, forcing herself to take deep breaths, releasing them in slow, controlled measures as her therapist had taught her. She needed to stop imagining worst-case scenarios. It wouldn't do anyone any good. She needed to conserve her energy for keeping her promise to Margot and not being too much of a nuisance to Jude.

She stared at her list. Seizing the Jason Diamond book, she read Jasper's bio and added 'cricket lover' to the list. Pulling her phone towards her, she started madly searching the Internet, losing herself in the research. She made lists of lists, eventually narrowing the selected charities down to five local—or at least local-ish—options for him.

She froze when someone jumped onto the stern deck and went cold all over. Was someone going to knock, try to break in?

The door opened...

And Jude appeared. Sagging, she glanced at her phone to find an hour and twenty minutes had passed in a flash, just like that.

His brows rose. 'Expecting someone else?'

'What?' She blinked. 'No! I've only just finished coming up with your five charities and I...'

'You?'

She surreptitiously covered the notepad with her hand. 'I got caught up in the research and hadn't realised so much time had passed.' She sent him a weak smile. 'For a moment there, I thought I might have to fight off a robber.'

He stared at where her hand rested on the pad and her stomach scrunched up tight. She nodded at the bags he held, hoping to distract him. 'What have you got there?'

When his attention turned to the bags, she pulled the pad onto her lap and pushed it down between the dinette seat and the wall.

'One pair of running shoes, size four.'

He set them on the seat beside her. She stared at them and

then at him. He couldn't mean…? 'I can't go running with you, Jude.'

'Sure you can.'

'If someone recognises me…' She rubbed her hands over her face. It'd be an absolute disaster. 'I can't risk it. I…'

'And in this bag are two wigs. Now, I know they'll probably itch, but it's better than you staying on board and climbing walls.'

She bit her lip. To be able to go for a run… But if she was seen… If she was seen *with a man* it'd be splashed across the front pages in an instant: *Cleo the serial dater.* And what if the press then dug deeper to find out who Jude was? What if they discovered he was Jasper Ballimore? He'd be unmasked. The scandal would explode! Margot would be devastated. And Cleo would've let everyone down—*again.*

'Cleo!'

She snapped to at the command in Jude's voice.

'Try the wigs on.'

He'd gone to so much trouble. The least she could do was try on the wigs. *Model passenger, remember?* She pulled the first box towards her and lifted the lid. Oh, wow. These were proper wigs, not cheap knock-offs bought for fancy dress. The first one was honey-blonde with long plaits and a fringe. She couldn't help grinning. 'Did you also get me denim overalls and a piece of straw to chew?'

Maybe Jude had a cowgirl fantasy. And maybe that would be kind of fun…

Gah! Stop it.

'The other one is, in my opinion, the real *pièce de résistance.*'

He uttered the phrase with the most deliciously perfect French accent and leaned back against the kitchen bench, the picture of relaxed ease, but she sensed an alertness, or perhaps an anticipation, in him that piqued her curiosity.

Pulling the second box towards her, she lifted the lid and her eyes went wide. The wig was a riot of light-brown curls that would hang down past her shoulders. She ran a light finger over a curl. 'This is really lovely.'

'The sales lady said you'd need to be careful with it if you wanted to maintain the curls, but nobody in real life has hair that perfect unless they've just come from the hairdresser. Messing it up would make the disguise all the more perfect.'

He reached out as if to do exactly that, but she held it out of reach. 'Let me try it on first. Then we can mess it up.' Racing into the bathroom, she tried it on and stared at her reflection. *Oh, wow.*

'Well?' Jude called out.

She moved back into the main cabin. Jude's jaw dropped. 'I wouldn't think you the same woman.'

His gaze travelled over her face in a way that had her nerves pulling tight and a pulse at her throat thrashing. Her breath caught as an expression akin to hunger stretched through his eyes, but then his lips thinned and he shook his head.

'It's all wrong with what you're wearing. This—' he gestured to her new mane of hair '—is too perfect, too formal. While this—' he gestured to the rest of her '—is casual and...'

And what?

'It doesn't work together.'

She wanted the floor to open up and swallow her. The only way Jude had been looking at her was as a problem he needed to fix. He wasn't looking at her as a woman he found attractive. She didn't *want* him looking at her that way either!

Lifting her chin and pasting on a smile, she said, 'That's easily fixed. Do you have an elastic band?'

Turning, he searched in a drawer and handed her one.

She gestured to the beanie sitting on the bench. 'And that.'

He handed it to her.

She tied the wig into a low pony tail and jammed the beanie onto her head.

He cocked his head to the side. 'With all of that hair pulled back, we can see more of your face now.'

Meaning someone might recognise her.

'You have another elastic band?'

He handed her a second one.

She shook out the wig and ran her fingers through the curls to frizz them up a bit, before fashioning the hair into two low bunches, pulling out wisps of hair to frame her face. 'How's that?'

He nodded slowly. 'That could work.'

His expression, though, told her that it was still a little too perfect. 'Wait until I do this.' Pulling the bands free, she grabbed his hairbrush from the bathroom and reefed it through the wig. When she was done, she held it out at arm's length. 'Now it's suitably frizzy.'

Without a word he handed her the blonde plaits. She pulled it on, the fringe tickling her forehead. He didn't say anything. Her hands went to her hips. 'Well?'

'I wouldn't have known it was you,' he finally said. He pointed at the fringe. 'It changes the shape of your face.'

Moving back to stare in the bathroom mirror, she frowned. 'Fringes don't do me any favours. Which, in this instance, is perfect. With a bucket hat and sunnies, no one will recognise me.' Even Margot would be hard pressed to recognise her in this wig.

'Except you can't run in hat and sunnies—not at night.'

She pulled off the wig. 'I'm not running with you, Jude. I can't risk it.'

'You're going stir crazy.'

Oh, God. 'Have I been bothering you?'

He rolled his shoulders. 'No.'

That clearly was a lie.

'The thing is—' he rubbed a hand over his hair '—you're going to have to sign for your laptop tomorrow. I should've told you to address the package to me. I don't suppose you did, by any chance?'

Her stomach plummeted. She shook her head.

'But with a wig, a pair of sunnies and a beaten-up bucket hat...' Rifling in a top cupboard, he turned and tossed her a navy number. 'No one will recognise you.'

What if he was wrong?

'Same with the jogging, even without hat and sunglasses. Plus, there won't be many people about, not at this time of year. The canal path is lit, but the light is dim. And you'll be jogging behind me.'

To get out and expend some pent-up energy would be heaven.

'And I don't want you getting sick on my boat. Nor can I imagine Margot being thrilled if you turn up on the day of her wedding looking like a ghost.'

She shifted her weight from one foot to the other.

'We'll have an early dinner, give it time to settle and then go running when most people are already tucked up inside.'

He made it sound easy. He made it sound doable. Ever since she'd screwed up three years ago, exercise had been her crutch. It had helped her deal with *everything*. It gave her the resources to cope.

'The fresh air will do you good.'

Hadn't she told herself earlier not to keep imagining worst-case scenarios? Jude wouldn't lie to her. 'Okay.' She gave a short nod. 'In that case, I guess I should get dinner on now.'

He moved aside to let her slide out of the dinette and then slid in to where she'd been sitting while she gathered up the wigs and shoes and dumped them on her bed. Returning to the galley, she began pulling ingredients from the fridge.

'Cleo?'

'Hmm…?'

'What's this?'

Something in his tone had her swinging round. He sat with his back to her. Between his fingers he held up the list she'd made. She froze: the list of the things she knew about him.

Something had gone cold inside him. He turned and whatever she saw in his face had her paling.

'Are you keeping some kind of a dossier on me?' Had she figured out *who* he was? Beyond Jasper Ballimore, that was.

Giving a nod that held a world of fate, she set the red pepper she was holding on the bench and pressed her hands together. 'Turn the page over and read it…and the one after as well.'

Turning his back to her, he did as she said. He closed his eyes as he joined the dots.

'I wrote down what I knew about you so I could…'

'Choose five charities…' That would have a connection to him.

'That you'd be happy and proud to support.'

He'd set her the mission, wanting to give her something to do—to keep her occupied and stop her from surfing news sites, or constantly checking her phone, hoping to hear from Margot. If she didn't stop that soon, she'd drive herself batty.

'You startled me when you returned from your shopping trip. I'd become so wrapped up in the search I'd lost track of time. You were upon me before I realised. I didn't have a chance to get rid of my notes. I know it doesn't look good, but the motive was innocent.'

He nodded. Behind him, she started slicing and chopping. He ought to make conversation, move them on from this awkward moment, but he couldn't manage it. Not when the facts of his life were written in black and white in front of him, stated so baldly and starkly.

'So...' The strain in her voice made him wince. 'Do you approve of said charities?'

Pulling in a breath, he stared at the final list she'd compiled. It included a literacy programme for adults, home help for the elderly, the UK Canal Trust, a charity that paid for deprived local young people to learn to drive safely and a struggling cricket club. When was the last time anyone had taken this much trouble for him over such a simple task? Anyone else would've simply listed the things *they* thought worthy.

'Of course, those aren't the only things I know about you.' The sound of spitting oil and the scent of frying onions filled the air.

Why did the fact that she'd taken so much trouble touch him so deeply?

'That's the thing when you ask yourself a question like that, isn't it? Other answers bombard you for days afterwards.'

More hissing and spitting sounded. More delicious scents rose in the air.

'I know that you're kind to damsels in distress, which means you'd probably approve of a donation to a women's shelter.'

He added it to the list.

'You have a sense of humour—the joke knickers are proof of that.'

He didn't know whether to wince or laugh.

'So maybe a donation to a comedy festival? It's a good thing to do, to make people laugh.'

He jotted that down too, then held his breath as he waited to hear what else she thought she knew about him.

'You're ridiculously reclusive, but I don't think there's a hermits' association you can donate to—though maybe fund-

ing a writers' retreat would suffice. Peace and quiet for writers is something you'd approve of.'

Absolutely.

'Also, you can't cook, so donating to some kind of life
skills programme might also be a worthwhile pursuit.'

Her observations were disconcertingly perceptive.

'And you understand the importance of exercise,' she finished. 'So in all likelihood an exercise education programme
would appeal to you too.'

He stared at the fourth item on her list again. Sliding out
from the dinette, he moved to the other bench so he was facing her. 'Matt was a good driver.' He didn't want her thinking
Matt hadn't been a a good driver. Or a good person.

She met his gaze and nodded once, before turning back
to the stir-fry, wielding her wooden spoon like a wand. 'I'm
sorry you lost your brother, Jude. I can't even begin to imagine.'

Her quiet sympathy, its sincerity, lodged in his throat, making it impossible to speak.

'And I'm sorry that it was stated there on my list like that.
As if…'

He raised an eyebrow, doing his best to look unmoved.

'As if it wasn't the biggest and worst thing that's ever happened to you.'

The edges of the room blurred. *The biggest and worst
thing.* That summed it up exactly. A laugh scraped out of
him. 'Want to hear the crazy thing? I was in the car when
it happened, and basically walked away without a scratch.
How wrong is that?'

He'd walked away while Matt…

Dead—in a split second—from hitting his head the wrong
way. The world had gone dark after that night. The light had
never come back.

Warm hands sliding into his brought him back to the present. He stared into eyes tempered with concern. 'What happened, Jude?'

He lifted a shoulder and let it drop. 'A deer. It raced out of the woods and onto the road.' He answered because he didn't know what else to do; he didn't want to lose the comfort of her touch. 'Matt swerved to avoid it.'

Her lips parted and a sigh escaped, low and sympathetic.

'We'd been at the pub.' It had been Matt's turn to drive. 'I was the one who called time.' His heart gave a sick kick. 'I thought he was drinking low-alcohol beer.'

She swallowed. 'He was over the limit?'

'Only just. If I'd waited half an hour longer…'

Her hands tightened in his. 'It wasn't your fault.'

Forget waiting half an hour; ten minutes, two minutes, would've made all the difference. Even sixty seconds! Then they'd have avoided that deer. And Matt wouldn't have ploughed the driver's side of the car into a giant oak.

He flinched as that moment played through his mind. If only he'd known Matt had been drinking full-strength beer. If only…

'It wasn't your fault, Jude.' Cleo shook his hands and leaned closer. 'It wasn't!'

Tell Elodie that.

He slid his hands from hers. He didn't deserve her comfort. 'He left behind a grieving widow and a three-year-old son.'

She rubbed a hand across her chest, as if trying to ease an ache there. 'Such a terrible tragedy.'

A tragedy he should've prevented.

'Jude…'

'Enough, Cleo. You asked what happened and I told you.' Realising how brutal that sounded, he added, 'But I thank you for your condolences.'

She bit her lips, her eyes throbbing into his.

'I just don't have the heart to keep going over it.'

With a nod, she rose and went back to their dinner. A short time later, she set a plate of chicken stir-fry and rice in front of him. Considering the subject they'd been discussing, he shouldn't have had an appetite, but the sight of the food—colourful and glistening—and the scented steam that lifted into his face had him ravenous.

He forked food into his mouth and closed his eyes to savour it. 'I wish I'd lied to the coroner.' The words left him unbidden, making him blink.

She acted as if his confession was wholly normal, spearing a piece of broccoli on her fork, popping it into her mouth and chewing thoughtfully. 'Which bit would you lie about?'

He tried to eat slowly, but the food was insanely good. 'The bit where I said he lied to me about what he was drinking.'

'I'd lie to keep Margot out of trouble. I'd help her hide a body.'

He huffed out a laugh. Her lack of judgement was unexpected, and unexpectedly welcome. It eased some tightness inside him.

'Keeping schtum about that wouldn't have changed a thing.' His fingers tightened around his cutlery. 'All it's done is mar everyone's memory of Matt.'

'Nonsense!' Chicken and rice slid off her fork to splat back to her plate. 'Is that your enduring memory of your brother?' She pointed her fork at him and proceeded to answer her own question. 'Of course it isn't. You think of the time you were both at the crease in a county cricket match and won the day on the last ball of the final over.'

That had never happened, but he'd once fed Matt a perfect pass in a football game. Matt had drilled the ball into the top-left corner of the net for a stunner of a goal. It had been a thing of beauty.

'And the day you were his best man at his wedding.'

His lips twitched. He'd never seen Matt so nervous; he

would never forget the look on his face when Elodie had appeared at the end of the aisle.

'And your grandmother would've remembered the day he graduated from university and…the time he burned down the back shed.'

Ha! That had actually happened.

'And his wife will remember the first time she met him and setting up house with him and the birth of your nephew.'

His chest clenched. To her dying day, Elodie would hold him responsible for Matt's death.

'You should've known he was drinking. You knew how much stress he was under at work. You should've taken on some of the responsibility. You should've been helping him.'

She was right on every count—he should've.

He pushed his plate away.

Cleo pushed it back. 'You'll offend me if you don't finish it.'

He glared. She shrugged. 'You want to know why I'm such a Jasper Ballimore fan?'

No. Yes.

'Why?'

She scooped up more of the deliciousness on her plate and ate it, chewing slowly, as if savouring it. He picked up his fork with a scowl. The food was too good to waste, damn it.

'Jason Diamond helped get me through the worst of my therapy. You, or rather your pseudonym, appeared on my radar after a particularly…rough session.' She wrinkled her nose. 'It's hideous, coming face to face with one's own failings.'

She could say that again.

'Anyway, there was a book my therapist suggested I read, so on my way home I dropped into the big book shop on Piccadilly. Your publicist was there and you had dialled in to talk with her about your latest book. I couldn't believe how many people had come to listen to you speak. I mean, it's not like you were there in person signing books.'

She spiked a piece of chicken with her fork, followed by a slice of pepper, a bit of carrot and a broccoli floret. He doubted she'd fit it all in her mouth. Setting down her fork, she rested her chin on her hands and stared at him. 'You spoke about your inspiration for Jason Diamond—how you'd always loved writing, how hard it could be but how satisfying too. And I thought to myself, here's a person who's living life on their terms, forging ahead with their dreams. And a tiny voice inside me whispered, *if he can do it, so can you.*'

He stared.

'It felt like serendipity—a tough therapy session and then stumbling into your inspiring talk.'

Inspiring? *Him?*

'So I bought the book my therapist recommended and your book too. I alternated reading a chapter of my therapy book with chapters of Jason Diamond. I swear his adventures kept me sane.'

That made him laugh.

He slowly sobered. 'I didn't give you enough credit when we first met. But, other than New Year's Eve, you hadn't appeared in the papers for...'

'Eight months. When Davide orchestrated that scene at the premier of a new movie and prostrated himself at my feet on the red carpet.'

His lip curled. 'That's right. He cried, claimed you'd destroyed all his dreams, or some such nonsense.'

'All news to me. We'd already parted ways, but I'd agreed to honour the public commitments we'd made. He did it for the publicity, to get his name in the papers.'

Men like Davide and Clay had preyed on Cleo, taking advantage of her kindness and good nature. And in return the world had pointed an accusatory finger and condemned her—himself included. She wasn't perfect—her terrible dating record proved that—but he'd written her off as a vapid starlet based on what? The media write-up? There was *so* much more to this woman. Cleo had hidden depths he suspected he'd barely scratched.

Not only that, she'd made significant changes to her life. She'd turned her back on the celebrity scene. Cleo wanted to move on; it was just the rest of the world wouldn't let her. She had, in fact, done an amazing job at turning her life around, at no longer being the 'wild child'. She ought to be proud of herself. Her *family* ought to be proud of her.

'I just wanted you to know I'll always feel grateful to you for Jason Diamond and his kick-ass attitude.'

She pushed her plate away. As she'd finished most of her food, he asked, 'You done?'

At her nod, he seized his fork and polished it off. The brightening of her eyes was his reward. 'Seriously good,' he told her, sitting back and patting his stomach. 'And, for the record, I think you've done a great job at turning your life around. I expect Margot recognises that too. We're not going to let anything ruin that, I promise.'

It was a rash promise. But all this woman wanted to do was to save her relationship with her sister. She deserved the opportunity to do that.

Rising, he took their plates to the sink. She followed and butted him away with her hip. 'I'll do the dishes.'

The heat from her hip burned against his thigh. He edged away, the scent of pears filling his nostrils. 'You don't have to wait on me.'

'But you're doing all of the boat driving and stuff. This is me pulling my weight where I can.'

He snorted. 'The difference is that you're paying me an absolute fortune to do "the boat driving and stuff".'

'Money which you're giving away.'

She pointed down towards his easy chair. 'Go and do your puzzles.'

'And then in an hour we're going for a run,' he reminded her.

Her eyes shadowed. Reaching out, he touched her cheek. 'It'll be fine, I promise.'

She moistened her lips and his gut clenched.

Her gaze fluttered to his lips. Her chest rose and fell... It'd be so easy to reach across and press his lips to hers. To...

They both snapped away at the same moment.

She busied herself with the dishes. Rather than grab a tea towel as he'd planned to, he retreated to the other end of the cabin and hid behind the newspaper. Nothing was going to happen between him and Cleo. He wouldn't let it. He might not be a hero, but she was alone and vulnerable. And he refused to be her next big mistake.

CHAPTER FIVE

'OH, MY GOD!'

Cleo clapped her hands and danced on the spot while Jude locked the door behind them. When he turned, she took a plait in each hand and twirled them, beaming up at him. He shook his head, but one side of his mouth hooked up.

'Not a single person recognised me!'

'There weren't enough people out there to recognise you.'

There'd been a dog walker and three other joggers, and no one had given her a second glance. She danced on the spot again.

Jude braced his hands on his knees, his chest rising and falling from the exertion of their run. She took the opportunity to admire the powerful lines of his body. He wasn't built like the musclebound cover model that graced the covers of his Jason Diamond books, but he was strong and lean without a spare ounce of flesh. And those shoulders...

He glanced up and froze at whatever he saw in her face. He straightened slowly, his gaze pinning her to the spot. 'What?'

'Nothing.' The word squeaked out of her.

A dark brow rose. It made her heart hammer harder.

'It's just that this—' she pulled off the wig and beanie '—was inspired, and I so needed that run, and I feel so much better for it—euphoric, you know? And for a moment there I was tempted to hug you.' *And more.*

She gripped her hands in front of her. 'But that's not a good idea, because we're all sweaty, and hugging you wouldn't be a good idea anyway, because…' *Oh, God, shut up now, Cleo.* 'You know…' *Floor, open up and swallow me.* 'I don't want to send mixed messages or give you the wrong idea…'

Jude closed his eyes. His lips turned white. She zipped her mouth shut.

'I'm in no danger of getting the wrong idea.' Those eyes snapped open. 'I've no intention of…' His hands made vague gestures, filling in the blanks. 'But no hugging is an excellent rule.'

She straightened. A rule now, was it? 'I couldn't agree more.'

She glanced at the ceiling, the floor and the wall—everywhere but at him. 'D'you want the first shower?'

He gestured her towards the bathroom. 'Knock yourself out.'

She showered, dressed in her cute though far from sexy pyjamas, bustled back into the main cabin and set about making hot chocolate. 'All yours,' she shot over shoulder, barely looking at him, sucking herself in as he eased past. Setting two steaming mugs on the table, she slid onto one of the bench seats—the one that ensured her back would be to the bathroom and Jude's bedroom. She didn't want to risk even the briefest glimpse of him emerging from the shower in nothing more than a low-slung towel, his skin gleaming…

Stop it.

What was wrong with her? Did she mean to spend her life lurching from mistake to mistake? Two days ago, she'd had a boyfriend!

Yeah, but he was a bad boyfriend.

Oh, right, so that means it's okay to immediately jump into bed with another man to soothe your hurt pride, for revenge sex?

She sipped her hot chocolate, letting its warmth filter into her. She didn't want to be the kind of person who did that. Given the circumstances, jumping into bed with any man was a bad idea. Besides the fact the media would have a field day if they found out, she'd had enough therapy to recognise a negative pattern when it slapped her on the head. The short-term satisfaction of sleeping with Jude wouldn't outweigh the damage she'd be doing to herself.

Where men were concerned, she was a disaster. She needed to work out why. And, once she'd done that, she'd work out what to do about it. If she'd been looking for love in all the wrong places, then she needed to start looking for it in the right places, or in different ways.

Besides, Jude wasn't interested in her like that. And who could blame him? He craved the quiet life. A woman like her—one who landed herself on the front pages of the news-papers with remarkable regularity—had to be his worst night-mare. And yet he *had* let her stay. Because he knew what it was like to lose a brother and he didn't want her losing her sister.

She picked up the notepad with the list of charities she'd collated. Behind his stern appearance and reserve, Jude was a bit of a softy. He didn't need to be messed with by the likes of her. Setting the notepad back down, she pressed her hands together. She'd abide by his rules. She'd be the easiest and best of boat roomies. She'd prove to Jude, her father and Mar-got—especially Margot—that she wasn't a hot mess. She'd prove that they could trust her. And maybe one day they'd even be proud of her.

Jude appeared wearing an old pair of tracksuit bottoms and a baggy, long-sleeve T-shirt that didn't plaster itself against his body like a second skin. Not that she'd have noticed if it had.

She gestured. 'I made you a hot chocolate. You don't have

to drink it if you don't want, but as I was making one for myself...'

Eyeing the mug as if it might bite him, he lifted it and took a sip. His brows shot up and something in his face lightened. 'This is good.'

She stuck her nose in the air. 'I'm an excellent hot-chocolate maker.'

It earned her a chuckle that made her breathe a little easier. 'You're also an excellent runner.'

He leaned against the bench; he *didn't* take the seat opposite, where their knees and feet might accidentally touch. She wished she hadn't mentioned hugging earlier. This was his boat, *his home*. He should be able to relax here. She needed to make things comfortable again.

'You'll find I'm excellent at many things.' That earned her one of those rare half-smiles. 'Therapy taught me the benefits of positive self-talk.'

'I think we can safely tick that KPI off the list for the day.'

She laughed. He could be funny when he wasn't concentrating on frowning all over the place. 'Running keeps me on an even keel—gives me an outlet for my excess energy, and the exercise endorphins are good for my brain. It's my number one strategy for staying on the straight and narrow.'

He crossed his legs at the ankles and stared at her over the rim of his mug, his eyes gratifyingly going glassy as he took another sip. 'You keep yourself on a tight leash.'

She didn't want to spiral out of control again. 'Thank you for making tonight possible, Jude. To be able to run is... It's everything.'

'I know.'

Something told her he understood exactly. What demons was Jude wrestling with? Did he really hold himself responsible for his brother's death?

She shook the thought away. It was none of her business.

It didn't take a rocket scientist to see that Jude Blackwood was a private man—a *very* private man.

He took another sip of his drink and a low hum sounded from his throat. It vibrated through her in an utterly delicious way. 'How long since you had a hot chocolate?'

'I honestly can't remember. If you'd asked me, I'd have said not to bother making me one.'

'And look what you'd have missed.'

'And look what I'd have missed,' he echoed, his gaze stilling as it rested on her...darkening when it lowered to her lips. Two beats passed. He jerked upright and reached for the list of charities.

Cleo tried to catch her breath, trying to calm the crazy racing of her pulse. The way he'd looked at her... No, no, he wasn't interested in her *that* way.

He slid into the seat opposite, careful to angle his knees away from hers. 'Which charity should I donate to first?'

'I'd start at the top and work my way down.'

'The literacy programme it is.' Pulling out his phone, his fingers flew over the screen. 'There, done.' He set it down again.

'What's the deal with that?' She nodded at the list. 'Why not choose your favourite from the list and give all the money to that one?'

He immediately removed his gaze from hers, and she wished she could retract the question. She was supposed to make things easy and light, be an undemanding travelling companion, not some nosy parker.

She opened her mouth to change the topic, but he spoke first. 'One of the last things my grandmother asked of me— made me promise—was, for the next year, to do one good thing every day.'

She stared at him. Her heart started to pound.

'And I reckon giving a thousand pounds to a worthy charity is a good thing to do. So, for the next five days, that's what I'm going to do.'

Her eyes burned. *Oh, Jude.* That would not have been what his grandmother meant; she was certain of it. He'd taken his grandmother's words entirely the wrong way.

A new thought slammed into her. *Oh.* Clasping her hands in her lap, she fought against the sudden burn of tears. 'That's why you let me stay.'

He hesitated, then shrugged. 'You needed help. You asked for help. And it's not like you were interrupting me doing anything important. Having a passenger might be inconvenient, but not unworkable.'

There you have it, Cleo: you're an inconvenience. Let that be lesson to you.

In her lap, her hands gripped each other so hard they started to ache. She was simply part of a to-do list he needed to tick off.

What were you hoping for?

She fought the urge to rest her head on folded arms. 'You hid me, you agreed to let me stay, you bought me the essentials and today you made it possible for me to go for a run. *And* for the next five days you're giving a thousand pounds to charity.' As she named each event, she flipped out another finger. 'Are you trying to get ahead or are you simply a high achiever?'

He scowled at the contents in his mug. 'I broke my promise. Between my grandmother's death and her funeral—five days—I did *nothing* good.'

'You were grieving. Your grandmother would've understood.'

'A promise is a promise.'

The haunted expression in his eyes caught at her. 'Jude...'

He stood abruptly. 'Thanks for the hot chocolate. Crossword and whisky time.'

She watched him settle in his chair by the wood burner, her heart aching, burning and bleeding a little. But she kept her mouth zipped tight. Every instinct she had told her he wouldn't welcome her opinion.

You're a smart and resourceful woman. Find a way to show him instead.

Smart and resourceful women didn't have their photos snapped throwing punches at their boyfriends. Smart and resourceful women didn't let their sisters down.

Swallowing, she seized her Jason Diamond book and lost herself in a comforting world of heroics, where right and wrong were easy to identify; where injustices were righted and the good guys always prevailed.

Cleo strode into the main cabin and lifted her hands. 'What do you think?'

Jude stared at her for several long *fraught* moments. Finally, he nodded. 'If I were a photographer on the lookout for Cleo Milne, I wouldn't glance at you twice.'

She let out a breath. She had on the curly wig, which after her ministrations now sported a realistic and somewhat unattractive amount of frizz. She wore yoga pants, a sweatshirt and had twined an old scarf of Jude's around her throat. Grabbing the new sunglasses, she perched them on her nose. It was a far cry from her usual attire of jeans and wool blazer.

'We are just nipping out to get the laptop and coming straight back?' she checked, trying to stop the panic from choking her.

He nodded.

Going out in the broad light of day was a far cry from jogging the canal path at night. She'd felt safe last night, with the darkness hiding her and Jude's back shielding her. But this felt risky.

He settled his hands on her shoulders. 'No one is expecting to find you in Berkhamsted.'

'There's plenty of speculation in the papers about where I could be, though. It's like a game of *Where's Wally?* Any journalist worth their salt will be keeping their eyes peeled.'

'You spend too much time on those damn news sites.'

He gave her shoulders a gentle squeeze. It put the heart back into her, and had her straightening her spine.

'You worry too much.'

True on both counts. But as soon as she had her laptop she could get back to work and stop fretting so much.

'Okay, let's do this.'

Standing on the towpath moments later, she tried not to fidget, but her stomach clenched so tight it almost cramped. Jude turned from locking *Camelot*'s door and frowned.

'Tell me a story.' The words blurted from her.

'A story?'

She nodded, keeping her gaze on the ground in case anyone should be around… lying in wait and watching for her. Her pulse sky-rocketed. 'God, Jude, please take my mind off impending disasters.'

He stepped onto the path beside her and she nudged him. 'You're a master storyteller. I had to force myself to put your book down last night and get some sleep. It's the second time I've read this book. I know what happens, yet it's still so compelling. So *once upon a time…*'

A hollow laugh sounded through Jude. A master storyteller? Not likely. A master storyteller could pick up a pen or drag a keyboard towards them and words would pour from their fingertips. A master storyteller could lose themselves in a story for hours at a time, could wrestle with a plot problem for days and then feel ridiculously victorious when they found the answer.

None of this applied to him, not any more. Where once there'd been creativity and an intriguing swirl of ideas, a burning fire to pick up a pen, there was now a black hole. He might not have been physically injured the night of the accident that had claimed Matt's life, but he hadn't been able to write since.

At first he'd thought it a symptom of his grief. After Elodie had made it clear how bitterly she held Jude responsible for Matt's death, though, guilt had stifled all inspiration and had laid a rotting blanket over the first tentative buds of his reawakening creativity. He'd found himself utterly incapable of writing a story of honour and courage for an upright hero like Jason Diamond.

He now doubted he'd ever write again. Despair threatened to descend in a smothering black cloud. The thought of never again experiencing the rush and joy, the challenges and frustrations, of writing a story... To have that door now barred against him...

What right did he have to such consolation, though? If he hadn't been so selfish, he'd have noticed how much pressure Matt was under. He'd have noticed that Matt had started to drink more. He'd have noticed *something*. Then he could've done something to help. But he hadn't noticed anything. He hadn't *done* anything, too engrossed with his own selfish needs and wants.

And the worst of it was that he wondered now if it was because he hadn't *wanted* to notice anything, hadn't wanted to be dragged into working for his family's firm, Giroux Holdings. Because he'd wanted to lead the life *he'd* wanted.

And now it was too late, all too late. And Cleo wanted him to tell her a story? He knew she was nervous. He knew she sought distraction. He knew she had no idea what she asked of him but...

'Did you always know you wanted to write thrillers with a good guy hero?'

He forced himself to focus on the question rather than the chaotic blast of emotions roiling through him. He mightn't manage a story, but he could probably answer the odd question or two. 'In the early days, I had no idea what I wanted to write.' He frowned. 'Actually, that isn't exactly true. I wrote whatever took my fancy, no rhyme or reason. I must have at least a dozen manuscripts that aren't JD books in various stages of completion—from entire first drafts to just a few opening pages.'

'A dozen!' She halted to stare up at him, her eyes wide, as if she thought a dozen a particularly amazing number. Despite everything, he found himself fighting a smile. Maybe it was her wide-eyed awe, maybe it was the hair that fizzed around her face, completely messing with her normal tidy lines.... Those eyes, though, were the same compelling green. And those lips...

With an effort, he dragged his gaze from her lips and forced his legs forward again, only slowing his pace when he realised she had to rush to keep up. 'And, if we counted actual ideas for books, we'd be talking three or four times that number.' Talking about writing was much safer than focussing on his reactions to this woman.

She heaved a sigh as if his words had evoked the happiest of thoughts. He worked hard at keeping his gaze on the path in front of them.

'What kind of trees are those?' She pointed to the tall stand of trees bordering the towpath.

'Beech—very common. Harder to tell with no leaves on them, though.'

She made a noise in the back of her throat. 'I'm terrible at anything botanical. I've never had a garden. But it'd be lovely to have one.'

It seemed a small enough wish, and an achievable one. 'You'd need a big garden for those.'

'But don't they look pretty? Actually, not so much pretty as grand.'

She turned, hands on hips, to stare back the way they'd come, and he realised someone was coming along the path towards them. *Right...* 'Your name for the rest of the day is Fran.'

Her lips twitched, but she didn't look away from the beech trees. 'Look at the way the light is filtering through the branches. It'd make a really nice image.'

'For what?'

Pulling out her phone, she snapped a couple of pictures. 'In my spare time, I muck around with creating website headers. Much like you do with story ideas.'

Did, not *do. Past tense.*

But he tried to see what she saw in the beeches, tried to see what had captured her imagination. 'It's...peaceful.' His shoulders loosened a fraction. 'A little bleak, but kind of timeless.'

She smiled up at him, as if he'd given her the right answer. Turning, she started walking again, mumbling a greeting to the couple as they passed, but keeping her gaze lowered.

'So, back to our conversation...'

What conversation?

'If you hadn't written the JD books—or if they hadn't been picked up by a publisher—which of your many projects would you have pursued instead?'

Her knuckles had turned white where her hand gripped the strap of her handbag. The couple hadn't recognised them— had barely looked at them—but her fear of being unmasked overrode what logic should have told her. If he couldn't find a way to help her relax, her tension would give the game away. So he told her what he hadn't told anyone. 'A young adult fantasy trilogy.'

Her hand abruptly unclenched. 'Like *Lord of the Rings*?'

Lord of the Rings was one of his favourite books. Did she like it too?

'It takes place in a kingdom called Ostana. No elves or orcs, but there are dragons and—'

'Are the dragons good or evil?'

'Generally good, but they're like people, in that they can be a bit of both.'

'Tell me more.'

'There's a mysterious dark force threatening the world, a boy who doesn't know he's a king, and a girl who doesn't realise she's a dragon rider.'

She did a funny little skip and clapped her hands. 'Tell me they fall in love.'

'Yep.'

'And that together they save the world.'

'Ah, but it's not that simple, is it?'

He led the way off the towpath and into the town of Berkhamsted. It was eleven-thirty, and the town was bustling. From the corner of his eye he saw Cleo swallow. 'Eventually they save the world, but there are a lot of ups and downs first.'

'Tell me more!'

'Well, he's timid and runs away at the smallest sign of danger, while she's too cynical to believe in happy-ever-afters. Plus, she's bossy. They hate each other on sight.'

'Of course they do. But fate forces them together?'

He couldn't *not* smile. Her eyes had lost their hunted expression, replaced instead with the avid interest of a true reader. 'Something like that.'

'Tell me this trilogy is written.'

Was she actually holding her breath? 'Books one and two are. The third has been started.'

'Tell me I can read it.'

'And here we are at the delivery place,' he announced, pulling them to a halt.

She tensed. Her hand clutched the scarf she'd wound around her throat.

'*Look... Fran*, you're an actor. Think of this as a role.'

'Did you see me act?' she snapped. 'I was terrible.'

His head rocked back. 'No, you weren't. Your character was troubled, but you brought out her vulnerability beautifully. You made her sympathetic. She did some awful things, but the audience wanted her to find her happy-ever-after all the same.'

Her jaw dropped. 'You watched?'

He wasn't admitting anything. 'I caught a couple of episodes. And in today's drama series you're an ordinary person with slightly frizzy hair collecting a parcel. You need this particular parcel for an assignment because you're a mature student at the local community college.'

'What am I studying?'

'Horticulture.'

Her lips twitched. Her death grip on her scarf eased.

'I'll make a deal with you, Fran.'

Her lips twitched again.

'You do yoga, right?'

She nodded.

'If you relax your shoulders—ease them down from around your ears, unlock your jaw and unclench your hands—I'll let you read the first chapter of my trilogy this afternoon.'

She immediately did everything he asked. 'You *so* have yourself a deal... Brian.'

Brian? He nearly tripped up the first step.

Chuckling, she leapt up them lightly and reached the door before him. For the briefest of moments he wondered if he could write a similar scenario into one of his books. It could be fun at some stage during the third instalment of *The Crown and the Fire Wielder* if Clement and Ruby had to don disguises—Clement having to pull on a mantle of command while Ruby had to act meek and downtrodden.

Cleo opened the door and the thought slipped away as they waited together in line. It took a while for the assistant to locate Cleo's parcel and he snapped into hyper-vigilance mode.

Like JD? Ha! He was no hero. But he had no intention of letting anyone blow Cleo's cover.

Eventually the parcel was located, signed for and handed over. Keeping his steps steady, he moved towards the exit and gestured for Cleo to precede him through the door.

Except she grabbed his arm and tugged him to the side; maps of the local area were lined up in neat rows in front of them. The pulse in her throat raced. 'Impending disaster!'

What the hell?

'Across the road. The man in the blue jeans and grey woollen jumper...'

'Journo?'

'Yes.'

Glancing towards the counter, his jaw clenched. The assistant stared at them, her phone to her ear. Cleo followed his gaze and swore softly. They'd been rumbled. And they needed to move fast.

Seizing Cleo's hand, he tugged her to the side door, shot out of it and set off down the street and into the bustling heart of the town. A shout sounded behind them and they broke into a run. Rounding a corner, he pulled her inside a huge discount fashion store, ones with racks of clothes everywhere.

Cleo took the lead and towed him to the back of the shop. They half-crouched when the journalist halted in front of the plate-glass window, ducking down when he turned to peer in their direction. Keeping low, Cleo led him to the fitting rooms. She collapsed onto a bench seat. He locked the door behind them and gestured for her to lift her feet onto the bench—in case anyone happened to look beneath the door.

Maybe he'd grown used to narrowboat living, but the room didn't feel too cramped. What he wouldn't give to be safely tucked away on *Camelot* right now, feeling cramped and unable to escape the mouth-watering scent of pears.

'What are we going to do?' she whispered. 'That witch of a sales assistant will have given him our descriptions. And he knows what we're wearing.'

Setting his backpack on the bench beside her, he rummaged round, emerging triumphantly with her blonde wig.

Her jaw dropped. 'You wonderful man!'

She immediately pulled off the frizzy wig and donned the plaits. The difference it made was remarkable.

'Here, put this on.'

He blinked when she shoved the curly wig at him.

'Hurry up.' She pulled the backpack towards her to check its contents. Grinning, she pulled out a battered beanie he'd forgotten was in there. 'Truly wonderful,' she murmured, pointing at him.

He didn't tell her the beanie was an oversight. It had been ages since anyone had thought he'd done anything wonderful. He pulled on the wig. He looked ridiculous, but she pulled a hair-tie from her handbag, gestured for him to turn around and made some kind of low bun at his nape. The touch of her fingers had hard darts of electricity zapping across his scalp. He had to clench his teeth and silently recite his eight-times table.

Once she was done, she pulled the beanie over the wig until it covered his ears, curls spilling out to frame his face. He blinked at his reflection. He no longer looked like a man wearing a woman's wig. He looked like a hippy…and that could work.

'D'you have a shirt on under your jumper?'

He pulled the jumper over his head, careful not to disturb her handiwork. She stowed the jumper in the backpack. 'I hate to ask you…'

He was already ahead of her. 'I'll go out there and get you a completely different outfit.'

'Then I'll do the same for you.'

He came back with oversized denim overalls, a multi-striped jumper in some kind of fuzzy fabric and chunky, dangly earrings. She grinned when she saw the ensemble. Taking the backpack, he moved to the dressing room next door. A few minutes later, she tapped on the door. He took one look and gave her a thumbs-up.

She blew out a breath. 'Okay, give me your sizes.'

He told her, taking her clothes to stow in the backpack. She returned with super-baggy black cargo pants, a tight long-sleeved T-shirt with a 'peace' sign emblazoned on the front… and a cardigan! He nearly snorted with laughter.

Her eyes danced as she pushed a big tote bag into his hands. 'That should be big enough to stow the backpack.' Which was when he noticed the wicker basket she held over one arm. *Perfect.*

'Give us a cover story,' she ordered.

'We're a couple who are into sustainable living. We have a stall at the local market where we sell handmade crafts, though we've both part-time jobs to help pay the rent. You work at a nursery while I'm a night-time shelf-stacker at a grocery store. And today we're…' he glanced at her wicker basket '…going on a picnic.'

Ten minutes later, they sauntered out of the shop as two completely different people. Cleo stopped at a deli and bought a loaf of sourdough, cheese, bananas and a bottle of sparkling water. She took his arm and they made their way back to the boat, looking like a pair of young lovers.

Back onboard *Camelot*, he ushered her down the steps,

pushed the door closed and slid the lock into place, before swinging to face her. She had to be frantic. She…

His mind blanked. She'd bent at the waist, both hands clapped over her mouth to stifle her laughter. 'Oh, my God, Jude. I should be beside myself, but that was so much fun.'

She said the words as if they ought to start with capital letters, so in his mind he gave them capitals: *So Much Fun.*

She was right. Which made no sense…

Her eyes danced and her lips curved upward, and it woke something deep inside him, shaking it free and making him glad to be alive. He could no more stop from leaning across and pressing his lips to hers then he could have stopped the tide.

CHAPTER SIX

CLEO SMELLED LIKE pears and tasted like freedom.

And she froze, as if taken totally unawares.

What the hell...?

Jude started to move away, but her fingers tangled in the ridiculous cardigan he wore, dragging him back, her mouth opening under his...

And he was gone. Cupping her face in his hands, he devoured her, learning the shape of her mouth, learning what made her shiver or brought a low hum to life in the back of her throat. Every time she sighed, moaned and deepened the kiss something inside him loosened and unfurled, forming an entirely new shape where before there'd been nothing but a hard, dark lump. Desire, need and the invigorating thrum of blood coursed through his veins.

Curling her fingers into his cardigan all the more securely, as if anchoring herself there, she devoured him back and all thought fled as things fizzed and sparked with an urgency that ought to have shocked him—that might have shocked him if he'd been able to think straight.

Growling with hunger and heat, he tried to temper the inferno that gripped him, tried to temper his strength, afraid of holding her too tight. As if she had no such concerns, she lifted up on tiptoe and flung her arms around his neck. The full length of her body pressed against his.

He backed her up until they reached the table, lifted her

onto it and settled between her thighs. He caught her soft cry inside his mouth and a rainbow of colour arced behind his eyelids as their bodies strained towards each other.

Her fingers dug into his buttocks as if to drag him nearer. His fingers dug into her hips as he pulled her as close to him as he could, air hissing between his teeth when small, seeking hands slid beneath his shirt to explore the contours of his stomach and chest, her palms grazing against his nipples and making him jerk.

It was too much too soon. He couldn't breathe.

Dragging his mouth from hers, he pulled in gulping breaths of much-needed air as they stared at each other, their chests rising and falling, air sawing in and out of their bodies.

Cleo couldn't pull her gaze from Jude's. The blue of his eyes was piercing and bright, and it sent a thrill circling through her.

How could a simple kiss be so *consuming*?

She touched fingers to her lips. It hadn't been simple, though, had it? That kiss had reverberated through her in a way a kiss never had before. His hands cupping her face had made her feel safe. They'd been gentle but strong—their strength had become her strength. And the kiss had sunk deep, the echoes of it imprinting onto muscle and bone. That had to mean something…

She blinked. It couldn't mean *anything*!

Planting her hand in the middle of his chest, she pushed him away, slid off the table and backed up a step. 'You said no hugging. It was a rule.'

She didn't recognise the voice that scraped out of her throat. She recognised the self-loathing that immediately smothered all the sparkling blue brightness in Jude's eyes, though.

Oh, no, Jude. Don't do that to yourself.

Kissing was a bad idea, but it didn't have to mean the end

of the world. He shouldn't hate himself for it. Rather than focus on the confusion raging inside her, or the desire coiling through her, she focussed on finding a way to rid that expression from his eyes.

Sliding in at the dinette before her legs gave way, she dragged off her wig and slanted a smile in his direction. She couldn't let him take the blame for what had just happened. That wouldn't be fair. *She* was the train wreck, remember?

'However, as we didn't hug—not really—I guess we didn't technically break any rules. So that's okay.'

He backed up to his easy chair, reaching behind to swivel it round before collapsing into it—as if he didn't trust himself to sit at the table so close to her. He was probably worried she'd jump him and kiss him again.

Her fingernails dug into her palms. He might have a point. It was exactly what her body was demanding she do. Except... she wasn't that person any more.

Don't ruin everything. Don't revert to type.

She *needed* to be better. She swallowed. *He* deserved better. And she needed him to not feel bad about this or it'd be another item on the long list of things to feel guilty about.

Sending him the tiniest of smiles, she shrugged. 'It was a hell of a kiss, though.'

He rubbed his hands over his face. 'I'm sorry, Cleo. I...'

'Don't.' Her smile faded. 'I was as into that as you were.'

'But I promised to look after you.'

'No, you didn't!' Her every muscle stiffened. 'You promised to give me a place to hide—*nothing* more. Jeez, Louise, you just went above and beyond in helping keep my identity secret, and I'm *really* grateful for that. But it is *not* your job to look after me.'

Pursing his lips, he stared at her. 'Is that why you kissed me back—because you were grateful?'

Her laugh might've held an edge of hysteria. She did her

best to rein it in. 'That was *not* a pity kiss, Jude.' *Nuh-uh.*
'That little adventure of ours, managing to avoid detection
and giving that journalist the slip... I haven't felt...'

Resting elbows on his knees, he leaned towards her.
'What?'

'It made me feel more alive than I have in...' *Seven years.*
'In a long time.' She moistened her lips. 'It went to my head
and I felt like...' She swallowed, clearing her throat. 'Celebrating.'

But that had been entirely the wrong way to celebrate.
Though now she had to wonder if, in keeping herself on such
a tight leash for the last few years, had she chased all joy
from her life? She pushed the thought away to deal with later.

'Also.' She pinned him with a glare. 'I don't give you permission to look after me.'

He straightened.

'By all means help me out if, like today, my cover is threatened, but I *can* look after myself. That whole calling myself
a damsel in distress was supposed to be a joke.'

Delicious frown lines deepened. Everything about this man
was delicious. It was enough to make a grown woman weep.

'You're going through a lot at the moment, though, Cleo.'

'So are you.'

The frown became a scowl. 'You just broke up with your
cheating boyfriend.'

She folded her arms. 'You just lost your grandmother.'

He paled and her heart went out to him. He'd been dealing
with the weight of the world.

'In my world, losing grandmas trumps cheating boyfriends
every single time.'

He blinked. Colour rushed back into his face.

She clapped a hand to her mouth. 'I'm sorry, that sounded
so much better in my head than it did out loud.' This wasn't
some kind of contest and she hadn't meant to make it sound

like one. 'I'm sorry,' she repeated. 'Don't ever put that in the book. I don't think readers would like it.'

He laughed, as if he couldn't help it. It wasn't a particularly joyful laugh, but she'd take what she could get. 'If you get to look after me. I get to look after you.'

Blue fire flashed from his eyes. 'I don't need looking after!'

She spread her hands, as if to say, 'I rest my case'. 'I'm starving. You want some lunch?'

He glanced at his watch and looked to be doing some kind of calculation in his head. 'I want to set off ASAP.'

An excellent idea; she wanted to put as much distance between them and that ruddy journalist as possible.

'But I'd appreciate it if you could hand me up a sandwich in half an hour.'

'Deal.'

Cleo spent the rest of the day working. Not on one of her many paid projects, but on an odd and sudden inspiration. Rather than stamp it out or ignore it, as had become her habit in recent years, she decided to indulge it. Because seven years of not having any real joy in her life…that was awful!

At seventeen, the acting out and partying had been an attempt to outrun the grief of losing her mother. It hadn't worked; therapy had helped her see that. But it now seemed she'd gone too far the other way, viewing fun, laughter and joy as things she ought to avoid.

She didn't want to live a joyless life. She could experience fun and gladness without descending into those old damaging patterns of behaviour. She needed to make room to let joy back in.

Late afternoon, Jude called down that they were docking in a marina and for her to stay out of sight.

A marina? Why? Was everything okay? Was there an issue with *Camelot*'s engine or…?

Oh.

Her heart dropped to her feet. He wanted to be rid of her, didn't he? He was going to ask her to leave. Because of that kiss. And because they'd nearly been unmasked. Because she was a mess, and he didn't want a mess like her in his life.

And she couldn't blame him, because if he was seen with her it would lead to speculation, and speculation could unmask his secret identity. 'You look like you've lost your best friend,' Jude said, coming below deck. 'Everything okay?'

She made herself smile and nod. A marina made sense. Jude was a decent guy; he wasn't just going to dump her on the side of the canal. He'd find her passage on another boat first. *Then* he could wash his hands of her with a clear conscience.

She had a crazy urge to yell and throw things, stamp her feet and cry.

'Cleo?'

Jude didn't deserve a temper tantrum. She'd be a model passenger if it killed her. 'A marina? Is all well?'

He frowned. 'Do you trust me?'

She might only have known him for three days, but in that time he'd kept her secret, had kept her hidden and he hadn't betrayed her when it would've been in his financial interests to do so. She nodded. 'Yes.'

If he thought now was the right time to part company, she'd accept it with all the grace she could muster.

'Here's the thing… After the incident in Berkhamsted, I think the media will start scouring the canals for you again.'

Oh! She should've thought of that. If that kiss hadn't completely befuddled her, maybe she would have.

Don't think about the kiss.

Letting out a slow breath, she straightened. 'D'you have a plan?' One that didn't include dumping her on someone else's narrow boat.

He opened his mouth then frowned. 'What smells so good?'

She gestured to the kitchen bench. 'Banana bread. I baked some earlier.' *For joy.* 'I found some flour. I didn't think you'd mind.'

'Of course I don't mind. I…' He shook himself.

'The plan…?'

He straightened. 'As long as you're in agreement, I thought of organising a car to get us as far away from here as possible.'

'*Excellent* plan.'

Her relief was due to the excellent plan and not the fact he didn't want to be rid of her. 'When?'

'We'll leave under the cover of darkness.'

Jason Diamond style? She grinned. 'You've always wanted to say that, haven't you?'

One corner of his mouth twitched, but then he sobered. 'I need to go out for a bit and make the arrangements. In the meantime…' he stalked into his bedroom and returned with the tote bag they'd bought earlier '…you'll need to pack.'

'Roger that.'

He headed for the door. 'Same drill.'

She nodded. 'Don't answer the door. Don't make any noise.'

'I'll be as quick as I can.'

Packing took no time at all. What else ought she do? They'd bought food for dinner. Was 'under the cover of darkness' before or after dinner? She paced for a while before pulling out her laptop and working on her fun project again to give her mind something different to focus on.

It was dark when Jude returned. 'A car will collect us at ten.'

That answered the dinner question. 'Where are we headed?' North was her guess—a remote farmhouse in Yorkshire or Northumberland would be perfect.

'Still being decided. Things are in motion, though. I'm just waiting to hear back.'

From whom? She didn't ask as he moved into his bedroom, presumably to pack his own things. And probably to avoid her. He'd barely looked her in the eye since that kiss.

They ate crumbed steak with mash and veg for dinner. She didn't pester him with questions about *the plan*. He seemed oddly keyed up, so she remained on her best model-passenger behaviour.

She also did her best not to notice the way his eyes half-closed on each mouthful, as if relishing every bite. It did strange things to her insides—made her stomach soften and her chest clench. It made her want to cook her entire repertoire of meals to discover his favourite.

He glanced up and caught her stare. 'What?'

She forced herself back to the mechanics of eating. 'Do you ever treat yourself to a pub lunch?' Wasn't that one of the things people did when cruising the canals—stop to enjoy the delights of a canal-side pub? Because Jude quite clearly enjoyed his food.

'Nope.'

'Why not?'

He didn't answer, just shrugged. Talk about excluding joy from one's life. He made her look like an amateur.

'I'll sometimes grab a pie from a village bakery.'

That was as much as he allowed himself? The admission had her wanting to cry.

Afterwards, they cleaned up and did the dishes. There was still nearly three hours before the car was due to collect them, though. And, while they didn't speak about it, now that night had fallen the memory of their kiss burned in all the spaces between them.

Jude retreated to his chair with the paper. She cut banana bread and made them hot chocolate, which they sipped in their individual corners. Her mind worked overtime. She waited until the contents in her mug had reached the halfway point before speaking. 'When I was in therapy, I had to keep a gratitude journal.'

He glanced up, watchful...silent.

'I scoffed at the time, thought it silly and gimmicky, but it really did help.'

He looked torn between saying something unfriendly such as, *So what?* or something supportive, such as *Good to hear.* In the end, he opted for silence—no surprises there.

'I think we should do that for as long as we're on this... adventure. I'll go first.'

The newspaper rustled in his lap. 'Why do *I* have to do it?'

Because it would help him focus on the positive things in his life. Because it would help him realise what his grandmother had meant. 'You don't. Not if you don't want to.'

His shoulders unhitched.

'But it would keep me company and make me feel less vulnerable and alone.'

Those glorious shoulders tensed again. 'I believe that's what they call emotional blackmail.'

She wrinkled her nose. 'I feel as if I've ruined your life.' His jaw dropped and she added, 'Not your whole life, just these couple of weeks where I'll be invading your privacy.'

'Cleo...'

'And knowing that there are some things in your life every day that you feel happy about and grateful for would help ease my guilt.'

He set his mug and the newspaper onto the small table beside him. 'You're making banana bread and real food. You've nothing to feel guilty about.'

'Hey, I said I'd go first!'

She stared at him in mock exasperation and he huffed out a laugh. 'You're incorrigible, you know that?'

She stuck her nose in the air, but her insides had started a little tap dance. 'I've been called worse.'

He shook his head, gesturing for her to continue.

'Okay, so we need to name three things each. First on my list: I'm ridiculously grateful we managed to avoid detection in town this morning. And this is going to sound a bit twisted, but it was also fun—edge of your seat stuff, like watching your football team surge forward in the last seconds of extra time and scoring a goal just as the final whistle sounds.' She folded her hands on the table. 'Incredibly exhilarating...but I really don't want to go through it again.'

'Noted.' Jude had no intention of letting anything like that happen again. 'First on my list is the banana bread and dinner—both delicious.'

She pursed lips that were pure temptation. The continuous effort to resist them left him exhausted. Leaving *Camelot*'s close confines would be a relief. His lips twisted; even if it did come with problems of its own.

'There are lots of things to feel grateful for, or that were good about my day, but there are two in particular—'

'Like what?' he cut in. Other than the amazing food she'd served up to him, he was struggling to think of anything else to put on his list.

She nibbled a corner of her banana bread. 'There are always the old chestnuts to fall back on—like, I have my health, my family have their health, I have somewhere safe to sleep, have food in my belly, clothes on my back, blah blah. And don't get me wrong; I *am* grateful for all of those things.'

He nodded. Not everyone was so fortunate.

'And there are more besides that might usually make my list—like our run last night. The air was crisp, it didn't rain, there weren't many people about and that stretch of the river was really pretty.'

It was why he'd stopped there.

'I'm glad I have my laptop, that I had a good night's sleep and that I made banana bread. That I'm no longer climbing the walls.'

She rattled them all off with such ease. He fought a scowl; it wasn't a contest.

'And I'm *really* glad my face wasn't plastered on the front pages of any newspapers today,' she added with a roll of her eyes.

Her name had appeared, though. That 'where's Cleo?' version of *Where's Wally?* continued to create speculation. It had to be playing on her mind.

'But none of those things made it onto your list?'

'Nope.'

He tried to not sound grudging. 'What's your number two, then?'

'I had an epiphany.'

He shuffled up a little higher in his seat. 'Which was…?'

She cupped her hands around her mug, though he suspected her hot chocolate had been drunk long ago. 'Our adventure today…'

'Some people would call it a misadventure.'

'Meh…potato potahto. It ended well, so I think we can drop the *mis*.'

He acknowledged the hit and gestured for her to continue.

'Getting away with it gave me a weird high and I suddenly realised that whenever I feel like that—'

'Like what, exactly?'

'Excited, jumping up and down with… I don't know.' She chewed on her bottom lip. He did his best to not notice. 'Glee, laughter, a sense of fun, delight… I realised I try to stamp those things out, try not to feel them.'

He leaned towards her and fancied he could smell pears. 'Why the hell would you do that?'

She stared at her hands. 'The first four years after my mother died, I was trying to hide from what I was feeling—the grief. I felt lost and I tried to hide that beneath a veneer of fun and partying hard. We already know how that played out and how I've since tried to turn over a new leaf.'

He nodded.

'For the last three years, though, I've equated things like glee and flights of fancy and lots of laughter with losing control. I've been so focused on keeping on the straight and narrow—trying not to do anything that would horrify and disappoint Margot and my father—that, basically, I've been murdering all and any high emotion that's bubbled to the surface.'

She mimed the stabbing knife from the shower scene of *Psycho*, her eyes rueful but with a hint of laughter in their depths, and he couldn't entirely smother a laugh.

'I hadn't realised that until today. And it struck me as kind of dense.'

'Only kind of?' He raised an eyebrow.

She poked out her tongue. 'Anyway, I'm through with doing that. Your turn.'

Cleo had let herself fully indulge in a moment of stress-relieving laughter, had gloried in her close escape, had let herself be wild and free—and what had he done? He'd gone and kissed her.

'No, no!'

Her voice broke into his thoughts.

'You're not supposed to look like that when we're making our gratitude lists.'

'Like what?'

'Angry...scowly.'

'Can we list regrets?' The words growled from him.

'Absolutely not! This is a gratitude list—things to feel good about, not beat ourselves up for.' Her eyes narrowed. 'And, for the record, that kiss shouldn't be a regret.'

'It sure as hell didn't make your list of things to feel grateful for.'

'Only because I was being tactful,' she shot back.

He stabbed a finger on the arm of his chair. 'It shouldn't have happened.'

'Maybe not, but it was a damn fine kiss all the same. One I'm not going to forget in a hurry.' Her lips curved. 'I bet I'll still remember it when I'm eighty. And, when I do, I bet I happy-sigh.'

His stomach clenched; *everything* clenched. The kiss had been hell-on-wheels spectacular. It had blown him open, and to deny that he wanted to kiss her again would be a lie. But it didn't change the fact that it shouldn't have happened.

He shouldn't play with that kind of fire. He'd had his heart shredded by a woman once before. He wasn't going to allow that to happen again. And even if Cleo was nothing like Nicole, his ex, she was still a hot mess. He had no desire whatsoever to be her next big mistake. He'd witnessed what loving and then losing his brother had done to Elodie. He wasn't going to open himself up to that kind of pain.

Cleo had boarded his boat and had promptly sworn off men. Given her situation, it was a smart move. He wouldn't mess that up for her.

'I refuse to regret something that has the potential to be a happy memory.' Cleo held her head high. 'It was just…a moment. We stopped when we should've, called a halt when we should've. It's only if I follow up on it now that it would become self-destructive. And we've already agreed we're not going to do that.'

Her words brought no comfort because he wanted to, with

his every fibre. But by this time tomorrow she'd know exactly who he was and...

No. Just...no.

'I don't think you ought to regret it either. And if you do then I don't want to hear about it.'

Her candour, delivered with sledgehammer bluntness, startled a laugh from him.

She raised an eyebrow. 'Okay, what's your number two?'

'I saw an otter.'

Her eyes widened. 'When?'

'Just before we pulled into Berkhamsted this morning.'

'And you didn't call me? Why not?'

Because he'd thought she was trying to stay out of sight. 'It was there one moment and then it was gone. It all happened too quickly.'

Her face turned wistful and he nodded. 'It's one of the best things about cruising the canals—catching sight of a kingfisher or watching swans glide by. And, when I'm very lucky I occasionally see an otter. I saw a badger once.'

'What about hedgehogs?' She gave a gusty sigh. 'I love hedgehogs.'

'From time to time. They're endangered now.' His plan meant otters and hedgehogs wouldn't be featuring on the agenda for the foreseeable future, though. His stomach churned again at how close he'd come to blowing her cover. After promising to keep her safe, he'd almost handed her to the media on a platter! If they'd been caught...

But they hadn't been. He let out a slow breath. They were still safe. Soon, though, this section of the canal would be crawling with journalists. It was time to get her well and truly out of their reach. He should discuss the plan with her, except it'd change her focus from her epiphany to her fears. And, once she knew the truth, everything would change.

'What's third on your list?' he asked instead.

A slow smile spread across her lips.

Don't focus on her mouth. Hmm, look—delicious banana bread, see? He shoved the last bite into his mouth in an attempt to distract himself, but all it did was stick in his throat.

'I did a fun thing. A fun work thing—only it wasn't work because it wasn't an actual job. It was a bit of play—for joy, you know? I had a ball. Want to see?'

Before he could answer, she lifted her laptop from the spot on the seat beside her where it was charging and lifted the lid. Retrieving a file, she turned the computer to face him. His jaw dropped when he realised what was facing him: a website home page...for *him*.

His Jasper Ballimore author headshot was a cartoon of an archetypal musclebound hero, and she'd clearly grabbed it from his current website, as it sat to the left below a header. This header was all swirling black shadows and golden fire, which managed to look both threatening and beautiful at the same time. Rather than Jasper Ballimore, the name Jay Ballimore emerged in various shades of teal and sapphire from the shadow and flame.

'Jay Ballimore?' he murmured.

'I thought, if you were writing a young adult fantasy series, you'd need to write under a different name than the one you use for your thrillers.'

She scrolled down. There was a paragraph beside the author photo that he couldn't read from this distance, and beneath that she'd created three mock-up covers for the trilogy he'd told her about as they'd walked into Berkhamsted.

'I thought "Jay Ballimore" sounded suitably fantasy-ish. Not all your thriller readers will follow you here—' she tapped the screen '—or vice versa, but you will get some crossover readers who adore the way you write.'

Was she one of them? He shook off the thought and gestured to her computer, his mind a tumble of confusion.

'Why...?' Why would she go to so much trouble? Why would she invest so much time in something that would never become a reality? Things inside him bucked at that thought, as if they hadn't given up hope of finishing the series. Which was odd, and not entirely welcome.

He rose. 'May I?'

At her nod, he took the laptop, retreated to his seat and read the paragraph beside his photo.

Let Jay Ballimore take you into a world of stolen thrones, ancient fire magic, cursed swords and majestic dragons in this brand-new fantasy series where a pair of seventeen-year-olds, who hate each other on sight and on principle, need to learn to work together if they want to save all that they love from destruction.

She made it sound like a done deal!

Well...? The inner voice sounded a lot like his agent's. He ignored it.

He glanced up and she shrugged. 'Like I said—it was fun. I love doodling around like this.'

Doodling? This wasn't doodling...

'And, while I love Jason Diamond, thrillers aren't my usual jam. Fantasies are, though. My fave authors are Naomi Novik, Tolkien, Sarah J Maas... Oh, and so many others!'

She rattled off names—his favourites featured among them; he'd never heard of the others, but made a mental note to check them out. It had been too long since he'd read a book, too long since he'd wanted to, but the urge swept through him now.

He clenched his jaw so hard it started to ache. He'd been as guilty as Cleo in cutting joy from his life, but he wasn't giving up reading for anyone. A man was allowed one comfort.

'That wasn't supposed to make you mad.'

He glanced up to find Cleo biting her lip, dismay etching lines into her lovely face. 'I'm not mad at you, I'm mad at myself,' he said.

Before she could ask why, he rushed on. 'This is amazing, Cleo. You're very talented.'

'Thank you. Like I said, it was fun. Though, of course, my ulterior motive is to spur you on to write the last book. I *so* want to read this series!'

He knew she said it to lighten the moment, but he couldn't laugh; he couldn't even smile. Write the last book? Impossible.

You sure?

She clapped her hands. 'Your turn.'

He dragged his mind back to the gratitude list. What the hell was the last item on his list? He contemplated using one of her old chestnuts and saying he was grateful he had his health and a place to sleep. But, no matter how much he wanted to, he couldn't do it. She'd given so much of herself. It wouldn't be fair.

'After I say it, there's to be no questions, no discussion... nothing.'

'Okay.'

He dragged in a breath. 'For the first time in nine months, it didn't hurt to talk about writing.' He still couldn't get his head around it. 'I'm grateful for that.'

Her jaw dropped, her eyes widening with a hundred questions, but true to her word she didn't utter a single one. And then she smiled, a beaming light of a smile that felt like the beginning of a fairy tale.

His phone buzzed. Picking it up, he read the message and, rising, he handed her the laptop. 'The car is here early.'

CHAPTER SEVEN

NERVES JANGLED IN Cleo's stomach. 'It's an hour early.'

Jude's phone buzzed again. He read the message and shrugged. 'Things are moving more quickly than expected.'

Um...okay. Trying to look composed, she stowed her laptop into the tote bag, donned the blonde wig and settled a beanie over it.

'What are we going to do with the perishables?' She gestured to the fridge and the pears on the kitchen bench.

'Leave them.'

'Which means you'll come back to—'

'There's not much left and I've a caretaker coming in to look after things.'

He did?

'Though we're not leaving the banana bread.'

Reaching across, he seized the banana bread and wrapped it in wax-proof paper and a clean tea towel.

'Here, put this on.'

She caught the mac he tossed to her and shrugged it on. He swung her tote bag over his shoulder, picked up the small case he'd packed for himself and stowed the banana bread under his arm.

'We're in luck. It's started to rain.' He pushed an umbrella into her hands. 'As soon as we reach the top of the stairs, open it and keep as much of your face behind it as you can. I'll go first. Just keep your eyes on my feet and follow.'

'Is there something you're not telling me?'

He swung back.

'Am I about to be greeted with the flashes of a hundred cameras?' If she was, she'd rather know that now.

'There aren't any journalists waiting to pounce on us, but after what happened earlier I'm taking every precaution; that's all this is about.'

Right.

'Ready?'

'Yes.'

They exited *Camelot*, and she followed him along a dock and across a small yard to a waiting car—big, black with tinted windows. Not that she got a good look at it. Jude ushered her before him, taking the still open umbrella and shielding her as she slid inside the car's luxurious interior, before following her.

She stared at him as the car pulled away on silent wheels. 'Have you worked as a bouncer or bodyguard? Because you did that like a professional.' It reminded her of her acting days when she'd been filming on location.

He sent her a wry smile. 'No.'

'Where are we going?'

His phone buzzed with an incoming text. He read it and grimaced. 'At the moment we're heading to the airport. The rest I'm still trying to sort out.'

The airport? Oh, God. He was going full Jason Diamond heroic on her. This had to be costing him a fortune. Reaching across, she squeezed his forearm. 'I want you to know that my rainy-day fund is at your full disposal.' She'd cover whatever costs she could.

Glancing up from his phone, something in his face softened. 'Cleo…'

The phone rang and he blew out a breath. 'I have to answer this.'

When they reached the airport she was ushered onto a private jet. Before she could splutter out a single question, Jude disappeared into the cockpit. From then, for all intents and purposes, they travelled separately. When the jet set down in Nice, two bodyguards ushered her to another car with tinted windows, drove her down to the harbour and escorted her onto a super-yacht.

A super-yacht!

She was shown into a saloon and the yacht immediately headed out of the harbour. She had no idea if Jude was on board or not.

Half an hour later, he strode into the saloon wearing an exquisitely tailored suit that fitted him to perfection, highlighting his broad shoulders and strong thighs. It was so unexpected, her jaw dropped.

Grimacing, he shrugged out of his jacket and irritably flicked open the top two buttons of the crisp white business shirt, like some kind of movie star. Her mouth dried while her pulse surged in giddy appreciation.

Don't.

She dragged her gaze away. She couldn't afford to indulge a single carnal thought where this man was concerned. As previous experience had proved, she was a terrible judge when it came to romantic partners. And he was just too *tempting*. Just... *No*.

He poured himself a Scotch from the polished blond-wood bar at the far end of the room, before sauntering down to sit directly across from her on the semicircular sofa—a bespoke white leather indulgence that fitted the curve of the room.

An acre of space spread between them—literally *and* figuratively. She lifted her hands. 'Who are you?'

Hooded eyes stared back. 'You didn't look me up on the Internet?'

It hadn't occurred to her to do any such thing. 'Is Jude Blackwood another pseudonym?'

Seizing his glass, he moved to sit beside her. Not too close, but close enough that she could see the exhausted lines fanning out from his eyes. Something in her chest clenched.

'Not a pseudonym, but my name isn't well known in England.' He sipped his drink. 'You've heard of Cesar Giroux?'

Everyone had heard of the Giroux family, though Cesar had died four years ago. 'What does he have to do with you?'

He stared into his Scotch. 'Cesar was my grandfather.'

Her eyes bugged. *No way.*

'*You're* the Giroux heir?'

The Giroux family were French industrialists who'd made their fortune several generations ago, and had been adding to it ever since. They were one of the richest families in France, feted wherever they went. Cesar had been nicknamed 'Midas', because everything he'd touched had turned to gold.

Random snippets of news reports came to her: Cesar's state funeral; the shocking death of the older brother, Matthew—Jude's brother; his mother, Cesar's only child, dying of a drug overdose when Jude had been a young boy; one of Cesar's nieces marrying a Scandinavian royal. The family was wealthy, powerful and influential, and their fortune legendary.

Her cheeks burned. 'I offered the *Giroux heir* the use of my rainy-day fund to help finance our escape? *Seriously?*'

'Cleo—'

'And when I crashed onto your boat and inferred you were living frugally and that some extra money might come in handy...' As if he'd been living a hand-to-mouth existence—how he must've laughed.

Floor, swallow me now.

Reaching out, he took her hand. 'You treated me like a real person. You judged me on our interactions rather than my family's fortune. You treated me like you would anyone else. I treasured that.'

The expression in his eyes had her heart flipping. She carefully reclaimed her hand and eased back a fraction, things inside her becoming too heated and needy.

'I wasn't trying to deceive you. I was just…enjoying my anonymity. I'm sorry I didn't tell you who I was sooner.'

She waved that away. 'Totally understandable.' She'd have done the same in his place.

'So…you don't want to throw your drink in my face or punch me?'

She tried to glare but failed. 'It should be too soon for that joke.'

He gave one of those crooked half-smiles that never failed to send her insides into a spin. She recalled that moment earlier when his lips had found hers…

She jerked back, horror dawning through her. 'You're *seriously* famous.' He was ten times the news story she was. 'You have to be one of Europe's most eligible bachelors. You—' she gestured at him and then to herself '—and me. If we're photographed together…' It would create a sensation of *monumental* proportions.

'I know.' Tilting his head back, he drained the contents of his glass. 'But you forget I've also the kind of wealth that can shield you from the media. And I'm going to use every tool at my disposal to do exactly that. I assure you, Cleo, no one is going to discover where you are and who you're with. You have my word.'

The yacht was amazing. When Jude took her for the grand tour the following morning, Cleo spent most of it trying to haul her jaw off the floor. Besides the spacious saloon with its opulent white leather sofa and blond-wood bar, there was an oak panelled dining room, a galley kitchen that was thrice the size of *Camelot*'s, and eight bedrooms, all with *en suites*. There was an office-cum-library and a gym.

There were staff quarters on a lower deck. There was a magnificent pool at the stern. There was a hot tub on the main deck, and the upper deck had a sky lounge—all clear glass and marvellous light. There were myriad outdoor seating and dining areas. As soon as the first helicopter flew overhead, though, she avoided all of those, along with the sky lounge. She couldn't get the image of a telescopic lens out of her mind.

She and Jude fell into a kind of rhythm. Because the yacht was operating on a skeleton staff, she continued to cook while he ate with the same relish he'd shown on *Camelot*. They worked out in the gym, and they set up their laptops in the yacht's generous office.

They danced around each other trying to act normal, *very* careful not to touch. Yet every now and again she'd glance up and catch an expression in his eyes—an expression of heat and yearning, sweetened with a strange tenderness. And her reaction was always instant and totally out of proportion— her skin would prickle with a heat that made her fidget, made her antsy. And it wasn't the kind of antsy that a hard session in the gym could ease.

No men. No romance. No making headlines.

She kept repeating it silently, like a mantra. She wasn't going to let herself down. She wasn't going to let her family down. And she wasn't going to let Jude down either. *Nothing* could happen between them.

'You don't have a French accent.'

It was their fourth morning on the yacht and Cleo was pounding the treadmill while Jude's legs furiously pumped the stationary bicycle.

'Didn't you grow up in France?'

He wore shorts and his thigh muscles bunched and flexed.

Her mouth went dry. With an effort, she dragged her gaze away. She had no idea how to mitigate the intensity of her *want*. She wanted him, with a fierceness that made no sense. She did her best not to think about it and tried to focus her mind on other things. Yet she'd constantly jerk back into the moment, realising she'd been indulging in flagrantly detailed fantasies of making love with him: slow sensual love-making; fast, furious love-making. Intense love-making…

She couldn't remember ever wanting anyone with this kind of intensity.

In perfectly accented French, Jude now said, 'My French is flawless.'

'Oui,' she agreed.

'My parents divorced when I was six and my British father insisted that Matt and I be educated in England. We spent most of our school holidays at the Château Giroux, though.'

She'd seen photographs of the château, located on the outskirts of Paris. It took grandeur to a whole new level.

'I was close to my maternal grandparents before they passed.'

She kept her gaze to the front. 'And you were close to your paternal grandmother too.' The one who'd made him promise to do one good thing a day. 'When did you get to spend time with her?'

She couldn't resist a quick glance in his direction to find her question had surprised a smile from him, which made her breath catch.

No, no, that was the exercise. She slowed her pace to ensure oxygen could still reach her bloodstream.

'When my father dumped me and Matt in boarding school, we barely saw him—or my mother. Gran upped sticks from London and moved to the town where the school was located. She insisted we spend every weekend with her.'

'Oh, what a lovely thing to do! She sounds wonderful.'

He nodded. 'She took two rowdy boys, who were pretty angry at the world at the time, in her stride.'

Of course they'd have been angry. They'd been ripped from all they'd known and abandoned.

'She made us into a family,' he finished simply.

Her eyes filled.

'If you start crying, Cleo, I'm throwing you overboard.'

'I'm not crying!' She picked up her pace again. 'You make me jealous. I've no memories of my grandparents.' She sent him a sidelong glance. 'I'm sorry, Jude. You must miss her enormously.'

'I believe you already gave me your condolences.'

The timer dinged and they both stopped, both breathing hard from the exertion. 'But now I know more about her, which means my condolences are more.'

'More what?'

'Just…more.'

Climbing off the treadmill, she reached for her towel and pressed it to her face and neck. Glancing across, she found Jude's hungry gaze glued to where she'd blotted the towel to her throat. The racing of her pulse nearly brought her to her knees. She deliberately turned away.

'What about your dad?' *Breathe, Cleo, breathe.* 'Do you ever see him?'

'He died when I was sixteen. A lorry blew a tyre on the motorway and slammed into his car.'

She swung back, her heart sinking. 'Oh, Jude, how awful.'

He rolled his shoulders. 'We weren't close.'

'That doesn't make any difference. It's worse in some ways, because now you'll never know what the future could've held.'

He stared, and for a moment she thought he might say more, but then he shook his head and ushered her through the door. 'I need a cold drink before hitting the shower. You?'

She nodded.

'It must be time for you to answer a few questions for a change. What about you? Were you close to your mum?'

Oh, God. Had she been asking too many questions? Of course she had. She needed to stop doing that...

'Cleo?'

Jude's eyes narrowed at the way Cleo had started frown.

She shook herself. 'Yes, really close.'

Hence the reason Cleo had gone off the rails so spectacularly after she'd died, he supposed. He handed her a bottle of water from the bar in the saloon and sprawled on the sofa. 'What was she like?'

'Smart, vibrant, fun. We didn't know what to do after we lost her.'

She paced around the room, her gaze fixed on the view outside. 'She brought out the best in us. She made Dad talkative, when he's not the most communicative of men. Margot has a tendency to be a bit too serious, and she got her to laugh and be a bit silly. She made them relax and have fun.'

She smiled, remembering, but she was still too keyed up, too tense. This woman needed to learn to relax. 'Cleo, sit. You've just spent an hour pounding away in the gym.'

She shook her head. 'I'm not sweating my dirty sweat all over your white sofa.'

'Why not?'

'Respect.'

'It's hard-wearing and easy to clean,' he shot back. 'And I insist.'

After the briefest of hesitations, she perched on the very edge of a seat. But he suspected she'd only done it to humour him. Maybe talking more about her mum would help her unwind. 'How did your mum bring out the best in you?'

She sent him a sidelong glance. 'You might not believe it, but I was a shy teenager. Mum brought me out of my shell.

Acting was her idea; she thought me joining a drama group would help me gain confidence.'

Confidence she'd lost when her mother had died. His heart went out to her.

She tapped a finger against her water bottle. 'You know, we've never really functioned properly as a family since.'

She stood again, strode across to the bank of windows and stared out at the view—at the hills of Nice rising up behind the terracotta tiles of the city. The sun glittered off a sea that sparkled silver and blue. 'I can't believe how beautiful it is here.'

'Come up on deck.' It was January, so it was cold, but not like in London or Paris. She'd been cooped up for too long. The fresh air would do her good.

She shook her head.

'Why not?'

'There are other yachts.' She pointed.

They were miles away!

She then pointed skywards. 'And haven't you heard the helicopters passing overhead?'

Was she worried they might be news helicopters?

'Anyway, I'm content inside.' She gave an excited wiggle. 'Do you know how amazing this is?' She turned on the spot, her eyes filled with a mix of awe and delight, and something in his chest softened. Some silly thing he did his best to ignore.

'I feel as if I've been rewarded for my bad behaviour—land myself on the front pages and get whisked away to the French Riviera.'

'Or maybe you were rewarded for sticking up for yourself. Clay deserved everything he got.' Reaching out, he gently squeezed her shoulders, her warmth flooding every pore. 'You deserve every drop of good fortune that comes your way, Cleo.'

She stared at him as if his words had momentarily immobilised her. Her gaze lowered to his mouth. Full lips parted, as if parched.

Hunger roared in his ears. To taste those lips one more time...

Cleo tugged herself free, leaving his hands empty. She backed up a step, and then another one, her eyes not meeting his. She pointed behind her. 'I...uh...shower.' Turning, she fled.

He clenched his hands at his sides and counted to twenty until he was certain she'd reached her cabin before heading to his own. His punishing cold shower should've left him blue, but barely took the edge off the heat banked just below the surface of his skin. He needed to tread carefully—very carefully. He'd sworn to himself that he wouldn't get involved with Cleo. It was just too...dangerous. There was a warmth beneath his desire that instinct told him would lead to trouble of the heartache variety. He wasn't opening himself up to that, no matter how much he wanted her, or how much he liked her.

He'd been burned before, and he wasn't interested in repeating the experience. Nor was he interested in opening himself up to the agonies Elodie now suffered.

While Cleo was doing her best to get her act together, what would happen the next time life dealt her a blow? Would she act with maturity, or not? What if he unintentionally provided that life blow? A bad taste coated his tongue. Their attraction had the potential to be monumentally destructive, materially and emotionally. His body might burn for her, but he'd burn in hell if he gave into the temptation.

'Okay.' Cleo put down her book—the third in the Jason Diamond series—and clapped her hands. 'Gratitude time.'

He held up his puzzle book. 'I finished the cryptic crossword.'

He'd had his staff grab a host of puzzle books from the airport. Just as they had on *Camelot*, he and Cleo continued to do identical puzzles and compared notes at the end of the day.

'No way! I need a clue for three down. It completely bamboozled me.'

She was a novice when it came to puzzles, but was smart and quick. Given enough time, he suspected she'd overtake him. Not that they'd be here long enough for that.

Stretching, he shifted on his seat. 'Go on, then, hit me with your gratitude list.' He wouldn't say he looked forward to doing this gratitude thing, but he'd started to find it easier. And the way her eyes lit up when she listed her items was a definite consolation.

'My beef stew was perfection.'

His mouth watered at the memory. 'It was.'

'I don't always get it right, but I did tonight, which was satisfying.'

He searched his mind for something to add to his list. 'I fixed an engine problem. It was a bit tricky, but it worked.'

She stared. He half-scowled. 'What? If you can have beef stew, then there's nothing wrong with me putting engine repairs on my list.'

'Absolutely *nothing* wrong with it. I thought you'd have an engineer for that.'

He did, but engines were another kind of puzzle, and he liked to tinker.

'It's just, you're so…*capable*.'

Their gazes locked and the air between shimmered. It took all his strength to wrench his away and lift his glass of whisky to his lips.

'I added a book page to the Jay Ballimore website.'

He glanced back.

'It was fun. Want me to send it to you?'

He stalked across to the bar and poured himself another finger of whisky. 'Sure, why not?'

'Say please.'

Her teasing made it hard not to grin. 'Cleo, could you please send me the new website page that you made today? I'm curious to see it.'

She wriggled in her seat. 'That acknowledgement almost makes my list, but I'm afraid it's trumped by Margot.'

He started to walk back to his seat but froze at her words. With an effort of will, he made his legs move again. 'That sounds…' *Promising? Ominous?* He sat. He had no idea.

'I've been emailing her every day with my gratitude list. Today she emailed back with hers. Nothing else, no other message, but it's a start.'

He swore.

She blinked. 'Did you just say *a very rude word*?'

He glared. 'Must you always over-share?'

She crossed her arms, her shoulders inching up towards her ears. 'It feels safe to share here. I…'

'It's not a criticism.' Her confidences made him feel privileged. He scowled: and beholden.

'I'm in awe, that's all,' he grouched. 'You seem to find it easy.'

She sent him the smallest of smiles. 'What happens on a super-yacht remains on a super-yacht. Same goes for narrow boats.'

Dragging in a breath, he nodded. 'I'm pleased you're making progress with Margot.' That was huge news.

'Thank you.'

She stared at him expectantly. His scowl deepened. 'Okay, there's to be no response to what I'm about to say, got it?'

'Okay.'

'I started the first chapter in book three of my fantasy series.'

Her eyes widened. Her hands slapped to her thighs. She leaned towards him…

He pointed. 'Not a single word.'

Her mouth snapped shut. Without uttering a word, she happy-danced, then she picked up her Jason Diamond book and opened it to the bookmarked page.

He couldn't have said why, but it made him smile. 'That's great news about Margot, Cleo.'

She didn't look up. 'Thank you.'

'The website page…?'

'Already sent.'

Margot was talking to Cleo again. He had to double every effort and ensure nobody discovered where she was. He wouldn't let anyone ruin this for her.

As for the writing… What the hell did he think he was doing? When he took his place as head of the Giroux family, there'd be no time for writing. There'd be only duty and responsibility. Duty and responsibility he had no intention of shirking ever again.

CHAPTER EIGHT

'THE POOL IS HEATED, Cleo. You can go for a swim if you want.'

Cleo turned away from the window with its view of the pool. It wasn't a plunge pool, but a proper pool—one any resort would be proud of. She suspected she'd been staring at it a little too wistfully. 'It's just hard to not keep admiring the view. I mean, the Côte d'Azur! I have to keep pinching myself.'

No matter how much she might want to, she couldn't go for a swim, even though there was a wardrobe of clothes in her cabin, including swimsuits. The pool was on the open deck, and helicopters continued to pass overhead with monotonous regularity.

She was Cleo Milne. Jude was the Giroux heir. And together they'd be tabloid gold. Margot deserved better from her. *Jude* deserved better from her.

He stood. 'Come on.'

'I'm not swimming, Jude.' It was too risky.

'I'm not talking about the pool.'

Another session in the gym? Excellent idea! Powering down her computer, she followed him. But he didn't lead her to the gym; instead, he led her to... *The hot tub? No way!*

Turning on the jets, he took her hand and plunged it into the water. 'Feel how warm that is.'

She nearly swooned. It was heaven.

Releasing her, he pointed to the awning above. 'This area is covered.' He pressed a button on the wall and shade screens lowered. 'A telescopic lens isn't getting through that lot.'

Still, she hesitated. It was hard enough being in the same room as Jude, working at different ends of the huge table in the yacht's office or sitting on opposite sides of the curved white sofa in the saloon, let alone jumping into a hot tub with him.

'You said you wanted more joy in your life. And yet here you are, still turning your back on it.'

'No, I'm not!'

'And I can't help wondering why.'

She rubbed both hands over her face. 'Because I don't want to keep making the same mistakes.'

He blinked.

'Surely you understand that? I want to find joy responsibly. I don't want to keep looking for it in the wrong places.' Especially not in the lead up to Margot's wedding. She couldn't afford to be reckless or rash.

He folded his arms. 'It's just a hot tub, Cleo.'

Which of course made her feel like a fool.

'And there's no chance of the paparazzi snapping a picture of you here.'

Even to her paranoid eyes, all looked safe.

'And I dare you.'

'You...*what*?'

He raised an eyebrow.

The hot tub was huge. Hitching up her chin, she pointed to it. 'I'll meet you here in ten.'

He was already in the tub when she returned, a cocktail glass in one hand, the picture of relaxed, and *potent*, masculinity. An identical glass rested nearby for her. 'But I don't...'

'Mocktail,' he said.

He'd made her a mocktail? That was kind of...sweet. Self-consciousness had her momentarily clutching her towelling robe to her chest, which was crazy. She'd worn swimsuits on her TV show. Thousands of people had seen her wearing a bikini. But she'd bet Jude hadn't been one of them.

Stop it. Get in the hot tub. Gritting her teeth, she dropped the robe onto a nearby chair and climbed in. Jude studiously glanced away, as if doing his best not to notice. She did her best to not notice him in turn.

Seizing her mocktail, she sipped it, tasting pineapple juice, coconut milk and a hint of lime.

'Delicious.' Setting it to the side and sliding up to her neck in the water, she closed her eyes and let the heat and bubble jets work their magic.

She didn't open her eyes. 'Okay, I'll admit it—this was an inspired idea.'

'I think we've earned it.'

She opened an eye and peeked at him. The hot tub was built on generous lines, but even from this opposite corner— as far away from him as she could get—the breadth of his shoulders and the golden perfection of his skin beckoned.

His jaw clenched, as if he'd sensed her gaze. Heat of a different kind gathered in all the places she didn't want it to. Gritting her teeth, she forced her eye shut. She wouldn't do anything stupid. She wouldn't do anything reckless or self-defeating. She'd caused enough havoc in Margot's life. Her sister deserved to have the wedding of her dreams. Cleo would hate herself forever if she cast the smallest shadow on the day.

A helicopter passed overhead and she forced herself to imagine worst-case scenarios—such as what would happen if she and Jude were snapped in a hot tub and the photograph plastered across the front pages of the newspapers. A slavering horde of paparazzi would then trail in her wake, catcalling and disrupting everything with their pointing cameras and impertinent questions. She imagined the hurt and betrayal stretching through Margot's eyes, the way her father's mouth would tighten as if he'd been stupid to expect better from her, and died a little inside. Was a brief fling worth that price? *Hard no.*

Anyway, what was it Jude had called love—an exercise in

deception, disillusion and despair? She shuddered. No way was she getting involved with someone with a worldview that bleak.

Which begged its own question. She stared up at the awning. 'Can I ask you something?'

'Hasn't stopped you in the past.'

Her stomach clenched. Had she been bothering him?

'Ask your question, Cleo.'

'It might be considered invasive.'

'I can't wait.'

His assumed nonchalance made her smile. Something had lightened inside him during the last few days and she was glad of it.

'How has your Jasper Ballimore identity remained a secret? How has one of your girlfriends not spilled the beans?'

When he remained silent, she lifted her head to glance at him. 'I told you it was invasive. It's just, girlfriends always have a way of finding things out.'

Turning his head, he raised a wry eyebrow. She forced herself to settle back again. 'Though, unlike me, you probably haven't had a series of disastrous relationships.'

'The problem, Cleo, is when your family is as wealthy as mine you never know if someone wants you for yourself.'

'Or whether you're a status symbol and a meal ticket.'

'Exactly.'

'Are you saying you've run shy of romantic relationships all your life?'

'It's my MO now.'

Which meant it hadn't been his MO once.

'I've no interest in marrying and being made a fool of.'

Overhead, another helicopter passed by. She couldn't see it, but glared in its direction. 'Was Matt disillusioned in love too?'

'Matt and Elodie were very much in love. But Elodie has been in hell since Matt died. It seems to me that love extracts a price, and it's not one I want to pay.'

It took every effort to not look at him. Someone had hurt him, and had hurt him badly.

'I did contemplate marriage once.'

She swallowed her surprise.

'However, the woman I considered proposing to...'

Had she cheated on him, betrayed him? Her heart clenched. Jude deserved better, and if she got her hands on the woman...

'She discovered my Jasper Ballimore secret and proceeded to name a price to keep it. I got my lawyers on it immediately.'

'The witch!'

'It was a small price to pay to get her out of my life. I'm grateful I didn't make the mistake of marrying her.'

She glanced across. 'I hope she rots in hell.'

He met her gaze and shrugged. 'It was a long time ago.'

The glance grew heated. She dragged hers away and resumed resting back and gazing upwards. That kind of betrayal would have left a mark. No wonder he'd become so cynical. 'I'm sorry you were treated so badly.' She swallowed. 'And thank you for not throwing me immediately off *Camelot* when I told you I'd discovered the secret too.'

'You're nothing like Nicole, Cleo. *You* have a good heart.'

She refused to let his words warm her. Reaching for her glass, she raised it in his direction. 'To a train wreck with a good heart.'

He raised his glass too. 'To good hearts.'

She sipped then set her drink aside. 'What I don't understand is why it's so important for Jasper Ballimore to remain a secret.'

He was quiet for a moment. 'I don't need the money from book sales, which has freed me from the pressures of publicity. I've been fortunate to enjoy the best about being an author without the downsides.'

Some people would have seen the fame as the best part.

'Also, Jasper Ballimore isn't on brand for the Giroux name.'

Not 'on brand'? Did he mean not serious enough? She straightened. 'Says who?' Had this come from his family? 'Your family should be proud of you.'

'They are—those who know about it.'

'So…this is a decision you took on your own?'

'Look.' He sat up. 'With great wealth and privilege comes great responsibility.' He recited it like a lecture. 'I need to carry on my grandfather's legacy. There's no room now for frivolous things like writing. Giroux Holdings is a family corporation. The head of the family needs to work hard to maintain that for the sake of future generations.'

'What? While everyone else suns themselves on a super-yacht?'

He stared, then grinned, as if her outrage tickled him. Her heart did a silly pitter-patter thing. 'Everyone pulls their weight, Cleo. There are no shirkers.'

She mulled that over. 'Being head of the family sounds like a big responsibility.'

'And one I left entirely on Matt's shoulders.' His mouth turned grim. 'The problem is, I inherited my grandfather's Midas touch. When it comes to business, I have his knack for making money.'

But it didn't feed his soul the way writing did. He didn't have to say the words out loud. She could see it for herself.

'Matt, though, encouraged me to pursue what made me happy.' His jaw clenched. 'But in doing that I left him alone to deal with everything. I could've helped him. I *should've* helped him.'

Oh, Jude. He held himself responsible for so much.

'That's all nonsense, you know.' She kept her tone conversational, but his glare turned glacial.

'You're not responsible for what happened to Matt. And being head of Giroux Holdings doesn't mean you can't write.

You're the boss now, you can arrange things however you want. You don't have to play the martyr.'

His jaw dropped.

'If Matt had asked for your help, would you have denied him?'

'Of course not. I—'

'Did Matt hate being the head of the family?'

'That's beside the point.'

It so wasn't. 'Don't make the same mistakes your brother did, Jude. Change things so your nephew never feels as hemmed in and restricted as you now do.'

His lips twisted. 'Ah, but that's not the traditional way things are done. We're a family who values its traditions.'

'Just because something is traditional doesn't mean it's good. Innovation has its place.' She flicked water at him. 'You want your nephew to be happy, don't you?'

'What the hell kind of question is that?'

She spread her hands. 'So change things to suit you all. You could establish a family committee to share the load. I bet you have uncles and cousins who have the necessary skills and would love more responsibility.'

She could see him mulling that over for two-tenths of a second. 'That would bring its own problems.'

'There will always be problems. No system is perfect.'

He glared. 'What else do you see in this utopia of yours?'

But the heat had left his voice and she bit back a smile. 'You might have to remain the titular head, but you can delegate, delegate, delegate.'

He rolled his eyes.

'You'd work part-time for Giroux Holdings and spend the other half writing. That way, you wouldn't be neglecting your responsibilities *or* what feeds your soul.' He'd be abdicating neither duty nor joy. 'In keeping the latter, you'll be better at the former.'

'That doesn't necessarily follow, you know?'

'I think it does. Anyway... *I dare you.*'

He rolled his eyes. 'Some people will hate the idea.'

'But I bet your nephew's generation will thank you.'

They were both sitting rather than reclining. It gave her the most spectacular view of his shoulders and chest—his *naked* shoulders and chest. Her bikini-clad breasts were visible above the water line too, and she noted the way he carefully averted his gaze. Her skin drew tight and fire raced through her veins. She forced herself back into a reclining position, sinking her entire body below the waterline. *Breathe.* 'What would Matt have thought of the idea?'

He didn't answer, not that she expected him to.

Overhead yet another helicopter passed. She glared. It was better than focussing on thoughts of hurling herself at Jude. She pointed skyward. 'What do you think they're hoping to find?'

Without warning, Jude rose and stepped out of the hot tub in a single lithe movement. Water sluiced down his body, his trunks plastered to the most glorious pair of glutes she'd ever seen. Her mouth went dry. She'd never wanted with the kind of want she now did. The man was *beautiful.*

'Out of the hot tub, Cleo.'

Her heart lurched into her throat. Had he seen...?

'We're leaving.'

Her heart settled back to beat erratically in her chest. 'Leaving?'

He gestured at the helicopter. 'It was a mistake coming here. I thought you'd be able to relax.'

'I am! Jude, you don't need to—'

'We're leaving for the Château Giroux. It's where I should've taken you in the first place.'

CHAPTER NINE

THEY DROVE THROUGH the iron gates of Château Giroux at seven o'clock that evening. Clean lines graced the palatial four-storey façade and four elegant towers rose at each corner. Cleo stared at the fairy-tale elegance and had no words.

Outside it was all white stone walls and black slate roof. Inside it was white marble and soaring ceilings, the walls lined with works of art intermingled with what she assumed were family portraits. There was elegant furniture, exquisite Aubusson rugs and antiques stretched for as far as the eye could see.

'It's beautiful.' She breathed, staring around, trying to take it all in.

The housekeeper sent her a smile as she led them up the grand staircase to a room at the top of the stairs, an enormous drawing room. A fire crackled in the fireplace and the furniture, while grand, had clearly been chosen for comfort. A little boy, maybe three or four years old, leapt to his feet, shouting, 'Uncle Jude!'

Racing across the room, he launched himself at the man beside her. Jude caught him easily and swung him into the air. The childish giggles made her smile.

After a hug and more tossing, Jude set the boy on his feet and turned him to Cleo. 'Oliver, this is my friend Cleo.'

Cleo held out her hand. 'I'm very pleased to meet you, Oliver.'

Oliver shook it. 'Are you going to marry Uncle Jude?'

She choked back a laugh, but for the life of her couldn't meet Jude's eyes. She fought to keep her tone light. 'Well, Oliver, as much as I like your uncle, I expect not. We're just very good friends.'

'Would you like to see my truck?'

'Yes, please, very much.'

Before he could haul Cleo across the other side of the room, though, a woman rose from one of the sofas arranged near the fire. 'Oliver, come here.' Her voice was sharp. 'Do not bother the lady.'

'It's no bother,' Cleo assured her. 'I like trucks almost as much as I like boats.'

The little boy grinned at her. The woman did not.

The touch of Jude's hand at the small of her back urged her forward and had warmth curling in her abdomen and circling lower in ever more concentrated circles. It took all her concentration to make her legs work. The burning, the need and want remained long after he'd removed his hand.

'Cleo, this is my sister-in-law, Elodie.'

'Pleased to meet you.'

'Delighted,' said the other woman, though her frosty gaze declared otherwise.

Cleo glanced at Jude. His clenched jaw and flared nostrils told their own story. A woman, presumably a nanny, entered to take Oliver to bed. The little boy kissed his mother, hugged his uncle and promised to show Cleo his truck in the morning.

'You're looking well, Elodie.'

'What are you doing here, Jude? You know I don't want you here. You're not welcome.'

Not welcome? But this was his home.

Cleo stepped forward. 'I needed a bolthole. Jude has very kindly played the hero and brought me here to hide from the paparazzi.'

At Elodie's questioning eyebrow, Cleo explained how Jude had helped her to hide from the paparazzi when they'd been chasing her.

'And how long are you planning to stay?'

Elodie directed the question at Jude, but Cleo pretended it had been meant for her. Lifting her arms, she turned on the spot. 'Now that I've seen the Château Giroux, I'm thinking forever.'

The light-hearted words were meant to dispel the tension, but they fell disappointingly flat. Elodie turned burning dark eyes in Cleo's direction. 'As for Jude playing hero? I find that unlikely.' And then she was gone.

Cleo's stomach dropped to her feet as pieces of the puzzle fell into place. It wasn't just Jude who blamed himself for Matt's death—Elodie did too. And the expression on Jude's face made her want to weep.

Don't hug him. Don't hug him. Don't hug him.

But not hugging him with the hardest thing she'd ever done. Swallowing, she kept her chin high. 'Aren't families grand? This reminds me of Christmas four years ago. It was a real barrel of laughs.'

A huff of a laugh left him. 'You're...'

'Let's settle on "incorrigible". It's more endearing than "irresponsible" or "irreverent"—which happen to be two of my father's favourite words when referring to me. Oliver is a sweetheart,' she added. 'He adores you.'

'It's mutual. Elodie, though...not so much.'

'Who'd have guessed your family would be so much like mine?'

'Let's not compare war wounds, Cleo.'

She was a guest in his house. She'd do whatever she could to make their time here as comfortable for him as possible.

'Let's eat.'

As if he'd magicked them from the woodwork, staff entered and set a table at the far end of the room with steaming bowls of French onion soup and slices of French bread topped with bubbling cheese.

Her stomach rumbled its approval, and one of those beguiling chuckles rumbled from Jude's throat to trace a tempting finger down her spine. She did her very best to ignore it. Instead, she chattered about mundane things until some of the darkness had receded from his eyes.

As had become their habit, they retired early. She'd never slept in such a luxurious room. She should've slept like a log, and yet she tossed and turned, yearning for the sound of lapping water and the slight rocking of a boat.

Jude's and her bedrooms shared a sitting room. On *Camelot* they'd been physically closer—they'd been able to hear each other moving about and talking in their sleep—and yet the knowledge that he was only two doors away…shouldn't be more tempting, more intimate. But that was exactly what it felt like.

Don't think about it. Instead, she replayed that moment when Jude had leapt out of the hot tub with the decision to bring her here to the Château Giroux. Because he wanted her to relax, to let down her guard, to feel completely safe.

She could see now why he'd stayed away. And yet he'd come here anyway…*for her*. It was one of the kindest, most stupidly unselfish things anyone had ever done for her, an act of open-handed generosity that created a warm glow at her very centre.

He was the most amazing man.

And he was only two doors away.

Don't think about it.

After another hour of tossing and turning, she gave up. Grabbing a throw and her book, she padded out to the living room. She pulled up short when she found Jude staring moodily into the embers that were dying down in the small grate.

He glanced across. 'Can't sleep?'

Dropping her book onto the coffee table, she arranged herself at the other end of the sofa, drawing her feet up, careful not to touch him. 'The bed is exceptionally comfortable, and I should be dead to the world, but...'

'You never sleep well the first night in a new place.'

She stared. He remembered...

He shrugged. 'It's an interesting character trait.'

She tried not to read anything into it. 'So what's your excuse?'

He turned back to the fire. 'Too many ghosts.'

'Matt,' she murmured softly.

'He and Elodie made their home here after they married.'

'And you?'

'My grandmother moved back to London when Matt and I finished school. I split my time between here and my flat in London.'

He hadn't wanted to abandon his grandmother. Her stomach softened.

'I have an apartment overlooking the Thames.'

Of course he did. They both stared into the fire. 'And yet you banished yourself to *Camelot* for the last seven months.'

'Not banished—I wanted peace and quiet. Wanted room to breathe.'

She understood that he'd needed to adjust to the new reality of life without his brother, but in his grief and misplaced guilt it seemed he'd shut himself away from everyone.

She turned to face him more fully. Inside her were things with jagged edges. 'When was the last time you were at the Château Giroux?'

'The day we buried Matt.'

She wanted to weep. 'Have you stayed away because of Elodie?'

He nodded. 'It's hard for her to see me.'

And then she was on her knees and so close the heat from his body beat at her. 'It's not fair of her to blame you for your brother's death, Jude. Or to punish you like this.'

'She has every right!' His eyes flashed. 'I should've realised Matt had been drinking. I should've taken the car keys from him. I should've insisted we take a cab home. I—'

'None of it was your fault!'

Her words rang around the room. Surely his grandmother had told him this, his cousins and friends? But maybe he hadn't been ready to listen.

'Jude, it was an *accident*.' He opened his mouth but she rode on over the top of him. 'It wasn't your fault Matt had been drinking. Of course you believed him when he told you he hadn't been. He probably thought he was fine to drive.'

He stared at her.

'And it wasn't either your or Matt's fault a deer raced across the road when it did. An *accident*,' she repeated. '*Nobody's* fault.'

His lips twisted. It took all of her strength not to reach out and touch him.

'And, as for feeling guilty about not having helped out more with the family business… Matt had a tongue in his head. If he'd needed help, he could've asked.'

'That doesn't change the fact—'

'Maybe not, but beating yourself up about it changes nothing. Nor is it fair of Elodie to blame you for it. You miss Matt too.'

'Yes, but…'

She pressed a finger to his lips. 'You can help now, though. There are some things you can do. For one, you owe it to Matt to have a relationship with Oliver.'

Eyes the colour of a turbulent sea throbbed into hers.

'And you can help Elodie move past this, Jude. Her hurt and bitterness are understandable, but it's hurting her. She clings to it because she's scared, because it's easier to be angry than to be heartbroken, but it'll eat her alive.'

He gripped her hand like a lifeline. 'How do you know this?'

Sitting back on her heels, she pulled in a breath. 'They didn't call me Wild Child for nothing. All of those late-night parties, all of the drinking and acting out—that was me trying to run away from my grief for my mother. Therapy helped me see that, helped me realise how self-destructive I was being. When I stopped doing those things and faced my emotions…'

He leaned towards her. Their faces were so close she could feel his breath on her lips and her heart stuttered in her chest.

'What?'

She had to swallow before she could speak. 'It let the good stuff back in. I began to remember the good memories. I started to feel hopeful.' She let out a shaky breath. 'I found a purpose, something to work towards, and I found a way to live with the grief.'

'You think I can help Elodie overcome her anger, and her resentment of me?' He shook his head. 'That's impossible.'

'It's not impossible, not for you. I know you don't see it, but you're amazing. Seems to me you can achieve just about anything you put your mind to.'

His jaw sagged. He hauled it back into place, his gaze throbbing into hers. Oh, so slowly, his gaze lowered to her lips. Hunger blazed in his eyes and things inside her throbbed to life.

She broke all the rules. Leaning forward, she kissed him.

The warm magic of Cleo's lips had heat filling Jude's every pore. He wondered now if this had been inevitable.

Sitting in the hot tub with her had been torture. Trying to look unmoved had taken all his strength. He'd been aware of her tension. Aware of the heat in her gaze when it had rested on him; her curiosity; her interest; her restraint.

And the way she'd tensed every time a helicopter had passed overhead... He'd focused on *that* rather than everything else. It had been the one thing he *could* act upon.

He'd hoped coming here would diminish what was happening between them. But he wondered now if they'd been building to this from the first moment she'd clattered onto his narrowboat.

He sank into the kiss like a starving man. Threading his fingers through her hair, he kissed her with an intensity he had no hope of tempering, and with a thoroughness he hoped told her what an extraordinary woman he thought her. Cleo gave so much of herself with no expectation of anything in return. With her silly, light-hearted teasing, her gratitude lists and her frank confessions, she'd felled all of his barriers. *And* she'd given him hope.

Her fingers tangled in his hair, pulling him closer, and fire blazed in his veins. Pulling her onto his lap, he pressed a series of kisses along her jaw and down her neck, her skin satin-soft, and she hummed her approval, the sound arcing straight to his groin.

Slow hands traced a path along his shoulders and down his chest, sparking heat and intensifying need. Cupping her breast in his hand, relishing its weight, he stroked his thumb across it and her nipple beaded to hardness with flattering speed. It had him hungry to draw it into his mouth, to touch her with his tongue. To taste her...to have her naked beneath him and arching into his touch, crying out his name...

He froze.

What was he doing?

'Oh, no, you don't.'

Cleo's ragged whisper scraped across his raw nerve endings. She straddled his lap and he had to force back a groan at the way her body slid against his with an intimacy that left him dry mouthed. His fingers dug into the soft flesh of her hips, though whether it was to anchor her there or to put her away from him when he found the strength to do so he had no idea.

Seizing his face in her hands, pale green eyes stared into his. 'Why are you hesitating? I know you want me, Jude. As much as I want you.'

He couldn't deny it, not with the evidence of his desire throbbing against her. He clenched his teeth and forced himself to breathe through the red heat. 'You came to me for help.'

'And you don't want to take advantage of me?' A dimple appeared in her right cheek.

'You said sleeping with anyone at the moment would be self-destructive. I don't want to do something that will have you hating yourself in the morning.'

Her smile faded. 'I don't leap into bed with men I barely know any more, Jude. I no longer use sex—or alcohol—as a way to hide from my problems. And you're not just *anyone*.'

His heart gave a kick that knocked the breath from his body.

'I know we only met a bit over a week ago, but we've spent every waking hour of that time together.'

True enough. He'd shared things with her he'd never shared with anyone.

'I know you better than some guys I've dated for months.'
Like that jerk Clayton Carruthers?

'What's more, I like you. And I think you like me.'

'Of course I like you!' Meeting this woman had changed his life. He was writing again. Whatever decision he made in regard to it, it was still a consolation of sorts. His heart kicked again—hard. She made him think it might be possible to fix things between Elodie and him.

'This thing—' she gestured between them '—isn't about me forgetting my troubles for a night or two.'

'What is it, then, Cleo?'

She braced her hands on his shoulders, smoothing the material of his soft cotton T-shirt over his arms. 'I like you and I want you. Neither one of us is in a relationship. We're free to indulge in a fling. I know you're not interested in a long-term relationship, so don't think I'll be mistaking this for anything more than what it is.'

He wasn't interested in anything long-term. He felt too broken at the moment; his life was going through too much change. Besides, parading any kind of coupledom happiness in front of a still grieving Elodie... It was out of the question. But a short-term fling...?

'This will be fun and pleasure and tenderness...' A smile trembled on her lips. 'And a happy memory.'

He would be a happy memory for this extraordinary woman! A fault line opened in his chest, letting in light and warmth.

She patted his chest with soft hands. 'Now, you may not feel the same, of course.'

She made as if to move off his lap, but his fingers tightened about her hips. 'I think you're the most amazing woman I've ever met. I burn for you, Cleo.'

She stared at him, her lips parting as if his words had taken her off-guard. Tilting up her chin, he slanted his mouth over hers in a scorching kiss that had her fingers digging into his biceps, before wrapping around his neck. She kissed him back with a fiery enthusiasm that had him breathing hard.

Lifting her in his arms, he strode into his bedroom, kicking the door shut with his heel. Tonight he would be the one to give *to her*. He'd give her body all the pleasure that was in his power to provide. He'd make sure it was a night she'd remember when she was eighty—a memory that would make her smile whenever she thought of it. A good memory she could pull out and hold close whenever she needed to.

He followed her down onto the bed and kissed her deeply,

slowly… Restless hands moved across his body, but he tried to ignore them.

'Jude…' She panted. 'I need you.'

'And you're going to have me, sweetheart—in all the ways you want me. But first…'

He flicked open a button on the satin pyjamas the staff had found for her and then another…slowly…until he had the shirt spread out and her beautiful breasts exposed to the air and his gaze. Need roared in his ears but he tamped it down.

A sigh left her as his fingers danced across her skin. 'But first I'm going to savour every delectable inch of you.'

A cry left her lips as his mouth closed over one nipple. He sucked, lathed and traced the shape of her with his mouth and tongue. She arched into his touch, the inarticulate noises in her throat making him hard and hot, yet he refused to rush. Her pyjama top fluttered to the floor as he kissed his way down her body.

He ran his fingers through the damp curls at the juncture of her thighs, teasing and tempting, deliberately avoiding where she most wanted to be touched as he divested her of her pyjama bottoms before kissing his way back up her body—ankles, knees, thighs… When he traced his tongue along the seam of her and circled the most sensitive part of her in slow, lazy strokes, her shocked cry, the way her body lifted, almost undid him.

But the sweet scent of her…the taste of her…the feel of her against his mouth and tongue and arms…

'Jude, I need…'

He slid a finger inside her, her silken flesh tightening around it. 'I have you, sweetheart.' He lapped at her with his tongue, slowly, rhythmically, hypnotically, until, with a cry and his name on her lips, she came.

Once the fluttering of her body had subsided, he eased away, rolled on a condom and lowered himself over her, bearing his weight on his forearms. He brushed the hair from her face. Heavy-lidded eyes opened and a sultry smile spread across delectable lips. 'I think I just died and went to heaven.'

He grinned down at her. This woman made him feel like Superman. 'I aim to please.'

Her fingers danced down his body, her fingers wrapping around him. 'You certainly do that.'

That wicked hand moved up and down with a gentle strength and purpose that had air hissing between his teeth. Seizing first her right hand and then the left, he trapped them beside her head.

She pouted up at him. 'Why can't I play too?'

His erection nudged her entrance, she lifted her hips to greet him and they slid together in a single smooth motion.

'Oh!'

Her whimper made him tense. 'Did I hurt you? I—'

'No.' Her head moved restlessly against the pillow. Tugging her hands free from his, she ran them down his body to dig surprisingly strong fingers into his buttocks and haul him even closer, her legs wrapping around his waist.

'It's just…' Her breathing grew ragged, sawing in and out of her lungs. 'I've never wanted someone so soon again… after…'

He couldn't not move then. The sensations built between them hard and fast. Her warmth and energy, her very essence, surrounded him like a blessing. She gave a final cry, her muscles clenching around him and then his body followed with a will of its own. His hoarse cry filled the room as a golden heat flooded him and stars burst behind his eyelids. Wave after wave of sensation spiralled through him—deep, intense pleasure—and finally peace.

Jude lay in bed and stared at the ceiling, Cleo a warm bundle curled against his side, and watched the early-morning light filter into the room, appreciating the soft-focus gentleness of it after a night of love-making that had left him feeling remade.

It wasn't just the love-making, though—it was the words Cleo had spoken to him. Words that had hope stirring in his heart.

He might feel guilty that he was alive when his brother was dead, but Cleo was right—the event that had claimed his brother's life had been an accident. He couldn't change it, no matter how much he wanted to. But he remembered the look in Elodie's eyes whenever they'd rested on him...

He felt the searing ache of missing his brother that refused to subside...and his regret that he hadn't helped more with the running of Giroux Holdings, that he hadn't taken some of the responsibility from Matt's shoulders. His lips twisted. Being a scapegoat had given him a role to play. But that didn't help anyone. It was no healthier than all the younger Cleo's drunken partying.

Matt would want you to have a relationship with Oliver. He knew the truth of that on a bone-deep level. He needed to be an admirable role model for his nephew; emotional cowardice wasn't admirable on any level. He also knew Matt would want him to give Elodie all and any support he could.

Cleo had made him see it was time to stop hiding. It was time to fight—to fight for his family in the same way that Cleo fought for hers.

Cleo stirred and a smile curved her lips as she blinked sleep from her eyes. A warm arm slid across his chest and she made a sound of approval. He immediately grew hard.

'Did I mention you have a great body?' she murmured.

'You might've mentioned it once or twice.'

He grinned. She grinned.

'I vote that this thing goes for longer than one night.'

He rolled her over and kissed her. 'I second that vote.'

CHAPTER TEN

JUDE TAPPED ON the open door of Elodie's private sitting room. Elodie's faced hardened when she turned. 'I don't want to see you. I don't want to speak to you.'

A hard knot formed in his stomach. He had to fight the instinct to turn and leave. Recalling the expression in Cleo's eyes last night, he pushed his shoulders back and nodded. 'I know.'

She blinked.

'The thing is, Elodie, your anger at me and your wish to avoid me don't seem to be helping. You're just as unhappy now as you were nine months ago.'

'Unhappy?' she spat. 'How can I be anything other than *unhappy* when my husband is dead?'

'You're no more *at peace*, then.'

Her eyes flashed. Jude rubbed a hand over his face. 'Running away hasn't worked out so well for me either.'

Striding across, she stabbed a finger at him. 'You don't deserve peace.'

Everything inside him burned. It took all his reserves of strength to remain where he stood rather than removing himself from her presence. When he spoke, his voice emerged low, the strain stretching it thin. 'I know you think blaming me is a way to remain strong, but I'm starting to think the opposite is true. Blaming me is stopping you from moving on. You're using all of your resources to remain angry at me, instead of using them to come to terms with your grief.'

She stared back stonily.

'What I've started to realise is that the truth is preferable to continuing in a lie, even when it isn't palatable.'

He ached to reach out and take her hands or hug her, but she held herself so aloof, he dared not. He could not force her to hear his words, *really* hear them, no matter how much he wanted her to. But he had at least to try.

'I'd do whatever I could to make your life easier, Elodie, but continuing in this lie isn't helping any of us. The fact is, I'm *not* responsible for Matt's death. I didn't know he'd been drinking.'

'The alcohol *had* to have affected him. You should've seen that!'

'I wish it had been evident, but it wasn't. The fact I didn't notice, that I didn't pay more attention, is something I will regret till my dying day.' He swallowed hard. 'But it doesn't change the fact that the accident wasn't my fault.'

She took a step back, her eyes widening.

'I've played it over in my mind so many times. Everything happened so fast—*so fast*. Matt's reaction was pure instinct. I don't know if he'd have done any differently if he hadn't had anything to drink. I don't know if I'd have done anything differently if I'd been behind the wheel.'

He dug his fingers into the hard knot of muscle at his nape. 'I wish he'd told me how much pressure he'd been under at work. I wish he'd asked for my help. I wish even more that he hadn't had to ask. I wish I'd seen it and leaped in to do what I could.' *That* would be the biggest regret of his life.

'What I do know, though, is that Matt wouldn't want me beating myself up and blaming myself for any of it. Even if I had been at fault, he wouldn't want me beating up on myself. He was always generous like that.'

For a fraction of a second something in Elodie's eyes lightened. In a heartbeat, it was gone again. He despaired that anything he said would touch her.

'He wouldn't want you miring yourself in all of this bitterness and anger either.'

'You have no idea what he'd want!'

'Not true,' he said slowly. And in some fundamental way that gave him back his brother. 'Matt would want me to support you in any and every way I could. He'd want me to have a good relationship with Oliver. And this will sound harsh when I don't want it to but, Elodie, Oliver deserves better.'

Her quick intake of breath speared into his heart. 'How dare you?' Her whisper was hoarse. 'I love my son.'

'I know you do, but Oliver deserves to have all of you, not half of you.'

She backed away from him, shaking her head.

'Do you want to know what it's like beyond the anger and bitterness?'

She stared, swallowed and glanced away. 'How?'

'It's not much different in some ways. I miss Matt every single day. So much, sometimes it's like there's a hole inside me.'

She pressed a hand to her mouth.

'But letting go of my guilt and anger—at myself and the universe—has forced me to accept that Matt is really gone for good.'

She stiffened.

'It doesn't matter how much I don't want that to be true. It's a fact. Matt isn't coming back.'

Her bottom lip wobbled.

'In its place I've been remembering some of the good times we had—some big, some small. They pop into my mind when I'm least expecting it. Like the week Gran took us on a yachting holiday to the Lake District. We were ten and twelve. It was magic.' He couldn't help smiling at the memory. 'Matt's excitement when he got into his dream college at Cambridge.' He waited for her to meet his eyes. 'The tone of his voice when he told me he'd met the girl he was going to marry.'

Elodie's shoulders started to shake and he did what he should've done nine months ago. He pulled her against his chest and held her as she cried out her grief and her pain.

Cleo stared at Jude sleeping. His face at rest looked more youthful, more at peace. She resisted the urge to reach across and press her lips to his. These last few days had been idyllic. She still couldn't believe that from so much disaster she'd found so much *joy*.

The thought had her swallowing. This was a temporary refuge. She couldn't forget that. She and Jude were finding temporary consolation in each other, nothing more. They'd become friends and then lovers. The former would hopefully endure, but the latter had an end date. In six days' time, she'd return to London and be the model of propriety at her sister's wedding.

Six days? She glanced at Jude again. Would she get her fill of this man in that time? Together they'd scaled heights she hadn't known existed. And yet it hadn't taken the edge off her hunger, or his.

The thought of leaving him... An ache gripped her chest. Slipping out of bed, she padded through to her own bedroom and changed into a pair of jogging bottoms. Jude considered love an exercise in *deception, disillusion and despair*. He had no interest in anything long-term. She had to respect that.

And anything beyond a clandestine affair was out of the question. For pity's sake, he was a hundred times more high-profile than any of her previous boyfriends. Think of the media frenzy. If their names were linked, it would create *so* much tabloid speculation. Exhaustion swept through her. She was tired of being in the limelight, tired of the derogatory in-nuendos, tired of no one taking her seriously.

She dragged on her trainers and pulled the laces tight. She'd sworn to Margot she'd fly under the radar. She *would* keep her promise. She simply needed a moment to get her scattered emotions back under control. They were running high today, which was to be expected. Letting herself out-side, she set off around the massive gardens at a fast clip, the air icy in her lungs.

Jude met her on the terrace on her return. He smiled, but his gaze searched her face. 'You had the energy for a run?'

She shrugged. 'A necessity. Your chef is a gem, and I've been indulging a little too much.'

'Come and have breakfast. You can shower later. Elodie won't mind.'

He'd told her about his conversation with Elodie. His cour-age in baring himself to the other woman had left her speech-less. The gulf had been breached, though, and both Jude and Elodie were doing their best to mend their relationship. She didn't doubt there'd be rocky times ahead, but nor did she doubt their ability to get through them. She'd been so happy for him.

'It's due to you,' he'd told her.

'Nonsense!'

'I've seen how fearless you've been in mending your rela-tionship with Margot. I've seen how determined you are to not let her down—the lengths you've gone to and the sacri-fices you've made.'

'She's my sister,' she'd said, as if that explained it all.

'*Exactly*. You refuse to let your own hurt or resentment or guilt stop you from doing what you can to fix things. Even when that turns your life upside down. Even when the de-mands made on you aren't reasonable. You've done it gladly, without complaint. Me? I just went into hiding.'

'You were grieving.' In his shoes, she'd have travelled those same depths of despair. 'You needed time, and now you've had it you're seeing what you need to do, and you're doing it. You should be proud of yourself.'

She'd kissed him then and there hadn't been talking for a very long time.

Afterwards, when she'd been luxuriating in a golden glow of contentment, Jude had turned his head on the pillow. 'Meeting you has changed my life, Cleo. For the better.'

She'd had to blink away tears. She'd nestled against his side and pressed a hand over his heart. 'Ditto, Jude.'

She followed him through to the dining room now, and Elodie's brows shot up when she saw Cleo's running gear. 'A run? Is it not freezing outside? Did not you and Jude use the indoor gym earlier in the week?'

'It was *bracing*. And I like the fresh air.' She grinned. 'I'm also aware I'll be walking down the aisle in a bridesmaid's dress in a week and I want to fit into it.'

Elodie laughed, but was it Cleo's imagination or had Jude's eyes clouded over at the reminder she wouldn't be here this time next week? She shook off the thought—definitely her imagination.

She glanced up a short while later to find him frowning at the way she picked at an omelette. She forced herself to lift a morsel to her lips and make noises of approval.

His frown deepened. 'Is something wrong?'

Elodie became instantly alert then too. Cleo abandoned her cutlery and willed the tears away. 'It's Saturday.'

They both nodded.

She tried to smile, but the sudden concern that flickered across Elodie's face, and the way Jude's brows lowered, made her think she hadn't succeeded. 'It's Margot's hen night tonight and...' She trailed off with a shrug. She ought to be there.

* * *

Jude and Elodie threw her a party. Jude surprised her with a designer dress in hot pink that he'd had specially delivered. Fun and flirty, it fitted like a dream and made her feel like a princess. And the relatives who'd travelled to the château for the weekend joined in the festivities with gusto.

The château's chef excelled herself. There were delicious platters of canapés—clever things made with prawns, bacon and asparagus—exotic salads and cold meats. Sweets included tiny crème brûlées in shot glasses and mini chocolate eclairs. There was non-alcoholic fizz to wash it all down.

There were party games that had everyone laughing, and dancing under the lights of a disco ball. Everyone wanted to dance with her, and made the most delicious fuss. Jude's family were warm and loving with the same bone-deep decency that ran in Jude's veins. Their enjoyment wasn't feigned, and it made Cleo realise what she lacked in her own life—a sense of belonging, a place where she could be herself and not always be so guarded and on her best behaviour.

'Would you like to record a message for the bride?' Jude asked later in the evening.

'Yes, please!' She handed him her phone to do the recording.

The volume of the music was turned down, though the disco ball continued to flash, and she stood in front of the crowd who all cheered and waved from behind her.

'Margot, I so wish I could be celebrating with you tonight. I hope you're having the most wonderful time and are looking forward to marrying the man of your dreams next weekend. You've been the best sister a girl could ever hope for and I'm lucky to have you in my life. Because I can't be there with you tonight, I'm celebrating you here with my new friends.' She raised her glass. 'To Margot!'

'To Margot!' everyone cried behind her, raising their glasses.

She blew Margot a kiss and Jude stopped the video. She immediately sent it and crossed her fingers that Margot would send her a reply—a happy reply.

An hour later, just as the party was winding up, her phone vibrated in her pocket: a text from Margot. Her heart picked up speed.

What is your gratitude list today?

Another text pinged.

Top of my list is my message from you. xx

'Everything okay?'

Jude watched her with bright intent and she doubted she could've blinked the tears from her eyes or stopped her smile—not even if there'd been a photographer's camera trained on her. 'From Margot.'

She held out her phone so he could read the text, her breath doing a funny little stutter in her throat when a grin spread across his stern features. Giving a whoop, he picked her up and swung her round, and for the briefest of moments it felt as if everything in her world had aligned.

'Happy?' he demanded, setting her on her feet again.

'Over the moon!' A moment later, she murmured, 'People are staring.' Though they were staring at him, not her—and in bemusement, not disapproval.

'Don't care.'

And why should he? These people, his family, were people he could trust. They'd accept him for who and what he was.

You can trust your family too.

Not like this.

Whose fault is that?

She pushed the thought away. She'd made things right between Margot and her again, which meant they'd be okay again between Cleo and her father. She'd be careful not to create more drama or scandal and everything would be just fine.

She clasped her phone to her chest. 'Thank you, Jude. Not just for this party, but for everything. For helping me save the day.'

'You saved the day yourself, Cleo. I just gave you a place to hide.'

'You came to my rescue more times than I can count. You let me stowaway on your boat.'

'Grudgingly.' He grimaced.

'You whisked me away to the French Riviera when it became clear journalists were on our tails.'

He shrugged, as if that was nothing.

'And then you brought me here because I couldn't relax with all of those darn helicopters.'

He gazed around, his face softening. 'It's good to be back.' He looked more content than she'd seen him.

And, just like that, every atom flooded with awareness: for the strong, lean lines of Jude's body that felt like silken steel beneath her fingertips; for firm lips that could be as gentle as a summer breeze through the fronds of a weeping willow, or as demanding as a surging tide; for the feel of his body moving against hers, as if the fact of them becoming lovers had always been inevitable. As if there were molecules in him and her that otherwise would've always remained dormant.

Dangerous, a voice whispered through her.

'This hasn't been one-sided, Cleo. If it weren't for you...'

His words petered out when he registered her desire and need. She couldn't hide it. Her body pulsed with it, on fire with an urgency she couldn't explain. The darkening of his eyes and the quickening of the pulse at his throat told her he felt the same.

'Party's breaking up.'

His hoarse whisper rasped across her skin. 'Do you think that means it'd be okay if we slipped away?' she whispered.

Taking her hand, he pulled her from the room.

'They're all going to know.' Her heart pounded in her throat. 'That was hardly discreet.'

'I don't care.'

Then she wouldn't either.

The moment they reached their suite, she slammed the door behind them and backed him up against it. Stretching up on tiptoe, she pressed her lips to the spot where his pulse pounded in his throat, lathing it with her tongue and drinking in the scent of him—all spice, fresh mint and warm musk, a heady combination that made her head spin.

As did the sound of air hissing from his lungs and the touch of his fingers at her waist.

'I wanted to do that all night,' she said, pressing a series of kisses along his jaw towards that beautiful, beguiling mouth.

'Want to know what I've wanted to do?'

He'd eased back a fraction so she'd have to stand higher on tiptoe to reach his lips, but his hands tightened on her waist and she couldn't move. She nodded.

He lifted the hem of her skirt in one motion until it was hitched around her waist, the move shockingly brazen and shockingly seductive. In a flash of movement, he whirled them around so it was her back pressed against the door. His fingers slid beneath the lace of her panties with a wicked intimacy—his fingers unapologetically bold and searching. She gave a shocked moan of need, her head lolling back against the door.

He swore softly in French, making her toes curl. 'I touch you like this…' that finger moved against her with merciless thoroughness that made her legs tremble '…and I'm in danger of losing control.'

'Please…lose…control.' Each word was ground out—a gasp and a plea.

'It's why I've taken to carrying condoms with me wherever we go.' He tore the corner of a foil packet with his teeth.

Cleo had given up speaking, too busy fumbling with his belt and then the zip of his trousers. He sheathed himself in the condom and lifted her. She wrapped her legs around his waist and he entered her in a smooth motion that filled her body, making her mindless, spiralling her to another place—a place of pleasure and delight where they both rode wave upon wave of pleasure that lasted forever.

She came back to herself to find Jude resting his forehead on the door beside her. Her arms were looped round his neck and her legs dangled loosely round his hips. Turning her head, she pressed a kiss to his neck. Very gently, he eased away and let her slide down until her feet touched the floor.

'I think I might've screamed loud enough for them to have heard me back in England.' She'd never realised she could be so vocal.

'I couldn't hear you over the noise I was making.'

He grinned. She grinned.

'Don't worry, Cinderella, the castle walls are thick.'

They made love again. Of course they did.

Afterwards Cleo watched as the light outside the window began to filter into the room while Jude slept beside her. She'd never had such a generous lover. She hadn't known that making love could be this good. But she was starting to feel as if it meant more to her than it should. She could feel herself wanting to plan a future with Jude.

She needed to knock that on the head because it simply wasn't going to happen. He'd warned her that he didn't do long-term. And last night she'd fully reconnected with Margot at last. Margot had finally forgiven her. She couldn't do anything to risk upsetting that balance. Acid burned her stomach—which another disastrous love affair with another high-profile man would absolutely do.

Silently she slid from Jude's bed and made her way to her own room to slide between smooth sheets that felt too crisp and cold.

'You returned to your own room this morning.'

Jude watched Cleo's face closely as she sipped her tea. The staff brought a pot of tea into the library at ten-thirty every morning. It was where he and Cleo had taken to working. Often an hour or more would go by without them speaking, both immersed in their work—she with her website designs and he writing the third book of his trilogy.

Dammed for so long, the words now flowed with a speed he could barely keep up with. He couldn't explain how, but writing again made him feel strong—gave him the resources to deal with other tougher things.

He couldn't stop thinking about Cleo's suggestion to change the internal structure of Giroux Holdings. He'd started researching what it would involve and had made a list of family members to approach. It had filled him with a new sense of purpose and a new optimism for the future.

Her gaze skittered away from his now. 'I was feeling a bit restless. I didn't want to disturb you.'

His heart sank. It was a lie—or at least not the full truth. He understood it, though. Their love-making had taken on a new edge—had become something deeper, both fiercer and more tender somehow. It had filled him with exhilaration. But, staring at Cleo's face now, he realised the other side of that equation.

'What?'

He blinked to find her frowning at him.

'You've turned grim,' she said.

'I didn't mean to. I just…' Moving from his desk and pouring himself a tea, he forced himself to sit in his usual spot on the sofa beside her, careful to keep some space between them.

'You just…what?'

'I just realised what you're doing. You're trying to create some distance between us, and I can see the wisdom in that.' Neither of them had made promises. Neither of them was looking for a relationship.

'Last night we were indiscreet.' The way they'd beaten a hasty retreat from the party wouldn't have gone unnoticed. In the cold light of morning, did Cleo regret that? Was she worried rumours would reach the tabloids? 'I promise you can trust my family, *and* the staff here. No word of this will reach outside ears.'

She turned back so fast, tea sloshed in her saucer. 'I trust you and them.' Setting her teacup onto the coffee table, she turned to him more fully. 'I love making love with you, Jude, but we were clear from the beginning about not making any kind of commitment to one another. We always knew that our…*amour*…'

His lips twitched at the quaintness of the word on her lips. She half-smiled too, and he found an odd comfort in that. 'We always knew our *liaison* had an end date,' he finished for her.

'Yes.'

She'd be returning to England on Friday—in five days' time, he realised with a jolt. 'You're worried I'll read more into our affair than I should.' As the words left his mouth, he wondered if she had every right to worry.

'I want to make sure *I* don't start reading more into it.'

Her hands twisted and it was all he could do not to lean over and cover them with his own.

'My past has proved that me rushing headlong into things without thinking is a recipe for disaster.'

And they had rushed headlong into their affair. He didn't regret it, but she was right: it was time to be sensible. It was time to remember the boundaries they'd set.

'Now that Margot has forgiven me, I can't afford to do anything to ruin that.'

His jaw clenched. 'You should live your life to please yourself, Cleo, not to make your sister and father happy.'

She reared back, as if he'd slapped her. 'It just so happens that those things are inextricably entwined. And you'd be lying if you said it wasn't the same for you.'

That was true, but it seemed to him that it was Cleo who made all the sacrifices and compromises in her relationship with her family, while Margot and their father made none. But it was none of his business and he had no right to criticise. He nodded. 'You're right.'

'I just want to get my life back on track.' She rolled her eyes. 'And *never* appear on the front page of a newspaper again.'

And being linked with him would mean living her life in the spotlight, which was everything she didn't want.

'Are you angry?'

He stared at her, shocked she could think such a thing. 'No! I'm thinking how right you are and how wise you're being. We didn't make promises for very good reasons.' His chest grew heavy as the weight of those reasons pressed down on him. 'My and Elodie's relationship has started to mend, but the equilibrium is...'

'Delicate?'

Exactly. It'd be cruel to flaunt any sort of romantic happiness in front of her when she was grieving for Matt. Had Elodie witnessed Cleo's and his exit from the party last night? He scanned his memory, sagging when he realised she'd excused herself earlier. But she'd probably hear the speculations of all those who'd been present.

He squared his shoulders. She wouldn't hear any more, though; he'd make sure of it. He glanced back at Cleo. 'I have so much I need to do, so much to accomplish. It deserves my best efforts.'

She nodded her understanding and drew closer. 'Okay, this is what we're going to do: for the next five days, we're going to be discreet.'

She was gifting him the next five days!

She tapped his chest. '*Seriously* discreet.'

Taking her face in his hands, he kissed her. 'Deal.'

CHAPTER ELEVEN

EVERY DAY CLEO'S departure grew closer, the darker Jude's world became. Was it because it meant the adventure would end? He'd never felt more alive than he had in these last two-and-a-half weeks.

She'd helped him see things so differently. Was he concerned they'd go back to the way they'd been? Was he worried about taking up the mantle as head of the family, or finishing the current book?

It all fell into place for him on Thursday afternoon. He couldn't let Cleo go. He'd fallen in love with her. Despite his best efforts, despite believing love an exercise in deception, disillusion and despair.

The thing was, Cleo had never deceived him. She'd eased the despair of his grief…and she'd turned his disillusion into wonder, and had made him see a world worth fighting for. His scowling and grumpiness had been no match for her teasing, her laughter or her frank confessions. And the thought of her leaving…

Of course she needed to go to her sister's wedding. But then *she had to come back*. Their attraction had taken them both off-guard. Was it out of the realms of possibility that love could take her by surprise as well?

She *liked* him. And the way she made love with him that evening made him dare hope.

Lying in bed afterwards, trailing his hand idly over the

soft skin of her back, he wanted this forever. 'Cleo, is it really outside the realms of possibility that after Margot's wedding we couldn't see each other again?'

'What do you mean?'

She looked warm and rumpled and utterly beautiful. 'You and I have always been honest with each other.' He frowned. 'Well, okay, I mightn't have told you who I was immediately.'

'We've always been honest about the things that mattered,' she agreed, sliding her hand into his.

Generous—that was Cleo. He pulled in a breath. 'Which is why I want to be honest with you now.'

Blinking, she sat up, drawing the sheet with her. 'Okay.'

He sat up too. 'I'd like to see you again.'

Something in her face softened. 'Oh, Jude. I've loved the time I've spent with you.'

Loved. She used the word *loved.*

But then she shook her head. 'I don't think that's a good idea.'

Was that because she thought he was toying with her... wasn't serious? 'Would it make any difference if I told you I've fallen in love with you?'

Her jaw dropped. She stared as if she hadn't heard him right.

He rolled his shoulders. 'I didn't mean for it to happen. It wasn't part of my plan. But I have and...' He petered off as he recognised the emotion dawning in her eyes: horror.

Backing away, she scrambled out of bed and thrust her arms into her robe, tying it tightly at her waist before turning to face him. 'You said your heart was safe! You told me you wouldn't fall in love with me!'

'I didn't know I had!' The accusation in her tone stung. 'I realised this afternoon, which is why I'm telling you now.'

She raked both hands through her hair. 'This can't happen, Jude.'

Leaping out of bed, he hauled on a pair of boxers. 'Why not?'

'We had rules!'

'Which we both kept breaking.'

Her gaze caught on his chest and she swallowed.

'Why not?' he repeated. 'I know you want me.' The expression in her eyes assured him of that. 'And I know you like me.'

'Of course I do! But attraction and like aren't…'

She broke off, and he went cold all over. Ice crawled across his scalp. He'd been reading too much into it all—her warmth, her generosity, her honesty—because it meant so much to him. And to imagine his world without her in it was unbearable.

'You do *not* need someone like me in your life, Jude. And neither does your family. Believe me, I am not *"on brand"*.' She made quote marks in the air.

What the hell…?

'Once the papers get wind of the story—' she gestured between them '—and things get real, you'd see that too.'

Did she think he'd abandon her?

'And what about *my* family, Jude? My notoriety reflects on them. It impacts their careers. They don't deserve to have their colleagues and friends whispering behind their backs every time my life is splashed across the papers. They deserve better than that. They deserve *better* from me.'

All his wealth and the power of his family name wouldn't be able to prevent the story from hitting the headlines once he and Cleo were linked. It was everything she didn't want; she'd told him that repeatedly. What part of that hadn't he heard and heeded?

'My family deserve me to lay low for a while.' She dragged in a breath. 'They deserve me to be whole and happy for them.'

He rocked back on his heels. He clearly wasn't part of a future where she saw herself as either whole or happy. His mouth tasted of ashes.

Her chin wobbled. 'I'd give a thousand worlds not to have hurt you—'

'I'm sorry I raised the topic,' he cut in. 'I shouldn't have said anything.' He could see that now.

Her knuckles turned white from where they gripped the front of her robe. 'I'm sorry, Jude,' she whispered.

She left, closing his bedroom door softly behind her. It felt as if every light in the world had gone out.

He drove her to the airport the following afternoon. What little conversation they had, they kept practical.

'Has your father organised a car for you at the other end?'

'Yes.'

'I've arranged a contact to take you to the first-class lounge.'

'That's very kind. Thank you.'

Her hands twisted in her lap. She bit her lip and stared out of the window. Her misery washed over him in waves. He should never have burdened her with his declaration last night. If he'd been thinking with any logic at all, he'd have waited until after the wedding—waited until she'd felt secure again. Then he could've orchestrated a meeting and they could've taken it from there. Instead, he'd told her he loved her, and now the guilt at being unable to return his feelings was eating her alive. For God's sake, he knew how beholden she felt to him!

He pulled the car into a space at Departures. 'Cleo, I want you to understand that knowing you has made my life better. I also want you to know that I'm going to be fine.'

She swallowed. 'Of course you are.'

'I'm disappointed, but...' He shrugged. 'I've much to keep me busy.'

She turned to him. 'I can't thank you enough for everything you've done.'

'Then don't. It's been a pleasure.'

Her gaze met his and she nodded, then she gestured out of the window. 'Don't come in with me. It'll be better this way.'

He wanted to argue, but didn't. 'Let me text my contact to say we're here. He'll take you the back ways the media don't know about.' He sent the text. The silence between them stretched. He found his fingers going to his pocket, reaching for her sunglasses as if they were a talisman.

'You know—' he held them up '—you never did tell me what the story was with these.'

She glanced at them and then smiled, truly smiled. His heart started pounding like a wild thing.

'They were my mother's.'

His jaw dropped. Her *mother's*?

'She loved those sunglasses; she took them everywhere. When she died, I asked for them. They've been my most treasured possession ever since.'

He thrust them at her, horror filling his belly. 'You must take them back!' He couldn't deprive her of her mother's sunglasses. He'd have never made that deal if he'd known...

She shook her head. 'She'd have been so proud of me for the deal I made with you, Jude. And that means more to me than anything.' Reaching out, she curled his fingers back around the sunglasses, touching her other hand to her heart. 'I carry my mother with me wherever I go. I don't need a pair of sunglasses to remind me of that, not any more. Keep them. Use them and enjoy them, and remember how you once helped a silly girl out of a pickle—that will make me happy.'

He put them back in his pocket. He'd treasure them forever.

Jude's contact appeared and opened Cleo's door. 'I will be pleased to be of service to any friend of Monsieur Blackwood.'

Cleo smiled her thanks, before holding her hand out to Jude. 'Thank you.'

He curved his fingers round her hand, fixing the feel of

her in his mind for the very last time. 'It's been a pleasure knowing you, Cleo.'

He watched her until she disappeared from view, the weight bearing down on his chest growing heavier and heavier.

Elodie took one look at Jude's face when he returned, and she lifted the coffee pot in a silent question. He shook his head.

She set it back down. 'Did Cleo get off without drama?'

'Yes.'

'She must be excited about the wedding.'

'Yes.'

He ached to talk about her. In equal measure he ached not to talk about her. 'Excuse me, Elodie, I have some calls to make.' Turning on his heel, he left the room.

It was just Elodie and him for dinner that evening. Unusual for a Friday night, but there was a glittering black-tie affair in the city that many of the extended clan were attending. Elodie cut into her perfectly cooked chicken breast before glancing across at him. 'When is Cleo to return?'

He kept his gaze on his food. 'She isn't returning, Elodie. Our business here is complete.'

Her cutlery clattered to her plate. 'That's nonsense!'

Elodie's lips had pinched into a tight line and his throat went dry. 'Why?'

'Anyone with eyes in their head can see the two of you have feelings for one another.'

All of this time he'd thought they'd been discreet... He rubbed a hand over his face. 'You must hate me.'

'Hate you? *Why?*' She blinked at whatever she saw in his face. 'Because I lost my love, you are therefore not allowed your love? Is that what you think?' When he remained silent, she slammed her hands on the table. 'Do you think me so ungenerous?'

'No! I just...'

'Did it not occur to you that seeing the people around me fall in love and find happiness might be a form of consolation?'

He closed his eyes and let out a breath. 'I might be in love with Cleo, Elodie, but she's not in love with me.'

Elodie gave an undignified snort. 'You did not see her face when she was telling me what a heroic Galahad you had been, saving her from all the journalists. You did not see how her eyes softened when she said how kind you had been to her.'

'And you didn't see her face when she told me she doesn't want the complication of a relationship with someone as high-profile as me.'

Her eyes narrowed. 'Did she tell you she did not love you?'

'Yes.'

'Did she say those actual words?'

He frowned. She'd certainly implied it.

'Tell me what she said, exactly—because I do not believe she does not love you.'

He told her as much as he had the heart to.

Elodie folded her arms. 'She told you what you needed and she told you what her family needed. She did *not* tell you she didn't love you.'

'That's semantics.'

'She is afraid she cannot fit into our world. She is afraid of letting you down. She is afraid of letting her sister and her father down. She is doing what she thinks is the best thing for everyone.'

She... His frown deepened and his mind raced.

Her panic when he'd said he'd loved her; the expression on her face at the airport; the fact she'd given him her mother's sunglasses: had all that meant something after all?

Wishful thinking.

'It seems to me that Cleo fights for everyone else's happiness.' Elodie glared at him. 'But nobody seems to be fighting for Cleo.'

He shot to his feet, his hands clenching and unclenching. Elodie was right. He hadn't fought for Cleo. He'd made his declaration, she'd panicked and he'd retreated into his shell like a scared little hermit crab. He'd let Cleo walk away without a murmur of protest. He hadn't told her that he loved her again. He hadn't told her that, if she changed her mind, to call him. He hadn't told her he'd be there if she ever needed him.

What he'd told her was that he'd be okay. As if losing her hadn't shattered his world. As if his broken heart was a small thing easily recovered from. Cleo might not love him, but she deserved a man who would fight for her. And, if there was the slightest chance of winning her love, he'd fight with everything he had.

Cleo arrived at the Dorchester under the cover of darkness and was whisked straight up to a suite of rooms her father had organised for the bride and her attendant.

Other than the butler on hand to ensure she had all that she needed, the suite was empty. 'Your things arrived earlier, Ms Milne, and have been unpacked.' She handed her a letter. 'Your sister asked that I give you this.'

Cleo took the letter. 'Thank you.' Where was everyone?

'Dinner has been ordered for you for seven-thirty.'

Would Margot and her father be joining her then?

'If you need anything, please ring.' The butler gestured towards the phone and Cleo managed a polite smile before the other woman left. She felt like a robot. Ever since she'd walked away from Jude, she'd felt like half a person.

It had taken all her strength to force herself out of the car and to walk away from him this afternoon. The real reason she hadn't wanted him to come into the airport with her was that she hadn't been sure her resolve would hold. She had been afraid she'd weaken and tell him she loved him too.

But what had loving her given anyone? Nothing but headaches and heartache. Jude didn't need a mess like her in his life. He'd been through enough. He needed all his energy and resources to take his place as the head of the Giroux family. She swallowed. He'd forget about her soon enough.

Which was just as well, because with her on his arm he'd be nothing more than a laughing stock. He deserved better. He deserved the best.

She rubbed a hand across her chest, trying to ease the ache there. Nor could she let her sister down again. She hungered to make Margot and their father proud of her. And she would! Regardless of what it cost her.

She gritted her teeth. Staring at Hyde Park through the French doors, she rested her shoulder against the door frame and tore open Margot's letter.

Cleo,
Dad and I think it's best if you spend the night in the hotel suite where journalists can't get to you, while I spend the night at the family home. We'll arrive at the hotel at ten a.m. on the dot, as will the hairdressers and make-up artists, along with the seamstress, in case last-minute alterations are necessary.

Do not step foot outside your room. Do you hear me? Do not mess this up for me. If you do—

That last half-sentence had been left unfinished and the words had been crossed out, but they blazed off the page like a threat.

I will see you tomorrow.

It was signed *M*—no love, no kisses, no thank you. Just '*do not mess this up for me*'.

The letter dropped from her nerveless fingers and floated to the floor. 'The seamstress won't be necessary,' she whispered.

Cleo gazed in the mirror the next morning and hoped the make-up artist was a magician. She'd barely slept a wink, and hadn't touched her food last night or this morning. She looked as lacklustre as she felt.

She practised a smile, and then another one, because the first was so appalling. She *wouldn't* ruin Margot's big day. But a growing sense of disquiet had been building inside her since reading Margot's letter. She'd thought Margot had forgiven her. She'd thought things were right between them again. She'd done everything that Margot had asked of her—*everything.*

There was a slim chance that Margot had turned into a panic-stricken Bridezilla, but the more Cleo thought about it the less likely that seemed. For heaven's sake, Margot had trained as an international lawyer and was embarking on a political career. The one thing Margot *did* have was nerves of steel. And yet Margot continued to avoid her.

Cleo made herself smile in the mirror again and, while the smile was better, the tears that filled her eyes completely ruined the effect.

She forced them down. She suspected she knew why Margot was avoiding her and it had nausea churning in her stomach. She flashed back to New Year's Eve, once again feeling the impact of her fist colliding with Clay's jaw after those dreadful words had left his mouth. If what he'd said hadn't been a pack of lies...

A knock on the door had her straightening. Margot and Dad were ten minutes early. *Smile*, she silently ordered herself as she rushed out of the *en suite* and through the bedroom to fling open the door . 'Margot, I—'

She stopped dead, her mouth working, but not a single syllable emerging.

Jude! Jude stood on the other side of the door, looking grumpy, dishevelled and utterly wonderful and she drank him in with a greedy thirst. His scowl deepened. 'Can I come in?'

Closing a hand round one strong forearm, she hauled him inside, glancing outside the corridor to make sure it was empty before slamming the door shut. Her fingers tingled from where she'd touched him. She had to fight the urge to fling herself into his arms.

'Jude! What are you doing here?'

'I needed to see you. I forgot to ask you something.'

The expression in his eyes turned her insides to mush. She did everything she could to harden her heart. 'You can't stay.'

Oh, God! Margot and Dad would be here any moment. If they found Jude here... Her heart stuttered. They'd think she'd reverted to type. That she'd been partying and drinking. They'd believe the lies the newspapers had printed about her. Their smiles would slip, their mouths would twist, a cynical disillusion would spread across their faces. Worst of all, it would cast a shadow and a stain on Margot's day that could never be erased.

'There's something I need to ask you, Cleo.'

She barely heard him. Her heart fluttered too fast, like the wings of a hummingbird. Everything was unravelling.

Jude's hands curved around her shoulders. 'Cleo, I need to know—'

A knock on the door and Margot's, 'Cleo?' had her wanting to cry.

Jude stared at the door. His eyes widened. 'I thought there would be time before the wedding prep took over.' He kept his voice low. 'The wedding isn't till four o'clock.'

Seizing the front of his shirt, she shook him. 'They can *not* find you here.'

He spread his hands in a gesture that said 'what the hell do you want me to do?'

She pushed him into her bedroom. *'Hide.'*

'Where?'

'The *en suite*, wardrobe, under the bed... I don't care!' Hopefully there'd be a chance to sneak him out when no one was looking.

Another knock came. 'Cleo!' Margot sounded impatient.

'Coming!' She pointed a warning finger at Jude as she pulled the bedroom door closed, then rushed to answer the door. Her father and Margot stood on the threshold, thankfully alone. The army of hairdressers, make-up artists and dressers were yet to arrive.

They both gave her perfunctory kisses on the cheek—no hugs, no warm words.

Why had Jude come?

'I was starting to wonder if you were here.' Margot's ash-blonde hair swung in a shiny curtain as she moved past.

'Of course I'm here. I received my orders and have been following them like a good soldier.' She'd meant to say the words lightly, but they held an edge that made her wince internally.

Margot turned with stricken eyes—as if Cleo had plunged a knife into her heart. Cleo made herself smile and shrug. 'I was in the bathroom, that's all. Now, should I order tea to be sent up? Or maybe you'd like a glass of fizz instead?'

Was it her imagination or did Margot look a little green?

Did you really just order Jude to hide?

Her father strode to the phone and requested both tea and champagne to be sent up, before settling on one of the sofas. Cleo couldn't drag her gaze from her sister's. Margot swallowed. 'I trust you had a pleasant night?'

She'd spent fewer more miserable nights in her life. She'd missed Jude with an ache that had made her chest cramp. She'd missed Margot and the fun of the night before the wedding. She'd missed their mother. *Everything* had felt wrong.

'Yes, thank you.'

Margot's and her gazes remained locked. She could tell

Margot wanted to break the contact, but couldn't. She recognised some of the emotions churning in the amber brown of her sister's eyes and for a moment she wanted to cry. Clay's ugly words went round and round in her mind.

'Cleo,' Michael Milne started, oblivious to the silent battle going on between his daughters, 'I wanted to say how impressed I am. You've handled yourself extremely well over the last two-and-a-half weeks.'

That had Margot swinging around. 'No thanks to you! I still can't believe you turned her out of the family home.'

Cleo smiled then because she knew in that moment, despite her fears, that she hadn't lost her sister. 'Clay told me you and he had kissed.' The words blurted from her. She wished she'd found a way to say them with more grace, but the air needed to be cleared.

Margot turned back, her pallor making Cleo wince. Their father rose to his feet.

'He put it far more crudely than that—called you something dreadful. And, before I'd even realised it, I'd hit him. Over the years I've heard a lot of bad things said about you, Dad, because of the politician thing, but I'd never heard anyone say anything awful about you, Margot. If you're going to be a politician, I'm going to need to work on that. I can't go around beating up everyone who says something mean.'

Margot's knuckles turned white where she gripped them in front of her. 'Cleo, I—'

'I didn't believe it at first. The penny only dropped because of the way you've continued to avoid me. I—'

'You kissed your sister's boyfriend?' Michael suddenly roared.

'Don't you start!' Cleo rounded on him. 'Margot has always tried to be perfect to make up to the both of us for losing Mum.'

He blinked.

'She looked after me when you closed yourself off, but who looked after her, huh? Not once has she ever rebelled. You've absolutely no right to judge her.'

His jaw slackened.

Grabbing Margot's hands, she squeezed them hard. 'The thing is, I don't care if it *is* true. You could do something a hundred times worse and I'd still forgive you. Look at all I put you through, and yet you still stood by me.'

Margot's face crumpled. 'I'm so sorry, Cleo. *So* sorry. I've never been more ashamed of myself. I—'

A knock sounded: the tea and champagne. Cleo gestured for it to be placed on the sideboard.

What was Jude doing here?

Only when they were alone again did she speak. 'I was never in love with Clay. You knew that.' She frowned. 'Why did you talk me out of breaking up with him?'

'I felt so guilty about what had happened. I blamed myself and that stupid kiss for your changing feelings for him. I was worried I'd wrecked things for you.'

'So you wanted me to give it another chance?'

'I just wanted you to be sure. The thing is, Clay really did love you. I felt a bit sorry for him.'

It was Cleo's turn to blink.

'I think it's why he kissed me—he was searching for comfort from someone he associated with you. It's not really an excuse, but...'

But it was a human thing to do.

Did you really just order Jude to hide?

She glanced at her father and gestured to the tea things. 'Do you want to play Mother?'

He moved across and poured the tea.

'As for me...' Margot stared down at her hands before meeting Cleo's eyes once more. 'I was having one of the worst weeks of my life. A parliamentary paper I'd spent months working on was sent back to the drawing board and the party had decided not to approve my nomination just yet.'

They'd what? 'But—'

'They changed their minds a few days later, but…'

She nodded to let Margot know she understood.

'Worse than that, though, Brett and I had a huge fight. We never fight, and it was unexpectedly fierce.' She grimaced. 'He made his excuses and didn't come to Dad's sixtieth birthday party.'

Ah, so that's why Brett hadn't been there.

'I thought we were over. You and a few of the other girls were talking about what we should do for my hen night and I didn't have the heart to take part, so I drifted off. I found myself alone with Clay in the library. It was obvious he felt a bit left out and…'

She shrugged, the skin at the corners of her eyes drawing tight. 'It was stupid. But for that brief moment we felt like two lost souls and we turned to each other for solace. We sprang apart a moment later, both utterly appalled.'

Cleo's heart burned for her sister, and a little bit for Clay too. Pulling in a breath, she pressed her hands together. 'I need to check—are you sure you want to marry Brett?'

Margot stiffened.

'And, while we're talking so frankly, do you truly want to be a politician or are you doing that to make Dad happy?'

From the corner of her eye, she saw her dad's gaze sharpen.

'Yes, and yes. I told Brett about what had happened between me and Clay. I couldn't lie to him. He was hurt, but was mature enough to point out that we hadn't made any formal vows to each other at that point. He was ridiculously understanding. He still wants to marry me, and he knows I love him.'

Cleo sagged.

'I'm the luckiest woman in the world.' Margot's smile told them she meant it. 'And I do want to be a politician, Cleo. I promise you I do. I want to make a difference, and it feels like the right platform to do that.'

Their father sagged then too.

Cleo clapped her hands. 'Look, we're all adults and it's time to start acting like it. We can't keep playing the same roles we have since Mum died.'

'Agreed,' Margot said.

Her father nodded. She pointed a finger at him. 'You need to be more present.' She turned to Margot. 'You need to stop trying to be perfect. And I—' she slapped a hand on her chest '—need to stop appearing in the papers. I know the tabloids love labelling me a wild child, but I need to stop providing them with fodder!'

Her father frowned. 'But the reason you landed on the front page this time was…due to someone else's bad behaviour.' His frown deepened. 'And the time before that too.'

Margot stared at her. 'And the two times before that it was due to Ewan and… Oh, that pretty boy! What was his name?'

'Austin.' Cleo nodded and swallowed. 'I haven't been a wild child since I was twenty-two. It's just that no one wants to believe it.'

Margot took her hands. 'Then *you* don't need to change anything.'

'Yes, I do,' she said slowly, remembering something Jude had once said. 'I need to forgive myself for past mistakes and stop trying to win everyone's approval. I need to learn to be proud of myself instead.'

Proud of herself? She'd just pushed Jude—a man who'd proven himself a true friend, a man who'd told her *he loved her*—into the bedroom and ordered him to hide, as if he was something she was ashamed of.

Her stomach churned. What kind of person had she become? 'There's something I need to tell you both.' She pressed her hands together. 'Jude,' she called out, 'would you like to come out here?'

CHAPTER TWELVE

JUDE STEPPED INTO the living room, his head spinning from all he'd overheard. The *someone* Clay had taunted Cleo with had been her *sister*?

Yet Cleo had still done Margot's bidding. She had done her utmost to ensure her wedding was everything she wanted. She'd effaced herself and put Margot's needs first. His heart pounded. Cleo loved so hard. If only he could convince her to love him just a little with that big heart of hers.

Cleo took his arm and faced her father and sister. 'This man helped me at his own personal expense when he didn't have to, just because he has a good heart. He went above and beyond.'

She dragged in a breath. 'He turned up here two minutes before you did and I panicked when you knocked, because I thought it might look bad if you found him here. I thought you'd be disappointed in me.'

She glanced up at Jude with burning eyes. 'That was an awful thing to do, Jude. I'm sorry.'

He shrugged. 'Apology accepted.'

'If it wasn't for this man, I'd have been plastered across all the newspapers *again*.'

Margot leapt forward and hugged him. 'Thank you for helping Cleo. I'm so grateful to you.' The warmth in her eyes had him understanding why Cleo loved her so much. She hugged Cleo too. 'I think we've been taking dysfunctional to a whole new level.'

'Nonsense.' Michael cleared his throat. 'This is just normal family...'

Cleo raised an eyebrow. 'Drama?'

'Dynamics?' Margot offered.

'Muddle.' He cleared his throat. 'When people care about each other they can get into the occasional muddle, that's all. And, while we're on the topic of being adults, Cleo, will you please introduce us to this young man?'

Cleo made the introductions.

Michael Milne's lips twisted, but there was a twinkle in his eyes. 'Now, in case you've forgotten, we're supposed to be having a wedding today, and the crew are impatiently waiting downstairs.' He held up his phone. 'I've been holding them off, but they're becoming increasingly frantic.'

Margot clasped Cleo's arm, her eyes going wide. 'I'm getting married!'

Cleo laughed. 'To the man of your dreams, remember?'

Margot's smile could've lit up an entire city block. Jude found himself grinning.

Margot wrung her hands. 'We have to get ready! I want it to be perfect!' She turned to Jude. 'Please come to my wedding.'

If it meant being near Cleo... 'I'd be honoured.'

'Come with me then, young man, and we'll get you sorted.' Michael clapped him on the shoulder.

Glancing back, he found Cleo watching him with eyes the colour of a still sea. Striding back, he squeezed her hand, the scent of pears engulfing him. 'Later,' he promised. He'd wait as long as he had to if there was the slightest chance of winning this woman's heart.

The wedding went without a hitch. The bride glowed while the groom couldn't wipe the grin from his face. Cleo, in a dress of dusky green that highlighted the colour of her eyes, was the picture of propriety.

Michael made a speech about how proud he was of his two daughters, how their happiness was his happiness, which barely left an eye in the room dry. The best man made a speech that had everyone laughing. And Cleo made a speech so heartfelt and sincere, it had a lump lodging in Jude's throat.

The cake was cut. The bridal waltz was danced. Jude's hands clenched as he watched the best man twirl a radiant Cleo across the dance floor. A young woman tapped his arm. 'We haven't been introduced, but Michael sent me over. He implied you'd be eager to dance with Cleo.'

He had?

'And as Cleo is dancing with my husband...'

Excellent.

'Shall we?'

He waltzed a direct path to Cleo. 'We're hoping to cut in.'

Cleo's eyes widened, but she moved into his arms without hesitation. 'Is it *later*?'

He nodded. Holding her so close, their bodies moving in harmony, had warmth encircling him and he closed his eyes to savour it.

'Why have we not waltzed before?' Cleo murmured, her left hand sliding further round his back so she could press herself closer.

Heat flooded his veins. 'Not much room for waltzing on a narrow boat.' And on the yacht they'd been too busy keeping their distance.

Mischievous eyes met his. 'It'd be fun to try, though.'

Images flooded his mind, making his nostrils flare.

'So...' She eased away a fraction. 'Are you enjoying the wedding?'

The wedding was nothing more than an interruption he had to endure before he could have Cleo to himself again. He hadn't prepared a speech, but...

Margot sidled up beside them. 'I seem to have torn the lace on my dress, Cleo. Can you pin it back up for me?'

Cleo stepped out of his arms with an apologetic wrinkle of her nose. 'Later is going to have to wait for a bit.'

He wanted to howl at the moon. He shrugged instead. 'For you, I'll wait as long as I have to.'

Her lovely lips parted, but then Margot tugged on her arm and Cleo moved away before he could kiss her which, despite the itch of impatience chafing through him, was probably for the best.

Cleo's heart pounded. What was Jude doing here? He'd said he'd wait as long as he had to, but...*why?* She'd already told him they couldn't be together. That had been hours ago. And, true to his word, he was still here—waiting.

And she loved it. *Loved him.* But she needed to fight that because the thought of letting him down at some future date and seeing his love turn to derision, realising she'd made his life worse instead of better... She didn't think she could bear it.

What if you don't let him down?

Yeah, right, and pigs might fly.

She did her best to focus on her bridesmaid duties. Margot and Brett were sent off with cheers and well wishes as they climbed into the white stretch limousine that would take them to a secret location. Cleo clasped her hands beneath her chin as the limousine pulled away. 'It was the most beautiful wedding.'

Her father rested an arm across her shoulders. 'It was a beautiful wedding, and your sister is a very happy woman. And, Cleo, I believe you will be too.'

She blinked when he took her arm and handed her inside a black cab that had drawn up behind the limo. 'Look after my girl, Jude.'

'I will.'

Jude slid in from the other side and her heart hammered, leapt and swooped. Her father pressed a kiss on her cheek, though she barely registered it, her mind too full of the man beside her. 'Give your dear old dad a call tomorrow, huh?' Dragging her gaze from Jude, she nodded.

The door closed, the cab pulled away and piercing blue eyes met hers in the semi-darkness. The breath squeezed from her lungs. She wanted him so much, she ached with it.

Don't focus on that.

'Where are we going?' she managed instead.

'You'll see. It's a surprise.' He threaded his fingers through hers. She stared at their linked hands. She ought to pull hers free…but she didn't.

They drove over Westminster Bridge and through Southwark. She'd assumed they were heading to his apartment. She straightened as the cab wended its way down to the Thames river-front.

Jude squeezed her hand. 'This is where we get out.'

He leapt from the cab and strode round to open her door. She took his hand and stepped out. There was a gate in front of them, but not one that led to an apartment building. 'Jude, where…?'

He led her through the gate and her eyes widened. A ramp led down to the water and the most spectacular… 'Is that a canal boat?' She couldn't call it a narrow boat—there was absolutely *nothing* narrow about it.

'It was the floating Customs and Excise Office. It's been decommissioned and is now a luxury house boat.'

She pulled to a halt. 'We're going on board?'

'I've leased it for a few days.'

He had?

'I thought it might appeal to you.'

It did, but… 'Why?'

'Why what?'

'Why are we here rather than your apartment, which has to be nearby, or my apartment in Fulham? Or in a private room at the Dorchester?' Why had he brought her *here*?

His face settled into familiar stern lines. 'It's *later* and I don't want to be interrupted.'

'But I don't have an overnight case or—'

'Your father had the staff at the hotel pack up your things. They've already been stowed on board.'

Her father had been party to this?

'Come and see.'

That lopsided smile could do the craziest things to a woman's pulse. She let him lead her down the ramp and onto the boat. It was two storeys of absolute luxury. Jude led her up the wooden staircase to an open-plan living room, dining room and kitchen. There was oak furniture, big, comfy sofas and bold art on the walls.

Walking across to the enormous windows, she stared at the view of Tower Bridge. 'This is bigger than my entire apartment!'

'It's something, isn't it?'

The boat rocked gently beneath her feet and she wanted to close her eyes and savour the familiar motion.

'No expense was spared restoring it. It can comfortably accommodate twelve. Sleeping quarters are on the lower deck— four bedrooms and two bathrooms. It puts *Camelot* to shame.'

Not true—she would *always* be grateful to *Camelot*.

'Would you like a cold drink, or something to eat?'

A platter of hors d'oeuvres sat on the table and drinks were chilling in a silver bucket.

'The pantry is stocked.' He started towards the kitchen. 'So if there's something else you'd prefer...'

She couldn't stand it another moment. It was taking all her strength not to stride across and kiss him, or say something she might regret, like *I love you*.

'Jude.' She pressed her hands together. 'You said there was something you needed to ask me.'

He stilled. 'Before we get to that...' He turned and moved back. 'Was Margot the "someone" Clay referred to?'

She couldn't decipher the expression in his eyes. She shrugged and nodded.

'You knew from the first that Margot had betrayed you?'

'No.' She pointed a surprisingly steady finger at him. 'And there are two things to unpick in that sentence. The first is, of course I didn't know. I thought Clay had lied. But when Margot kept avoiding me...' She swallowed. 'It clicked into place when I returned to London last night and found we were staying in different venues.'

He didn't say anything. It made her fidget. 'I had no plans to confront her with it, but the moment she clapped eyes on me...' She winced. 'The guilt was eating her alive. It was better to get it out in the open.'

'It was brave.'

'Nonsense.' She straightened. 'And the other thing you need to understand is that Margot didn't *betray* me. She was desperately unhappy and did a stupid thing. She didn't deliberately set out to hurt me. She didn't think to herself, "what's something I can do to hurt Cleo?"' Blue eyes throbbed into hers. It took everything she had to remain where she stood rather than sway towards him.

'You meant it when you said you'd forgive her something a hundred times worse.'

Of course she'd meant it. Margot was her sister!

He leaned down until they were eye level. 'Your father refused to let you hide out at the family home?'

She huffed out a breath. Where was he going with this? 'Look, I understood his frustration and his impatience. It was a classic case of my past coming back to bite me.'

'This past you continually refer to, Cleo, was over three

years ago. Since then you've turned your life around—changed jobs, been sober, been a responsible adult. Your only crime,' he added when she opened her mouth, 'was to date a few untrustworthy jerks.'

She folded her arms. 'Your point being?'

'That you harbour no resentment towards your family for not realising that earlier.'

She folded her arms harder. 'Families can fall into patterns. They came to think of me as the problem child. Don't forget, they were grieving for my mother at the time too. Dad had no idea how to help me. And he's not the kind of man who takes kindly to feeling helpless. Margot just wanted to make everything right for everyone. All of us made mistakes.'

She hitched up her chin. 'It's taken me years to see that, though.' *And a lot of therapy.* 'So, no, I don't feel resentment towards them.'

Jude widened his stance. 'So you don't want them feeling bad about how they've dealt with you in the past? You don't want Margot to keep beating herself up for kissing Clay?'

She gaped at him. How could he even think such a thing?

His face darkened. 'Then why don't you cut yourself the same slack? Why aren't you just as kind to yourself?'

That had her speechless for a moment. 'I...'

'Since I've known you, you've continually beaten yourself up and blamed yourself for putting your family through the wringer. Over the last three years, though, you've done nothing to be ashamed of. So what if you've dated a few bad eggs? We've all done that. Unlike the majority of us, though, your romantic woes were splashed in the newspapers—*not* your fault.'

She didn't know what to say.

'The things you did when you were younger were understandable.'

'It doesn't mean I condone them!'

'When are you going to forgive yourself for them?' His

hands slammed onto his hips. 'The way you've forgiven the mistakes your family have made?'

She took a half-step back.

'Earlier today you said you needed to forgive yourself. *When* are you going to do that?'

Her heart hammered. He spread his hands and scowled, but she saw the exhaustion behind it and it had tears pricking her eyes.

'What if I backslide?' she whispered, blinking hard. 'I can't afford to do that. I don't want it for me or my family. Keeping a catalogue of my sins at the forefront of my mind and reminding myself of the damage I did ensures it won't happen. It keeps me on the straight and narrow.'

His face gentled. 'Oh, Cleo.' He reached out as if to touch her, but his hand fell back to his side. Her pulse jumped and jerked. 'What if that mindset is stealing your joy?'

Maybe that was a small price to pay. His eyes narrowed, as if he'd read that thought in her face. 'Do you think Margot will ever kiss another one of your boyfriends?'

'*No.*'

'Do you think your father will ever again refuse you sanctuary?' When she remained silent, he continued, 'So why can't you believe *you* won't make the same mistakes you once did?'

She moistened her lips and frowned. Actually...that was an excellent question.

'You're not an angry teenager any more, Cleo. You now have the strategies you learned in therapy to help you cope. Isn't it time to start trusting yourself?'

Very slowly, she started to nod. The thought of treating anyone she loved the same way she'd been treating herself had her breaking out in a cold sweat. She rubbed a hand across her chest, acknowledging silently that she didn't want a life devoid of joy.

'On Thursday night you told me I didn't need someone like you in my life.'

Her gaze flew back to his. She'd walked away from him. It was the hardest thing she'd ever done. But if she was going to start trusting herself...

'When you said I didn't need someone like you in my life, I know that you meant someone lumbered with your kind of notoriety.'

He was the head of a family with a proud heritage. He was good, kind and honourable. He deserved the best.

'But in my eyes that meant I was being deprived of someone like you—a person who has the most generous heart I've ever had the privilege to meet. It meant being deprived of your kindness and your humour and your teasing—all of which lighten my load. It meant being deprived of seeing the world through your eyes—because your way of seeing it gave me a different perspective, and that helped me find my way forward.'

Tears burnt a hole in her throat.

'On Thursday night you told me what I didn't need in my life and what your family didn't need in their lives, but what you didn't tell me is what you needed in your life, Cleo.'

Tears spilled from her eyes.

'And you didn't say you didn't love me. So the question I came here to ask you today, Cleo, is...do you love me?'

She couldn't speak. Her throat was too thick and her voice had deserted her. But what she could do was nod and throw herself into his arms.

He crushed her to him as if he meant to never let her go. She sobbed incoherently into his shoulder for several long seconds. Lifting her head, she cupped his face. 'I love you, Jude—so much. You're the most amazing man I've ever met—the *best* man. You make my life better, in every way.'

'Cleo.' Her name was a groan from his lips.

'In my mixed-up way, I thought you deserved better than me. I thought I'd just cause chaos in your life and you'd had enough of that. I didn't know...'

His fingers travelled down her cheek. 'What didn't you know?'

'That you feel exactly the same way about me that I feel about you.'

His smile, when it came, was the most beautiful thing she'd ever seen. She suspected her smile was just as radiant.

'I love a good epiphany,' she whispered.

He nodded, his head lowering to hers. Their kiss had stars bursting behind her eyelids.

Lifting her in his arms, Jude lowered them to the sofa, keeping her in his lap. She rested a hand against his cheek. 'Thank you for coming back for me.'

He half-scowled and shrugged lightly. 'I couldn't not come back for you. I fell for you the moment you crashed onto my boat and held a finger to your lips as you hid behind my chair. You've had me in some kind of spell ever since.'

She grinned. 'You were so grumpy.'

'What did you expect? You'd turned my world upside down in under ten seconds flat.'

Her grin widened. 'You were so kind, though you tried to hide it.'

He shook his head, as if still befuddled. 'I went from agreeing to hide you for an hour, to agreeing to drop you further along the canal path, to letting you stay for a week...and then a fortnight.'

Her chest fizzed with so much emotion, she could hardly breathe.

'It should come as no surprise to either one of us that I can now not let you go, that I want you in my life for good—that I want a lifetime with you. You also ought to know that I asked your father for your hand in marriage.'

The edges of the room blurred.

'Not that we need his permission, but I wanted him to know I was serious. I want you to know that too.' He cupped her face. 'You love so fearlessly. You showed me how to love fearlessly too.'

Something too exceptional to be called happiness bubbled up through her. 'I am going to be the best wife you could ever have, Jude. I'm going to make you the happiest man alive.'

He stared at her and then he grinned—*really* grinned. 'Was that a yes?'

She grinned back. 'It's most definitely a yes.'

Could a person have been any happier than she was at that moment? Hooking a hand behind his head, she drew his face down to hers. 'I love you, Jude. I love you with my whole heart. It's all yours.'

Their lips met in a kiss that was both tender and intense, fierce and loving. It was the kind of kiss that lifted her up on a wave of optimism and *joy* that didn't lower her back again— as if her world now was bigger, better…truer.

It was a kiss that she'd remember for the rest of her life…

* * * * *

If you enjoyed this story,
check out these other great reads from
Michelle Douglas

Tempted by Her Greek Island Bodyguard
Claiming His Billion-Dollar Bride
Accidentally Waking Up Married
Cinderella's Secret Fling

All available now!

PRINCE'S REUNION
IN PARADISE

FAYE ACHEAMPONG

MILLS & BOON

PROLOGUE

THIRTEEN-YEAR-OLD DAMICA FOYE studied the Dani DoRight doll, unsure about whether she wanted to cradle the plastic toy human in her arms or rip its entire head off.

She's not me. I'm not her, she chanted to herself again and again.

For a handful of imaginary handclaps Damica forgot about the aroma of cleaning chemicals and the silent city of shaggy mopheads, surface cleaner bottles and supply carts surrounding her. The new song she'd accidentally made up was a welcome distraction from the unexpected misery that came with playing one of the most recognisable fictional characters in the world. She'd become so recognisable that she preferred to hide.

The door guarding the conference building's maintenance closet betrayed her, opening with a trespassing click. Reflexively, Damica's hand flew up to protect her face from the cameras and she braced herself for a tidal wave of barks.

'Smile Dani!'

'Over here, Dani!'

'Put your hands on your hips, Dani—not both, just the one.'

'Look over here—at me only, sweetheart, forget the others.'

Instead, she was cowering away from a solitary silhouette in the non-threatening brightness of the hallway.

A...boy? Shorter than her. With dark wavy hair and bronze-coloured skin. He appeared to be around her age, but the confident style and cut of his suit suggested he was cosplaying someone more mature. The shock in the width of his brown eyes outdid Damica's astonishment.

She was actually relieved.

The event photographers or, worse, her mom, hadn't found her yet.

Only Prince Dorian of Concarre.

'This hiding spot is taken!' Damica squeaked, sticking her head out of the unlit space to peep left and right.

The coast was clear. For now. She wondered if she should be bowing or offering him a handshake—that was how everyone else at the Youth Today, Leaders Tomorrow conference had reacted to his presence.

'Pick another... Your Highness.'

That sounded polite enough, didn't it?

The Prince peered past her, inside the dark otherworld of the cleaners' closet. He took in the nozzles protruding from the spray bottles and the exhausted aprons hanging from their hooks like ghouls.

Authority overrode the confusion of his round face and the unbroken pitch of his voice. 'There seems to be plenty of room.'

'No, there isn't.' Damica shook her head stubbornly.

He crossed his arms. 'Yes, there is—'

An army of walkie-talkie beeps and serious codewords echoed in the distance. Bodyguards searching for the young royal who had escaped their watchful eye.

The children were immediately united in their terror. Their disagreement was replaced with the common dance of hopping frantically from foot to foot and a wild choreography of gestures that included repeatedly jabbing a finger over their mouths.

Panic took over as Damica dumped her doll into the nearest bucket, then grabbed Dorian by the lapels of his suit jacket. Pulling him inside the cleaners' closet, she ignored his triumphant smile.

'See, I told you there was room…'

'Shh!'

They were cloaked by darkness once Damica had closed the door as quietly as possible. She put her ear to the surface, listening for the sound of footsteps coming from the other side. Nothing. Crisis averted. Phew!

Suddenly she was bathed in unwelcome light. The closet's flickering lightbulb managed to come alive at the command of the pull switch now manned by Dorian. With a sigh, Damica tugged the string so that the light was turned off.

The Prince turned it on again.

Off. On. *Off.*

Finally he got the message and the safety of the shadows remained uninterrupted.

'Wow…this really looks like you.'

She turned around to see Prince Dorian holding the Dani DoRight doll, squinting at its form.

That was another reason Damica was so comfortable with the closet's dim interior—she didn't have to deal with how dumb and toddlerish her clothes looked. Frowning down at her tutu, jeans and ballet flats, she longed for a more stylish outfit. She wanted to try make-up and high heels and miniskirts like regular thirteen-year-olds did.

Self-consciously, Damica shrugged. 'Not really. She's not me. My name's not even Dani…it's *Damica*. With an M and a C.'

The nothingness that followed only made her feel more awkward. He wouldn't understand anyway. He was a prince. Royal people probably got to do and wear whatever they wanted to.

She looked up, her gaze connecting with Dorian's. He watched her as if he could see her clearly.

'I wish I had another name,' he confessed, looking as lost as he sounded. 'People think they know me because they've heard of me. I don't get to introduce myself. It's weird.'

'Having two names is overrated, so you're not missing out on anything. No one cares about the real me any more… they're only interested in the new version,' she told him, surprising herself with her own honesty.

Slowly Damica sank onto the floor, sitting down cross-legged and leaning back against the chilly brick wall. Dorian joined the descent, settling with his legs straight. She observed him tapping the heels of his smart-looking shoes together, so the leather clapped, creating a tune.

'Choose one,' she said.

He paused. 'Pardon?'

'A new name.'

Being alone with him wasn't so bad, she decided. They were more similar than she'd thought.

'Oh.' His posture straightened whilst his fingers plucked at the air, as if he was concentrating hard on conjuring up a… 'Wilbur.'

Damica snorted. She slapped a hand over her mouth, but that did little to stop the giggle fizzing up inside her.

'What?' Dorian demanded. 'What's wrong with Wilbur?'

She scrunched up her nose. 'It's so—I dunno—*old*!'

'Pick something that suits me, then.' He'd deflated into a relaxed state instead of a sad one.

'Okay. You look like a…' Damica cleared her throat and pumped her fists to add some pizzazz. 'Romeo!'

He laughed. 'No, I do not.'

'You do!'

And that was that. They were familiar enough to banter with each other…share feelings that were supposed to go unspoken about and ask questions that usually fell upon deaf ears.

Damica didn't know if she'd spent twenty minutes talking with Dorian or several hours. What mattered most was that this was the most fun she'd had at Youth Today, Leaders Tomorrow and she wanted it to last longer. By the time his security team raided the haven of the cleaners' closet she'd opened up about how she was scared her mom cared more about the Feir Channel pay-cheques than her.

In return, Dorian had confided in her about how he missed his dad a lot, and was only able to get his attention by pretending to be 'macho'.

One of Dorian's guards escorted Damica back to where her mom was pacing around like a headless chicken. Just as Damica had predicted, she was greeted with a scolding lecture about setting a bad example and the whereabouts of the lost doll before the conference's scheduled presentations continued for the day.

Somewhere between the interpretative dance promoting wildlife conservation and the speech about running for Youth World Government, the kid next to her nudged her shoulder and dropped a folded sheet of lined paper clipped to a ballpoint pen on her lap. The message was addressed to her, however she didn't recognise the penmanship.

Damica scanned the hall, packed with child activists, musical prodigies, young royals and teen starlets, until she detected Dorian seated at the very opposite end of her row. He sent her a shy wave and pointed at the message he'd sent out into the sea of attendees.

She grinned back, then read the contents of her delivery:

Do you have email?
From...maybe Giorgios???

Damica hadn't got to say goodbye to him before, when they'd been so harshly separated, and she'd accepted that they would never meet again and trusted that her secrets would be safe with him. Now, shimmering with hope, she realised that she and Dorian would never truly be apart from each other if they became pen pals.

She freed the pen, pressed down the button and started to write her email address...

Age Thirteen

From: mrdoryfish7@inbox.com
To: damidiamondzzz@inbox.com
Subject: READ ME... IT'S URGENT!!

Hi :D

From: damidiamondzzz@inbox.com
To: mrdoryfish7@inbox.com
Re: READ ME... IT'S URGENT!!

Hello!!

PS Did you get the email chain I sent to you? Who did you forward it to?

PPS Is your email name coz of *Finding Nemo*? I had to go to the premiere... Premieres suck! I hate it when the men with cameras shout at me...

From: mrdoryfish7@inbox.com
to: damidiamondzzz@inbox.com
Subject: READ ME... IT'S URGENT!!

Um... I'm not going to tell you that! Don't want seven years bad luck!

Try hiding from them again? They can't take pictures if they can't see you.

When I'm travelling I sometimes lie down in the car boot. Works every time!

:D

CHAPTER ONE

Twenty years later

THE FIRST RULE of looking after a child: do not lose said child.

Damica was already off to a terrible start.

The soles of her platform flip-flops thwacked against the stone ground, rivalling the hammering of her speeding heart, during the frantic search of her nephew. She'd looked away for literally *a minute*, assuming Jalen would be fine whilst she brought him a cone from the counter at the resort's ice cream parlour. However, she was now paying the price for underestimating the four-year-old boy's energetic streak and thirst for adventure.

He'd taken his auntie's lack of supervision as an opportunity to dash out of the parlour and explore the resort all on his own.

Under prolonged exposure to the Maldivian afternoon sun, the once chilled scoop of mint and milk chocolate ice cream was now a pathetic green-brown blob. Streams of melted ice cream oozed down the softening wafer cone and onto Damica's hand, causing her to pull a face. Sighing, she slowed down to dump the dying delicacy into a nearby bin and shake away the mess.

How could she call herself a functioning adult when she couldn't even handle the responsibility of caring for her own nephew?

Immature. Selfish. Irresponsible—

Damica closed her eyes and ran through the breathing exercises introduced to her by her therapist.

Inhale for four seconds, hold for seven seconds, exhale for eight.

You're free now, she reminded herself.

Her Dani DoRight days were long behind her, as was the overwhelming control of her mother. Plus, Damica had fulfilled all contractual obligations to her record label and concluded her music career with a worldwide tour just five months earlier. This holiday in the Maldives with her close family was way overdue. At long last she was free. Life was good. Normality was all she'd ever wanted.

She stood up straighter and readjusted the dark lenses of her designer sunglasses. There was no time to enjoy the summer heat, the crisp cerulean blue sky and salty sea air. And there was even less time to care about the passing vacationers—friends, families and couples—who reacted to the white patches on her brown skin with typical quizzical glances.

Damica focused on scrutinising the picturesque landscape of the Étoile Privée Resort. The path before her branched off at consistent intervals, leading to the elated squeals and chlorinated turquoise rush of the water park, or the contemplative silence of the resort boutique. Down on the beach, the members of a yoga class executed poses with such stillness that they might have been mistaken for a collection of statues parked on the vastness of the golden sand.

No sign of Jalen, though.

She'd already checked the marina, the fitness centre and the reception building to no avail.

Damica prayed that Jalen was at least still on the main island, and wasn't sobbing in the jungle area with a scraped and bloody knee—or, worse, floating face-down in the sea...

Fear and gut feeling guided Damica straight ahead, towards the sharp architecture of the ocean-front villas, which were bisected by a wood-planked pier that seemed to stretch on for ever. Explaining to her younger sister Taylor and her brother-in-law that she'd lost their only child wasn't an option.

The slap of Damica's flip-flops fired up again, and her sundress swished around her legs as she moved with purpose. Pumping adrenaline made her all the more aware of her surroundings: of the cool shadows of the looming palm trees growing sparser as she approached the water. Of the faraway trilling of a bicycle bell followed by sombre calls to be careful. Then, unfiltered boyish laughter that was instantly identifiable.

'Jalen?' Damica shouted at the blurry figures cruising in her direction along the wooden walkway.

Someone on a bike, and a person jogging behind, struggling to keep up. From a distance, she was able to pinpoint her nephew. He was having the time of his life, sitting on the wicker basket fixed to the cycle's handlebars.

'Jalen, there you...!'

The projection of her voice fell when the cyclist's features came into clear view.

Dorian Saadoun Sotiropoulos.

The joyous shine vacated Dorian's facial expression and alarm invaded once he saw Damica. Taken with equal shock, his hold on the bike slackened and it toppled from side to side. Jalen screeched in excitement, clinging to the basket for dear life as he mistook Dorian's action for an added thrill to the ride experience.

The chaser's thudding footsteps decelerated as he neared. Heavy hands protectively landed on the Prince's shoulder and the bicycle saddle just as Dorian planted a shaky foot on the ground.

Despite drowning in sweat and the self-inflicted furnace

generated by his all-black attire, the bodyguard muttered stoically, 'Careful, Your Highness.'

'Thank you, Ravi.' Dorian's eyes refused to part from Damica as he spoke.

She couldn't stop observing him either.

The last time she'd seen him in person had been when they were both on the cusp of teen hood. Still kids.

He looked exactly the same, but somehow different. In so many different ways—subtle and obvious—that it was near-impossible to process them all at once. The reassuring brown of his irises and the slight hook of his Roman nose remained. But his wavy hair was much longer now, the ends finishing at the nape of his neck and curling outward, giving him a regal sort of charm.

Their difference in height was the same. She must have had about two inches on him—even more so with her platform shoes on.

New was the lean edge to his build. A thin chain necklace had residence midway down his chest, the sun's glare and the half-buttoned state of his short-sleeved shirt attracted her attention downward.

An embarrassed flush wormed its way through Damica's body as he drank in her changed appearance with the same interest. On the tip of her tongue, a joke about Dorian finally sprouting the chest hair his father had so badly wanted him to have immediately formed. However, she knew that its delivery would only make this reunion more tense.

She recalled the finality of their last email exchange. How she'd obviously no longer had a place within the strict, regulated boundaries of his life. Damica hadn't realised at the time, but the abrupt end of their friendship had been the best outcome for them both. In hindsight, their falling out seemed like a juvenile case of miscommunication. Nonetheless, the overarching message had been that they were heading for very different trajectories in life.

Dorian was destined to be the sovereign ruler of Concarre—a small but prosperous nation situated in the Mediterranean Sea, midway between southern Greece and Egypt. Polite behaviour, sacrifice and protocol were on the cards for him.

As for Damica…it would be a cold day in hell before she relinquished control to another person or a greater cause again.

'Again! Again! Again!'

Jalen's chanting faded in, breaking up the pair's deep study of one another.

'No. You've had enough fun today.'

Damica charged up to the bicycle and lifted her nephew out of the large basket. After his small feet were reunited with the wooden planks of the pier, she crouched down so they were eye to eye. She cupped his cheeks, making sure to keep her hold gentle but firm as he whined and attempted to wriggle away from accountability. His features—a healthy head of tight curls, expressive eyes that creased at the corners and a round face—were the perfect summarisation of Taylor and her husband Leroy.

'You almost gave me a heart attack. Don't run off like that again.'

Judging by the way Jalen stilled and looked down shamefully, she'd perfected her 'mommy voice'. No sense of pride completed this victory, though. Only a building nervousness as Dorian closely watched the exchange, his stare clinging to Damica like a second skin.

She wrapped a hand around one of Jalen's and stood up again. Checking that she was still protected by the dark lenses of her eyewear, Damica pulled on a false mask of indifference.

'What are you doing here?' she asked Dorian, not meaning to sound as breathless as she felt.

Her efforts were ultimately in vain. She would have blamed the weather, but she'd always preferred hotter climates.

'Taking a sabbatical.'

Dorian dismounted from the bicycle, smoothly swinging his leg over the seat. Quickly, he handed over the two-wheeled vehicle to his bodyguard, so he could allocate all his attention to Damica and Jalen.

'And you?'

'Family holiday.'

The less she said the better. She couldn't embarrass herself further that way.

Nine years had passed since she'd last heard from Dorian. Almost a decade. Damica had assumed the wound of their separation was well and truly healed. But something as simple as their contrast in motives for their stay here caused the resurfacing of a tender soreness that was too familiar. Even the way Dorian strode undecidedly towards her and Jalen, whilst the bodyguard shadowed him, informed Damica that a restoration of their previous relationship would be impossible.

She could forgive him if she wanted to...but forgetting about their clashing principles? Unlikely.

'How...how are you?' Dorian's focal point jumped between her blank face—she was working overtime to give nothing away—and Jalen, who was restlessly tugging on her arm.

She dodged the question entirely and pivoted. 'Where did you find him?'

'Here. Running up and down.'

To demonstrate, Dorian pointed down the stretch of the jetty and made his fingers sprint through the air.

'Initially, I didn't want to interrupt—he said he was hiding from his aunt, so I assumed there was a game of hide-and-seek happening. But then he got distracted by my bike.'

Damica was temporarily lulled by Dorian's version of events. A distinct accent still underscored his words. However, his tone had matured considerably into a deep, engaging articulation. The boy from the janitor's closet was long gone.

As she noticed the stubble framing his mouth, Damica wondered if he was still obsessed with poetry. She remembered the essay's worth of emails he'd sent her from his boarding school library, chronicling his analyses…

Stop.

'We were about to take him to the concierge desk,' Dorian concluded, utterly oblivious to her slipping resolve. He regarded Jalen with fond confusion. 'Is he your…?'

'Nephew?' She finished off the sentence, watching inexplicable relief, hurt and then guilt play across his demeanour. 'Yes,' she added quietly.

Huh? Had Dorian thought Jalen was her son? If so, his reaction didn't make any sense. She hadn't been attached to any pregnancy rumours since she was a teenager, and keeping a child secret from the press would be highly unrealistic.

Clearly it was just she who checked the tabloids occasionally, to see how he was doing, knowing full well that the updates would be inaccurate. But something was better than nothing. Although now she could see it had been a useless venture.

As if sensing the uncertain shift in energy, Dorian furrowed his brow in regret. 'Damica—'

'Say *thank you* to Dorian and his friend.'

She ushered Jalen in front of her and positioned both hands defensively on his shoulders. The source of Dorian's sadness was none of her business. Discussing feelings was something friends—which they no longer were—did.

'Thank you, Dorian's friend! Thank you, Dorian!' Jalen waved enthusiastically at the Prince and his bodyguard, garnering a respectful nod from them both.

Dorian raised his palm, inviting the young boy to give him a high five. With no delay, Jalen reached up to slap the surface of his hand against Dorian's. The variance in size and the affectionate curve of Dorian's smile triggered a squeezing sensation between Damica's lungs.

Clearing her throat, she announced, 'Let's go...'

She pulled Jalen away, directing him back towards the main island. He whinged in protest, but eventually conformed.

They were still within earshot of Dorian's closing comment. 'Nice to see you again.'

An itch pierced between her shoulder blades before dipping lower. Damica could feel him contemplating her retreating back, but she feigned ignorance. Believably too.

The impulse to return to Dorian lessened with the growing distance. As she and Jalen walked back together she made sure to swing their joined hands, to keep him entertained. Jalen beamed at the motion, falling for the distraction. And so did Damica for a short while.

The Étoile Privée Resort website boasted that its twenty-two-acre grounds in the Maldives were optimal for high-profile guests who desired privacy. Damica prayed that she would in future experience the full extent of this geography, and blamed her reunion with Dorian on mere coincidence. The probability of them running into each other again was zero. This holiday was designed for her to reclaim her free time, bond with Jalen and figure out who exactly she was outside of being a world-famous entertainer.

She'd already missed out on so many milestones due to work. The summer ahead would be dedicated to what mattered most: creating new memories and reconnecting with her identity.

Whatever that was.

Nothing and no one would get in the way of that. She'd make sure of it.

Age Twenty-Four

From: damidiamondzzz@inbox.com
To: mrdoryfish7@inbox.com
Subject: Sorry and Save the Date!

Dorian,
Hey! how have you been lately?

Sorry that it's been so long since my last email. Between all the music video shoots, photoshoots, meetings and recording sessions, it's like I barely have a life any more.

But that will all change tomorrow night—maybe the evening on the day after. The date hasn't been finalised!

Me and Zak are getting married! In Vegas!

We want the affair to be super-small and intimate, so only our close friends are invited. That includes you. It would mean everything to me to have you present at my wedding. You've been one of my best friends for so long, and I love you so much, so it's a no-brainer that you're getting this email.

Diana is more than welcome to join us too. I can't wait to finally meet her, and to actually see you in front of me! This has been a long time in the making…

Seeing as I'm both the bride and the wedding planner, I'll accept your response as your RSVP, or whatever they are called. LOL!

Love ya!

Dami xo

From: mrdoryfish7@inbox.com
To: damidiamondzzz@inbox.com
Re: Sorry and Save the Date!

Hello, Damica,
I'm well. It's nice to hear from you again.

I regret to inform you that I will not be able to attend the ceremony in Vegas. Although I am currently on leave from any royal duties, it would be most inconvenient for me to travel out of the country at such short notice. My foundation, the people of Concarre, my future wife and children—whoever they may be—need me, and it is my responsibility to serve them to the best of my ability.

Many congratulations on your engagement to Zak. I hope you have a happy marriage.

Best,

Dorian

From: damidiamondzzz@inbox.com
To: mrdoryfish7@inbox.com
Re: Sorry and Save the Date!

Aw, boo!

I know I shouldn't push you to change your mind, but… this is me, pushing you to change your mind!

This is basically the first time in for ever that our schedules are matching up and you're choosing to stay home?

Think of all the Elvis impersonators, alcohol and cake you'll miss out on. Even better, think of the wild story you'll get to tell your kids when you tuck them in at night, years from now. You've gotta prove to them that their daddy wasn't boring!

What went down in the last seven months?

I know this is all super last-minute, but me and Zak will pay for everything, so don't worry about the cost. Just get over here.

Dami

PS Cake depends on whether there are any cake stores around that can finish our order within such a short turnaround.

From: mrdoryfish7@inbox.com
To: damidiamondzzz@inbox.com
Re: Sorry and Save the Date!

I'd rather not delve into any specifics, but Diana and I have mutually agreed to part ways. During this time I have come to treasure the work I do with CYAF, no matter how strenuous it may be—this may come as a surprise to you, considering your disdain for most work.

Now that I am actively crafting a legacy of my own, I realise that sacrifice comes along with the construction of something far greater than myself. Unfortunately, missing your ceremony is a part of this sacrifice.

Please try to understand this.

From: damidiamondzzz@inbox.com
To: mrdoryfish7@inbox.com
Re: Sorry and Save the Date!

Don't preach to me about the meaning of hard work, Dorian. Whatever you get up to at your vanity project isn't the same as working twelve-hour days as a child, and dancing so hard you have blisters on your feet.

If I wanna 'sacrifice' everything and put myself first for just one night, I will.

From: mrdoryfish7@inbox.com
To: damidiamondzzz@inbox.com
Re: Sorry and Save the Date!

I take it your mother has no knowledge of your plans? Doesn't she hate Zachary? I mean… I thought you caught him going through your wallet last year.

From: damidiamondzzz@inbox.com
To: mrdoryfish7@inbox.com
Re: Sorry and Save the Date!

That was a misunderstanding!!!

I don't care what either of you think. I sleep with who I want, orgasm as much as I want, show as much skin as I want. And I'll continue to do what I want.

From: mrdoryfish7@inbox.com
To: damidiamondzzz@inbox.com
Re: Sorry and Save the Date!

The last thing I want to do is control you. All I'm doing is advising you to think before making such a rash decision.

From: damidiamondzzz@inbox.com
To: mrdoryfish7@inbox.com
Re: Sorry and Save the Date!

Well, if the options are being Daddy's little puppet, like you, or a reckless mess, I know which one I'm choosing!
    :)

From: mrdoryfish7@inbox.com
To: damidiamondzzz@inbox.com
Re: Sorry and Save the Date!

Have a nice life, Damica. Don't bother to come crying to me when Zak reveals himself to be the lowlife he's already shown himself to be.

Not every sensible decision exists to be an inconvenience to you.

From: mrdoryfish7@inbox.com
To: damidiamondzzz@inbox.com
Subject: About Yesterday...

Damica,
I apologise for the comments I made previously. Tension was running high, and we've both experienced a world of change since we spoke last.

Perhaps it would be beneficial to discuss everything in a video call? What time of the day would work best for you?

Yours,
Dorian

CHAPTER TWO

DESPITE FINDING THE phrase 'Heavy is the head that wears the crown' incredibly unoriginal, its sentiment rang painfully true for Dorian Saadoun Sotiropoulos.

As evening shrouded the paradisiacal resort, the Crown Prince of Concarre strolled through one of the four restaurants on site. The name of this particular eatery evaded his mind, nonetheless its modern décor and bespoke menu, specialising in the finest Japanese and East Asian cuisine, had left a lasting impression on his senses.

Melancholy occupied the space beside him like an invisible companion, prompting him to remember that he had no one to share this experience with. He wanted to count Ravi as a sort of travel buddy, but the bodyguard was a stickler for formalities. And procedure dictated that the professional boundaries between security staff and the Concarri royal family were uncrossable.

The Prince sighed to himself, breathing in the idle clink of cutlery against ceramics and the inviting aromas wafting from the open counter in the process. Kanou-style paintings lined the walls, along with leather booths accommodating several other guests. In a far corner sat none other than Damica and her nephew.

Dorian changed course immediately, sidestepping to seek refuge behind a potted plant.

Fortunately, she hadn't spotted him.

Jalen was fussing with his ketchup-stained napkin, and Damica was busy using a knife and fork to cut up katsu chicken into digestible pieces for him. The scene was an instant hit of dopamine, helping Dorian to escape the sobering aspects of his life.

A polite tap on his shoulder made him flinch.

'Do you still intend to dine here, Your Highness?' Ravi enquired discreetly.

Dorian's response was an unbothered wave. The private dining room and all those empty chairs could wait.

In his head, he cursed at how suspicious he appeared in his current predicament. No better than the paparazzi who routinely camped out in the bushes neighbouring the palace back home.

He still couldn't quite believe that he and Damica had crossed paths again. Once had been luck. Maybe twice was a sign that they were supposed to reconcile?

The aftermath of their fallout had stalked him into his late twenties and beyond. The morning after their heated email exchange had consisted of him refreshing his inbox every hour, on the hour. He had no idea whether she'd read his last message and deliberately ignored him thereafter, or if she'd simply stopped visiting her email account altogether after he'd essentially ended their friendship.

The mysterious way she'd conducted herself during their latest interaction had confirmed little, leaving him with no other option but to revisit the event under the precision of a magnifying glass. Now it was painfully easy to lose himself in the elegant slope of her neck, and the way she scrunched up her nose ever so slightly...

Self-inflicted suffering wasn't really Dorian's style, but the dull twinge awakened by Jalen was worth it. Dorian loved children. Mandatory school visits had always been the highlight of his duties. He adored the simplicity with which children viewed the world, and their lack of shame. Kids were beacons of creativity and playfulness and he'd always be willing to tend the flames of that.

Perhaps his negative experiences with his own father had spawned Dorian's wishes to be a parent himself, so he could right all those wrongs. Before receiving devastating news from the royal household physician Dorian had eagerly anticipated the day he'd become a dad. Now burdened with the knowledge of abnormalities in his sperm's shape, he was questioning if that blessing would ever arise.

And, if it did, would he be co-parenting with a woman who was genuinely attracted to him in spite of his shortcomings in fertility?

Digging around in the pockets of his shorts, Dorian sought catharsis in the form of a toothpick. Typically, he'd light a cigarette. But habitual smoking was likely the cause of his problems 'downstairs', so he'd had to retire that pastime for good.

Dorian's hand resurfaced empty: he must have left the toothpick box in his villa.

Determined not to drown in his issues, he ventured out of his hiding spot and drifted towards the booth Damica and her nephew were seated in. With Ravi on his tail, Dorian did his best to keep his stride casual. Once he reached the table, he hovered at its edge, suddenly grappling with his own awkwardness.

Jalen perked up and his bright inquisitiveness greeted Dorian like an old friend. Simultaneously, Damica's quiet acknowledgment of him—and Ravi—was tinged with caution. Dorian second-guessed his intentions in coming over. The inexplicable pull that had directed him to her side wasn't something he could voice without sounding over-familiar. They weren't children and nor were they friends any more.

'Good evening...'

To buy himself enough time to come up with a believable

excuse for his intrusion, he gesticulated at the half-eaten dishes on the tabletop. Their dinner. The private dining room included in his resort package became a useful asset all of a sudden.

'I'm about to have my evening meal and I was hoping you would join me.'

Gasping in excitement, Jalen placed his fork down and began scooting out of the booth.

'Jalen, sit still, please,' Damica ordered.

'If you'd like to, of course,' Dorian added hastily, taking note of the exhaustion marking her tone. 'I'll understand if not.'

He looked to her for final approval, and was pleasantly surprised to find a ghost of a smile waltzing across her lips. Under his inspection, she squashed it with stolidness, narrowing her eyes at him as if she could tell he was improvising. Which he was.

'Can we, Auntie Dami?' Jalen pleaded. 'Please, please, please, please?'

'Hmm…fine,' she agreed, still avoiding eye contact with Dorian.

He was glad her eyes weren't concealed by her sunglasses this time around—the almond shape, upturned corners and haunting shade of brown were just as he remembered them.

Unhurriedly, Damica got to her feet and selected a few plates to take with her. Dorian rushed to provide his assistance, discerning the scent of cocoa butter lotion and rose perfume scent in the midst of picking up whichever dishes she pointed to.

With renewed optimism about his scheduled getaway, he broke away to lead the small group to his private dining spot.

They resettled at the long rectangular table in the dining room booked for Dorian. Ravi blended into the background, taking up a post by the door, sacrificing comfort and a hot meal for optimum viewing of all the space's exits and entrances whilst the staff finished serving up a banquet's worth of food.

Jalen dug in, paying no mind to the rising steam. A glass wall revealed the setting sun bleeding across the sky in various hues of orange, yellow and pinks. Having already become accustomed to the view, Dorian observed Damica admiring the Maldivian evening sky with unrestrained awe.

The innocence of her expression transported him back to their first meeting at thirteen years old. And he still prided himself on being able to grant her freedom—all three seconds of it—from the way they'd both been losing their entire childhoods to adult responsibilities.

The moment ended swiftly.

Realising she was under the microscope of his surveillance, Damica stiffened and quickly sought diversion in teaching Jalen how to blow on his food to cool it down. The shift in her body language jogged Dorian's memory of how she didn't care for being stared at. Attracting attention was a phenomenon that predated Damica's rise to fame. In their emails, she'd opened up considerably about living with vitiligo since the age of four.

Although her autoimmune condition wasn't the subject of his current musing, Dorian was apologetic. Redirecting his focus to his own choice of meal—Thai fish cakes with sweet chilli sauce—he raced through the contents of his mind for a conversation-starter that would bridge the gaping silence between them.

He flattened the impulse to admit aloud that he'd been overjoyed by the reports that she'd annulled her marriage to that opportunistic fool whose name hadn't been worth remembering.

Dorian glanced at Jalen, who was happily munching away on some Peking duck pancakes.

Definitely not. Any contributing factors to the demise of his and Damica's friendship would best be spoken of in private. Plus, any comment on her relationship history would expose the fact that he'd read numerous articles about her over the years—which was hardly a step above his current behaviour: gawking at her as if she was a restored Michelangelo painting.

So much for being better than a creepy photojournalist...

Instead, he opted for a safe, inoffensive topic that surely he couldn't go wrong with. 'Congratulations on your retirement.'

Damica took her time before replying, chewing on the last of her vegetable spring rolls. The soundless grind of her teeth outdid the anticipation of any regular countdown, and it was during this suspense that Dorian realised he'd in fact unveiled his awareness of her presence in international news. Although her exit from the music industry had made headlines all over the world, so he could still feign casualness if needed.

She swallowed, drawing him back to the point of her chin and the bobbing of her throat. 'Thank you... I...er...' Grabbing the large serving spoon protruding from the closest bowl of sticky rice, she gave herself another helping. 'Sorry to hear about your engagement.'

She waved the utensil towards his near-empty plate. Spoon or olive branch? Regardless, Dorian was intent on turning this drop of conversation into a bucketful. Her mumbled answer also suggested his online stalking wasn't one-sided.

Dorian nudged his plate over, sounding happier than one might assume a heartbroken bachelor would as he said, 'Thank you.'

Damica raised an eyebrow.

'Convenient arrangement,' Dorian explained. 'Ultimately, we worked better as friends.'

Sophie was the type of woman that everyone expected

him to marry: private-school-and-university-educated like himself, someone who ran in aristocratic circles, was experienced in charity work. Their friendship with 'benefits' had made matters easier too—they'd skipped the whole getting-to-know-each-other charade. They'd made each other happy enough. Intercourse had been satisfying enough. The public reception they'd received had been good enough.

For men like Dorian, romantic love would always be nothing but a fairytale. Archaic tradition dictated that all marrying royals had to undergo fertility testing, to check that they would be able to continue the line of succession. Dorian's results may as well have read 'failure', because that was how he'd felt. When the time had come to involve Sophie in his discovery…he'd choked. He hadn't been able to bear the thought of her, or any more people, knowing what he was.

Blaming his decision on something nonsensical, he'd ended their engagement. She hadn't been particularly devastated. Concarre had briefly mourned the death of 'Dophie' and taken the royal communications office's lie-infested statement as the truth.

Dorian would have thrown himself into his royal duties with full force afterwards, to assure himself that he could still serve the Kingdom of Concarre, but the test results had called his ability to provide an heir into question.

'I'm guessing your father wasn't pleased?' Damica tapped the spoon against Dorian's plate, depositing a scoop of rice.

They both gritted their teeth at the mention of Concarre's reigning king. Dismay eclipsed Dorian's elation over Damica's lowering guard. Luckily, his father had not been privy to the test results. To avoid a brutal attack on his masculinity, Dorian had omitted the real reason for the breakup during the King's interrogation.

When in Concarre, do as the royal family always does:

hop on a plane to the Maldives, to avoid further discussion with your father.

Shaking his head, Dorian recounted, 'I think he broke the world record for the highest usage of the word "coward" in a single conversation.'

'Yikes.' Damica continued eating.

'In retrospect, it could be argued that he wanted to marry Sophie more than I did.'

Dorian paused to wolf down a portion of his meal and wash it down with some wine. Over the rim of his glass, he gently posed a question.

'How did your mother react to your news?'

'We haven't spoken since she stopped managing me.'

The hurt flashing across Damica's features, contradicted the indifferent rise and drop of her shoulders.

'My sister's tried passing on a few messages for me, but I never get a response...'

She inhaled, as if preparing to spill more. But the further outpouring of emotion never came.

Protectiveness stirred inside him like a beast evaluating whether or not to pounce on an invader.

'Don't let her ruin this,' he said. 'I know this—it's what you've always wanted.'

'It doesn't feel like I thought it would. It's like...' Damica's head tilted from left to right, as if she was searching for the right description. 'Like...there's something missing, y'know?'

A loud scrape caused their eyes to dart around the room until they discovered the source: it was just Jalen, pushing back his chair. Together, Damica and Dorian watched him journey along the curve of the table in pursuit of the windows.

'Do you think you could ever forgive her?' Dorian near-whispered.

Whatever her answer was, it would be for his ears only. Just like in their email friendship days.

Do you think you could forgive me too?

'I don't know,' Damica murmured. 'She held my hand and stuck by me through so much. Was that for her own gain sometimes? Sure. But she's my mom. There are days when I just want a hug from her. We went from talking, arguing—whatever—pretty much every day to…nothing. I miss her, but I have to move on. And I can't be around her without the past looming over us, so…'

Remorse weighed down Dorian's heart. He imagined it must have been tough for Damica to read his passive aggressive jabs at her rebelliousness, when that same rebellion was the only freedom she'd ever known.

Jalen was now stationed by the glass, deliberately fogging up the surface with his breath and drawing smiley faces in the condensation. The animated curves were a direct contrast to the more subdued stretch of Damica's mouth.

'He really likes you.'

Dorian blinked. 'Hmm?'

He ached to run his fingers reassuringly along her forearm. But touch had never been a component of their relationship, and he didn't want to infringe on her personal space.

'Jalen,' she clarified at a barely audible volume. 'He hasn't shut up about you since you let him play on that bike a few days ago.'

A feeling of fulfilment flickered within Dorian, warming him like the beginnings of a sparking fire. 'Really?'

'Seriously—I'm not exaggerating.' Damica bit down on her lip, though the action was ineffective at dampening the quiet pride she glowed with. 'He's so energetic *all* the time… I miss being like that. Sometimes he's a handful, but he's a hundred percent worth it.'

'I understand…'

Only partially, though. The possibility that he might never have the fully-fledged honour of fatherhood pained him. But despite this sobering reality, Dorian was more concerned about the possible opportunity dangling before him, just within reach. The chance to repair the damaged relations between himself and Damica while spending time with her adorable nephew.

It would be a perfectly crafted distraction to help him forget about his failings as a man. An escape from how lonely he was in paradise. Three birds, one stone.

Dorian took aim, hoping that he wouldn't miss the shot.

'How long are you here for?' he enquired as casually as possible, so as not to raise Damica's suspicions.

To make use of his hands—which had grown clammy—he picked up his fork and resumed eating his meal.

'The next three weeks,' Damica confirmed, taking a sip of her water.

'Interestingly, so am I.'

Dorian was pleasantly surprised by how the timelines of their vacations were aligned, and momentarily disturbed by the jittery sensation breaking out across his stomach. Butterflies were the symptom of a nervousness that he hadn't experienced since mustering up the courage to ask out his boarding school crush. There was no place for that here, with his friend.

Did they still qualify as friends?

'I don't mind helping you look after him—if you ever need help, that is.'

There. The ball was firmly in her court now.

Damica tapped a manicured nail on the edge of her plate. The acrylic-ceramic combo produced a pinging effect that twanged at Dorian's valour.

'Are you sure?' she asked.

'Positive.'

How ironic, he thought, that he knew some of her deep-est secrets and fears, but she was like a stranger to him in other ways.

'Well, okay... I don't see why not,' Damica agreed non-chalantly.

An uncomfortable silence followed, wherein Dorian fished for a response and emerged with nothing. Was this the part where he should crack a joke? About what, though? And if she didn't find him particularly funny, his efforts would be counterproductive...

Instead, Damica extended him a new invitation. 'Getting him to wind down at bedtime has been a...challenge. Maybe you could come over to our villa and help out?'

'Absolutely. I'll be there,' he said, with lifted spirits and a grin that spanned from ear to ear.

Clearly blown away by his eagerness, Damica smirked but kept her gaze lowered, dodging connection with his vi-sion. Her reservations about him were mostly unshaken, it seemed. Nevertheless, a willingness to trust him was start-ing to peek through—which was better than being turned away altogether.

Dorian could work with this.

Noticing that Jalen had wandered back to the table, Dorian clapped his hands together mischievously, making a show of rubbing his palms together. 'Who wants dessert?'

'Me! Me! Me!'

Jalen jumped up and down, springing to heights that grass-hoppers would envy.

Dorian couldn't help but chuckle at this—and at Damica's consequent warning about the dangers of too much sugar.

CHAPTER THREE

DAMICA FINISHED ANOTHER circuit around the living room, then determined the probability of the carpet being worn down by her restless feet. Craning her neck, she monitored where Jalen currently was—cocooned in a blanket at the intersection of the L-shaped cream-coloured sofa, teetering on the edge of sleep.

Her worries softened into a need to nurture and she changed course. Being mindful not to startle him, she eased down onto the leather couch and slowly put her arm around her nephew. After wiping away a string of drool and fixing his durag, she tucked him into the crook of her arm and listened to the steady rhythm of his breath.

Dorian is right, she realised.

Despite her scepticism about letting Jalen gorge on his pick of desserts, the large meal, new surroundings and general excitement had been more than enough to wear the infant out.

Damica gave props to the origins of her late-night fidgets, only to be lured into the whirlpool of overthinking for the umpteenth time.

Dorian was sexy now.

Objectively, there had never been a time when he had been 'bad' looking. But the pulse of desire ignited by his attentiveness and the soft, intimate hum of his voice over dinner had felt weird and...and *wrong*.

Probably just intrusive thoughts, she told herself. Her therapist said they were the junk mail and spam of the human mind.

When was the last time she'd had sex? Her libido was simply desperately mining for prospective partners to sleep with.

Right?

Right.

Haven't seen him in twenty years...

Meaningless attraction...

Nothing to see here...

Bound to end in resentment and tears...

A formal knocking at the door overpowered Damica's speculation and the forgotten cartoons airing on the TV.

Scrambling to her feet, she left Jalen to entertain himself with the television. On her traipse across the spacious living room, she willed herself not to pull down the hem of her shorts or fiddle with her bonnet.

Dorian was her friend. Just a...

She flung open the villa's door, ready to give the Prince and his bodyguard a cool greeting. But her larynx temporarily fell short of speech upon seeing Dorian right there... looking exactly the same as he had a few hours ago. His stance—hands buried in his pockets and eyes appraising the neighbouring holiday homes—was casual.

All light had vacated the sky, transforming it into an ominous sheet of black that twinned with the water. The single glowing lantern that was fixed to the front of the villa illuminated all the dips and points in his striking side profile.

And, of course, Ravi was firmly posted behind him, glaring over at Damica to weed out any signs of threat.

She kept her words succinct. 'Hi.'

'Hello.' Dorian inclined his head and put his hands together briefly, as though in prayer. He kept his eyeline respectful—way above her chest and pert nipples, which she knew were visible through her tank top due to the chilly night air. 'How is he?'

'Practically asleep,' she reported with a playful undertone, moving aside so he could enter. 'You'd better get in here and work your magic.'

Ravi beat him to it, blocking the doorway and declaring soberly, 'I'll need to perform an optical sweep of the premises first, ma'am. Standard procedure.'

Damica's warmth vanished, leaving only a dry echo. 'Procedure…?'

It was a much-needed reality check.

Leaning around his bodyguard's immovable form, Dorian winced apologetically at Damica. 'Any chance we could skip this part, Ravi?'

'Standard procedure, Your Highness.'

Damica waved Ravi inside. 'It's fine.'

Naturally she was familiar with security detail routines, having often hired personal protection for herself in the past. Damica couldn't blame the guy for doing his job. Although his request had opened up a trapdoor to a basement of worries.

Attraction to Dorian came right alongside limited freedom. Additionally, true privacy would always be a finite resource. If being babysat by guards didn't bother them now, the constant surveillance from the media, royal correspondents and fans would smother them both later down the line. Frantic pleasure in exchange for a lifetime of restricted liberty wasn't a worthy trade-off.

'Don't forget to check under my bed,' she snarked softly. 'I definitely planted a bomb back there.'

Dorian's disapproving headshake did little to dim his growing amusement. Luckily, Ravi was out of earshot. 'Don't.'

'There's a crossbow and arrows too,' she added in jest, crossing her arms.

Random bursts of small talk kept them entertained during their wait for Ravi to give the all-clear on the house, and the oh-so-dangerous four-year-old still hypnotised by cartoons. Once he did so, Dorian wasted no time in following Damica's lead to the living room sofa.

Their visitors' entrance was akin to an energy boost for Jalen. Suddenly gone were his yawns and impending drowsiness, replaced with a new thirst for the night hours.

Damica tracked down the TV remote on the coffee table and punched the 'off' button with her thumb, whilst Dorian scooped up Jalen.

Like a duck taking to water, Dorian relocated to the child's bedroom and tucked him under the duvet. Damica trailed behind, leaning against the doorway and marvelling at how much of a natural Dorian was in a caregiving role. He'd even prepared a special bedtime story for Jalen—an epic tale about a young boy who ventured through a meadow of sheep. Clever.

During the strategically placed counting of sheep, Dorian's eyes sought her out and he requested her close company with a simple wave. The way he held her gaze made familiarity twang at her heartstrings.

Damica didn't know why this fatherly spirit came as any surprise. If Dorian was still the same man of his emails, then his reverence for children was still going strong.

She sidled over to the bed and eased down on the edge, careful not to disrupt Dorian's storytelling too much with the sudden deposit of her bodyweight on the mattress. With Jalen nestled between them, the adults waited patiently for sleep to come calling...

Damica and Dorian migrated to the back porch, creeping away from the adorable string of drool glistening along Jalen's chin and the soft snores zigzagging to the ceiling.

They reclined on a pair of sun loungers whilst Ravi skulked in the shadows by the ajar door to Jalen's bedroom.

An enclosed swimming pool which resembled a Tetris piece was slotted perfectly between the villa and the all-encompassing ocean. In the darkness, the liquid might have been a walkway that spanned the parameters of for ever, venturing deep into the unknown and far beyond.

Her insignificance among the forces of nature should have squashed Damica's fears. Nonetheless, they flooded back into her psyche with the severity of a burst pipe. Taylor and Leroy were enjoying the resort's live music night, which would undoubtably involve lots of dancing and public displays of affection. Jalen was only a few yards away—he was safe…she wouldn't lose him for a second time. Better yet, she'd successfully got Jalen ready for bed tonight, which was very aunt-like and accomplished of her.

Damica could do this.

She could successfully be someone other than a celebrity.

She would.

She was in control.

Suddenly aware that she was almost lying next to Dorian in utter silence, Damica rushed to fill the auditory gap with noise.

At the same time as him.

'Do you—?'

'I was—'

The clash was instantly defused by the quiet harmony of their laughter. Alas, the peace was short-lived. In the darkness, Dorian's chuckle and the constant sigh of sea water was like an unanticipated caress. Panic lanced through Damica's nervous system.

'You go first.'

Oblivious to her inner turmoil, Dorian gestured at her.

Those nimble fingers attached to those artistic palms only stroked the flames of—

Control.

She had lots of it.

Did she, though?

Dorian had swept in and not only put Jalen to bed, but also read him a bedtime story like some sort of childcare pro. Dorian knew exactly who he was outside of being a prince. Unlike hers, Dorian's identity was clearly set in stone: prospective father and lover of the arts.

'Just so you know, I still haven't forgiven you. I probably never will,' Damica blurted out.

She knew that she'd come across as petty and childish. *Good.* That was her aim. It was low-hanging fruit, but destroying any progression between them meant she could predict the outcome.

'I'll apologise as many times as you need me to,' he vowed without hesitation.

Urgh.

Why did he have to be so noble?

'What I want…' Damica closed her eyes, intent on blocking Dorian out. Internally, she wished for the impossible— then blew out the flame representing her want for him with all her might. 'Is to go back in time…to before you ended everything.'

'Technically, it was you who finished the friendship between us.'

The crease bisecting Dorian's brow deepened with each passing second, as though a knife blade was probing at his brain. Remorse bloomed in Damica's conscience. Was it really worth it? Excavating old memories to distract her from her own sexual confusion?

'You weren't the only one who lost a friend that day. I

kept waiting and waiting for you to reply to my last email and you never did.'

'It's not like I could have. My marriage didn't even last for seventy-two hours—the whole world was laughing at me,' Damica justified emptily.

Unsurprisingly, once discovering the nuptials between her and Zac, Damica's mother and the management team had forced the lovebirds to sign annulment papers.

'Wedding gate' had been the straw that broke the camel's back. Damica hadn't been able to resign herself to living a life where she couldn't even dictate her subpar love-life. Taking a plunge, she'd fired her mother and replaced her entire team. An era of daring artistic decisions and scandals had followed.

'Hey…'

Something smooth and cool captured her chin, keeping her anchored to the present. Dorian's thumb curled over the underside of her jaw, gently turning her face to meet his. Their eyes connected. She hated how her sadness was on full display for him. But in turn, his sorrows were reflected in the shine of his brown orbs.

'I'm not the whole world,' he said.

The fuel required for her to lash out was running low, and a hollowness that she was well acquainted with crept in. It was the very same void that she'd desperately tried to fill with party-girl antics. And expensive alcohol. And controversial fashion choices. Anything that was bound to soil the 'good girl' image her mother and the Feir Channel had crafted.

Damica shifted further along her lounger, removing his touch. 'You're really gonna sit there and pretend that you wouldn't have said *I told you so*?'

Dorian emitted a long breath, which carried the weight of his repentance. 'I swear to you, I didn't mean half of those things I said.'

A loud and ugly scoff escaped Damica. 'You cared enough to type them out, though.'

'I wasn't thinking clearly!' Dorian insisted.

'You're being too loud…'

She suddenly became conscious of how far their noise might travel. The last thing she wanted was for Jalen to be woken by their arguing.

Dorian sat upright and turned his body towards her, planting his feet on the deck in the process. Disappointment contorted his features, sucking away all the joy and leaving a pinched husk in its wake.

Stress has aged him, she noted.

It had withered them both, her moral compass reprimanded her. And here she was, shoving away the only other person who could empathise with the pains of her upbringing.

Readjusting his volume to an appropriate level, Dorian took a new approach. 'Besides, you're hardly the only victim here. What you said about my relationship with my father—after I confided in you about him—was hurtful.'

'I…' He'd got her there. 'I'm sorry.'

'Even if I had attended your wedding,' Dorian went on, appearing to be trying to convince himself, 'security would have been a nightmare, and someone would have alerted the press…which would have created an even bigger mess.'

'In hindsight, it was never really about the wedding…'

She owned up to her past behaviour, confronting the ash and smoke left in the wake of her interpersonal wildfire. The dull ache of embarrassment cancelled out any of his magnetism.

'I don't think I even loved Zac. I just wanted to feel like I was in charge of something in my life at the time…and I wanted to see you.'

'Over the last—what? Nine years? Refusing to arrange

that flight has been one of my biggest regrets,' said Dorian, making a revelation of his own.

'One of them…?' Damica zoomed in on that particular phrase. 'Good to know I made that shortlist,' she said gravely.

Dorian seemed to have developed a newfound fascination in the lifelines branching out over his open palms.

'First place goes to Daddy Dearest. Naturally,' he proclaimed wryly, although the accolade was tinged with a darkness that Damica was afraid to investigate. 'As much as I loathe him, we are cut from exactly the same cloth. His influence on me is inescapable. I should've fought…should still fight harder to be free of him.'

'You did, in your own way.'

Damica's selection of the past tense was carefully intentional. She wasn't qualified to speak definitively on the man he was today. Only the boy she'd grown up with.

A bittersweet tang came with this realisation, leaving her with no choice but to stomach it. She'd made her choice.

'You made a whole new identity for yourself through your art. Is that something you still do?'

'Yes.'

Dorian frowned. Damica damned herself for how eager she was to know the verdict of his quasi palm-reading. She couldn't even commit to the stupidity of her petty little grudge. Her aversion to discipline evidently ran deep.

'I recently submitted one of my paintings for an exhibition,' he went on. 'Under a pseudonym, so no one knew I was the artist. It was a nightmare trying to remove all traces of the oil paint from my skin…but worth it. The piece ultimately got to hang in Concarre's National Gallery.'

'Dorian…!'

Damica was momentarily rendered speechless at how casually he'd recalled a career-affirming achievement that other artists would likely commit murder to attain.

'That's…*sensational*. And so, *so* well deserved.'

As though it was yesterday, her mind was cast back to the email in which he'd first described his love of the medium of oil painting. The attached photos had been of pieces characterised by bold colour schemes and ambiguous brush strokes. It had been impossible for her to decipher whether he'd intended to depict a fox or the Eiffel Tower…

'My favourite part of it all is that I actually earned my place there—like everyone else.' Dorian's satisfaction was unmistakable. 'And my father wasn't in my ear, complaining about how painting is a "feminine interest". My talent opened that particular door for me—not *my title*.'

He enunciated each word as if it were scarlet and bloodied from the shameful history of war and colonialism that was inseparable from Western monarchies.

'You're lucky that your title gives you access to so many things,' Damica said, delivering a gentle, much-needed reminder of Dorian's privilege.

He might have been within touching distance, but the glaring difference in their claims to wealth and fame meant they were worlds apart sometimes. Right now, for instance. Their childhoods were a point of bonding, but Damica's working-class background, race and relationship with hard labour couldn't be erased or overlooked.

'Things most people would die for.'

Dorian ran a hand through his hair, tousling the composed waves. His head sank even lower—in shame—and he scratched at the back of his neck. 'I know…'

'Have you ever thought about giving up being a royal?'

She dug a fraction deeper, unsure of whether she would uncover a rock-solid royalist, firm in his ways, or a man who was malleable to differing political outcomes.

'You could escape from your dad and everything that way.'

'I've thought about it. Many times.'

He glanced over his shoulder, chancing a look in Ravi's direction, as though he fully expected to be arrested for treason. Just entertaining the idea of forfeiting his title was akin to a serious crime.

Ravi was unmoved.

Despite it being Dorian's political livelihood lying on the other side of her question, it was Damica's heartbeat that spiked and dipped. His answer would uncloak so much. About his morals. About the type of man he was. About how she would classify him moving forward.

Upon hearing him say, 'I doubt I would ever step away', she felt her buoyancy deflate.

She remained silent, out of fear that she would give away just how invested she had been in his reply. This was just a conversation between the two of them. Yet she felt as if she'd been thrust into a time machine, doomed to relive exactly the same crushing sensation she'd suffered when first reading that size twelve Segoe-font-typed email confirming that Dorian's duty and chains of obligation would always outrank her.

She'd be stupid to think otherwise.

Duh. Water is wet.

'On the surface, it seems like such an easy choice. Just leave. Simple.'

Dorian's justification was an unforeseen resuscitation.

'But in actuality I'm choosing between a gilded cage or being hunted down like an animal for the rest of my life. The devil you know is marginally better than the one you don't. I've been primed for one lifestyle only.' He appeared to be convincing himself, as well as convincing her. 'I won't survive in any other environment. See?' He clicked his tongue. 'Just like him.'

King Constantine VIII of Concarre was the image of tradition, and it was no secret that his son, as heir apparent, would follow in his footsteps. Ascension to the throne and reigning over his nation was Dorian's birthright.

Their physical similarity was certainly a popular subject amongst devout fans of the Sotiropoulos family, with side-by-side comparisons of Dorian and the young Constantine going viral every other week.

Nevertheless, where the King was a staunch champion of Concarre's ancestry and imperial legacy, Dorian represented the face of a nation with a liberal future. Or at least journalists seemed to think so. They consistently ran pop culture commentary pieces with headlines such as: *Monarchy, but Make It Woke: What Royals All Over the World Can Learn From Prince Dorian of Concarre.*

And it didn't hurt that he was a thirty-something male specimen who was easy on the eye.

Fourteen Reasons Why We're Totally Crushing on Prince Dorian this Valentine's Day!

Damica was inclined to remind Dorian that although he shared familial roots with Constantine, he was budding into being his father's polar opposite. The fruits of these efforts, the Concarri Youth Arts Foundation—or CYAF, as Dorian had commonly referred to it in his emails—was a fitting example to cite. After a long battle with his father, Dorian's foundation had taken down all the statues memorialising colonisers and replaced them with artworks by up-and-coming sculptors of Afro-Concarri descent.

Now that she was aware of Dorian's media sleuthing in regard to her, making her own internet spying known to him was no longer such a humiliating prospect. The symmetry of their actions showed that a level of care still remained, even though they'd been on bad terms for so long. It was as if a part of him had always been with her, in spite of the self-righteous, self-deprecating art enthusiast and poetry-reader vacancy he'd left behind after their separation.

She would be a fool to divorce herself from such a kindred spirit.

Their past had a beginning, middle and end—a predictable outline that most stories abided by. They would never be teenagers again. Presently, they were easing into their thirties: a new decade of life and the opportunity to start anew was available.

Sleeping with him would cheapen their connection and expose her to a grey area, Damica rationalised. Strictly platonic friendships were more fun anyway. Solid. Dependable. And above all, she'd be guaranteed a commanding role at the steering wheel for the entire voyage of their relationship.

'It's never too late to control your narrative,' she told him. 'All the charity work you're doing speaks for itself anyway, but…'

She lowered her emotional guard and surrendered all weapons, communicating with him the way that had always worked best. Her therapist had surmised that Damica's ability to joke about things was a coping mechanism developed during her childhood, in order to deal with the trauma of growing up under the intense scrutiny of the world's stage. The therapist was highly educated and likely correct.

Notwithstanding that, for Damica and Dorian, cracking jokes had always been their version of a digitally transferred hug.

'Fan fiction's always an option,' she went on.

'You…cannot be serious,' Dorian deadpanned.

His fading frown lines and the restored twinkle in his eye were a giveaway that his spirits were rising. And it was Damica who was driving this particular forklift and lifting them.

'As serious as a heart attack…'

Rotating at the waist, Damica swung her legs off the edge of the reclining chair. Her knees lightly bumped against his. However, she centred her attention on sliding her feet into her flip-flops. Not on how the innocent brush of their skin made heat flood her flesh. His rearranging of his thighs so that they bracketed both of hers *didn't* make her bones sigh. At all.

She pressed her legs together, double-checking they were firmly closed. 'Keep it simple. You versus your father. Wrestling AU.'

'And AU means…?' He leaned in slightly, signifying his interest.

Damica dug her nails into the cushion of her seat, anchoring her line of thinking. 'Another universe.'

As if he was genuinely tickled by the idea of him and his father reimagined as theatrical fighters, circling each other in a squared ring, a ridiculous chuckle erupted from the pit of Dorian's stomach.

And together they leapt into a rabbit hole swarming with tropes, terminology and internet memes…

It wasn't until her entire body was jostled, and shards of light tapped impatiently at her closed eyelids, that Damica realised that she'd fallen asleep whilst chatting with Dorian. What had started as minutes had extended into hours. The moon had since long departed, and the sun had embarked on its climb to the sky's peak.

A secure pair of arms was carrying her somewhere, bride-style… *Inside*, she barely managed to deduce. In a far-off place, two men were conversing in rapid Concarri. The pillow beneath her ear wasn't a regular one, but something like a wall that strained and vibrated. The slow, repetitive tempo of a heartbeat played in her ear like a private lullaby. A chest?

Mustering up every scrap of energy, Damica opened her eyes a smidgen. Through those slits of blurry vision she detected Dorian, right above her. His hair, messy. His lower jaw moving in sync with one of the voices. It must have been him who was cradling her so protectively.

Dorian's smell—an oud and bergamot fragrance—intoxicated her senses and lured her deeper into a slumberous oasis. Warm, earthy, fresh, sweet…

Damica surrendered once again to unconsciousness.

Between falling asleep at her computer and waking up to keyboard impressions marking her cheek, and this, there was no competition.

She nestled deeper into Dorian's warmth, welcoming dreams and nightmares and whatever else awaited her with open arms.

Age Fifteen

From: mrdoryfish7@inbox.com
To: damidiamondzzz@inbox.com
Subject: Hmm…

Dear Damica
Heyyyyy! I love you. I love you so much!
   Everyone always leaves.
   My mother left me, but you stay.
   I keep waiting for you to send emails…
   And I keep replying…respondink…and I just don't understand…

From: damidiamondzzz@inbox.com
To: mrdoryfish7@inbox.com
Re: Hmm…

Hey Dorian,
Are you DRUNK?
   LOL!
   What is going on here?
   XD
   Dami

From: mrdoryfish7@inbox.com
To: damidiamondzzz@inbox.com
Re: Hmm…

Dami,

My deepest, deepest apologies for my last email. You must have been so confused. Please don't take anything I typed seriously. I can barely understand it myself.

Yes… I was drinking.

One of the day students here at my school managed to smuggle in a few bottles of vodka. The toilets are one of the few places we have any privacy, so someone stood watch at the door there. The rest of us passed the bottle round until it was empty.

Fun in the moment, but not in the morning. My head feels like it's being pounded. The worst part? I have to hide the hangover, because if the nurse finds out, everyone involved will get into trouble.

My bodyguard, Ravi, already knows, but he promised not to tell any of the teachers.

So, I'm safe! For now.

How are you doing? Tell me what life on tour is like.

From,

Dorian

From: damidiamondzzz@inbox.com
To: mrdoryfish7@inbox.com
Subject: Hmm… Part Two

I've heard of drunk texting before, but drunk emailing must be a new one.

LMFAO!

Very princely of you.

Life here isn't as exciting as you would think. We're currently in London, and I'm dying to go sightseeing, but all the shows and travelling make me really tired, and then I have to fit in the hours with my tutor, so I've mainly been sleeping and watching TV shows at hotels.

NEVER *Dani DoRight* or anything on the Feir Channel, though. I get enough of that already.

It's…hard. But performing is always fun.

Sometimes I wish I could sing my own stuff, but literally anything is better than school. I never miss it. Back when I still went, the other kids treated me like I was contagious because of my vitiligo. Now people stare and I give them a reason to, whilst doing something I actually enjoy

:)

Good luck on your mission of not getting caught! One time, my cousins let me drink with them and Mom caught us. She was not happy, but she's only happy with me when I'm working, so…

From,

Dami

From: mrdoryfish7@inbox.com
To: damidiamondzzz@inbox.com
Re: Hmm… Part Two

Okay, so apparently alcohol makes your breath smell!?

Mission failed.

I got called to the headmaster's office. I took all the blame, and now I have to spend my extracurricular hours volunteering at the school library.

It's not as boring as I thought it would be. And my friend Dario is here keeping me company because he is also in trouble. He says hi by the way!

:D

If you ever want someone else to read your songs and

give a different perspective, send them my way. I started reading the work of Nizar Qabbani, and I'm learning that poetry can actually be interesting and cool. Songwriting and poetry are basically the same thing, right?

I need as many distractions as possible right now. Someone must have told the press about my drinking...and the headlines are not on my side. Neither are the people of my country. I made the mistake of reading a comments section or ten. Weirdly, Father sent me a letter saying how 'pleasantly surprised' he was by my behaviour, and how he hoped it 'put some hair' on my chest.

How is that now almost everyone hates me, he decides to be proud of me?

From: damidiamondzzz@inbox.com
To: mrdoryfish7@inbox.com
Re: Hmm... Part Two

Dear Dorian
I went through something similar, but in reverse, so I feel you. I've always known who my dad is. He and Mom broke up after my little sister was born, and he chose not to be in our lives. He got back in touch after *Dani DoRight* got big, though...

Obviously, I didn't want to speak with him—none of us did. Next thing I knew, he was on all the big talk shows talking about how spoilt I was and saying that I'd forgotten my roots.

It was like he was suddenly everywhere, and everyone had something to say about the way I was treating him. But Mom was by my side the whole time...which was confusing, but not confusing.

For as long as i can remember it's only been the three of us. Mom and Taylor don't say it, but it's obvious that it's my job to earn money for all of us. I like acting and every-thing...the pressure is a lot to deal with, though. I feel like i can never quit because then Mom will be mad at me. How-ever, she gets mad at me a lot these days. Disappointed might be better...

I never forget what our life was like before, when she would stress over bills and stuff. That's why smoking is good, I think. Once i got over the chicken noodle smell, it was relaxing and fun. Just for a while I can forget about everything, chill and be normal.

So, yeah, I get what you're going through.

I'm not gonna tell you to just keep your head up, because I hate that phrase, and you might too.

From,

Dami

PS Thanks for offering to take a look at my songs. I've at-tached a few. Lemme know what you think! Not sure if it compares to the work of a poet.

CHAPTER FOUR

'AND THEY'RE OFF!'

Dorian gave a live commentary on the flurry of children dashing across the beach in pursuit of the sea. The mini stampede conjured up a collective cloud of sand grains with its demanding feet. Dorian might as well have been a grand prix spectator, viewing a party of racing cars zooming around the grid—after all, each and every kid was a personalised machine, fuelled by energy and an eagerness to win.

Amongst them, in the lead, was Jalen. Dorian had pulled a few strings to get him a place in Club Enfant—a group within the resort that organised fun activities for any children currently visiting. By 'strings', he meant royal influence. Unsurprisingly, the overworked summer staff had been more than happy to accommodate a last-minute enrolment on behalf of Concarre's prince.

Dorian supposed he was being a hypocrite, having complained about the crippling woes of being born into elite power and privilege last night to Damica. Although providing some fun for Jalen felt like a worthy cause. Being able to contribute to the care of a young child was a reward. Life itself was a gift. And if Dorian didn't have the full capability of procreating, he wanted to be able to pour his love into any child that was in his presence.

'I'm blue and I'm deep…you can find me by the sea.' Damica recited the first clue in the Club Enfant treasure hunt, the reason for the racing competition. 'Let's go.'

Dorian hitched the handle of his parasol higher, taking the portable shelter and shade with him as he followed the kids. They'd been informed by the club staff that parents, guardians and carers were welcome to participate in all activities. Not wanting to cramp Jalen's style in front of his new friends, they'd opted for inconspicuous supervision at a distance, with none other than Ravi bringing up the rear.

Dorian's sandalled feet sank into the uneven shore, making the journey uneven and more laborious than he'd expected. Granular gold sand unforgivingly invaded whatever and whichever gaps presented themselves—namely the gaps between his toes. He winced slightly at the piercing heat of the sunbaked sand on the sensitive grooves of his skin.

Beside him, Damica's arm accidentally bumped into his own. His heightened senses interpreted the innocent touch as a searing stroke. The tumble of her braids around her shoulders attracted his attention to their bareness. His piqued vision latched on to the way the thin strap of her blush-pink dress was teetering on the very edge, threatening to slide down her upper arm...

This was highly inappropriate.

Dorian cleared his throat suddenly. Loudly. Mainly to catch at his wandering concentration. Far, far away at a signpost planted at the sea's edge, the children had congregated, already working on solving the next clue.

'Very straightforward riddle,' he said. 'A bit too easy. I know they're young, but...'

What was he even saying?

'The poet aficionado has spoken,' Damica teased him—which, in all honesty, only fanned the flames of his nerves.

At the same time, he couldn't help flirting with fire. Once

would hardly maim him. After all, romance was incredibly fleeting. Sexual urges to a higher degree.

But friendship was the best setting for them. The foundation was firm, built to last, and it had evidently survived the last storm they'd weathered. He'd missed their joint talent for conversing so easily about a deep, personal topic in one breath, and something silly and inconsequential in the next.

Dorian feigned modesty. 'You're too kind...'

'In my opinion, *"replying...respondink"* is your best work by far,' Damica quipped, calling back the drunken message that had once been a running joke between them. 'Your magnus opus.'

He sent her a wink. 'I'm planning to publish it soon. You won't be disappointed.'

They picked their way across the scorching sand until they reached the soothing tide of the water. Along the way, they made sure to stick within the cooled cocoon of the parasol's shade to move as one.

Damica's vitiligo meant she was susceptible to sunburn, so Dorian took the responsibility of providing her safety very seriously. Keeping the umbrella poised over her head, he slipped off his shoes and hooked them onto the fingers of his free hand along with the opaque water bottle filled with the protein shake recommended by his nutritionist. Not necessarily his preferred drink of choice.

After taking a second to appreciate the frothy white waves rolling over their bare feet, and the azure expanse up above, Damica flipped over the laminated card attached to the post.

'I'm very tall and have green leaves,' she read aloud. 'You can see me where there's lots of...'

'Trees.' Dorian solved the clue effortlessly.

He gestured at the island, which was laden with evergreen and shrubbery, situated within the ocean's stretch. The objects suspended from his fingers knocked together but thankfully nothing fell.

The speedboat zapping across the water was critical proof that he was correct about the next location. Inside the vessel, the youngsters and the club leaders—all wearing lifejackets—faded into obscure orange blobs. Their endless chatter blended in with the retreating sound of the engine.

Going... Going... Gone.

'We can get a boat from the marina,' Damica advised.

No map needed, they plodded along the wet shoreline, liquid sloshing around their ankles as they inched further along the resort's coastline towards where a group of boats, yachts and jet skis were roped in the harbour. The watercraft bobbed as if in anticipation. The sporadic movement caused sunlight to blink harshly off their sleek surfaces, inviting Damica and Dorian to come forth.

Dorian's exhilaration swelled to new proportions. He marvelled at how a simple daytime children's treasure hunt could make him feel like an adventurer depending on the North Star.

'This is fun.'

'Very.'

Her eyes snagged his, and her tone mirrored his enthusiasm. The casual swing of her arms and the dangle of her flip-flops fed into their shared pleasure.

'I thought you'd be more competitive,' he said.

Curiosity sparked in him upon the realisation that, despite knowing her from the ages of thirteen to twenty-four, there was a whole chunk of Damica-related knowledge missing from his personal records. Dorian was well versed in the ins and outs of the mistrust she felt towards her father, and the extensive lore of her songwriting. However, when it came to other matters...like whether she preferred to drink coffee or tea in the mornings...he was coming up blank.

The nine-year deficit in their relationship exposed his familiarity with the girl of the past, not the woman at his side now. No amount of internet research could compensate for that.

Did she still dream of matching mother and baby outfits?

'I can be competitive…' She made a *so-so* motion with her hand. 'When a situation requires me to be.'

Dorian found that he was surprisingly desperate to unlock this side of her. To unwrap all the possible dimensions of her personality so he could appease the gluttonous monster formed of his inquisitiveness. His want was so intense it sucker-punched his gut, triggering nausea.

Wrong. Everything about this was wrong.

Why was he so intent on soiling the one thing that was going right?

Grappling with logic, he sought out the nearest sign that pointed to how incompatible he was with Damica on a romantic level.

'Ravi?' He addressed his bodyguard, who was a breath away behind them on a dry stretch of the sand. Fully clothed, he was a pillar of black material and muscle. The only signifier that the heat was getting to him was the folded handkerchief he was dabbing his damp forehead with. 'You can take your shoes and jacket off, if you wish. Enjoy the weather with us.'

'I'm fine, Your Highness. Thank you, though.'

Ravi's conviction was flimsy, at best, but Dorian knew better than to prod.

Besides, his turn to sweat arrived when they neared the marina. A guest transportation system of sorts was in effect, whereby a rotation of speedboats manned by resort staff travelled to and from the mainland and the island. They'd already missed the Club Enfant's ride, and if the queue forming on the dock was anything to go by they would have to wait a while for the next available speedboat.

Sensing Damica growing angsty at the prospect of Jalen being away from her view for that long, Dorian fished for a solution.

Thinking quickly, he flagged down the harbourmaster and sweet-talked him into renting them a rowing boat. That was the easy part. The real challenge was getting Ravi to hand over the proverbial reins.

Dorian couldn't blame the bodyguard for taking his role so seriously. He could only imagine the severity of punishment awaiting Ravi if the future sovereign of Concarre was to be put in harm's way under his supervision. Nonetheless, he failed to see the fun in having to bargain for his freedom on his own holiday.

Their negotiation process was one he was all too familiar with. Varying terms would be shot between them like bullets from the guns at a cowboy shoot-out.

Dorian cheerily proceeded to where the sailboat was waiting for them. The trick was to open discussions by demanding way more than he knew he would receive.

'I'll row us there and back,' he said.

'That won't be possible, Your Highness.'

Ravi overtook him, plonking down onto the craft. Then a rarity occurred. He landed heavily amongst the wooden oars, and his thick arms flapped in the air to help him regain his balance. The moment vanished just as quickly as it transpired. Once Ravi's equilibrium was restored, he lifted his elbow, offering himself as a handrail to assist Dorian in stepping down onto the boat.

In mutiny, the Prince backed away into the shade cast by Damica's parasol. 'I'll just row there, then.'

'Don't forget to put your lifejacket on.'

'Only if you let me row us there. Take it or leave it.'

'I have no issues with us staying here on the mainland, Your Highness.'

'Whoa… We can't *not* go!'

Damica's alarm powered the broadness of Dorian's smirk. Little did she know he had Ravi exactly where he wanted him.

'I can row us there. Lifejacket on. And tomorrow we'll have a lazy day at the pool, so I'll be easy to watch.'

Ravi was betrayed by the twitch of one of his eyelids and the pesky bead of sweat sliding down the side of his face to hang off his chin. The hot weather was taking its toll on him.

Dorian banked on the fact that Ravi was a man unmoved by favours or bribes. Practicality was the only way to win him over. The guarantee of an easy workload tomorrow, especially in a climate such as this, would be irresistible.

'We…have a deal, Your Highness.'

As predicted, Ravi caved.

Dorian pumped a victorious fist. The exaggerated roll of Damica's eyes did little to suppress her peals of laughter.

Accepting the lifejacket she shoved in his direction, Dorian put on the inflated nylon garment with the pride of a superhero.

'We'll definitely be taking a speedboat back to the mainland,' Ravi ordered sullenly.

Dorian saluted him. 'Sir, yes, sir.'

Ignoring the assistance of his bodyguard's arm, he descended from the dock and into the boat independently. The insinuation that he was made of glass, especially in front of Damica, bothered Dorian more than it should have. A tiny worry pricked at his ego, about how she might side with his father in his assessment of Dorian as weak and wimpish.

Under his feet, the boat rocked. However, he was so expectant of the jolt that it simply spurred him on.

Elaborately, he presented a hand upward to Damica. 'My lady…'

His outward humour countered the onslaught of inner shyness triggered by her close analysis of his palm. Her touch hovered over his, as though she feared she was about to come into contact with an unverified substance. The feather-light graze of her smooth, soft skin sent a pleasant heat up Dorian's forearm and bicep.

'Why, thank you, kind sir.' Damica's lips twisted into a sheepish smile, and she adopted a British accent to play along with his façade of chivalry. Only for Dorian it wasn't pretence.

She gracefully pressed her hand into his, allowing him to help her on to their new mode of transportation. His fingers clasped hers dutifully, his thumb closing around her knuckles like the snug fit of an envelope seal.

See—he *was* strong.

To his disappointment, an awkward shuffle around Ravi forced him to release Damica.

Lowering herself onto the bench stationed across from Dorian, she tittered. 'I can't believe how seriously you're taking this.'

'Because I've never done this before.'

Dorian gingerly took the glossy wooden oars awaiting him from their thick collars. His very first attempt at rowing gave the phrase 'a fish out of water' new meaning. Nonetheless, he simply tried again.

'I'm like a kid in a candy shop!'

His chuckles were intertwined with the audible strands of Damica's happiness, creating an inseparable structure.

As soon as he got the hang of the rhythm, he indicated for Ravi, who was situated in the hull, to untie the rope mooring the boat to the mainland marina. More confident in his ability this time, Dorian pushed and pulled at the oars. Their movement soon synced with the water's, and the boat drifted further out to sea.

Under the blaze of the sun, and in the throes of such heavy exercise, Dorian felt a thin layer of perspiration break out over him. Beneath his lifejacket, his shirt clung to his chest. He made sure to keep his breathing measured and consistent.

Damica's quietness and her steady examination of his flexing biceps threatened to derail the systemic to-and-fro of his movements. Yet he was enjoying being subjected to what he sorely hoped was her admiration.

The periodic splashing, the creak of the wooden oars and Dorian's breathing pattern were the only components bridging their noiselessness. His rowing persisted—with more vigour. Up and down. In and out. Coming and going. Did he appear confident and capable and manly, from her viewpoint? Because that was how he felt.

From under the heavy shadow of her parasol, Damica's dark eyes bored into him. He matched their glowing intensity, well aware that he was infringing on dangerous territory. If this was a siren's call, then he wasn't a poor, unsuspecting sailor, but rather a willing sacrifice.

The point of her tongue emerged from her mouth to wet her soft, parted lips…

And then the spell was broken as something flickered across Dorian's visual field.

A blink later, and Damica was one-handedly rummaging around the collection of objects scattered over her lap. Dorian put down the oars, using the opportunity to regain his strength and identify the source of the intervention: a pesky lock of hair had fallen over his face.

By the time he'd tucked it behind his ear and dried his sweaty hands on his shorts Damica was waving his drink bottle at him. Her downcast eyes and her preoccupation with the container's spectacularly uninteresting design exhibited how flustered she was. Apparently, he wasn't the only one who'd got a little carried away.

'Here. You should take a break.'

The tightness reigning over his muscles switched from

being provocative to something to be feared. Stiffly, he took the bottle from her and unscrewed the lid. The glare of the stainless-steel lining made him tense up even more, as though the light attracted even more attention to the bottle's contents. Meanwhile, his activity meant the boat was gradually being ushered off-course by the jumping waves.

'Everything all right, Your Highness?'

Ravi put forward the hushed query, from his corner of the vessel.

'I'm fine.'

The swig Dorian took was mostly for show. His tastebuds barely registered the smooth blend of raspberries, banana, kale and various other ingredients. Their ingestion solidified in his stomach like a stone of shame. Shoving the resealed bottle on the floor somewhere behind him, he carried on rowing, this time closing his eyes.

The poisoned chalice might be out of his sight, but out of mind it was not.

A sturdy fitness regime and diet plan were meant to be a practical long-term solution to improving his reproductive health. But no matter how much this domestic illusion he was in with Damica felt like a quick fix, it wasn't.

They could never be.

Plus, who was he to assume that Damica would even want to commit to him romantically? The fact that his little swimmers couldn't swim properly was intriguing at best and devastatingly emasculating at worst.

He could take being a plaything for the Concarri national press and media. And as much as he hated it he'd learnt to tolerate his father's countless jibes at his artistic endeavours. But his friendship with Damica had always been his safe space. Nothing could ruin that for him. Not the faintest whiff of a dalliance. Definitely not a serious relationship. And certainly not her finding out about his infertility.

It wasn't until he brought the boat to a safe stop at the island marina that Dorian felt he could exhale properly. After the docking process, he fulfilled his duty of helping Damica alight from the watercraft, and used the little composure he had left to stretch out his sore muscles.

The three of them approached the jungle, basking in the coolness provided by the network of trees. Light filtered in through the intricate lattice of branches and leaves overhead, which gave everything a green hue. Dorian was so overpowered by his own awe that he didn't immediately realise Damica had fallen a step behind.

'Everything okay?'

He paused to seek her out, meaning Ravi halted too. A chain reaction was now in effect.

'I just need a minute,' she told him, pressing the button to close her parasol. Slinging the collapsed canopy over her shoulder as if it was a bindle stick, she spun around. 'I love it here.'

The circular billow of her skirt, the languid purr and high praise for their new environment made him think of a Channel Feir princess. Given her history with the Feir conglomerate, Dorian knew she would heavily oppose any association with them. But her delight was so pure and magical. There was no other way to describe it.

'I can tell,' he remarked fondly. 'Do you want me to get a picture of you?'

'I forgot to grab my phone on the way out this morning.'

'I think I have mine…'

Dorian patted the front pockets of his shorts. Then the back. Nothing. Uh-oh. Amidst the rush to shed his lifejacket, he hadn't bothered to check whether he had all his belongings. Speaking of which, where was his bottle…?

Damica's extended arm looked all the more tempting when he noticed that she was in possession of his drinking container. Her blush-pink manicured nails were distinct against the royal blue. A sick reminder of the two worlds he wished to keep segregated at all costs.

Panic caused him to walk towards her more quickly than he would have liked. Oblivious to the cause of his anxiety, Damica danced away from his lurch.

'Damica…' He chastised her gently, walking over to her new spot.

'Yes?' She played dumb, side-stepped out of his range.

This was an immature game she was playing, and yet he entertained it. If her aim was to stress him out, she was winning.

Dorian froze…then struck when she least expected it. 'Give it—'

'Need something?'

She jumped away in the nick of time. Dorian's fingertips swept past her swishing braids.

'Give it back!' He tried again, but his effort was futile.

Impassive as ever, Ravi trod towards Dorian to keep him within close range. The domino effect wasn't lost on Damica. A mischievous glint dawned in her eyes before she took off down the nearest trail.

'Damica…come on! Seriously?'

Without a second thought, Dorian sprinted after her. As might have been expected, his hurried footfall was echoed by the uniform thump of Ravi's boots. Embarrassingly, his bodyguard's stamina made Dorian's panting seem all the more loud.

Damica was a faster runner than Dorian had presumed. The joke was on him for underestimating her. She led them down a turn here…around a corner there. She even had the audacity to giggle, which made Dorian's blood boil with the fierce flavour of competition.

He *would* catch her.

Pushing through the unheavenly burn of his quads and his calves, Dorian galloped over a spindly tree root obtruding onto the footpath. Woefully, Ravi didn't see the same obstacle quickly enough. An angry string of curse words punched at the air, followed by a calamitous smack and a skid.

'Your Highness—Dorian—stop!'

A crossroads of decisions presented itself.

Follow the rules or break the rules.

Obey the commands of his bodyguard and stay under his scrutiny like a good little boy.

Or keep on with Damica's bizarrely fun game of tag.

Deeper and deeper into the web of paths and thick forestation Dorian went, keeping the swoosh of Damica's skirt and the flashes of her bare thighs within his sight. Ravi's shouts were replaced by the bird calls reverberating from the treetops.

Dorian mimicked their sounds, succumbing to a juvenile nature he'd never been allowed to fully acquaint himself with. It, tag, hide-and-seek—whatever the name of this game was—was highly thrilling. A brief, much-needed deflection from his worries over his father's appraisal of his manhood and whether he would ever be fertile enough to become a father the good old-fashioned way.

All that mattered was that he was with Damica, fooling around.

She vanished around yet another bend. Taking a risk, Dorian chose to jog down a path that ran parallel to her route. Through the greenery, he spied her slowing to a stop, mistakenly assuming she was safe.

'Give up!' he yelled menacingly, between gulps of oxygen, 'Never!'

Caught by surprise, Damica started up again, traipsing onward—only to reach a dead end. She winced, and then hotfooted it back down the path.

However, Dorian was speedier. He retreated to the place where the two pathways diverged. 'Aha!'

'No!' she whined at her defeat.

'Oh, yes...'

He must've looked like a madman, spreading his arms wide and jigging on each foot in his attempts to block all possibility of her escape. A far cry from the controlled Prince who could never afford to put so much as a foot wrong. And if Damica was repulsed, she was expertly hiding all traces of disgust behind that same unreadable, beautiful expression she'd worn on the boat ride over.

She pulled back. Dorian prowled towards her, this time unhindered by the way his hair was flopping over his eyes. A hunter's instinct eclipsed his rationale for a nanosecond. He could go in for the kill right now and snag her plush lower lip between his teeth.

Not that he ever would.

But it was a positively electrifying prospect, he admitted to himself. In this place where there were no witnesses...

In an instant, Dorian was back in reality and mindful of the rattling of liquid and a faint prodding at his sternum. His bottle. Half full of a possible improvement to improving his sperm's health. Yes. The object of this wild goose chase. Damica was yielding the prized object, pressing the plastic cylinder to his breastbone with an audaciously innocent smile.

Dorian snatched it back, chest still heaving from the unforeseen workout. The ease flooding his nervous system overrode any anger.

'What are you playing at?'

'It worked.' She turned away to inspect the seat of a nearby bench, then dusted off the back of her dress. Sinking down, she noted, 'You look a lot more relaxed without a bodyguard attached to your every move.'

'So…you're telling me…this was part of a…grand plan to…?'

Suddenly Dorian's tunnel vision vanished, uncloaking the area where they stood and revealing a clearing of sorts, right in the heart of the labyrinthine jungle. The space looked boundless—even more so because he knew he was free to scale a tree without Ravi interrogating all the wildlife beforehand.

'To break you out of your castle and show you the world outside? Yes.'

Damica crossed one leg over the other, wriggling her dangling foot. The rotation of her ankle enticed his view to climb higher, to her shin and beyond. Instead, he pivoted his focus to his own feet which, like Damica's were caked in a mix of sand, dirt, dust and sweat.

Dorian wiped a hand across his jaw to get rid of the gathered moisture and the silly grin. 'Ravi's going to be furious.'

'Enraged!'

'Seething.' His mirth only tripled.

'We both know how the saying goes…' Damica patted the empty spot next to her on the bench. 'Ask for forgiveness. Not permission.'

Dorian trudged over to the wooden seat, wincing at how sore his leg muscles were. Collapsing onto the seat, he told her facetiously. 'There will be serious ramifications for the Maldivian government if anything happens to me on their soil…'

'Which it won't. I'm a pro at this,' she bragged, whilst giving his arm a reassuring squeeze.

He rested his eyes. His muted senses made the smell of Damica's signature perfume even stronger.

'I figured.'

'And I was lying before. I did bring my phone.'

Dorian's right eyelid opened a smidgen, so he could see

her take her touchscreen device out of her drawstring shoulder bag.

'We can contact Ravi to tell him where we are.'

'He's going to be so ma-a-ad,' Dorian sing-songed, causing them to fall into another fit of giggles.

'Yeah…the fallout is usually the worst part. But the brief moments of peace always make it worth it.'

She closed her bag and copied his manner of sitting, leaning on the support provided by the bench's backrest and tilting her neck back slightly.

'Like when we first met.'

Dorian kept on sneaking the occasional sideways peek in her direction. He couldn't have agreed more. Defiance with Damica was a sweet escape from the constraints he'd known his whole life and the string of anxieties bonded together by his royal obligation. The result of was…this. A quiet, insulated life, in which Dorian could cater to the whim of his inner child, whilst fulfilling his other wish of caring for a child of his own.

This was a perfect dream.

He wasn't ready to wake up just yet.

Dorian reflected on ways to preserve such a peaceful, precious moment, and Damica served as the perfect muse. Snapping a picture seemed instant and distasteful. And furthermore, the idea of breaking down her complexities into basic paint blobs of blue, red and yellow—the primary colours—felt almost insulting.

Not even his thinnest brush could reproduce her damp glow and the curled spring of her baby hairs. Plus, he hadn't packed any painting equipment for the trip. All he had was his trusted sketchbook and a tin of pencils ranging from HB to 4B. So, a drawing would have to do.

A gust of birdsong broke through nature's quiet and the utter serenity of Damica's upturned face. She squinted up at the rustling treetops and the jungle vine sprawled across the chunky bark like emerald scales.

'Asian Koel. Resident birds here,' Dorian said, educating her. 'Also known as *dhivehi koveli*.'

Damica expressed how impressed she was with a hum. 'Okay, Mr Discovery Channel… Does Sir David Attenborough have some serious competition now?'

'Not quite. I just read it in one of the resort brochures.'

It was during this amateur wildlife lesson that they noticed the next treasure hunt clue, nestled in the intersection of two tree trunks. And so on to the next location—the tennis courts—they went.

Dorian's newfound disobedient streak continued as he rowed himself and Damica back to the mainland to collect Jalen from the concierge desk. Once more like a kid in a candy store, he feasted on this bad behaviour at the ripe old age of thirty-three. Such delinquency was some compensation for all the childhood holidays he hadn't got to have. This was what he was owed.

He regretted ever asking for permission, and the begging for forgiveness from Ravi was all for show.

CHAPTER FIVE

'ARE YOU SURE this thing is safe?'

Damica was unable to hide her scepticism as she eyed the surf simulator set up in the middle of the beach. According to the Club Enfant timetable for Saturday morning, catching a few machine-generated waves was the perfect activity to commence the day.

'Says the woman who left the Met Gala mid-event on the back of a motorcycle!' Dorian guffawed. 'With no protective headgear.'

'That was my interpretation of that year's theme.'

'Fantasy and Fashion...?'

'Are motorcycles not the motor vehicle equivalent of dragons?' she asked, trying to legitimise the link. 'And there weren't any kids involved—back me up here, Ravi.'

Straight away, Damica felt remorseful about dragging the royal bodyguard into her light-hearted quarrel with Dorian. The only acknowledgement he gave was a rebuking glower, and his scornfulness notified them that their promise of a lackadaisical day by the pool and an uneventful remainder of the week wasn't an apology that was proportional to his tumble on the jungle island.

Damica and Dorian were inclined to agree, and so Ravi's silent treatment went largely unchallenged.

'We can investigate it ourselves,' Dorian declared, taking

her hand and gently dragging her over to the aqua blue simulator. 'It's open to adults too, remember?'

Without thought, she laced her fingers through his as they made their way past where the instructors were helping the group of excitable kids into lifejackets and trying to talk them through the health and safety measures.

She could see that any distrustful parents and guardians were indeed welcome to have a turn on the simulator. Up close, Damica made note of the machine's diagonal angle, and how the jets lining the sides sent water cascading down the slope. The instructor in charge presented them with the mandatory lifejackets and some facts about the machine's design. Damica perceived most of it as unintelligible, but Dorian seemed engrossed by the ins and outs of its engineering.

After the impromptu Q&A session had drawn to a close, Dorian kicked off his flip-flops and helped Damica onto the simulator.

'Turn that frown upside down!' he said.

A glum Ravi stayed on the sidelines, dwarfing the simulator instructor, who was attempting to make small talk. Never would Damica have guessed that she'd find common ground with the bodyguard through cynicism.

There had been a pronounced change in Dorian since their defiant dash through the jungle. He was louder…and looser… and less concerned with upholding a respectable image. Secretly, she'd never been prouder of being a 'bad' influence. Their fight to exist as two normal human beings for an afternoon had been worth it. Just like all the other unruly outbursts that had dotted her adolescence.

Now, they crossed the slanted terrain of gushing water, shivering at the cold their bare feet were subjected to. Damica gingerly climbed onto the surfboard fixed to the floor—its surface was already slick.

The hold Dorian had on her hips vied with the snugness of

her bikini bottoms. The press of his fingertips into her flesh seemed to correlate with the delicious heat blossoming at the pit of her stomach. But she hastily disregarded the sensations altogether, clinging to the stability of his shoulders instead.

'Are you okay?'

'I'm good!'

They shared a comforting smile until she was confident enough to stand on her own.

However, in the short time it took for Dorian to sprint over to the matching surfboard, a few meters away, she felt a yearning ache leak into her wits.

Was that his version of trying to cop a feel?

Should she be mad about his hypothetical fondle?

She *should* be, but...

Having clambered onto his own surfboard, Dorian gave her a shaky grin and a thumbs-up. 'Ready?'

With no forewarning, the board swivelled and jerked underneath her feet, robbing her of the chance to speak. The only sounds her larynx could produce were pathetic whimpers. Out of desperation, Damica bent her knees and thrust out trembling arms, desperately seeking to centre herself amid the chaos that had been introduced to her equilibrium.

The simulator was now in full force. Even the water settings had increased and had gone into a new mode, with liquid streaming down the blue flooring in hefty bursts.

To her left, Dorian's cackling was continuous—despite the fact that he was only mildly better than her at combating the onslaught of unpredictable movement below him.

Damica's jaw dropped. 'Seriously?'

Their circumstances hindered her ability to hurl any coherent accusation his way.

'Huh?' Dorian was goading her.

'You...*you*!'

'Yes?'

He was *laughing* at her.

She couldn't allow this disrespect to continue.

The dormant competitiveness that resided deep within her was harshly awoken. Tapping into her performer's instinct, she determined to treat her movements on the surfing simulator like a complex dance sequence. She looked ridiculous, sticking out her tongue, flapping her arms about and drawing erratic shapes with her waist, but gradually, she got the hang of things, distributing her body weight and balance to the necessary parts of her feet at any given time.

From her heels to the balls of her feet and back again, she met the frantic gyration and revolving of her surfboard, finally cracking the code. But in order to concentrate so intensely she'd decluttered her mind of all obstructive data, so she wouldn't get sidetracked—her apprehension about the simulator's safety included.

Just as she asserted her dominance over this realistic imitation of one of nature's most powerful elements, a blurred mass slipped, slid and then hurtled downward in her peripheral vision.

'Dorian!'

Damica was so terrified that the sequence of Dorian's accident unfolded in muddled order. Her knees crashed down into the shallow pool of water and droplets flew everywhere—into her hair, eyes and open mouth. At lightning speed she was kneeling beside him, where he was sprawled out on the floor like a woozy starfish. At some point the simulator had stopped.

The pounding of her heart and a panicked rush of blood inhabited her eardrums. Her heart jack-hammered against her ribcage. Her tongue was a useless organ, weighing down her mouth.

'Dorian…?'

'Your Highness?'

That was Ravi. He delicately elbowed her out of the way, so that he could check Dorian's wrists and neck—feeling the pulse points to see if he was still alive...conscious.

Oh, thank goodness—he was still breathing.

Unsure exactly what to do with her quaking hands, Damica tented them around her nose and mouth. Was she praying? She didn't classify herself as religious. But if there was the tiniest inkling of a chance that any higher power existed, she was reaching out and imploring that they save the man she loved from harm.

When she'd longed for freedom, she hadn't meant the removal of—

'Dorian...stay with me. How many fingers am I holding up?'

Ravi's gravelly rasp had been reduced to the kind of frail whisper that nurses used on ailing patients. He was holding up three digits before Dorian's bleary eyes, conducting a further examination of the Prince's condition.

Dorian lay on his back. So still. So...serene. He was thoroughly drenched. The soles of his feet and his fingers were wrinkly and prune-like. His hair was plastered to his skull.

Although unlikely, she speculated over the possibility of those strands protecting him from concussion. The fibres of the lifejacket formed a bulky layer over his chest, so it was difficult to judge the inhale and exhale of his lungs by eye alone.

The Prince's fall had garnered the attention of the children, the Club Enfant staff and other parents and guardians. More and more people were flocking to the simulator entrance, peeping over the blue wall as though they were participating in a communal coffin-viewing.

Ravi barked at the instructor, demanding—with a few expletives tossed in—that they bring him a first aid kit and call for an ambulance.

Medical intervention meant this was serious. Serious enough that any injury Dorian had sustained would mean repercussions for the Maldivian government. Protests? Economic sanctions? War?

Suddenly Dorian's unmoving state was ruined by a faultless chuckle. The corners of his closed eyes creased, and the corners of his lips curled upward.

'I'm fine. Everybody can relax.'

Suspicious about the Prince's miraculous recovery, Ravi repeated his order for an ambulance.

But Dorian undulated his arms and legs in perfect unison, as if that was enough proof of his good health. The motion caused the water to ripple all around him.

'Not quite a snow angel, but close enough,' he said.

Damica sagged, her bottom connecting with the floor—which was a lot softer than she would have expected. Perfect for breaking falls and absorbing the energy of high-speed collisions. All at once her body's adrenaline supply was disconnected, plunging her into what should have been relief.

She didn't know whether she wanted to punch him...or kiss him.

Soon after the mishap, Dorian grudgingly agreed to hang out in among the picnic benches, out of action's way but within breathing distance of the surf simulator. Jalen had decided he was a young medical professional, and had provided him with a towel, so that he could dry himself off, and an ice cream to sweeten his stomach.

'Thank you, Dr Jalen,' said Dorian, playing along.

Sitting across from the small boy, he waited for Jalen to finish making his 'medicine'. Stirring runny ice cream with a plastic spoon clearly deserved alchemy-grade precision, and the adults respected his process.

Damica took a sideways glimpse at Dorian, who was invested in Jalen's pretence with the utmost sincerity. The towel hung around his neck like a scarf, the material the only barrier to his bare chest now that his lifejacket had been discarded. He absentmindedly pushed a hand through the damp mass of his hair and she seized the chance to appreciate his tanned face. Kind eyes. And his nose—which luckily wasn't broken!

The ebb and flow of her distress had lessened substantially now that it had been confirmed he was all in one piece. However, Damica had no choice but to reckon with the knowledge her dread had unmasked.

She…*loved*…him.

Fidgeting on her perch, she extended her neck and looked around the umbrella pole attached to the tabletop's centre and over Jalen's shoulder.

'The group's about to start surfing. You don't want to miss it, do you? Get over there,' she chided her nephew tenderly. 'Forget about him!'

Dorian puffed in faux offence. 'Rude!'

Jalen was visibly torn between work and play.

'Go…' Damica took charge of the ice-cream potion. 'I'll take care of him for you.'

'Give him two and a half dollops only.' Jalen gave her strict orders, accentuating the syllables of the required amount. Testing her listening skills, he lobbed his orders at her again, remixed as a quickfire exam question. 'Two and a half what…?'

'Dollops.'

She passed with flying colours.

Jalen rotated his legs out of the picnic table's legroom gap and careened towards the queue for the simulator, conjuring up a mini tornado of sand as he went. When he rejoined his new friends, a Club Enfant staff member plonked a helmet on Jalen's head and buckled the straps under his chin.

Dorian's fall hadn't been in vain. To commemorate his plummet the kids were being suited up with extra protective gear—which pleased Damica and the other carers.

Ravi angrily planted himself in the space Jalen had vacated. The wooden picnic table reverberated under his weight. Like Dorian's, the bodyguard's clothes and hair were saturated. He hadn't taken the occurrence in good humour. Obviously, he had no reason to.

Under the table, she felt Dorian brace a defensive hand on her knee. First the jungle dash, and now *this*? They awaited Ravi's reaction. A strong-worded lecture, perhaps?

Damica forecast being verbally struck down by a surge of epithets. She was well acquainted with this pattern because of her mother, to the point that she had become an active contributor in the cycle.

Act up. Get screamed at. Scream back. Be iced out. Repeat.

Soon Damica had mastered the art of instigating the 'act up' phase. That way, she was usually ahead of the curve. Being shouted at wasn't so bad when she knew that she owned the keys to her own misfortune.

Admittedly, she'd been caught off guard by her impact on Dorian's devil-may-care attitude of late. Nevertheless, Damica was tensed and ready to retaliate with her own unique brand of insults. The trick was to be so weirdly specific that their creation became a fun game, detracting from her wounded feelings.

Dorian must have sensed how strained she was feeling. His palm glided higher, rubbing soothing circles on her thigh. Meanwhile, he unleashed a word-vomit to shatter the icy quiet.

'Ravi, if you're going to assign blame to anyone let it be me, and me alone. I understand you may be nervous about your job security should this attract any media attention, but—'

'Fortunately, the press are prohibited from this resort, so

the odds of that happening are low.' Ravi addressed them both in a slow, monotonous manner. 'I won't waste my breath on lambasting you, Your Highness. I don't have the jurisdiction, after all. But I had hoped you at least respected me—and yourself—enough to act responsibly. I see now that I was deeply wrong on that account. That is all.'

Giving them the cold shoulder, he positioned himself in a way that exiled Damica and Dorian to the outermost range of his sight.

There was a sharp intake of breath from Dorian that Damica distinguished as lethal. Genuine disappointment from her mother had always been deadlier than rage. Fury came in short bursts that she could always duck and out-manoeuvre. Being the cause of genuine dismay had far greater haunting power. It made her re-evaluate her ethics and shamefully conclude that the end rarely justified the means.

On no account was the relationship between Dorian and his bodyguard one of equal footing to her and her mother. But upsetting the man he'd peacefully co-existed with for the last twenty years was not a happy thing.

In an effort to prevent the escalation of their confrontation into a full-out fight, Damica did her duty and started feeding Dorian with the melted ice cream. He'd be physically unable to say anything he might regret if his throat was preoccupied with swallowing.

Two, three, four spoonsful. Definitely over Jalen's recommended dosage. But, hey—who was she to let free ice cream go to waste?

Damica scooped up as much lukewarm ice cream as the spoon would allow, and Dorian co-operated by opening his mouth. His tongue swirled around the dip of the curved plastic, licking it clean. The fuzzy moustache and beard outlining his cupid's bow of a mouth and his chin showcased how appetising his wet lips were. Audaciously, he held her gaze and maintained his consistent caress of her leg.

She'd assumed Dorian had initiated this tactile mode of comfort for her benefit. Although how anything this electrifying could instil calmness was beyond her. She understood now, after pondering on alternative motives, that Dorian was touching her in order to self-soothe...

That was what people who loved each other did.

Love.

But of course they had a special adoration for one another. They were friends. She didn't need to be a mind-reader to know definitively that Dorian loved her, but it was through no other channel but platonically.

Damica was fixated on the tub's contents, scraping the corners for the very last dregs of ice cream.

'You're...um...going to be an amazing father one day,' she told him. 'It's like you're a kid-whisperer.'

The tingling pressure on her thigh vanished as Dorian let go.

Sensibility twanged back into her brain with the force of a boomerang. And since she couldn't go to her therapist, she'd have to provide psychological guidance to herself...something about self-sabotage.

Yada-yada.

She wasn't used to being 'normal' and she was having trouble adjusting. Having acclimatised herself to chaos throughout her thirty-three years of living, it made sense that she was addicted to havoc. Now that she'd retired, her neurological pathways were struggling in the absence of the dysfunction that was usually intrinsic to her very being.

In other words, she was bored and looking for a problem. Agonising over the prospect of being in love with Dorian was a self-imposed dilemma.

She'd gone from working twenty-four-seven to lazing

around in paradise. No wonder her under-stimulated mind had concocted a whirlwind romance with her best friend.

'Is there a Nobel Prize for looking after kids?' she asked. 'You're probably eligible.'

And Damica didn't stop there, driving a further wedge between their contradicting lifestyles.

'The next generation of Sotiropouloses are in very capable hands.'

'I would hope so…'

She was confused by how unconfident he sounded—nonetheless, she didn't let this minor puzzlement detract from her overall aim: to give prominence to her and Dorian's lifestyle differences. There was no questioning whether he would father children. The only answer was 'yes'. Anyone with a brain knew that he had an obligation to continue, and in turn strengthen, the Sotiropoulos bloodline.

Thankfully, Damica had no such responsibility or rigid expectation.

'That's one of the things I like the most about you. How passionate you are about kids,' Damica went on. 'When you take off your crown, you can still identify exactly who you are. A man, an artist, a future dad…there's so much to choose from. At our last session, my therapist suggested that I look up some evening classes online and pick three non-performing arts subjects that interested me. But I couldn't even—'

Realising that she was rambling, and veering slightly off topic, Damica shut herself up. They were talking about Dorian—not her ongoing identity crisis.

'Everyone is someone away from their work,' he reasoned slowly. 'When I look at you, I see…'

Damica sighed at his hesitation. 'See? You can't think of anything right away.'

Dorian pushed onward. 'I see someone who loves her sister and nephew very fiercely. A loyal sibling and aunt. There are so many possibilities for you. You're stunning, and you know how to turn heads. You could start a clothing brand if you wanted to. Become a mother if you wish. Maybe combine the two with a mother-child fashion line?'

He might as well have described an alien.

She reflected on the possibility of being a mother. 'I mean, I hated being a child, so I want to make sure I have my life together before I have my own children...so they don't suffer. Whenever I do become a mom, I just want as few complications as possible. Simple conception. Simple pregnancy.'

Realistically speaking, Damica was aware that 'parenthood' and 'simplicity' was an oxymoron. She'd experienced the struggles of motherhood second-hand, when she'd been commodified at a young age in order to provide for her entire family.

'What are your opinions on IVF?' Dorian asked.

Case in point. Not all parents could conceive naturally.

'That's definitely something to consider. A couple of years back a friend of mine had IVF...it put so much stress on her body. And don't even get me started on the relationship with her partner. My heart goes out to everyone undergoing the procedure. It's tough. I don't think I could do it. I know the whole adoption process is tricky, but I think I would try that.'

Damica stopped twiddling with the empty ice cream pot and spoon. Braving a brief look over at Dorian, she was relieved to discover that he wasn't paying attention to her. Whilst towelling down his hair, he was watching the kids taking turns on the simulator. His expression was a mixed palette. The frown lines etched around his mouth harboured loathing, while hurt pooled in his pupils.

'There's a law back at home that excludes adopted royals from the line of succession.'

Blood purity. Another feature of the institutional beast that was royalty.

Some monsters should not be tolerated, only slayed...
What did Dorian's readiness to dance with this particular
dragon for the rest of his life say about him? And what did
her entire friendship with Dorian say about her? Was she in-
directly endorsing bigotry?

Damica curbed her interrogation before her identity issues spiralled into a morality crisis, but she did ask, 'Can
the law be abolished?'

'Royalty and politics are an ever-changing game. Cut off
the head, and three more the same will grow from the wound.'
With his words, Dorian painted an image of bleak resigna-
tion. 'Even if the law were to be rightfully changed, the media
and the royalists would still never let the adoptee forget their
origins. I would hate to expose any child to that. Every child
should be loved and embraced, regardless of their biological parentage.'

'Does it ever scare you? How much power you'll have as
a king...and as a dad?'

'All the time.'

'One missed Christmas recital and *boom*! Your kid'll have
low self-esteem and commitment issues for life,' Damica
quipped, keeping her tone light and airy. 'I think we'll do a
better job with our children, though. Our parents gave us a
masterclass of what *not* to do, right?'

'Right.'

Dorian's lips twisted into a mournful shape, triggering another crop of confusion to come creeping back into her. This
recurring strain was more potent. New questions arose. She'd
thought Dorian liked children—so why was he so saddened
by her mention of him raising his own. How could he be saddened about something that should make him happy? Or perhaps it was her ambiguous phrasing that had unsettled him?

By 'our children', she hadn't really meant *their* children.
Obviously Dorian would have no romantic future with her...

Here she was *again*…manufacturing her own unrest.

Determined to exterminate the weird energy between them, she decided to muster up the courage to ask him what was wrong.

Now or never. Put it all on the proverbial table. Better to speak your piece than wallow in silence, right?

She gave herself that mini pep-talk and then drummed her nervous fists on the wooden surface of the picnic table. Just as she was about to verbalise everything, Dorian got to his feet.

Jalen's turn on the simulator was calling for a standing ovation.

Like a proud father, Dorian whipped his mobile phone out of the pocket of his swim trunks. It was a miracle that the device could still function in the wake of such a crash as he'd had, but the cracked screen blinked into life under the bossy flick of his finger. After another flurry of swipes, Dorian was filming Jalen's first steps onto the blue slope in pursuit of the fixed surfboard.

Pushing aside her inquisitiveness, Damica stood up to join Dorian in his overt support of Jalen. Seemingly his weirdness over the possibility of having his own kids had vanished. Maybe she'd been overthinking, over-analysing and over-hypothesising and there had been nothing wrong to begin with…

Noticing the two adults eagerly awaiting his simulator debut, Jalen sent them a giddy wave. Damica returned his greeting, just as Dorian threw him a thumbs-up.

'Here we go…'

Dorian was watching Jalen with the kind of intensity that Hollywood directors reserved for blockbusters. She'd definitely been reading too much into his behaviour. The saying *If it ain't broke don't fix it* was especially fitting for this occasion. Dorian's excitement over Jalen was so…wholesome. Their time together at the resort was warm, soft and safe, an escape away from the world's problems, and Damica owed herself some peace too.

So she wouldn't burst her own bubble by conjuring up wild scenarios and romantic feelings for Dorian.

Age Fifteen

From: mrdoryfish7@inbox.com
To: damidiamondzzz@inbox.com
Re: Hmm... Part Two

Hi Damica,

I like your use of simile, especially when comparing yourself to a bird that must fly away to freedom. It's very effective.

There's a full breakdown of my thoughts in the attachments. I'm honoured that you wanted to share this with me. Hopefully, I didn't go overboard with the analysing...

It's just that, in a way, reading poetry and creative writing sort of reminds me of my mother. I don't remember much, because she died when I was so young. The memories of her reading to me before bed have always stayed with me, though.

Nowadays, I find myself thinking about her a lot. About what she would think of me.

Sometimes I fear she would be ashamed of me, like the people of my country seem to be.

The whole reason I joined in with the drinking in the first place was because I wanted to forget the trip Father and I took to England during the school break. Coincidentally, we went to London. Don't worry...you didn't miss anything amazing. Although Madame Tussaud's is cool if you avoid your own wax model.

Then we stayed with a family friend in the countryside who is a big fan of hunting. Him and Dad failed to tell me about the initiation ritual they perform on first-timers, where they dunk their heads into the belly of a fresh deer corpse...

It didn't matter how many showers I took or how much I brushed my teeth that night. Whenever I closed my eyes there was blood blocking my nose and mouth all over again.

I've thought about telling the school counsellor this... Did I mention before that school has made me have sessions with her? But even though she's nice, and lets me sit there in silence, I just can't trust her. When I have a child, I don't want things to be like that between us. I want them to feel free enough to speak with me about whatever they wish. Anything.

And there'll be no hunting and dead animals for us. No... every summer we'll take a trip to the coast, where we'll ride on our bikes near the sea and eat ice cream sandwiches for dinner.

Also, you are right! I can't stand *Keep your head up*. It's right up there with *Stay strong*.

From,

Dorian

From: damidiamondzzz@inbox.com
To: mrdoryfish7@inbox.com

Dear Dorian,

Ooh, yeah!

XD

Stay strong... Keep your head up... And the final boss... *I'm always here if you ever need someone to talk to.*

I had to go to appointments with a therapist too, around the time Dad popped back into my life. Did your therapist give you that little speech about having to tell your parent if they thought you were a danger to yourself or others?

I've never thought about doing anything like that, but

when I found out that she could snitch on me to Mom I knew I'd never be able to open up. I could just imagine how everything would go wrong if I didn't say the right thing. She'd tell Mom. Feir Channel would find out somehow, and they'd put out all these statements to the media, and even more people than before would be talking about it and it would never stop.

When I'm not on stage I just wanna be invisible. All the comments never stop, and I wish they would.

Thank you for making time for me and taking notes on my song. This means a lot!

I know we've been joking about hating all these phrases… but the hunting story and all the blood sounds like a scene from a horror movie. I hope you're okay now?

<3

Your future kid is gonna be so lucky to have you. If I think hard enough, I can see myself with a daughter. Always a little girl, for some reason. And we're wearing matching tracksuits.

:D

From,

Dami

From: mrdoryfish7@inbox.com
To: damidiamondzzz@inbox.com

Dear Dami,

Thanks for asking. I think I'm doing all right now. There's so much to do here, so I don't have much time to remember it any more. I can't decide if the situation was more mortifying than frightening.

Yes, the school counsellor gave me the same warning.

Honestly, my death would only attract more attention to me. When my mother passed, people spoke about her so much it felt like she was still living. There were pictures of her everywhere too, from the palace to literally every street in Concarre.

Time travel doesn't exist, for obvious reasons. However, I like to think there was true peace in the moments before I was ever created. I simply didn't exist. No name. No cells. Nothing. So there was nothing to criticise or pick apart.

If I could, I'd go back to that.

The downside would be that I couldn't eat my grandmother's *yazdi* cakes ever again, or get to see the *Mona Lisa* in person. We wouldn't have met either. So maybe not...

Message me whenever you want. It's always good to hear your thoughts. Doesn't matter if it's in an email or in a song.

Cheers,

Dorian

CHAPTER SIX

DAMICA LET OUT another aggravated sigh. Never in his life had Dorian heard so many expressions of frustration in the timespan of just thirty minutes.

'This requires patience…' he assured her in a low tone, inclining his bent head towards her whilst maintaining the steadiness of his fingers. 'You'll get the hang of it.'

'Easy for you to say.'

Dorian peeped upwards, in time to see her casting a cynical glare on his growing collection of artfully folded palm leaves. Baskets. Crowns. Animals. You name it—Dorian had made it.

'You're naturally good at this,' she told him.

Clearly giving up hope, Damica released her grip on whatever it was she was trying to construct. Its formation only survived for a few seconds, before unravelling into a chaotic mass of glossy green leaves, with points sticking up at various angles. Her shoulders slouched in defeat.

They were stationed in a quiet corner of the Club Enfant house, on the outskirts of one of the kids' afternoon craft sessions.

Following his embarrassing fall on the surfing simulator a couple of days prior, Dorian had been forced to apply some structure to his life on the resort. Mornings were dedicated to physical activities—swimming, scuba diving, playing tennis over on a different island and the like. Afternoons were for creative and intellectual enrichment—hence this designated arts and crafts time.

By the time the evening rolled around their minds were stuffed with brand-new experiences and everyone was ready to progress to dinner. 'Everyone' being himself, Jalen and Damica.

Their collective company had become a lifeline for Dorian. Now that he was tasting the fruits of domesticity, he could no longer comprehend how he'd survived the clinical confines of his royal upbringing. Existence within this imitation of a functional family unit was so utterly blissful that he knew returning to normal was destined to come with astounding withdrawal symptoms.

Dorian abandoned his latest creation—an incomplete fish—in favour of picking up Damica's work. Cupping it in both of his hands, he carefully lifted the tangled leaves up.

'A unique specimen…full of character and life…nowhere near as bad as you think.'

In response to this glowing review, Damica raised a perfectly arched eyebrow and crossed her arms. She echoed his description dryly. *'"Full of character"?'*

Dorian almost burst out laughing. 'Yes.'

'That's a nice way of saying it's shi—*bad*.'

Remembering she was within a shared radius with children, Damica censored her use of a rude word. Ravi's scowl of disapproval from a few seats away was confirmation that she was in danger of being overheard.

'Bad,' Damica insisted.

'I don't think that at all,' Dorian said. 'I'm being one hundred percent truthful.'

He was. In all honesty, he didn't think he possessed the discipline nor the conviction to classify any of her actions as negative, because he'd grown so infatuated with her. He knew better than to admit such an affliction aloud, though.

'Since you're an artistic guru, tell me what I was making, then, O Wise One.' Damica's sarcasm strengthened.

But Dorian wasn't the type of person who gave away an upper hand without putting up a fight.

'A car...obviously,' he retorted arrogantly.

Damica's eyes widened. 'Wow...'

Wow, indeed.

Her expression magnified the upward slant of her eyes and the marble-white of her sclera. Had her irises always been this mesmerising? Dark brown wasn't the right categorisation for their colour. No, it was a rare, complex hue that bordered obsidian. And her eyelashes... Each and every hair was naturally arranged in a way that reminded Dorian of delicate flower petals. Awe-inspiring by design.

His drawing hadn't done her justice.

'Wrong.' For added effect, Damica mimicked the sound of an error buzzer.

'Ah...' Dorian swallowed, zooming out of his fantasy. 'I see your intended vision now...'

'Which is...?'

'An...insect.'

Another buzzer sounded. 'Wrong again.'

'All this secrecy is killing me. Enlighten me.'

Damica plucked the knotted mess of palm leaves away from Dorian. 'It's a bird!'

'Ah. Right...' He knew the winged creatures had always held so much significance for her.

'I'm gonna have to throw it away,' she said.

'No, don't. It's fixable.'

Dorian quickly hooked his ankle around one of the legs of the kid-sized chair he'd had to contort himself to sit on. Scooting himself closer to Damica, who also dwarfed her seat, Dorian calmly slid his hands over hers. Under his touch, she went still. No longer prodding at the palm leaves, she stared down at the way their fingers worked together.

'If you fold this part through here…just like that… Perfect!'

Dorian whispered his instructions and they worked together to restore life to the mangled palm leaf bird. Damica's skin felt soft and addictively smooth under his fingers. Cool too. The ceiling fan was whirling on its highest setting, and in conjunction with the ocean breeze emanating from the open set of double doors it created a chilly haven. The swaying curtains, Ravi's gloom and the cacophony of childish squawks not far off seemed to dim, unable to compete with the centre of Dorian's activity.

As the restored bird took new form, Damica's nose scrunched up. A troop of wrinkles gathered at her T-zone, turning her attentiveness into the world's greatest show. Just like when she'd been surfing, the tip of her tongue made an appearance. She was in the zone, and Dorian was a charmed spectator.

He helped her weave the palms until she got the hang of it on her own. 'Good…there you go…'

'You're good with your hands,' she whispered.

He conveyed his agreement by absentmindedly trailing a fingertip from her wrist to her knuckle. The deft graze elicited an involuntary shiver from Damica that threw Dorian off-kilter—more violently than the simulator. Back then, he'd had a brush with possible concussion at worst. Right here, right now, with both his feet on solid ground, Dorian was hit with a truth much more disorientating.

This was the closest he would ever get to consummating his attraction towards Damica. He'd been deluding himself into thinking he was loving this mirage of stolen touches and lingering looks. In actuality he was pushing down his desire for more and clinging to their friendship because he was deathly afraid.

Everything between them was destined to change should he open up about his uncertain ability to procreate. All it would take was a confession about his compromised sperm and her nose-scrunching would become an indication of disgust.

Dorian was no seer or fortune-teller—he didn't have to be, because most of his social scripts were highly predictable. If he'd learnt anything from his father's diatribes, it was that being 'a real man' came with a lot of expectations and preconceived ideas. Yes, he might feel the pressures of prince hood were eliminated when he was with Damica and Jalen. Yes, they stripped back his royal armour and afforded him humanity... But underneath it all he was still a *man*. And, as stereotypical as it was, Dorian found that he enjoyed providing for Damica.

A calculated guess had led him to assume that she had a set of rigid characteristics she found attractive in potential partners...just because most people did. Wasn't all attraction discriminatory and inflexible to some degree? Would she bend her rules for him?

His inner realist had reached the conclusion of a resounding *no*. All the open-mindedness that carried their friendship would drain away should they decide to open the bedroom door, and Dorian didn't want to be anywhere else other than in her high regard. He'd lost her once, and he couldn't bear to lose her again.

Oblivious, Damica let go of him so she could marvel at their finished product: a proper bird. A defined beak and tail feathers jutted out proudly on opposite sides of a body in a series of interconnected triangles and angles.

'Look at this beauty!' she exclaimed. 'It's definitely a *her*. I'm gonna call her Birdy—subject to change.'

Fishing around in a nearby bowl, Damica rummaged for a pair of googly eyes.

Dorian schooled his expression to conceal his inner anguish. 'See? Never doubt the Guru.'

Even in an alternative timeline, where she reciprocated his feelings and became a royal bride, he knew they would still struggle. Damica's opinions of pregnancy and having a family had imprinted themselves into his memory. She wanted to conceive and raise her children under easy circumstances—understandable, given her childhood. Dorian could never grant her those wishes. There would be little rest or respite for the woman *he* married. Her body would be poked at and fiddled with until she was able to conceive and carry a royal heir to full term. And Dorian's fertility issues would make the journey more difficult.

He was aware that he was galloping leaps and bounds ahead, but nevertheless it was necessary to cull any inklings of hope before they grew lives of their own. Embarking down a romantic avenue with Damica was a lose-lose situation. All possible roads led to despair.

Damica, who'd finished dabbing PVA glue on Birdy's face and sticking down the eyes, fanned the bird with her hands in hopes of speeding up the drying process. Dorian scraped his chair back to its original place, although really he wanted to join in with the flapping. Mainly on the off-chance that their skin would touch briefly in passing. Being near Damica was a sure way to bring him comfort and help him communicate the many things he could never say aloud.

Whether or not she understood this new language was a mystery to Dorian. And, honestly, he'd come to favour this wondering status above the confirmed rejection that awaited him on the other side of this unverified limbo.

More pressing matters barged their way to the forefront of his mind. 'I have something to tell you,' he told her.

'Okay…' Damica slowed her movements as if in anticipation of his news.

'I might have…' He threw himself headfirst into building suspense, dragging out the pause. 'Volunteered us…as chaperones for the Club Enfant party…tomorrow night.'

'Chaperoning? Us as chaperones?'

Damica tested the responsibility as though she was trying on a dress. A doubtful scoff from Ravi notified them both that the eavesdropping bodyguard thought they were an ill fit for the job.

'I don't know… This is pretty short notice.'

Dorian sheepishly acknowledged that. 'I was feeling spontaneous. And Jalen was upset when you told him he couldn't go I thought it would make things easier for you to let him go, knowing that you can watch him the whole time.'

The celebration had been strategically scheduled to take place during the early evening, freeing carers and parents to explore the post-sundown entertainment the resort had to offer. Damica's reservations stemmed from the party coinciding with Jalen's bedtime.

Damica's hands dropped into her lap, further proving her astonishment. 'You're spoiling him too much.'

'I can't help it.' Dorian shrugged. 'Plus, if I recall correctly—which I always do—you've always wanted to go to a school dance.'

She shook her head in amusement. 'We're on a summer vacation…'

'With some *school-aged* children,' Dorian pointed out. 'Let's use our imaginations.'

'I…' Damica looked around, as if seeking justification for why she should deny herself excitement and finding none. 'Fine.'

Asking her to dine under the stars with him—and Ravi—whilst a private band serenaded them was obviously out of the question, but appeasing their childhood selves was harmless, thought Dorian. *Healthy*, in fact.

'Spectacular. I'll stop by your villa, so we can walk over together.'

Damica would have been maddened by Dorian's short notice if not for her increasing inability to stay angry with him and her long-time love of impulsivity.

Double Dare was the name of her highest-selling album for a reason: partying had been an authentic part of her brand and her being. A sheltered and fun-deprived adolescence had evolved into a hedonistic regime that had conquered her twenties. But tonight, at thirty-three years old, she was ready—and ironically better equipped—to fulfil her childhood wants.

'Can we go now, Auntie Dami? Is Dorian here yet?' Jalen tugged impatiently on her skirt.

She prised his fingers away from the tassels and patted his shoulder. 'Not yet.'

Unable to curb his excitement, the boy spun around. His small, sandalled feet tapped against the villa floor in a summoning rhythm and his blazer-clad arms performed what looked like an obscure form of wizardry. The mismatch in his dress style was self-inflicted, and the result of a last-minute shop at the resort boutique. The party had no dress code, but the formality of hunting new attire was a game that both nephew and aunt had enjoyed playing.

Jalen paused to alter the angle of his bowtie. 'How about now?' He pressed her for an update.

'He's on his way, Jalen.' Damica smiled. 'Be patient.'

'Boo!'

Jalen gave a thumbs-down signal, then jogged towards the living room for instant gratification from his favourite cartoons. He passed his mother, Taylor, in the doorway, and acquiesced to a hug and a kiss before disappearing.

'Thank you...*thank you...thank you*.' Damica's youngest and only sister pecked her cheek in the middle of her dash to the hall mirror. Using her reflection as a guide, Taylor put on a pair of gigantic hoop earrings.

'I'd say don't stay up too late...' Damica told her. 'But that's the entire point of me taking Jalen to the kids' party.'

Her consciousness diverted to her own evening plans with her husband, Taylor shouted, 'Babe! Hurry up! We're already late for the show!'

A gravelly voice hollered back something indecipherable, and the toilet in their shared bathroom was flushed.

In the oval looking glass, Taylor's winged-eyeliner-framed gaze fluttered to Damica. 'Are you sure you don't wanna come with us? We've barely seen each other this entire vacay. Dorian's welcome to tag along...'

'Positive.'

Damica had given up wondering whether her sister's string of invitations was being extended out of kindness or guilt— remorse for saddling the sister who'd already singlehandedly financed her whole life with her son.

Their relationship had never been conflict-proof. But Damica was now forthcoming enough to confront how she'd envied Taylor's freedom. Fame had meant she'd missed out on birthdays, funerals, graduations... Her sister had got to have the kind of life that Damica never could. Looking after Jalen on this holiday wasn't enough to replenish the empty well of experience, but Damica was being nourished by the quality time she'd accumulated with her nephew. She was also learning that taking care of a child was no walk in the park, and that parents needed a break sometimes.

Leroy hurried into the hall, zipping up his trouser fly and making a beeline for the door. Following her husband's lead, Taylor grabbed her leather shoulder bag and shoved an arm through the chain strap. Her high heels clicked at irregular intervals.

'Text me if you need me. I *swear* I'll drop everything in a heartbeat—'

'We'll be fine, Tay,' Damica vowed, straining against the nerves bubbling in the pit of her stomach like a soft drink fizzing with an abundance of carbon dioxide.

Her tone was honeyed, but she knew the evening was full of explosive potential. She didn't know which particular phenomenon to ascribe this exhilaration to: Dorian's impending arrival or the general itinerary of the evening ahead...?

Better to leave this particular stone unturned, she concluded.

Leroy leaned around Taylor's frantic gestures to give Damica a tight-lipped smile and a cordial wave. Then he opened the door...to reveal Dorian.

The commotion of bodies took a while to clear, but greetings served dually as farewells and Damica's party moved aside to let her sibling and brother-in-law exit the villa. It wasn't until Damica neared the now unobstructed doorway that she got a better view of Dorian.

His style was just the right balance of smart and casual. The crisp fit of his jacket accentuated the lines of his shoulders, and the dark material made the loud pattern of his Hawaiian shirt and the twinkle of his favourite gold necklace stand out.

Those tender hands were outstretched, with a bouquet and a roll of paper in them.

The airways in Damica's lungs constricted at the sight of the ornate cluster of folded palm roses.

'Dorian...' She was almost at a complete loss for words. 'This is... *Thank you*.'

Damica took the bouquet from him, blaming the tremble

caused by their overlapping skin on an imaginary post-sun-set chill and the convenient timing of Jalen whooshing past.

Dorian handcrafting her flowers was a gift all on its own, but her wonder expanded once she'd unfurled the accompanying tube of paper. Its firm texture and contents confirmed her suspicion that the sheet had been extracted from some kind of sketchbook.

'Dorian! You're here!'

The four-year-old launched himself at his grown-up friend. Meeting him halfway, Dorian crouched down to pick him up. With Jalen's legs wrapped around his midsection and his arms locked around his neck, Dorian ascended back to his full height. Hoisting Jalen up higher, he provided the child with extra support by closing a secure arm around his waist.

They exchanged some words, but Damica was too enchanted by the flowers and the detailed drawing to listen in. In her hand, the whirls and grooves of ivory leaves merged into green, as though visually representing the contentment suffusing her system. The leaves on the curled page housed a heart-warming group portrait featuring herself, Dorian and Jalen.

Every possible shade of pencil had been exploited, from the dark hue of everyone's textured hair to the glint that completed all three smiles. The result was a near-3D creation of the treasure hunt adventure's ending.

Jalen sat atop Dorian's shoulders, preserved mid-cheer and pumping a small fist. Dorian was holding on to Jalen's thighs, his mouth was twisted into a wolfish shape that mirrored a pirate's growl, and his pupils were angled sideways, tracking directly to where Damica was standing beside them.

Her head was thrown back in amusement, connected to her stretching neck adorned with stylish veins. The hand she rested on her stomach appeared to be a placement to contain hysterical laughter. Through Dorian's eyes and under the tip of his pencil she looked positively radiant—nothing like the sweaty mess who had run around the resort's jungle island for an afternoon.

Damica had seen Dorian bestow life upon a plethora of artwork countless times, but this…this was special. For her specifically.

She surfaced from her deep-dive inspection—only to nearly drown in the unnamed intensity pooled in Dorian's stare.

Detaching herself quickly, Damica brandished the palm leaf rose bouquet and the drawing at him. 'I hate it that I don't have a vase or a frame to display these in. They're stunning—I'm stunned!'

'That you have something I've made is enough.' One side of Dorian's mouth was weighed down in humility, making a lopsided smile that nurtured her happy buzz.

Damica laid the flower arrangement on the hall dresser, then melted back into his vicinity to address the child so at home in his arms.

'Jalen, look. Isn't this cool?' She pinched the corners of the curled paper between her fingertips and held it up for the boy to view.

Jalen gasped in fascination at his likeness translated into art. Eyes bright, he relived his treasure hunt fame with a bent arm and a celebratory swing of his fist. 'Argh!'

The trio chuckled harmoniously at Jalen's pirate impression.

Spreading the joy, Dorian chipped in with, 'Yarr! Shiver me timbers!'

Wild expressions replaced his handsomeness with a goofy distortion that only compelled Damica to admire him even more. It seemed fitting that a man so in tune with his own silliness and creativity had the power to present her with the most beautiful drawing she had ever seen.

For Damica, the world's finest jewels were relatively easy to come by. If she wanted them, all she had to do was make a phone call. Dorian's gifts to her were uniquely cultivated, with a type of care that money could never buy. And tonight he was granting her the most priceless gift of them all: the coming-of-age experience that she'd never got to have in real time.

CHAPTER SEVEN

DAMICA MIGHT HAVE been physically standing with Dorian, but he knew that she was mentally elsewhere.

The Club Enfant clubhouse had undergone a makeover. Gone were the majority of the tables used for craft activities and workshops. The survivors had been renovated into a home for paper plates, stacked plastic cups, punch bowls and a snack spread that put the resort buffets to shame.

The surface of the tropical fruit punch rippled, retaliating against the obnoxiously loud Y2K-inspired pop tune pouring out from the co-ordinated speakers perched at each corner of the room. The dance floor was swimming with young partygoers no older than ten years of age. Their small statures were deceiving. Teeming with sugar, they aggressively danced and threw shapes—shapes Dorian hadn't even known existed—under a sheet of gossamer lights projected from the disco ball hanging overhead.

Although Dorian considered himself a competent caregiver, this party was turning into a bootcamp in the art of patience. When the kids weren't crying, they were arguing. If they weren't arguing, they were running around at a zillion miles per hour. Truth be told, he'd severely miscalculated the difficulty level of being chaperone. His well-thought-out surprise for Damica had devolved into… Well…*this*… He couldn't fault her for withdrawing.

Their spot on the dance floor's perimeter gave them a

comprehensive view of the vicinity. A damp patchwork of paper towels marked the spot where a boy had vomited up his sausage rolls an hour prior. Another chaperone was battling against the clock to escort a girl to the bathroom before she peed herself. Mere feet away a group of children were squabbling amongst themselves over the correct moves for some TikTok dance routine. Damica was hugging herself as she observed them rehearsing.

As if aware of Dorian's quizzical glances, she grinned over at him. Alas, her smile was dimmer than the shimmering gold of her dress, which was a telltale sign of her waning happiness.

He needed to fix this.

Immediately.

Promptly, his hand gravitated towards hers like a moth drawn to a flame. 'Come with me.'

The snug fit of their interlocking fingers administered a welcome rush to Dorian's bloodstream, and he indicated for Ravi to track them from a distance.

Damica's gaze ricocheted between the compliant bodyguard and his prince. 'What's...?'

'You'll see.'

Dorian withdrew from the party, pulling back to the very edge of the sidelines until his back met the closed double doors. Giving the handle a testing rattle, he held down the lever and pushed until one of the doors opened. Its creak was smothered by the music and bustling celebration.

Trust me, he mouthed at Damica.

Still holding on to him, she followed.

The two of them slipped out into the night. The cool air and the dramatic dip in noise welcomed them like a delayed exhalation.

Dorian led her across the small garden area, squeezing her fingers persuasively. Together they navigated the obstacle course of discarded toys and swept aside the low-hanging leaves frilling the quiet pathway leading to the nearest beach. The lulling *shush* of the ocean waves steered them through the darkness, and the view that opened up was even more tranquil.

A deserted beach awaited them. The moon was comfortably posted at the sky's pinnacle, reigning over the scattering of stars. Its light reflected sharply off the sea's breadth and illuminated the safe passage of damp sand.

Dorian paused, allowing Damica to take in the breathtaking scene. 'I thought this might make you feel better.'

'Thank you… But I'm fine,' she mumbled.

Dorian was unconvinced. He released her hand and moved to stand directly in front of her. Spreading his arms elaborately, he took up all the space of her visual field, making himself impossible to ignore.

Damica crossed her arms and tossed him a scowl. 'What are you doing?'

As usual, her nose was scrunching up, as if in distaste. But Dorian knew it was mostly for show this time around.

He lobbed a disarming smile her way, kicking off his loafers and saluting the soft, grainy sand with his bare feet by curling his toes. Without removing his eyes from Damica's, Dorian jogged backwards, using nothing but his intuition to move himself to the heart of the shore. The party's playlist of current songs had been reduced to a distant memory, its replacement the never-ending hush of waves.

That was good enough for them. Perfect, actually.

'Come and dance with me!' he called, presenting his hand.

She didn't shout back…which technically wasn't a rejection.

Dorian waited. Waited so long that an ache started to build in his arm muscles—biceps, triceps and company.

From where he stood, Damica's form looked no larger

than a toy figurine. Nonetheless, he was positive he could see the tension bleeding out of her shoulders and her armour cracking inch by inch. As she drew closer, she grew larger. She stopped briefly to dispose of her shoes, flinging her high heels onto the shore. Confidence clearly increasing, she broke into an easy run.

Her long braids streamed out behind her as she hurried over to him. Her gold fringed mini dress sparkled and glimmered in solidarity with the moonlight, which bathed her in a delicate glow. Meanwhile the stretch and brightness of her smile eclipsed the stars. She was free. She was breathtakingly beautiful. She was...*his*.

All his.

And he was in love with her.

In tandem with his realisation Damica crashed into Dorian with a hug that sent him staggering backwards.

'Okay...maybe you're right. I do feel better now!'

The unfiltered and slightly unhinged pitch of Damica's laugh occupied his entire ear as he fought to reassert his physical and cognitive stability. Although with her pressed up against him so intimately, Dorian was a lone soldier in a losing battle.

Once he was firmly upright, he returned her embrace by circling his arms around her waist.

Dancing, he reminded himself. *They were meant to be dancing.*

Dorian swayed hesitantly, and Damica joined in with his awkward movement. She incorporated her feet into the sequence, so soon they were stepping from side to side, making a tentative rhythm of their own.

Damica hung her head, pretending to monitor their uncertain legs. But Dorian had already noticed the dwindling magnitude of her smile.

'My first time at a school dance. Am I doing this right?'

she asked sardonically. 'The closest I've been to one of these things is the *Dani DoRight* prom episode.'

'There are no rules,' he promised, his lips purposefully skirting along her earlobe.

Damica's rhythm lost momentum for a split-second, but she covered up the falter by wrapping her arms around him even tighter.

'If it's any consolation, I spilled punch all over my shirt at my first dance,' he told her.

She gasped sympathetically. And because their chests were pinned together, Dorian felt Damica's sharp intake of breath and the press of her breasts when she exhaled. The sensation bulldozed through his declining sense of awareness.

Easing his touch lower, Dorian let his hands find a new home at the flare of her hips. He was suddenly a teenager again, experiencing his first foray into romance. His heart was ratcheting inside him, threatening to burst free of the anatomical tissue holding the vital organ in place.

Growing bolder, he rested his chin on Damica's shoulder and let one of his palms ascend to the bare slope of her exposed back. She arched into him, causing him to raise his head.

'Should I stop…?'

Before he could lift his head she raked a hand through his hair, her nails grazing his scalp. The encouragement spurred his second dive—this time his face burrowing into the connection where her neck and shoulder met. She let out a loud, shaky breath as his nose trailed up the column of her throat, relishing the delectable scent of her perfume—an exclusive personalised fragrance he'd come to know.

Under the resting place of his lips, her pulse point hammered in arousal.

All Dorian had to do was move his mouth up a few inches.

His breath ghosted over Damica's jawline and chin, stopping at her lips. 'And now...?'

They came to a standstill on the sand, their dance long forgotten. Mere slivers of space separated their closely drawn faces. Dorian could perceive his own reflection in the dark mirrors of Damica's pupils. He read in them the depths of her pining. And her panic.

He knew a kindred consternation was projected by his own gaze. For he and Damica were two souls destined to pass each other periodically but never collide permanently. Or fully.

As if suddenly caving in to her impulses, Damica smashed her mouth to his quickly.

It was over in a heartbeat. More of an impersonal peck than an exchange of intimate passion.

She kept her eyes wide open the whole time, and her trembling fingertips dug into the back of his neck. Dorian didn't dare speak or move, save for dampening his lips with his tongue to savour the rushed taste of her,

Damica's clasp resettled at the sides of his face to cup his cheeks. She kissed him again. Then once more. Another, just to be sure. Each one lasted longer than its predecessor, stamped with the similarity of their unrelenting eye contact.

Although unvoiced, they were clearly in agreement that all this could amount to was a gratifying fumble in the dark. She was a retired star with a thirst for control, and he was a black hole of monarchist baggage and fertility complications.

A match made in hell.

Dorian couldn't afford to lose his head.

But shutting his eyelids came with the risk of missing out on the entirety of...whatever this was.

He'd best make the most of it...

The experimental brush of their lips evolved into something more as their searing breath ramped up the heat. Seeking more tactile sensation, Dorian slid his desperate touch back down to the small of Damica's back and beyond. His tantalising stroke over the incline of her ass earned him an invigorating sigh.

He tilted his head to the left, to deepen their next kiss, just as Damica pitched to the right.

Her right.

In an accidental clash, their foreheads banged together. The impact of the collision reverberated through his skull with an unpleasant tremor, interrupting the synchronicity of their embrace.

Conjoined souls was out of the question, but Dorian was neither pleased nor pleasured by this painful alternative.

CHAPTER EIGHT

DAMICA WAS SEEING STARS. Disappointingly, not the orgasmic kind, but dancing lights of the dizzying, disorientating variety.

She stumbled away from Dorian, her palms flying up to bracket her throbbing forehead. Her eyelids squeezed themselves shut and she hunched forward, propping her hands on her knees. A self-protective instinct took over, instructing her to accept sanctuary at ground level and the steadiness of the Earth's core.

'I am so, so…sorry!'

'Don't be—it's fine.'

'I'm not usually so clumsy—'

'My fault too.'

'Are you—?'

'Seriously, I'm *fine*.'

Her own voice sounded so distant and cold. Was that really her snapping at Dorian?

In for four seconds. Hold for seven seconds. Release for eight seconds.

Damica religiously carried out each step of her breathing exercises. But what use would anxiety-alleviating respiratory patterns be against almost bashing her head in? She couldn't connect the dots at this time. Nevertheless, they were fixed and familiar and difficult to get wrong.

She was messing up a lot of good things lately.

Namely, one of the only dependable friendships she'd ever had.

Dorian was rubbing her back in an effort to provide stress relief. However, his show of affection only rebooted every single nerve-ending in her body. And they collectively pushed for a continuation of her and Dorian's rushed make-out session.

Damica jerked upright, further separating herself from the source of her arousal by marching back across the sand to scout out her shoes.

'Damica...?'

Dorian was right on her heels, and she knew he wouldn't be content with anything other than definitive proof that she was fine. The after-effects of him fondling her behind still sparked down her spine. Euphoric hormones still raged through Damica's system. And she was *this close*—so close—to crumbling and dragging his mouth over hers so they could kiss some more.

Divine intervention materialised in the form of Ravi, with Jalen in his arms. The bodyguard had been posted at the opening in the palm trees that Dorian had ushered her through earlier. How much earlier exactly, she couldn't determine.

Had Ravi, the shadow that he was, been watching from the wings whilst she slipped up with Dorian? If he had, she knew they could trust him to not ask questions. Her saving grace was that Jalen was fast asleep in his arms and facing away from the beach.

Damica's face burned with shame. She'd been so lost in her lust—like a randy teenager exploring her sexuality for the very first time—that she'd neglected her responsibilities. Dorian wasn't the only person with duties. Damica had an obligation to look out for her nephew and she'd failed him.

Not wanting to forsake anything else, she slowed her steps,

inviting Dorian to walk by her side. 'I think about you a lot,' she blurted out. 'More than I should.'

As much as she wanted to, Damica wasn't going to run away from this problem. Independence wasn't just fun and games—there were terms and conditions too. One of them being that *she* had to deal with the consequences of her own actions. Her mother wasn't here to pen a fake apology because Dani DoRight had been busted buying contraception with her boyfriend. Mom couldn't swoop in and fix her marriage by pushing for an annulment on the grounds that both parties had been intoxicated.

Damica had to handle this all on her own.

'I lost control of myself and... Well, *that* happened.'

Alcohol wasn't a plausible excuse. Damica was stone-cold sober. She flapped her hands about—another manifestation of her own embarrassment.

'It won't again—happen again, I mean. You're you and I'm me. It's completely one hundred percent certifiably crazy to even think we could go there with one another...'

The end of her rambling appeared on the horizon at long last. Damica resisted Dorian's heavy stare and the skim of his jacket-clad arm as he pulled ahead of her.

They'd happened upon one of her shoes. He got down on one knee to retrieve the lone silver pump.

'Certifiably crazy? Hmm...'

His rendition of her words sounded blank and detached. Plus, his lowered stance made it near-impossible to see his face. Was he in agreement? Or worse... Gosh, she hadn't *upset* him, had she?

'You are not my type,' she said. 'At all.'

Real diplomatic, Damica.

She was only digging a bigger hole for herself here.

Dorian unearthed the pricey high heel, dusting the build-up

of sand off the satin before digging around inside. Stray pebbles and shells were evicted, falling back onto the sand bed.

With him squatting at her feet, Damica felt…inexperienced. She hated it that Dorian's consideration for her footwear reminded her of Prince Charming discovering the slipper left by Cinderella after the ball. Because that would make her the Princess in this ludicrous equation.

Prim and proper? No, thank you.

'And…and I'm not the right fit for you either!' She prattled onward.

In her peripheral vision she spied a silver heel elsewhere on the shore. Damica slogged over to where the first shoe's companion lay alone at an unbothered angle. Her abrupt parting from Dorian would end all possibility of him performing some fairytale re-enactment.

Firstly, that would be dumb. Secondly, she'd only hobble around with one shoe on until she sank pitifully into the sand. Her high heels were sorely incompatible with the low-density ground. She'd acquired this knowledge on many occasions—her girlish dash into Dorian's arms being one of them. Ironically, the 'sinking heel' analogy applied to her and him perfectly…

Damica snatched up her other heeled pump, granting it an apathetic excavation, then saw Dorian sitting down several yards away, having detected both of his loafers. After calming herself down, Damica traipsed back into his range and plopped down next to him.

He wasn't Prince Charming…he was just Dorian. Her best friend Dorian. A man with Daddy issues, who was born with a silver spoon in his mouth, and a curiosity that came at the expense of his own safety. He was a lot shorter than the guys Damica was typically attracted to. But more morally upstanding…sometimes boringly so. More…caring.

It wasn't till a cape-like gathering of cloth descended upon her bare shoulders that Damica realised she was shivering. Dorian styled his jacket around her upper arms so she was deeply enfolded in its warmth. Then he handed her the missing shoe.

'I wouldn't categorise that as the best kiss I've ever had,' he said. 'But you're unquestionably in contention for Most Memorable.'

Wryness tugged at the corner of his mouth, culminating in a goofy grin that made her eyes flick upward. A novel shyness had cast its net over Damica, but at least they were back to chasing up discomfort with jokes.

So...did this mean the two of them were good?

She hoped so.

Ruminating on the root cause of her pooling angst, Damica could only guess it was a knee-jerk reaction to her rejection of the boxes that so many people had pressured her into. Refusal to comply had always come with a punishment. When she hadn't played her role as someone else's puppet, the would-be puppeteer had always cut ties with her in some way. Emotional or physical.

Her own father had left her for the *second* time once she'd declined to play the part of a doting daughter. Her mom had struck her down verbally for swerving out of her designated role of Family's Golden Goose. And how could Damica forget her soured reputation amongst the Feir Channel execs every time they'd been forced to remember that their favourite child star was human too?

She'd made advances towards Dorian and then changed her mind—which wasn't a crime. But that had never prevented men who felt entitled to sex from viewing denial as a whopping violation. Just because he was a good friend, it was no guarantee that he'd make an excellent lover. Damica couldn't be sure.

All the more reason why dating him was a bad idea. Another unaccounted variable.

'Better leave it as a memory, then,' Damica countered quietly, after what felt like a lifetime of silence. She fussed with the skirt of her mini dress, twirling the tassels around her nervous fingers. 'Another one will never be able to match up.'

'Can't argue with you there.'

Dorian abandoned his study of the sea and the skyline to turn his loafers upside down. A stream of sand spilled back to its origins. Late-night luminescence cast its magic over Dorian's upstretched arm, making the shadow in the inner crook of his elbow stretch to maximise the appeal of his muscles.

Damica grasped the lapels of Dorian's jacket, bunding herself up tighter with the fabric. She was content with her present state.

Dorian's arm moved down again, taking its potential to distract along with it. He regarded her closely. So closely that she was unable to assert any authority over the temperature of her cheeks, which had skyrocketed under his speechless enquiry. He zoned in on her eyebrows and hairline, to the extent that she was frustrated with herself for feeling self-conscious.

She was Damica Foye! The one and only! Men became pathetically bashful in her presence, not the other way round.

'I should get you and Jalen back to your villa,' Dorian said. 'Although after our clash of heads I think maybe I should keep you awake for another hour or so. Just to be on the safe side.'

His inspection was earnest, swaying Damica's conclusion that he was only checking to make sure she had no bumps, marks or outward signifiers of a concussion.

'Yeah, my head was knocked around a bit—but your head's not *that* hard,' she reassured him firmly. Damica curled her fingers into a fist and gave his forehead a light, good-natured rap with her knuckles. 'Don't worry. I'm good.'

'Wow.' Dorian blinked dramatically, capturing her wrist. 'Does my being a patient under the established Dr Jalen not mean anything to you?'

'I'm sure he'd give you an A for effort...'

In unison, they turned to take note of the esteemed four-year-old clinician, who was still snoozing, uninterrupted, in Ravi's embrace.

Damica decided to make a bid for the royal bodyguard's fellowship. She would've made a beckoning signal, for emphasis, but she didn't want to risk losing the sweep of Dorian's thumb over the inside of her wrist.

'Come and sit with us?' she invited.

To both her and Dorian's surprise, Ravi acquiesced, and the stony safeguard of his demeanour prevailed as he stalked over to the open sand next to Dorian, his actual employer. Despite his large build and the sleeping forty-pound body he held, setting him up to sink into the beach's soft surface, he moved with the lithe quickness of a jaguar. It was an evolutionary step away from his previous flounders in the holiday climate.

Ravi soundlessly alighted on the spot adjacent to Dorian whilst Jalen stirred, snorted, and used his broad shoulder as a pillow. Ravi made no other move to acknowledge Damica's existence—not that she'd expected him to. But she managed to sneak a peek at him, verifying the suitability of his arms to go on supporting Jalen's bodyweight.

'Ah. I see how it is!' Dorian soothed the prickly atmosphere with a witticism. 'Can't steal my heart, so you're robbing me of a bodyguard instead.'

Under the wooing skim of his thumb, Damica's pulse skipped. Was...was Dorian *flirting* with her? She shouldn't be enjoying this. And yet...

She had her fill of the glimmer hovering in his mocha-brown eyes before taking her wrist back. Then, scooting closer, she reclined her head onto his shoulder. With ease, Dorian draped his arm around her, completing the circuit.

'Some see it as robbery,' she said. 'I see it as a loan between friends.'

She spoke into the distance, cherishing the sight of the boundary where the night sky met the ocean. She knew that, like this late-night wonder, all good things came to an end. A favourite song. The last drawn-out bites of a comfort dish. Her time here at the Étoile Privée resort with Dorian. That didn't mean she couldn't hang on to the dregs of pleasure before they drained away, though.

'I may not seem like I do, but I can hear you,' Ravi grouched.

Damica and Dorian's childishness bubbled up, producing hushed tee-hees and conspiratorial smiles. 'Sorry, Ravi,' they crooned in unison.

For now they were two kids, staying up way past their bedtimes, drunk on the milky night and the endless possibilities of their own leisure. When sleep made its rounds it would be heavy and halting. But Damica wasn't ready for this good thing with Dorian—whatever it was—to cease just yet.

Age Seventeen

From: damidiamondzzz@inbox.com
To: mrdoryfish7@inbox.com

Hey, Dorian,
You've probably already seen all the embarrassing stories about me in the news. I still can't believe how me and Liam got caught. We were super-careful. We were both wearing hoodies and sunglasses. He was in the store for five mins max and I stayed in the car the whole time.

What kind of weirdo hangs around in the condom aisle taking pics of customers?

Paula made me sign that public statement saying I'm sorry, but I'm so confused. I don't see what I've done wrong here…

We had a 'special' meeting about it and everything… All the *Dani DoRight* producers were there, some PR people, plus a load of serious people in suits who I didn't recognise. Paula, too, obviously.

I don't even remember most of what was said because it was so humiliating. Everyone in the room looked at me like I was dirty and I hated it.

Mom didn't have my back. When we got back home she gave me this long lecture about being irresponsible and putting our future in danger.

:(

Another thing that confuses me is that sex is overrated.

Whenever Liam has sex with me I mainly just lie there and wait for it to be over. It doesn't last long, but the whole time I'm thinking, Is that it? This is what all the singers sing about? What famous writers write about?

IDK…

Maybe I'm doing something wrong.

Kissing him is really fun, though!

Have you had sex yet? What's it like for you?

Dami x

From: mrdoryfish7@inbox.com
To: damidiamondzzz@inbox.com

Dami,

I'm very sorry. I hate it that you're being treated this way.

Your mother sounds a lot like my father. He threatened to have all my paintings thrown out of the palace if I don't join a sports club. In his opinion, a king has a duty to be athletic and strong. He says no one will take a 'flowery' leader seriously. He never lets me forget.

I have an embarrassing story to share as well: I have never had sex.

When I was still living in the boys' dormitory I'd always nod my head and make the odd comment whenever the topic came up. Just enough so I didn't stand out too much. No one wanted to ask too many questions or risk upsetting me because Ravi was always nearby in a room just down the hall. Some days I'd feel like he didn't give me room to breathe. But I'd never been more grateful to have him close by then.

My friend Dario's had plenty of girlfriends…sometimes multiple at the same time. He told me that sex is better when both people are really enjoying it, and that's the only way it should be. Therefore, it sounds like you have nothing to blame yourself for.

Apparently there's this book called *The Kama Sutra*? It's supposed to help with stuff like this. Check the attachments. I've sent you pictures of the pages!

I thought I might ask Jimena to be my girlfriend. But the palace head of security showed me proof that she's been talking to journalists. So now I know that it was her who told the press about how I vomited all over her lap during our last date.

I wish I could be angry at her. But I've had so many 'friends' betray me that I'm becoming numb.

I'm happy that I have you, Dario and Ravi.

There's a girl in my English class who I might ask to the next dance, if I even decide to go. I like hearing her opinions on Sylvia Plath.

I'll let you know if anything unfolds.

Yours,

Dorian

from: damidiamondzzz@inbox.com
to: mrdoryfish7@inbox.com

Dorian!

Forget about Jimena and her loose lips. Put the books down and ask this new girl out! You're kind and funny and artistic and extremely easy to talk to, so I already know that she's gonna say yes.

　:)

Thank you for those *Kama Sutra* pics.

First of all...

W. O. W.

I shouldn't have opened those attachments from your last email when I was in Hair and Make-Up. I had to lock my phone ASAP once I saw all those bodies in those positions! I was so shocked they made me spill my juice!

Luckily, I didn't ruin my outfit for the day, because then Mom would have shouted at me even more. Plus, the lady doing my hair was very understanding. I don't think she saw anything on my phone...but she also didn't look me in the eye for the rest of my time in the trailer.

Anyway, none of that is important. I've decided that I'm never going to have sex again. You're not missing out on much.

Liam broke up with me over text. He said he hasn't been asked to return to the set and that he's probably being written out of the show because of the condom thing and me.

I wish I didn't have to be here... But I've just got to keep telling myself that I'll be free after we finish filming this season. Once I'm eighteen I'll be able to do whatever TF I want. Mom will have more than enough money.

I wish I could be with you instead. School dances sound really fun! I'd be an amazing wing woman or third wheel! You are going to ask her out, right? LOL

We could dance until our feet are sore and we can't even remember your dad or my mom. And drink so much punch that we throw up everywhere. The full experience.

Now, I'm trying to imagine you dancing, but my mind's gone blank. Are you a robot dancer or a two-step kind of guy? Do you even know what those are? LOL!

Dami xxx

From: mrdoryfish7@inbox.com
To: damidiamondzzz@inbox.com

Dami,

I think the best I can do is a shoulder shimmy! Leave me alone. Not everyone is a skilled trained dancer like you!

Have you ever considered that, for me, reading books and writing to you is exciting enough? Plus, exams are coming up. I have to think about my future.

I was going to apologise for juice spillage, but since you've insulted me so much I don't think that I will.

:P

You'll be happy to know that I *did* ask the girl I was telling you about to the dance. Her name is Diana, and I think you'd really like her. This is me promising to take loads of pictures of the party, so it feels like you're right there with us, having the best time.

I've decided to keep any information about Diana from my father for as long as I possibly can. Firstly, as much as I like her, I'm not going to get my hopes up about this leading to anything more. Secondly, whenever Father knows that I'm dating someone he always finds a way to make a snide remark about us 'doing each other's make-up'.

Painting on a canvas...painting faces. They are apparently the same thing to him. And, of course, whenever I confront him he insists that he's only joking and I'm being too sensitive. I can never win with him.

This is probably inappropriate of me to say, but I'm over-joyed that Liam isn't in your life any more. I know I'm not physically with you, but your words always felt so sad when-ever you spoke of him. Similar to when you describe your mother.

Just know that I'll always support you, and I want you to be happy. Maybe, when you're finished with your show and I've completed school, we can try and meet up secretly. What do you think?

Yours,

Dorian

CHAPTER NINE

DORIAN WASN'T THE only Concarri whose inhibitions were being stripped away by the Étoile Privée resort, layer by layer. Time really did reveal all. Case in point: Ravi's ability to commentate on his prince's current condition with a degree of accuracy that hinged on invasiveness.

The sun was beating down unforgivingly on his temples and the late-morning brightness threatened to blind him. Hangovers and drug comedowns weren't valid scapegoats for this sensitivity because he hadn't consumed a single recreational substance over the last twenty-four hours. Not unless Damica's lips qualified...

Dorian slapped a mental lid over that tangent for now. His squinting eyelids flickered and, frazzled, he ran a hand through his hair, covering up the fact that he was scratching his head in confusion. Maybe he'd misheard Ravi's latest prognosis.

'Excuse me?'

'I said, you don't know what her reaction will be until you actually tell her.' Ravi tucked his arms behind his back, casually vocalising his thoughts as if he might be talking about something insignificant. Like the weather. Not the personal life of his literal employer. 'Whatever it is you're keeping a secret from her, that is, Your Highness.'

Dorian furrowed deeper into his defensiveness. 'What... what makes you think I'm keeping a secret?'

One of Ravi's eyebrows jerked a minor fraction, and his cheek twitched.

'Am I really that obvious?' Dorian groaned.

His hand flew up to his face and he massaged his forehead. Feelings of exposure and mortification aside, he was grateful that he and Ravi's camaraderie of sorts was piecing itself back together. Especially after the disruption generated by Dorian's recently developed streak of recklessness. Given the number of bangs to the skull he'd taken during this leave of absence thus far, he needed someone to have his back.

'No. But I wouldn't be doing my job if I didn't notice these things, Your Highness,' Ravi replied, giving himself further legitimacy.

Dorian couldn't conceive of a world in which he would ever fire his bodyguard for simply doing his job effectively. Truth be told, it was impossible to consider a life without Ravi, full stop. The assignment of differing guards to the young Crown Prince had been a revolving door that he'd never liked going through. But Ravi's indefinite allocation to the end of the corridor leading to Dorian's boarding school dorm had marked a welcome delay. Using his title to influence the roster and keep Ravi as a permanent guard had been one of Dorian's first exertions of sovereign power. And he was yet to regret his choice.

Ravi gave the word 'discreet' a fresh definition. He'd seen all of Dorian's grapples with boyhood—from his sloppy first kiss with a date on the school lacrosse field to his illicit introduction to cigars—and had uttered a word to no one. By virtue of doctor-patient confidentiality, Ravi was ignorant of the ins and outs of Dorian's reproductive health. But Dorian trusted that if Ravi ever became privy to this information he would approach it with the same subtlety.

Dorian swivelled his head, working out the kinks in his neck muscles with calculation for the activity ahead.

'What Damica doesn't know won't hurt us—not that there ever will be an "us". We're just friends on a— How do the British refer to it?' He snapped his fingers. 'Ah! A lads' holiday.'

As though conjured up by the mention of her name, a low drumming started further up the pier.

The polite resolution in Ravi's next utterance was a tip-off that this would be the last time Dorian would be hearing from him on such a topic. 'I'm not sure Miss Damica would appreciate being referred to as a "lad", Your Highness.'

The striking of flip-flops against the pier's wooden planks amped up in both tempo and loudness, as though rolling out a carpet in auditory form ahead of its owner's grand entrance.

Dorian turned to give Damica a warm reception, and she responded in kind with a modest wave. He wanted to attribute her bashfulness to their kiss, but figured the absence of her usual young, lively associate was a more realistic source.

Jalen was notably missing this morning—his parents had reclaimed custody of him for a day, and the adult pairs were switching places. Damica's sister didn't want her booked activity slots to go to waste, so as a thank-you she'd passed them on to her sibling. Being the thrill-seeker that she was, Damica had jumped at the chance to make full use of the jet ski reservation. And, ever her devotee, Dorian had concurred.

He was trying his best not to dwell on how he and Damica were effectively acting as proxies for Taylor and Leroy—a happily married couple—when last night had eliminated all prospects of them being amorous, let alone bound by wedlock. Damica had pronounced that Dorian was leagues apart from what she usually considered appealing, which had... hurt. But the reality check had been sorely needed.

'Do you want the good news first or the bad news?'

Damica curved her palm and braced it on her brow, forming a natural visor to block out the jarring sunlight. Dorian had always considered her to be pretty. But today the generous residue of her recently applied sunscreen made her dual-toned skin glisten, and her face was free of make-up, lending substance to how naturally striking she was. To class her as 'one of the lads'—or however it was that the Brits phrased it—was truly an insult to Damica's beauty.

'Surely it can't be that bad…?'

Dorian assumed a mellow approach, which should have been easy given his choice of company. Nonetheless, his insecurities were worming around under the surface of the well-put-together, well-to-do facade he was sporting.

'Well, you said it, not me…'

And Damica launched into an abridged recap of her chat with the resort dock master.

'All their jet skis are booked right now. Not really a surprise that they're so popular. Because of that, the staff can't give us a third jet ski. So we're gonna have to split two between the three of us…'

She turned to Ravi, who was reading himself to supply his typical forewarning about procedure and whatnot.

'I know… I *know* you can't stand and watch us from the pier. And I'm guessing you and Dorian don't wanna buddy up either. So, it's gonna have to be me and Dorian sharing a jet ski and you on the other one. Ravi?'

'That's fine with me.'

Dorian nodded definitively and drew up his shoulders, trying to exude a semblance of dominance. He wasn't feeling especially majestic, but he'd resolved to fake it till he made it so. His bodyguard might be keeping tabs on his every move, but it was the Crown Prince who ultimately called all the shots. Moreover, close proximity to Damica could never score as a loss…

Moving their conversation along, he wondered aloud, 'So what's the good news, then?'

'Isn't it already obvious? We're going jet skiing… Hello?'

The excitable hand-clap and ponytail sway that coincided with Damica's chirp only added to her innate charisma. In a further burst of elation, she discarded her flip-flops and advanced to where the jet-propelled vehicles in question awaited them.

Dorian followed suit and helped her untie the ropes that were keeping those bad boys tethered to the marina. When they were done, he motioned for her to mount what was essentially the watercraft equivalent of a motorbike.

'Ladies first.'

Its design was a brash one. The sprightly red panelling on the shell was overwhelmed by its black counterparts, and the deceptive curve of the body's apex bore a strong resemblance to a shark's nose.

Damica shot Dorian a lingering smile before climbing onboard. He took to his own seat afterwards. Their seating order meant that he was positioned rather intimately behind her, with his crotch meshed against her backside and his arms around her waist.

The vehicle bobbed subtly in accordance with the tide as they bided their time until Ravi was safely aboard his solitary jet ski. Neither of them seemed to mind the delay. Damica settled back against the support of his life-jacket-barricaded chest. The pressing of their spread legs seemed to coerce her bare thighs to mingle with the nylon of his swim trunks.

The last of Dorian's practicality crumbled. The boy who had once so chivalrously assisted an unrequited crush with boarding a watercraft at this very same marina was dead and buried. His first kiss with Damica had awakened a man with alarmingly simple wants.

The primary one being Damica.

Everything else—his royal life and his doubts about being able to conceive an heir—would have to be secondary for the time being. With Damica, anything felt possible. Why waste the opportunity to be happy with her on this holiday? For ever was impossible for them…so a short while would have to suffice.

Damica peeped back at him over her shoulder, mindful not to whack him on the nose with her braids, which were tied back into her ponytail. 'Ready?'

'Always,' he breathed, looking down pointedly at the minimal gap between their lips.

She gulped, her focus boomeranging between his suggestive gaze and his mouth. An arrogant rush of pride bloomed in his ego, but his face betrayed nothing of the inner workings of his mind.

He jutted his chin towards the jet ski's handlebars, which she was holding on to for dear life. 'I think you need to turn it on first…'

'Right. Of course…'

A dazed Damica cut off their stare-down to fish a pair of gloves out of the jet ski's glove box. With no further heads-up, she shoved the accessories on and jabbed her thumb on the vehicle's ignition.

The pair were lurched into action, zooming away from the marina in an eruption of aggressive engine revs and explosive water that unfortunately bathed Ravi.

In the midst of the thrill and the whizz Damica and Dorian seemed to morph into a single entity, concerned with screaming at the top of their lungs and chasing a high.

Gone were Dorian's father's diatribes now—because none of them were true. Dorian wasn't some feeble dweeb who substituted poetry and art for human interaction. Quite the contrary. He was a hot-blooded male who knew how to pursue a woman. He'd topped virtually every fan-voted poll relating to the world's most eligible bachelors…so he must be a lot of people's type. And pretty soon he would be Damica's.

* * *

If Damica hadn't known any better, she'd have thought that Dorian was on a top-secret mission to seduce her.

She did, though.

Know better.

In the real world they were just two friends, strolling into the resort's spa for their scheduled session with a professional masseuse. Hardly a storyline worthy of being included in a soap opera.

Nonetheless, it warmed the lining of Damica's stomach just like a comfort meal that had been cooked to perfection. And, as though fashioned to prove her wrong, the side of Dorian's hand targeted her with an accidental nudge that sent a train of tingles shooting up the stretch of her arm.

The nanosecond of skin-to-skin contact transported her back to how he'd cuddled her from behind on the jet ski hours earlier, the intimate press of his body and his howls in her ear facilitating her spiking adrenaline. And then she thought back to the deserted beach the previous night, where they'd shared those chaste, introductory pecks bathed in moonlight...

'Welcome to the Étoile Privée Spa. How can I be of service?'

The Zillennial woman behind the podium at the entrance addressed Damica and Dorian.

Ushering out the disturbance of her rose-tinted daydream, Damica jumped in to explain her and Dorian's circumstances. 'Oh—hi, we're here for—'

The receptionist rephrased her salutation in French, and then in German and Mandarin, and finally Dhivehi—the national language of the Maldives. Her oration was so well-rehearsed that Damica almost thought she was interacting with an automated machine.

A short phase of quiet ensued, perhaps to make way for any requests for more translations. When nothing else followed, Damica gave the woman Taylor and Leroy's booking details.

A sequence of computer mouse drags, clicks and keyboard taps played out, mismatching with the *boduberu* drum instrumental pouring out of the sound system. After reading the relevant information from her computer screen, the receptionist smiled accommodatingly.

'Mr and Mrs Williams. We're so glad you are able to join us. If you require a live demonstration before your session commences, our expert masseuses will be happy to assist you.'

Damica was temporarily rendered speechless. Not by the calibre of customer service—she expected nothing less with the resort's five-star rating and rave reviews. She was confused by the staff's willingness to provide a demonstration of how they did their jobs to a pair of guests.

Why would she and Dorian need a demonstration?

'I'm sorry...would you mind checking the booking. We're just having a couples' massage, right?'

'Er...yes,' the receptionist confirmed. Her eyeballs darted from left to right as she looked through the data. '"Couples' Massage Honeymoon Hands-On Package",' she read.

Recognising Damica and Dorian's bafflement, she kindly supplied them with a spectacular pitch. 'This package is designed to boost relaxation and intimacy between couples. A bespoke selection of the world's finest massage and body oils will be at your disposal, so you can be masseuse and masseur to each other. This hands-on experience is one of our most popular treatments here at the spa!'

A string of taps moved across her wrist, like temptation licking away at her self-restraint. Discerning Dorian's incessant finger as the culprit of the stimulation, Damica awarded him her full attention. He tipped his head urgently towards the closest corner of the reception area.

Damica updated the receptionist on their pending status as spa visitors. 'We'll be just one minute! Lots to talk through!'

'No problem. Take as long as you need Miss Foye—*Mrs Williams*.'

The young woman cringed at her slip-up. However, being identified took up the least of Damica's headspace. The majority of her energy was being channelled into keeping an unyielding lid over the desire stewing in the very pit of her stomach.

Her footfalls synced with Dorian's until they made it to the privacy afforded by the corner of the room.

Dorian whirled around, propping his fists on his hips as if preparing himself to get down to business. A deep frown line cleaved the centre of his brow, illustrating just how seriously he viewed this quandary.

'We can cancel if that would make you feel more comfortable,' he told her. 'I could do with a nap before dinner anyway.'

Their daylong experience was set to conclude with an evening reservation at the resort's seafood restaurant. Drawing inspiration from its menu, the outdoor dining area was daringly constructed on stilts that were planted in the ocean.

'I'm comfortable with whatever you're comfortable with.'

Damica gave him her vague answer whilst she contemplated the crossroads that represented her needs and her wants. The sensible route included the cancellation of the couples' massage, the overwater dining and the big fat cocktails that were to be thrown in for good measure. The road less travelled was more of a wildcard…

The worst-case scenario ended with Dorian's tongue down her throat. Which wasn't really a negative at all. Was it?

With an absentminded swipe of her tongue, Damica wet her dry lips. Dorian's eyes lowered to latch on to the movement, further shrinking her self-discipline.

Urgh! He was her own personal cookie jar! She'd digested a few bites, but that wasn't enough. Her hunger wouldn't be satisfied until she'd devoured every single chocolate chip, crumb and calorie in the glass container. Her old hedonist ways had taught her that the label of the forbidden increased a person's appeal tenfold.

Ever the gentleman, Dorian averted his gaze from her mouth immediately and dispatched a friendly salute to the admin podium, where the receptionist and Ravi were waiting. He kept his tone hushed as he spoke. 'Would you be comfortable if we did…?'

He left her to fill in the blank. The missing chunk of his enquiry hung in the air, adding to the unbearable tension that had been increasing since…

She wanted to blame their kiss. But a frightening honesty with herself unveiled that she'd craved him—her best friend—since their heart-to-heart on the waterfront. Their first evening together at the resort.

Unflinchingly, she confronted his considerate stare, and along with it the fortnight's worth of pent-up pining and self-imposed frustration. No more dodging, ducking and diving.

'I wouldn't be…*un*comfortable.'

To an outsider, it might appear that she was talking in code. But her subtext—of which Dorian was and had always been a fluent speaker—was loud and clear.

Damica observed the thin layer of hope brightening his eyes, like a film that had been restored to top quality. In lieu of pouncing on the opportunity, he looked deeply into her eyes for any hint of hesitation. His pause amplified the attraction she felt towards him.

'We can stop at any time. Just tell me and we'll get dressed…'

Reframing her perspective, she reordered the timeline of events leading up to her choice. What if last night on the beach hadn't been the catalyst but the final necessary step before taking a leap of faith. What if her feelings for Dorian weren't an obstruction, but actually a feature of her new life post-fame?

They were two single adults vacationing at a luxury holiday resort devoid of paparazzi. There would be no significant harm in giving in to the gravitational pull. Dorian had just broken off an engagement. A wife and kids probably weren't his primary concerns—and he'd never cast her as a wife. Damica would be able to have fun with him without forfeiting her freedom.

'I trust you.'

Adding credibility to her point, she placed her palm on his chest, gifting it with a light and playful pat. Her heart bounced in retaliation to the attack of arousal initiated by her simply coming into contact with his upper body. Likewise, the promise of more seemed to have outmanoeuvred Dorian's qualms, splitting his serious countenance with a slow-growing grin.

She beamed back at him. Her mind was made up and so was his. 'Come on, it'll be fun!'

CHAPTER TEN

DORIAN COUGHED, the display so hyperbolic it sounded as though he was on the verge of hacking up a lung.

'I'm ready for you now, milady.'

Any remaining flecks of Damica's nervousness were successfully sucked into the vacuum of Dorian's foolishness. She emerged from behind the room divider wearing the allocated spa robe, which was embroidered with Étoile Privée's world-famous logo.

'Shut. Up.'

Dorian gasped. 'Is this how you deign to treat a service worker at your beck and call?'

She lazily swung the hanging tie of her robe as if it was a lasso. 'If I find out you've been speaking to journalists about this, you're fired.'

Dorian's humour was a beloved tactic, but it was an ineffective distraction.

'Ouch! Worst boss ever.'

Laughter quaked through Dorian's exposed chest. The dark hair all over his torso congregated to form a trail that disappeared below his waistline. A fluffy white Étoile Privée towel sat low on his hips, acting as the lone preventative barrier to full-frontal nudity on his part.

Quashing the procrastination that was delaying the inevitable, Damica pulled at her belt. The bow at her midsection came loose, and she tugged the garment down her arms.

The robe slithered to the floor, landing around her ankles in a pool of flannel. She wasn't just stripping naked in front of him, she was shedding a skin.

'Where do you want me?'

He reciprocated her steadfast observation, extending their stare-off until the atmosphere was ripe with yearning.

Dorian read her like a book, learning her body in as much depth as his humble eyes would allow. Their adoring shimmer highlighted the symmetry of her soft breasts. His respect underlined her differing skin tones. And his unbearable longing lapped at the tips of her erect nipples and the triangle of hair guarding the apex of her supple thighs.

Unable to move himself from her line of sight, Dorian signalled to the massage table situated somewhere behind her.

Tearing herself away, Damica ascended what could be more accurately described as a *bed*. She lay on her front, settling on the padded white surface and aligning her frame with the curved dips designed to accommodate her breasts and knees. She folded her forearms under the rolled cushion at the head region, and let her cheek sink onto the plush surface.

Dorian came to her aid and drew a covering towel over her lower half, inducing an enticing tingle that outlined the backs of her legs and the swell of her ass.

The retreating sun spared some light for the room, which was a spotless white-and-cream-themed space with a premium fibre thatch roofing. All the doors facing the ocean were wide open to hail the expanse of cerulean water and its fresh, salted tang. She'd seen the Indian Ocean more times than she could count throughout this holiday, but she would never tire of it.

Only Ravi, another recent staple of her surroundings, was missing. He was conducting his duties from the hallway, allowing her and Dorian to be truly alone together for the first time since reuniting.

At the stand beside the massage table Dorian ummed and ahed over the rows of bottles lined up in a display box. An unscrewing sound, a pop and then a wet spillage on her back enlightened her to the fact that he'd made a selection.

Confidently, his palms glided over her exposed flesh, distributing the oil's moisture from the peaks of her shoulder blades to the very base of her spine and then the firm muscles in her neck and shoulders. They moved over the soft slope and rise in the middle of her back. Again and again. Over and over. Leaving no inch of her skin untouched or displeased.

The contented throb strumming at her core aligned with the building tempo of her heart, and goosebumps were awakened by his tactile expertise.

'You're good at this,' Damica said sleepily.

His talents didn't come as a surprise to her, after having witnessed his deft fingers bringing life to his artworks over the years. And under his sure hands, right now, she felt unequivocally safe.

Dorian kneaded the dimples at her lower back, using his thumbs to treat the knots of stress. He leaned down to whisper playfully in her ear. 'And *you* are tense.'

The heat of his breath tickled her ear canal, and Damica found herself intoxicated by his personal scent—fresh bergamot and oranges with rich, earthy oud.

He was so close…

Now was her chance to tell him how she felt.

She started off vague, lifting her head to correct her tilted view of him. 'I've got a lot on my mind.'

'Care to share?' Dorian drifted away to the opposite end of the table to reposition the towel and work on her calves.

Was she supposed to just come out and say it? Read out the entire novel of tenderness and need and angst she'd penned about him in her psyche. She wasn't well versed in how these sorts of things went. Usually, her romantic exploits didn't require much: a quick You up? text at three a.m. or a provocative glance from across a club.

'I've been thinking about how much I like being here with you. Like…really, *really* like being here with you.'

No, that isn't right.

She cringed at herself.

The hundreds of emails she'd written to him had always come with the option to backspace and edit her deepest thoughts to her heart's content. In person, she was nowhere near as concise or eloquent. How she'd managed to condense her emotions into a digital message and a handful of emojis was a grand mystery.

Irrespective of her tongue-tied trip-up, Dorian seemed to be trying his best to understand her.

His fingers drew intricate patterns into her calves, heading nowhere in particular. Damica had never regarded that part of her body as erotic, but Dorian's fingertips seemed to ink whorls of pleasure into her bare skin like…like some sort of sensual tattoo.

'I enjoy your company too,' he said.

This heart-to-heart slugged forward at a torturous pace.

Dorian's touch encircled her ankle next, and her entire body seemed to hum in approval.

'Um…that's good…'

Who was she kidding?

Talking would achieve little. Actions would pass on the message infinitely better than words ever could. Knowing Dorian, she believed he was principled to a fault. The chances of him falling on his own sword were far greater than of him rehashing last night's lip-lock. Even more so when he factored in that she'd explicitly said he wasn't her type…

So what? Types were changeable…they weren't laws. What was she doing?

'Damica, what are you *doing*?' she chided herself out loud, breaching the limits of her rationale.

Dorian immediately retracted his hands from her body—which was the polar opposite of what she wanted.

'I think we should stop,' he said. 'I don't know what's wrong, but—'

Damica scrambled upward, so that she was sitting on the edge of the massage table with Dorian standing between her dangling legs. The scrap of modesty granted by the towel fell away, brunching around her waist—although she didn't care in the slightest about that. The elevated surface meant she had to lean down to get to his mouth. But he eagerly met her halfway, stepping deeper into the invitation of her open thighs and tipping his head back.

Their ready lips collided, forming the beginnings of another messy, imperfect kiss.

Damica kept her eyes closed this time, surrendering wholeheartedly to their shared passion.

With one hand, Dorian securely held the back of her neck, intent on keeping her close whilst he sucked and nipped at her lower lip. Needy for more, Damica yielded and bared her all to him. Everything she wasn't fluent enough to express through words.

Walking away from him at the end of this vacation would kill her.

Whether Dorian could actually interpret the exact contents of her confession was unconfirmed. But he might as well be reading her mind... The slow caress of his lips persisted, in cahoots with the slow, intimate flick of his tongue against hers. Damica moaned into him, equalling his fervour and clutching at the dependable width of his shoulders.

She almost teetered into a disappointed whine when Dorian tore his mouth away.

'Shh…' His forefinger connected with his swollen lips, then jabbed at the closed doorway. On the other side of which stood Ravi.

Dorian's irises shone with a daring glitter, and he shot her a conspiratorial smirk before bending his head to track more kisses down the path of her exposed neck. Her bated breath verged on another crescendo when he journeyed lower to worship her breasts.

His grip on her thighs impelled her to tighten her legs around him. Frantic fingers threaded themselves through his hair and her back arched, pushing the peaks of her breasts further into the generous lapping of his tongue. They were a closed circuit, and an electrifying charge pulsed through Damica, thrusting her pleasure-points towards explosive consequences.

Dorian momentarily came up for air, responding to her gratified sighs with a breathless smile. He wanted this too.

She chanced another peek at the closed door, imploring the heavens that Ravi wouldn't come bounding inside.

Dorian was lost in his reverence of her breasts, and a low groan escaped him. The mist screening Damica's already non-existent inhibitions thickened.

Adulthood had come with many lessons. The most resounding of them all being the realisation that, on occasion, her happiness was lodged in unexpected places. But she knew that, once discovered, she should cherish it with all her might. For as long as the time constraints of their private session would allow.

Her shaky touch roved past his gold chain, accidentally snagging on the metal on its way to his taut back. Dorian's high praise persevered without interruption, his mouth developing a new obsession with her collarbone. Damica's fingers skirted boldly along the frontier of the towel concealing his lower body and…

* * *

Fraught with anxiety, Dorian lurched away from Damica. Those captivating thighs locked around him gave way at his struggle. To make matters worse, his elbow rammed into the box in which the extensive array of massage oil bottles were stowed. The box plummeted to the floor—but not before jostling a neighbouring vase that housed a cluster of decorative white orchids.

Damica tried to save the vase, but it canted out of her reach and succumbed to gravity.

Its final fate was a devastating smash that made the china fragment into a dozen sharp pieces.

A timid yelp unlike anything he'd ever heard from Damica before pierced the air. She scrabbled around the massage table for her towel, so she could cover herself up.

'Your Highness…? Your Highness…?'

Ravi was checking in with him, maintaining enough composure for the both of them. Funny… Dorian had missed him barging into the room.

'Dorian?'

The temporary paralysis holding him hostage was lifted. The first thing he noticed was the unpleasant stickiness binding his toes. Massage oil.

The crate was upended and its entire contents were scattered all over the ground. Poorly closed bottles—he'd cracked open a fair few to smell them earlier—had rolled astray, spilling liquid everywhere. The faux straw stuffing that had served as the objects' padding was now a dispersion of sad, soggy clumps that were beyond saving.

'Nothing to see here, Ravi. I got ahead of myself, that's all,' Dorian muttered, blazing in the flames of his humiliation.

Throwing a temper tantrum wasn't his style, nor appropriate for a man his age. But then again, how could he refer to himself as a man in good faith when he couldn't go more than half an hour without the supervision of a glorified nanny?

Damica, scantily clad in her towel, was helping the spa receptionist to collect and properly fasten the fallen bottles.

'Please don't worry, Miss Foye—I mean *Mrs Williams*. These kinds of incidents happen all the time,' the resort employee assured the group.

Never one to let other people clean up his messes, Dorian stooped down to assist with gathering the tumbled articles. Coincidentally, he and Damica made contact as they zeroed in on the same bottle. The aftermath of their tryst singed through Dorian, inducing a giddy warmth. However, Damica yanked her hand away as though she'd been scorched.

He angled his face strategically to catch her eye, but she kept her vision downcast, denying him at every turn.

What else had he expected? The commotion he'd caused had been so loud that anyone might theorise it was a deliberate act of sabotage. And they would be partially correct in thinking so...

Somehow his body had viciously divorced itself from his mind the second Damica had tugged on his towel. She'd wanted him to take it off, and Dorian had been highly in favour of the suggestion.

In his head only.

Averse to this idea, his body had shut down all possibilities of that happening. Because nudity would lead to sex, and sex would lead to him underperforming.

He hadn't been sexually active...not since receiving his semen analysis results. The doctor had spoken with him at length about his options going forward, and dispelled any myths about a low sperm count leading to impotence. However, that talk had been a mere blur in a previous lifetime, outpopulated by fear and stress.

If the human body was a temple, as the bible dictated that

it was, then Dorian's wasn't in the right state to receive any worshippers.

And Damica deserved the very best.

Now she dumped the last of the debris into the box, which had been reincarnated as a makeshift bin for the ruined goods.

'I'm gonna just…put my clothes back on. See you at dinner.'

The latter end of her hesitant announcement was aimed more at Ravi than him. Damica scooped up her spa robe—the last piece of evidence tracing back to her frolic with Dorian. Then she disappeared behind the dressing screen to recuperate from the whiplash Dorian had inflicted upon her.

Desperation ordered him to chase after her, to beg until she spared him enough time to adequately plead his case. Yet self-loathing had staked its claim, sealing him to his spot on the floor and holding him captive.

In this context, would she find his truth believable, or would she find his explanation too outlandish?

Dorian mustered enough poise to rise to his feet, and subtly he made sure the towel around his waist was positioned to remain in place. The material going rogue was both the last thing he needed and the last ingredient required to transform this already catastrophic ordeal into a full-on nightmare.

A hopeful intake of breath attracted Dorian's crumbling awareness to the mobile phone the spa receptionist was taking out of her uniform pocket. He knew what she wanted, even before she was able to finish voicing her ill-timed request.

'Mr Sotiropoulos—'

'Your Highness,' Ravi interrupted her with a clipped tone.

Dorian knew Ravi smacking the device out of her hands wasn't appropriate, so his trademark irritability would have to do.

'Sorry, Prince Dorian—'

'Your Highness.'

'My apologies… Your Highness.' She had the decency to appear contrite as she held out her phone like a beggar petitioning for pennies. 'Would you mind taking a quick selfie with me? My whole family—especially my mama—are massive fans…'

She recited a few impressive facts about the Concarri Youth Arts Foundation, the crown jewel in his charity endeavours.

'It would be my pleasure.'

Dorian parroted the standard response that he had delivered so frequently it was branded into his lexicon, and hoisted up the towel…loincloth…accessory to his vulnerability, and clamped his hand over the fabric, just to be on the safe side.

Functioning on autopilot, he shuffled to the girl's side as she prepared her phone to snap a picture.

The shot was perfect, consisting of what Dorian classed as his 'model smile'—a feature of a thing, devised to be looked at. He was a national treasure with universal appeal and a beam fit for public occasions. When in private he didn't have much to smile about.

CHAPTER ELEVEN

IT CAME AS a surprise to no one that Dorian did not, in fact, see Damica at dinner. Citing exhaustion from the jet skiing, she kept to her villa for the evening.

Her correspondence with him was still active, albeit distant: the odd emoji in reply to selfies of him nursing a cocktail and pulling comically mournful faces to poke fun at his solo dining experience. But he'd take a solitary crying-in-laughter emoticon over painful silence any day.

She didn't mention the episode at the spa. And Dorian didn't push her to do so. As unfamiliar as their romantic path was to him, he knew her well enough to respect that she hated being smothered.

So he would wait until she was ready.

However, that didn't change how lonely he was. At the overwater restaurant, outnumbered by tables housing happy families, couples and friendship groups, Dorian was reintroduced to a feeling he hadn't undergone since that fateful night he'd asked Damica and Jalen to join him. He'd taken one miraculous step forward, only to flounder down a full staircase.

How beautiful could a paradise like Étoile Privée truly be without a partner of equal footing to enjoy it with? What use was a life with all the world's riches at his disposal if there was no partner or children for him to share them with?

His life was in no way a fairytale, but the similarities

mocked him. Like a knock-off Pinocchio, no matter how much he postured and deluded himself into creating a more masculine mould, he would never be a real man. The setback at the spa was proof.

In spite of all this, Dorian was well acquainted with the notion of breezing his way through adversity. And with a brand-new day came a brand-new chance to convince Damica—and himself—that he was worth the hassle.

His text message didn't go unanswered. Neither did his request for her to meet him on the beach adjoining the Club Enfant clubhouse after breakfast. She showed up.

Jalen bounded ahead of her on the shore, while she hung back armed with her sunglasses and the protruding shadow of her parasol. If the boy's return was a tool to render Dorian defenceless, it worked like a charm. He sank to his knees in the sand, all set for when Jalen catapulted into his arms in a detonation of beach toys and chatter.

At the rate of a thousand words per minute, Jalen recounted his day away from Damica and Dorian, and Dorian hung on every detail.

The day's sandcastle construction project was well underway before he was able to slip away unnoticed. Without prompting, Ravi replaced Dorian, taking up an abandoned spade and shovelling the sand to deepen the moat engineered by Jalen.

Dorian moved over to where Damica was sprawled on a beach towel in the shade. Upon his arrival she tensed, but inched sideways to make room for him. He lay down, propping himself up on his elbow, hoping he appeared in some way suave.

'You were missed last night,' he said, testing the waters.

'So, your clawed friends decided not to stick around, then?' she mused quietly, referring to the crab and lobster spread he'd ordered for one. He'd joked about them secretly being still alive, and hatching a plot to run back to the refuge of their natural habitat.

'Quite the opposite…'

Dorian's gaze bored into the impenetrable lenses of her sunglasses, battling with his own distorted reflection. The dark mirrors inflated his forehead and diminished his eyes.

'Between my meal and Ravi's crabbiness I had more than my fill.'

Her commiseration was hollow. 'Yikes…'

'Yeah.'

Dorian's charm offensive was about as stable as a house of cards. He usually regarded all the literature he'd consumed about romantic love to be full of gross exaggeration. Artistic licence gone wild. Embellishment for the sake of art. But the unbearable silence between himself and Damica revealed the truth behind every cliche and then some.

Without the bright rays of her smile he was trapped in a rainy day, his heart was bludgeoning at his chest walls and he would gladly trade his soul to have it back.

Damica sat up to fish around in her bag, widening the distance between them physically and emotionally. She uncapped her sunscreen. The plastic bottle farted as she squeezed a blob onto her arm. The ridiculous sound only worsened the void dividing them.

He was losing her…

And he had a dearth of functional relationships to coach him through this.

His arrangement with Sophie had been that of two adults allied by lust and common charitable goals.

Outside of lambasting him for not taking part in any sport, Dorian's father took a one-size-fits-all approach to his son's rare pleas for general life advice.

Feeling nervous about giving a speech to the nation? Man up, smoke a cigarette and get over it.

Unsure what to study at university? Throw away those pathetic paintbrushes and man up.

Over thirty and still single? Man. Up.

The closest he'd got to genuine fatherly guidance had been Ravi's observation.

'You don't know what her reaction will be until you actually tell her.'

He could disclose everything—from the profundity of his love for her to his infertility diagnosis—and let the cards fall where there may. It was so simple that it was *scary*. As well as being the very antithesis of the manly ideal he'd been chasing to no avail. But all else was failing, and Dorian had little left to lose and Damica to gain by adopting a different strategy...

'About yesterday, Damica...'

Giving in to the mounting pressure, Dorian let his true emotions out of the floodgates. But seemingly, Damica had done away with her own restrictions too, resulting in a clumsy clash of speech from them both.

'Did I do something wrong...?'

'...for making you feel uncomfortable...'

'Heat of the moment...'

Dorian caught bits and pieces over his own incomprehensible babble about how much he hated this and didn't want to be apart from her ever again. Because he...he...

He fell silent, figuring he was grossly mishandling his revelation and would be better off lending his ear to her. When his turn to speak came around, he'd trust his own capability to speak about his infertility with patience and sensitivity.

You've lamented to her about fame, parental issues and the suffocation of human existence...why would this be any different?

Dorian struggled to calm his jittering nerves.

Damica neatly tucked her ankles underneath her body and sat on her knees, thoroughly rubbing the last of her sunscreen into the skin of her forearm. 'I know I'm not exactly princess material...' she began.

They circumvented the directness required for eye contact, instead settling for watching the recurring movement of her palm over her skin. Dorian was inundated with an awakening heat upon recalling her hushed moans in the spa and his mouth on hers...

'You're right. Princess material you are not.'

He laid his hand over hers, driving her to look at him. Finally. In close range, the transparency of her sunglasses exhibited the dejected droop of her wide eyes.

'But I'm in no position to shame you for that. I can't really be categorised as prince material either. When I said I was here on a sabbatical, I wasn't being truthful with you. I'm here to recuperate because I've received some news about my health... I might not be able to father children...'

Damica's face darkened a shade. Not with anger or repugnance, but because of the stranger suddenly standing over them and thus barricading the sunlight. Brightness rimmed the figure's silhouette and bounced blindingly off the glass screen of his mobile phone.

'Damica? Huge fan! Any chance I could get a photo?'

She conveyed her gratitude to the nameless fan, and politely declined the photo opportunity. But it was too late. The twosome's zone of safety was compromised. The insulated bubble in which he was just Dorian, and she was just Damica, was ruptured. This man—whatever his name was—was a storm cloud, tailored to bring a swift end to the sunshine they'd blissfully enjoyed so far.

'Oh, come on! One picture—just one!' The intruder shook his phone at Damica, sounding less like a fan and more akin to a press photographer.

His choice of holiday attire was inconspicuous...perhaps calculatedly so. Right down to the price tag still attached to his shorts. As though they had been purchased for the sole motive of blending in at the resort. It took a rule-bender to recognise a fellow rule-bender. Was this a paparazzi loophole to counter Étoile Privée's no-photographers-no-journalists policy? Checking into the resort pretending to be a guest... like some sort of Trojan Horse?

'What—too good for your fans now that you've got yourself a prince boyfriend?' the man went on.

Damica swerved the invader's incessant attempts to capture her in a photo, video, or any other pixelated format without her consent. Refusing to spare him an iota of attention, she promptly collected her bag and personal belongings.

'Jalen! Time to go inside, baby!'

Making himself useful, Dorian uprooted the parasol handle from its place in the sand and seized up the towel. In a shuddering heartbeat Ravi was by his side, to usher the Prince away from the scene unscathed. His allegiance lay with the heir to the Concarri throne and no one else.

'No...no...' Dorian veered away from his bodyguard's custody. He wasn't leaving. Not without Damica and Jalen.

The pap in disguise had wedged himself in between the child and his aunt. Damica had her hand splayed over her face as she tried to get around him, however he kept skidding into her path, intent on hounding the superstar into a headline-worthy outburst.

His frantic footsteps and belligerent questioning created an uproar of sand so petrifying that Jalen curled up in a ball, clapping his hands over his eyes.

A compulsion to protect raged in Dorian. He marched over to the 'guest'—no, the bloodthirsty vulture.

'Hey!' he barked, serving himself up as a decoy.

The Étoile Privée resort was an oasis full of celebrities and high-profile clientele. But this particular hound knew he had struck gold with Dorian. Gluttonous for a scandal, he dialled

his speculation up to a more obnoxious level. 'That your secret love child, Prince Dorian? Conceived before your...uh...
manhood failure, Your Highness?'

Vexation, panic and blind fury bubbled over the tidily
drawn margins of Dorian's brain. His sense of responsibility dictated that he fall back, let Ravi do his job, gather up
Damica and Jalen and bolt to safety. Nonetheless, his baser
nature—all the anger he'd spent nearly three decades squash-
ing and suppressing and silencing—won out.

Evidently he was already an object of ridicule to this...
this monster of man. Soon he would be a walking, talking
spectacle for anyone who had access to the worldwide web.
Far right commentators would make him their punch bag.
Talk show panellists would gossip about him shamelessly.
His father would balk. Advisors would talk his ear off about
in vitro fertilisation, medical research, cutting edge treatment and so on.

This peaceful alternative reality at Étoile Privée, with
Damica and Jalen, would be over.

If the time to say goodbye was upon him, Dorian swore
to put up a fight until the bitter end.

'A prince with no balls, huh? Sounds like something made
up by the Brothers Grimm!'

Dorian smacked the phone out of the imposter's grasp,
sending the device somersaulting through the air. It landed
meters away in the sand, demolishing the carefully crafted
towers and turrets of Jalen's sandcastle.

'What the—? That's my private property!' the harasser
complained.

The small window of opportunity available for him to
point out the irony of this whinge quickly expired. Wrestling
out of Ravi's restraining hold, Dorian raced to the place of
demolition, where the photographer was scouring the crumbled sand clumps for his weapon of chaos.

Both men homed in on the hurled phone gleaming in the sand as though they were pirates tussling over legendary riches. Uninterested in playing fair, Dorian elbowed his opponent out of the way and kicked at the mobile phone with the technique of a professional soccer player. The pain erupting in his instep was cancelled out by his contentment in watching the phone fly off into an incoming wave.

'You've destroyed my property! I'll be sending you a bill for all damages caused!'

Playing the victim, the fake guest keeled over and gingerly touched his gut—the location where Dorian had jabbed him during their heated contest. In the eyes of their growing audience, Dorian supposed he did fit the stereotypical mould of a movie villain. Mothers shot him dirty looks, whilst calling their children over and holding them close. Friendship groups ogled his blow-up with raw bemusement.

What they thought of him, Dorian acknowledged, was out of his control. Never mind. It was Damica and Jalen's dignity and honour he was scrimmaging for anyway.

For a second time, Dorian closed in on the instigator of all this upset. Ravi inserted himself into Dorian's warpath, pushing him back and roaring commands to stand down. But his bodyguard's conflict defusion tactics were in vain. Still filled by his own wrath, Dorian determined to go *through* Ravi, seeing as he couldn't get around him.

He charged, dedicating his energy to ramming through six feet of rippling muscles, flesh and bones. As expected, he failed, and his imperious order for Ravi to move out of his way went disregarded.

Since clawing his way over the immovable bodyguard would be a pointless endeavour, Dorian hurled a caution over the human fence in front of him. 'Stay away from them or I'll… I'll…' His index finger jabbed at the air over Ravi's shoulder.

'Is that a threat, Your Highness?' the photographer queried at full volume—for his own benefit as well as for the viewing pleasure of their witnesses. He lifted his palms, leaning into his performance of surrender. Only the predatory shimmer winking from the very bottom of his hungry, pitiless eyes exposed his smoke-and-mirrors show. 'I just wanted a picture of your lady. I meant no harm to the kid. It was you—'

Hellbent on shutting the creature up once and for all, and banishing him to whatever dwelling he'd dared to scuttle out of, Dorian shouted, 'Stay away from my family! You foul, abominable—!'

'Enough!' Ravi whispered. 'I advise you to step away, Your Highness. If not for me, then for Jalen…'

The child's cries dissolved into Dorian's hearing and everything else—the end of Ravi's lecture, the photographer, the bystanders still staring—faded into oblivion. They were not demure sobs but wounded wails that sucker-punched Dorian in the throat, making him wobble backwards. Undoubtedly, *he* was the cause of such distress.

So much of his time recently had been assigned to licking his wounds and anguishing over whether he could conceive a child the traditional way that Dorian hadn't evaluated the thought of a child ever feeling proud enough to refer to him as their dad.

Right now, the prospect was an unequivocal thumbs-down. He was no better than his sorry excuse for a father, who was ruled by his ill temper without any basic compassion.

Once Dorian's hesitation presented itself Ravi pounced, slapping a hand down on his shoulder and directing him towards the beach's closest escape route. The weight of his talon-like clutch was irrefutable. Dorian couldn't wriggle his way out of this one, regardless of the context.

Damica's sun umbrella and towel lay on the sand in twisted shapes, like the casualties of a fatal crime. And their owner hugged her inconsolable nephew to her hip, trying to hide him away from the cause of the harm and vitriol that had led to their neglect.

Him.

CHAPTER TWELVE

ONCE UPON A TIME, when Damica had fantasised about inviting the Crown Prince of Concarre into her sleeping quarters, it had been in the lead-up to more pleasurable events. The current situation they were tangled up in was anything but that.

She left the bedroom door open a crack, so she could survey Jalen where he was sitting cross-legged on the living room rug, under the spell of his favourite cartoons. Ravi worked around him, amassing the scrunched-up tissues used to wipe the boy's tears and snot. Somewhere in her and Dorian's much-needed chat Damica planned to advocate for the security guard to receive a substantial pay rise.

Incapable of delaying the unavoidable for much longer, Damica took off her sunglasses and turned to face Dorian.

'"My family…"?' She duplicated the wording from his meltdown on the beach, but went easy on the yelling of it out of fear that Jalen might overhear. '"Stay away from my… *family*"?'

Dorian started to walk around the hastily made king-sized bed, then immediately retired this course of action. He stayed firmly in his own territory, near the sliding glass wall that overlooked the villa's swimming pools. Although his arms were tucked respectfully behind his back, his pose held more self-restraint than royal honour.

'Damica, I can explain…'

'Yeah, please do!' She chuckled uneasily, still compar-

ing the irate mortal on the beach to the picture of civility
before her.

'Uh… I love you.'

'Love you too,' she fired back casually. 'Always have.'

'No, allow me to clarify. I am in love with you—in every
comprehensible way that one human being can love another,'
Dorian asserted.

Damica said nothing. At the spa, in the thick of foreplay,
she'd been ready for this. She'd been naked, writhing, basically offering herself up on a silver platter, begging for
Dorian to take her.

And he'd spat her out as if she was a toxin.

Following his disclosure that he was having trouble with
his…y'know—something that was clearly tough and burden-
some—Dorian's U-turn made sense. But then the slate had
been wiped clean and a new narrative had suddenly been in
motion. One she hadn't been privy to.

While he'd screamed with such certainty that she and Jalen
were his family, Damica's confidence in knowing him wholeheartedly had diminished.

'So you meant "family" as in husband, wife and child.
Not…not siblings or whatever. Good to know.' She dumped
her sunglasses on the bedside dresser, just so her aimless
hands would have something to do. Darkly, she added, 'Because I'm pretty sure brothers aren't supposed to play with
their sister's tits.'

Normally being crude brought her little shame. In this instance, though, she almost choked on what she'd intended to
be a droll and snarky comment.

Dorian's face was pinched with remorse. He was clearly
aware that the severity of his misstep was leaps and bounds
beyond simply kicking a pap's phone into the ocean. All it
would take was one anonymous tip to a celebrity gossip pub-
lication or forum and their privacy would be gone. Nothing

got people talking like a royal romance—especially the unconventional kind.

'That was a…a Freudian slip. Please accept my deepest apologies.'

Heading back towards her safety zone near the door, Damica grasped the door knob, as if dependent on the coolness of the metal. She was in danger of overheating…her brain activity was computing too many optics and requests, and…

The amplification of her voice dipped, to sever all chances of her nephew eavesdropping. 'Keep them. Or, better yet, give them to Jalen.'

'I…'

Dorian's face was awash with grimness. Bringing up Jalen's well-being was probing a soft spot…and perhaps a low blow. But Damica's guilt for dressing up her true sentiments as the hypothetical hurt feelings of her infant nephew was only partial. Any surviving culpability was cancelled out by the fact that she was correct.

'We both know how this is going to go. When this vacation is over, you're gonna fly back to Concarre and marry a model citizen. You'll have about three children—an heir, a spare and an extra—via the latest fertility procedure that unleashes biological warfare on a woman's body. Then you'll toss Jalen aside like he was nothing—'

Out of breath, Damica cut herself off to recoup.

Dorian called her out flatly, before she could recommence her escalating rant. 'You're hiding behind Jalen.'

A minute bud of hope sprouted in the same place where Damica's childhood happiness had wilted.

Maybe…maybe he did like her for her? How else would he be able to read her like a book?

All the better to control her with.

She killed the shoot of optimism, yanking at its roots and detaching herself from such naivete.

Her denial was harsh. 'Am *not*.'

'Are too,' Dorian insisted, refusing to release her from the impassioned stare-off he'd locked her in.

She squeezed the door knob so tightly that she almost lost all sensation in her fingers. Suddenly the high-ceilinged bedroom was too small and the walls too constricting. They weren't in a Maldives villa, but a breathtaking dolls' house: Dorian's fictional dreamland. Every tale needed main characters for the storyteller to boss around, and in this story Damica was the cookie cutter girlfriend/wife/love interest/mother of his imaginary children. To him, she wasn't a person, but rather a vessel enabling him to live out his fantasies.

The frantic shake of her head was useless in drying her welling tears. 'You…you don't really love me.'

'I do, Damica!' he exclaimed.

Oh, he wanted to get loud? She could get loud.

'Dorian, wake up! I am a single woman of childbearing age. You're a man, desperate for a family.'

She gestured at the door, on the other side of which Jalen still sat. So much for keeping quiet. Damica tugged the door closed, to at least muffle the contents of their argument. There was no way she was letting an almost-but-not-quite-breakup cause Jalen's loss of innocence.

Walking over to the bed, Damica speared a knee into the mattress and reached for the wall above the headboard, where she had exhibited Dorian's artful drawing depicting himself with her and Jalen. In light of the new information, she saw that what she'd initially interpreted as a sweet gesture was obviously the sum of Dorian's projections.

Her rushed hand resulted in a careless extraction that tore the drawing's corners, leaving tiny, jagged triangles of sketchbook paper and balls of sticky tack attached to the wall.

After fighting to stand up, she rolled the piece of paper

into a tube and prodded it at Dorian, urging him to take his gift back.

'Please take it.'

'No, I drew that for you and I want you to keep it.'

'W-we're just temporary Band-Aids that you're using to heal a long-term problem. And when you discover we don't fit your made-up expectations you'll be disappointed.'

She despised the fact that her voice waited until that very moment to crack. She pierced her lower lip with her front teeth to halt its tremble.

Here we go again.

Damica buckled into her metaphorical seat belt and gathered all her other protective mechanisms to shelter herself from incoming hurt.

Her past was repeating itself in the present, and she had the foresight to accurately prophesy how their 'romance' would cross over into tragedy. Back then, the Feir Channel execs and her mother had had big business plans for her—their family-friendly product—and there had been repercussions when she wouldn't bend to their every will and whim. This time around she could save herself from unnecessary heartbreak.

The real her—Damica Foye—could never match up with the fictional ideal that existed in Dorian's head. She could never be his perfect princess bride.

But Dorian's stance didn't waver, and the stubborn clench of his jaw grew more defined. 'There's nothing temporary about what I feel for you.'

'Look me in the eyes and swear to me that you're not using me and Jalen to live out a fantasy, Dorian,' Damica demanded, refusing to believe him. She tapped the roll of paper against her thigh impatiently.

The silence that followed spoke volumes.

Damica let out a guttural scoff, holding on to her stomach so she didn't keel over. His reaction was incredibly informative. But so what? At this point, if she didn't laugh, she would cry.

'See? Look, you can't even deny it!'

Dorian pushed a hand through his bedraggled hair in a poor attempt to smooth out the mess he'd caused. 'At the start I did—'

'Wow!' Damica's heart shattered. Having suspicions was bad enough, but confirmation was a death sentence.

'But I realised that wasn't fair to you. Or to Jalen.'

It was a strong finish. He'd pieced his tenuous reasoning together convincingly. However, the damage had already been done.

Damica's voice was flat and devoid of any life. 'I think we should stay away from each other for the next few days. I need time to think.' Time to add insult to her own injury. 'The media isn't gonna let me breathe when I get back home. Us being seen together is only gonna add fuel to the fire.'

'I love how rebellious you are…and how you stick out your tongue ever so slightly when you're concentrating on something very deeply. You have a spectacular way with words, and I love the way you make fun of me. I love *you*—not some archaic notion of what a woman "should" be!'

It seemed Dorian was fighting to restore the zest and sparkle of their connection. But the elephant in the room was only reincarnated into a larger, sturdier model that reminded Damica that this wasn't her or Dorian's first time at this particular rodeo. He'd ditched her before, when she hadn't met his goody-two-shoes standards. How could she be sure he wouldn't get rid of her again?

Seeing that she was unreceptive to his declaration, he strode over and held her delicately by the shoulders. She didn't dare look anywhere other than at the sorrowful chasm behind his inspection. Dorian was desperately seeking reciprocation…and she was giving him nothing.

'I will give up my crown for you. Anything. Just say the word and...just let me fix this, Damica.'

Now he was just throwing promises at the wall to see what would stick and make her change her mind. She didn't get it. Why place her on such a high pedestal only to knock her down later down the line?

But Dorian seemed genuinely distraught over her pulling away, which scared her even more. The trap he was setting for her was so temptingly sweet that it was too good to be true. Like all candy, his promise was overwhelmingly sugary and doomed to rot her. Dorian would resent her when she failed to match up to the kind of domestic bliss he hungered for...wouldn't he?

In her lifetime, Damica had endured a lot—too many unfavourable conditions. But she knew with certainty that she wouldn't be able to survive Dorian falling out of love with her. Just the thought of him hating her was petrifying.

'Damica...?'

This was too much. With tensions and stakes running so high, she was beginning to feel boxed in. The Maldives getaway was supposed to have been a new start, an escape from the scars of her old life. Yet now the Étoile Privée resort had become an air-tight bubble in which she was being forced to confront her deep-rooted anxieties.

Well...there was ownership, agency and power in choosing which battles she wanted to fight, wasn't there? She was in over her head with Dorian—perhaps the mature thing to do would be to back away.

Her panic subsided a little with this line of thinking. So she would go all in.

Say something—anything to get him to back off.

Realising that her mouth was uncomfortably dry, she swallowed nervously. She held Dorian's fragile gaze, respecting him enough to look him in the eyes.

'I need time to deal with…your…your junk being…broken,' she lied.

Her wording was clunky and ungraceful, but the implication was explicit.

She might as well have stabbed him in the gut with a sword.

She watched Dorian's composure splinter, revealing a preview of his inner turmoil and agony. It went without saying that his fertility complications would cause a lot of controversy with his father, the royal advisors and the people of his country. It must be eating him up inside.

The skin on Damica's shoulders dropped in temperature as Dorian let her go, removing his naturally warming touch. She turned and spun the paper tube in her hands, ashamed of pretending not to wholeheartedly accept his fertility status.

'Take as much time as you need,' he said. 'I'll be at my villa.' He was covering up his dismay with formal politeness. 'When…if you're ready.'

Dorian's reconstruction of himself was quick, but Damica was well aware that her comment had floored him.

Too ashamed to speak, she stepped aside, freeing up the route to the closed bedroom door so he could get away from her. Her movement was concurrent with his, and they were suddenly snared in an awkward shuffle in which they were trying to get around each other, but stepping into each other's paths.

They both surrendered, stilling to let the other person pass first.

Dorian sent Damica a tight-lipped smile that was far removed from his classic radiance. He seemed to be analysing the structure and contours of her face, as though committing them to his memory. Then he leaned in to press a tender kiss to her cheek. So tender that she was terrified she might break into a million irreparable pieces in front of him if he prolonged his exit any longer.

She hung on to the familiar smell of his sweat and his cologne. Bergamot and oud.

With a defeated tug, he gently reclaimed the drawing from her guilty fingers.

And then he was gone, slipping out of the bedroom, opening and closing the door with a subdued click.

You made the right decision, she told herself.

Closing her eyes, she exhaled deeply before taking an uneven breath. She prioritised the regulation of her erratic breathing pattern over wiping away the wetness dotting her cheeks.

Inhale for four seconds, hold for seven seconds, exhale for eight.

You made the right choice!

Then why did she feel so wrong on an atomic level?

CHAPTER THIRTEEN

Believing that he and Ravi would be able to continue their stay at the Étoile Privée Resort after the public spectacle he'd made of himself on the beach was wishful thinking. Yet Dorian clung to the edges and points of hope, as though he was a passenger on a shooting star. Present for a short while. Subsequently gone. In the blink of an eye.

The door separating him from Damica closed with a terminating click. Ravi shot to his feet, standing tall and rigid. Such formality exposed the fact that he'd overhead...

Dorian realised that he couldn't even refer to him and Damica's argument as a 'lovers' spat'. She would actually have to love him back for the word 'lovers' to correctly apply to them. Adding on to that, there had been nothing trivial about their impassioned debate. The noun 'spat' did not resonate.

His first taste of true romance had doubtlessly been eventful. He felt as though he'd been chewed up and expelled. He wondered how on earth people in their right minds could so eagerly chase this devastating emotion.

'Dorian...can we go and get ice cream?' Jalen tugged restlessly on the leg of Dorian's sand-crusted beach shorts.

'I think it would be better for you to ask your aunt.' Dorian knelt down so that they could converse on an equal level, eye to eye.

'But you and Auntie Dami were shouting at each other,' Jalen pointed out with youthful disdain.

Dorian got the impression that his and Damica's split was a major inconvenience to Jalen's appetite. The child's simple view almost made him burst out laughing, despite his current feelings of ruination.

He did wince, though. 'I'm sorry you had to hear that.'

By the sofa, Ravi let his eyes dart to the villa door discreetly. Dorian knew what that meant.

Wrap this up quickly, Your Highness. We must vacate the premises.

'I love you and your aunt very much, Jalen. No matter what happens next, I want you to remember that.'

Jalen's confusion at this took the form of a pronounced pout. Nonetheless, he agreed to Dorian's request for a hug. He kissed the boy's forehead and held him protectively.

Damica was wrong. When he looked at Jalen, he didn't see a placeholder for the child he might never be able to have. He saw the face of a unique child, overflowing with adventure and demands for the world around him, who had a bright future ahead of him. But Damica had also been right... It had been unfair to pursue her and Jalen's company with the intention of using them as a salve.

He wasn't healed. In fact, he was far from it.

If Dorian wished to mend himself on a psychological front, he needed to learn to accept his infertility diagnosis. The summoning to do so was swift.

'I've just received a lengthy, angry voicemail message from the palace communications office,' Ravi gravely informed Dorian, once they had departed from the family's rented villa.

They had left Damica still sequestered in her bedroom, and Jalen with his head stuck in his blissfully ignorant world of animation and high-action storylines.

Ravi gave the Prince a succinct update on the fast-progressing aftermath of his confrontation on the beach. 'Someone was filming. They uploaded the video to a social media site.'

'How bad is it?' Dorian asked, although he could already foretell the severity level.

Astronomical.

Jaw clenching in irritation, the bodyguard thrust his mobile phone at Dorian. 'Here. I've lost all hope that anything I say to you will matter, Your Highness.'

OMG! Prince Dorian of Concarre has gone berserk!! #good-boygonebad

A shaky hand had managed to capture the infamous 'stay away from my family' line, and Dorian, Ravi, Damica and Jalen hurrying away from the scene.

The view count was climbing rapidly. But what crushed Dorian was the footage of him reaching for Damica's hand in an effort to portray a united front and her shifting away from him.

Ravi stuffed his phone back into the pocket of his sandy blazer. The two men marched down the connected wooden pathways, following the quickest route back to Dorian's waterfront villa.

'I must speak with the security team as soon as possible to devise the best strategy for your safety, Your Highness. That video is geotagged, and we are sitting ducks here at the resort with no extra backup. I know you want to spend more time with Miss Damica and little Mr Jalen, but we may have to leave—'

'And I will go willingly,' Dorian interrupted with a clipped tone.

Dorian and Ravi were standing in the main reception building bright and early the next morning, to check out of the Étoile Privée resort. However, the only light experienced by

Dorian was that of the Maldives' natural climate. Sunglasses covered his twitching, unfocused, sleep-deprived eyes and he was tempted to rearrange his numerous suitcases around him to form a hut, and collapse within their enclosure.

'Thank you for visiting us here at Étoile Privée the Maldives,' the male receptionist said pleasantly as Dorian handed over his villa key card. 'We wish you and your companion safe travels.'

As though on cue, Ravi barked into the mouthpiece of his mobile phone. Something about how the car transporting them to the private airfield was moving at a snail's pace.

Dorian mustered up his finest smile, although a mournful jerk pulled at the corners of his lips. 'Thank you. May your day be delightful.'

He turned away just as an urgent yawn invaded his jaw. The automatic doors of the foyer glided open, prompting Dorian to check the identity of the entrants for the umpteenth occasion.

Not Damica and Jalen.

A silver-haired oil tycoon, whom Dorian had met before once or twice, meandered inside with his young wife and children. The youngest of the three kids cantered ahead to the concierge desk situated nearby and pressed belligerently on the polished bell. The patriarch took off his wide-brimmed hat and replied to Dorian's stare with a friendly nod and a self-deprecating roll of his eyes.

Dorian couldn't tell whether the child's constant dinging of the bell or the family's matching sun visors were the targets of this father's joking response. Irrespective, he found both elements undeserving of dislike. In fact, he was congested with envy.

'I also need time to deal with...your...your junk being... broken...'

'Being...broken...'

'Broken...'

The rich family went on their way, and Dorian wrestled with his self-pity. He wasn't broken. Damica hadn't given him the validation he'd needed so badly, though, which burned with the severity of a bayonet assault. All his preconceived fears had come to fruition right then and there. In her eyes, the deficiency of his sperm meant he was incomplete and fragmented, and there was no point in refuting her belief any further.

Those hours he'd spent drawing, encapsulating all her nuances, had amounted to nothing.

His outlining the hollows, heights and extremities of his love for her hadn't evoked a positive reaction either.

And he suspected that his spur-of-the-moment pledge to renounce his title as Crown Prince and Heir Apparent had been the final nail in the coffin.

If he loved her as he'd so boldly claimed—which he did!— then he was obliged to listen to everything she said. And she wanted to be apart from him.

He wouldn't defy her or read between the lines, or try and psychoanalyse her. But in spite of this Dorian had a strong hunch that she'd vetoed his bid for mutual love because she was convinced that he was just like her mother and all those Feir Channel decision-makers. By stupidly admitting to pigeonholing Damica and Jalen at the very beginning of his stay, Dorian had accidentally implicated himself in a far greater crime: a covert plot to control Damica.

That blundered confession had been all the evidence she'd needed. Dorian had seen no good in voicing this and prolonging their disagreement, so he'd let her go. He couldn't manipulate her into saying she loved him.

His hand delved into the pocket of his shorts and his fingers brushed the folded edges of the goodbye letters he'd spent the duration of his sleepless night penning.

He'd been telling the truth when he'd let her know that he would wait for her at his villa. But now, with Ravi, the palace communications office and his father simultaneously breathing down his neck, Dorian knew he was unable to stall for much longer.

Damica hadn't called him during the night, nor had she stopped by his villa that morning. There was no telling if she would come over the coming days. Maybe she'd elected silence to speak on her behalf.

Dorian would sooner have words speak for him.

The automatic doors of the reception building coasted open again. However, Dorian didn't bother to scrutinise the newcomer.

Ravi did. 'Finally,' he complained aloud. 'I thought you had taken a detour in order to go sightseeing. Would you like a drink now that you are here? Our situation is not one of urgency, after all.'

The new arrival was their driver. Registering the magnitude of Ravi's hostile and sarcastic greeting, the man made a beeline for Dorian's suitcases, bowed, then started piling them onto one of the silver luggage trolleys provided by the resort.

He apologised profusely. 'I am so very deeply sorry, Your Highness. I know any excuse I give you will not be good enough—'

Dorian put up a hand to curb the employee's incessant grovelling. 'All is fine, I assure you. Please...'

On this holiday he'd experienced a semblance of normality in spending time with Jalen and Damica. The imbalance of power between himself and his driver was now...disconcerting. Suddenly being waited on hand and foot, to the point of worship, wasn't only extremely infantilising, it also felt wrong.

Under Dorian's orders, the driver shut up immediately and got to work, wheeling the trolley outside to the open boot of an official state car.

Although the vehicle was stationary, Dorian was metaphorically already inside it, cruising along and pondering over an intersection that would not be visible through the window. The road leading to Damica had been blockaded—and she'd laid the bricks and cement herself. The other route presented a lonely existence, fenced inside stifling tradition.

These two bleak options couldn't be all life had in store for him, surely?

Dorian revisited the concrete foundations of his life as the Crown Prince of Concarre. Red-blooded, patriotic, old-fashioned masculinity was one of the core building blocks. Nonetheless, the bombshell of his worrisome sperm motility had caused Dorian's world to come crumbling down. There was now a giant hole for him to crawl out of—to freedom, should he wish for it.

Proposing that he would give up his crown for Damica had been an insane amount of pressure to put on her, and an easy way out for Dorian. What he needed to do was walk away from royal life because he wanted to.

He was not broken. The spotlight on his fertility status wouldn't result in his ruination. It was simply a magnifying glass over the workings of his body, and a vital chance for him to learn about himself. With such knowledge came the power to make informed decisions relating to his own health. It was a set of doors that would open up wider public conversations about male infertility. Dorian was the one in control.

But by no means did he feel confident about how to navigate whatever came next. He was only secure in his call for something new. A third avenue.

The driver deposited the last of Dorian and Ravi's luggage into the boot. After pushing the lid shut, he trooped around the vehicle and opened the back door for the Prince.

'Are you ready to leave, Your Highness?' Ravi checked with him.

Dorian strummed the corners of the pieces of paper in his pocket, undecided over whether he wanted to pull them out.

CHAPTER FOURTEEN

THE TIME HAD come for Damica to face the music.

'Jalen, slow down!' she called.

Unsatisfied with her rate, he'd streaked ahead towards their destination: Dorian's villa.

Moving her watchful eyes between the boy in her care and trying not to trip over her own two feet, Damica shifted through the crumpled and dog-eared pieces of paper in her hands. The sheets—decorated at the top centre with a tiny star with wings, the Étoile Privée logo—had been worn down by her restless fingers. Likewise, her blurry vision was symptomatic of the hours spent agonising over the wording and memorising paragraphs upon paragraphs of her own scribbled handwriting.

Less than twenty-four hours had passed since her faux pas with Dorian, but it might as well have been a century—and Damica was desperate to make amends.

Scraping at the wall that overlooked her bed was only so useful... Four small sticky-tack stains refused to vanish, as if objecting to the missing art piece. And Damica had further tried to tidy away the remnants of the volcanic afternoon by distracting herself and Jalen with ice cream. But their ice cream parlour visit had quickly devolved into an unforgiving interrogation.

Why had she and Dorian been shouting together?

Because…because he'd said something special to her and she hadn't believed he was telling her the truth.

How did she know he wasn't telling the truth? Did she have a mind-reading machine like the super-villain in one of the cartoons Jalen was obsessed with?

She hated to burst his bubble, but no, she did not have the power of telepathy.

Oh…well, could she and Dorian just make up and be friends again? Jalen wanted to go back to the beach and re-build the sandcastle wrecked by that strange shouty man with the phone.

Damica had been tickled by her young nephew's lack of complexity. Inspired by it, too.

She didn't have any mind-reading prowess, and she didn't have a third eye that could see into the future either. Ergo, there was no definitive way to verify whether Dorian was deceiving her, or to know if any romantic relationship they had would really crash and burn.

Without meaning to, Jalen had bulldozed the line of think-ing she'd so religiously been parroting to herself. All the pieces were now scattered into newer categories. What she did know versus what she didn't know.

Damica had three unquestionable points.

Point One: Since she'd come together again with Dorian, he had conducted himself towards her with a reverence that was consistent and stable.

Point Two: When he'd confidently listed the ingredi-ents that contributed to his love for her, she had felt terror-stricken.

Point Three: She'd referred to his fertility troubles as 'broken junk', but she hadn't meant it.

Damica's arranging and rearranging and additional rearranging of her reasoning had kept her up for half the night. What had started as a basic record of her thoughts had turned into a fully-fledged written admission of her fright and her feelings for Dorian.

She *did* love him.

To allow dread to dictate her life meant that she was still being restricted and controlled. The very thing she didn't want. Dorian had never imposed any physical or psychological limits on her. Quite the opposite. For the entire time she'd known him, and over the last few weeks, he'd been an advocate and supporter of her independence. But he wasn't a blind follower either, and would call her out when they didn't see eye to eye.

Surrendering to the uncertainty of romantic emotion was the wildest and freest thing she could do.

Calling Dorian broken had been pure projection on Damica's part. *She* was the one who was messed up. So messed up that she couldn't fully appreciate a good thing when it was right in front of her.

She hoped it wasn't too late to make amends.

Just like when she'd attended all those music industry award shows, she'd pre-planned exactly what she wanted to say, so she wouldn't become a pile of disjointed, incoherent sentences.

By the time she joined Jalen on the doorstep of Dorian's holiday villa, the young boy was leaping up and down on the 'welcome' doormat. Damica placed a stilling hand on his jumping shoulder and signalled for him to knock on the door.

The impact of Jalen's small fist on the wood caused it to drift open. Damica's brow crinkled. Why was the door already open?

The droning suction of a vacuum cleaner meandered from

within the rented home, and a resort maid stuck her head around the corner that marked the entrance into the living room.

'Good morning,' she addressed them diplomatically. 'Housekeeping.'

'House...keeping?' Damica parroted, just to make sure she hadn't misheard what the maid was telling her.

The employee nodded patiently.

An eraser seemed to be rubbing over the neat, precise calligraphy Damica had used to mentally choreograph today's heartfelt reconciliation.

Dorian was supposed to be here, with a pen tucked behind his ear and a heavily annotated literary classic tucked under his arm. And Ravi would be plonked in the doorway like some sort of sacred Easter Island statue, devoted to the villa's main entryway.

'I don't get it.' Jalen's head ping-ponged between his aunt and the uniformed woman in her fifties. 'Where's Dorian and Ravi?'

'I don't know...'

You don't know? You do, though.

'I'm sorry, there are no guests currently staying at this villa. I recommend visiting the concierge desk to check whether any messages were left for you.'

Dorian had left without so much as a goodbye.

Damica's hip connected awkwardly with the doorway as Jalen barged past her and ran out of the villa.

'Jalen, where are you—?'

Damica quickly uttered her apologies to the maid they'd disturbed and restored the villa's door to its slightly open position. Hopping out of her flip-flops and collecting them speedily, she bolted after her nephew.

Jalen was scampering ahead, but still firmly within view.

Somewhere during the unexpected workout she scrunched her pieces of paper into a ball, ready to cast her unrealistic optimism in the trash.

Naive. Foolish. Gullible.

Those things were what she was. Dorian had played her, and that whole Nice Guy monologue, with its assurance that he would be waiting for her at his villa, had clearly been bull.

Suddenly a splinter of wood wedged its way into the underside of her big toe. Damica cried out in pain, the momentum of her velocity slowing down into a limp.

You deserve this, crowed a tiny voice in her head that relied on dysfunction. *Karmic punishment.*

What had she expected? That he would welcome her back with open arms? How? She'd rejected him on the grounds of his undetermined fertility...which was scathingly personal. Every person had their limits—even Dorian. Patience was like an hourglass. The supply of sand seemed endless, but eventually the last of the grains would spill through the gap and no time, nor sand would remain.

Damica had run out of chances, and there was no option for a redo.

She hissed in discomfort as she extracted the splinter from her tender skin. When she had recovered, she managed to spot Jalen vanishing into the Étoile Privée reception building.

Damica hobbled through the parting automatic doors, luxuriating in the cool of the air-conditioned space. She closed in on her target: Jalen, in the queue of guests at the concierge desk. He was currently second in line.

'How many times do I have to tell you to stop running off, huh?' Damica snapped at him.

The authoritative, ill-tempered bass in her voice was unlike her, but she was at her wits' end now. Clamping a penalising hold around his elbow, she pulled him towards the exit. She reserved her strength, hoping her no-nonsense demeanour would do most of the heavy lifting.

Silly mistake.

Jalen wrangled himself out of captivity and scarpered to reclaim his position at the front of the forward-shuffling queue. 'No!' he yelled.

'Jalen…' she cautioned. 'You have three seconds to get over here or I'll…'

Do what?

She was only role-playing a demanding parent—although her frustration at the disobedient kid was oh-so-real.

Her nephew stamped his foot. 'I want Dorian!'

'Well, he's gone—and he's not coming back so…so get over it!' she shrieked. At herself more than at him.

They were causing a scene now. The very thing she *didn't* want to do. She was supposed to be lying low and doing ordinary things. Not falling in love with princes of foreign nations and getting involved in public arguments. Not being a poor caretaker for her family or having her hopes lobbed about only seconds before they were smashed to smithereens.

Holidaying at Étoile Privée had been a grave misreading of her needs.

Damica's swimming tears smeared the faces of their audience into indistinct blobs.

Jalen was up next at the concierge desk. He bounded up to the flawlessly polished counter and asked outright, 'Have you seen my friend Dorian?'

Wetness streaked the back of Damica's hand as she wiped her eyes. She walked unevenly to the concierge desk and quietly queried the attendant as to whether any messages had been left for her. She gave her full name and villa number—for show rather than diligence.

With a downcast stare, she distracted herself with a mean-

ingless analysis of the gleaming silver counter bell. The eager
tapping of Jalen's feet made her stomach clench with angst.

Damica was already equipped to hear the employee say,
no. Jalen, on the other hand, would be crushed. She'd tried
her best to shield him from the devastation, but now he would
have to live through it firsthand. Damica would do everything
in her power to help him pick up the pieces…

'Ah, yes. One message here for you!' The receptionist
whipped out a thin pile of folded sheets of paper.

A disorientating lightness overcame Damica, so that she
forgot she had arms, and her flip-flops, the screwed-up paper
ball—everything—nearly went clattering to the floor.

'There…is?'

The next interaction with the concierge was a blur.

Paper in hand, Damica virtually sleep-walked over to
a corner of the resort reception area and collapsed. Jalen
plonked himself down next to her, fussing over the written
correspondence in Damica's grip.

'What does it say? What does it say?'

After a while, his fickle attention span migrated to the
ball-shaped mass of paper composed of Damica's practised
declarations.

Forcing herself to extend her curt, rapid breaths into longer, more relaxing inhalations and exhalations, Damica
opened the makeshift booklet.

Comfort spread over her taut chest when she saw the abundance of lines written in Dorian's orderly, looped handwriting.

He'd left her a letter.

Dear Damica,
In the wake of everything that's happened between us…
every stutter, every blunder and mishap…it's fitting that

I return to the way in which you and I communicate with each other best. The written word.

Let me start off this letter by clarifying: if you are reading this, I am likely no longer staying at the Étoile Privée resort. Ravi has informed me that it would be dangerous to remain in residence after my latest exploit.

I know I would deeply regret exposing you and Jalen to any more harm, so I have made the difficult decision to depart the Maldives and return to the royal household in Concarre. Please believe that it was my intention to wait for you at my villa until you were ready for us to discuss the scope of our feelings.

Whilst we may be physically parted, I hope that an emotional convergence of some sort can take place between us, if you wish.

When I first laid eyes on you, twenty years ago, in that stuffy maintenance closet, I fell truly, madly and deeply in love with you. It was, and still is, a love full of friendship and great admiration.

Before you, I did not know what it meant to have a confidante who made me feel unequivocally safe and cherished. Who would entertain my tedious rambles about Monets and Klimts. Who understood the endless burdens of growing up under such an unrelenting public microscope.

I desire to bring you this kind of stability tenfold— not to satisfy my own ego, but because this is simply what a friend should do. My romantic regard of you is admittedly a newer and unfamiliar development, but I trust the foundation that we've built together.

If our splendid time together at Étoile Privée has taught me anything, it's that pleasure sometimes lies on the other side of risk. Whether exploring each other in-

timately, running through a Maldivian jungle, or hiding in closets, I would like you to be my partner, Damica.

I recognise how unfair and unjust it was of me to project my insecurities onto yourself and Jalen. Along with my appreciation, please see my apology. Swearing to forfeit my title in exchange for your love was a gross display of my desperation and a grave misinterpretation of your character.

Again, your fierce independence is one of your many inspiring traits. I failed you by treating your mind like something that could be easily swayed. Furthermore, I accept that whilst I aspire to be a recipient of your love, I cannot place any responsibility on you to affirm my manhood.

That task begins and ends with me.

What exactly will come next, I am unsure of. But I am confident that I have loved you for so long that I do not know how to go on without caring for you.

The media wildfire I have caused has ruined the possibility of a slow and peaceful meeting in the outside world, so I will keep my distance from you. There are plenty of matters for me to attend to in the meantime, the most urgent being whether my future is compatible with that of my nation.

A year from now, if there is any room in your heart for me, I would very much like to visit.

For ever and always yours,

Dorian

PS Please give Jalen a hug for me...

Damica shifted through the pages, rereading her favourite phrases and deriving new meanings from others.

There was an extra sheet at the back, which she assumed contained additional paragraphs of Dorian's words. However, upon closer inspection she found a well-known picture: the drawing of herself, Jalen and Dorian. Damica beheld its familiar aspects—Dorian lifting Jalen, whilst devoting himself to her—and visually digested the new.

An assembly of crease folds ran through the paper, and the shading was beginning to smudge. Not to mention the torn off corners. This image was less picture-perfect family and more...*real*.

At the bottom right corner was an email address that was undeniably a mature upgrade from mrdoryfish7@inbox.com.

The giggle puncturing Damica's throat thinned into a relieved sob.

Blindly, she felt around for Jalen and roped him into a hug.

EPILOGUE

One year later

DORIAN PULLED HIS bowtie loose, so that the silk-satin material hung freely around his neck. Blood circulation was restored to his head, and his shoulders relaxed when he undid not one, not two, but three buttons at the top of his dress shirt.

The red carpet for the Man of the Year Awards carried on uninterrupted, and Dorian took a moment to treasure the simple luxury of adjusting his uncomfortable outfit without having to consider the Concarri Royal Code of Conduct.

He followed his assistant to where the next interviewer was waiting with a microphone, a camera person and an ambitious smile.

'The night is young here at the Man of the Year Awards in Los Angeles! And I'm honoured to be joined by none other than His Grace Dorian Saadoun Sotiropoulos, Duke of Mirenz. Your Grace, you are set to receive the Gamechanger Award tonight—how are you feeling?'

Dorian was a picture of gallantry, in spite of the microphone being plunged into his face. 'Blessed…truly…'

Whilst some aspects of Dorian's life had changed beyond recognition, others remained the same.

After his speedy departure from the Maldives to Concarre, he'd booked a lengthy appointment with his father. As expected, the King had branded his son 'weak', 'insolent', and every other synonym for 'less than'. Instead of shrinking in the face of such abuse, as his reflexes had demanded, Dorian had stood his ground.

Renouncing his title as the nation's prince, publishing a memoir and partnering with a health charity to create a campaign focusing on men's infertility had been a wholly improvised reinvention. But Dorian had committed himself to making this rough design a reality over the last twelve months. In truth, he was still a work in progress, but overall he was lighter without the crippling pressures of prince hood.

All businesses had a PR front, and the royal family of Concarre was no different. The official statement it had released expressed sorrow over Dorian's decision to 'take a step back', and wished him the best in his upcoming ventures. He was no longer the Crown Prince, heir to the Concarri throne. He was now a lower-ranking duke—essentially a made-up title to help soften the blow of his monumental choice and leave the door open should he ever want to return.

A jeweller was only as profitable as his diamonds. Although he would have preferred a complete severance from his royal lineage, Dorian was willing to make this compromise. However, being called 'Your Grace' was still grating to his ears.

Halfway through the PR response he'd created with his assistant, Dorian became aware of his interviewer's slipping attention. 'I'm not boring you, am I?' he jested.

'No, Your Grace! Not at all!' The interviewer laughed. Looking straight down the rolling camera, he said, 'But it wouldn't be an award show without a jaw-dropping entrance!'

Damica wasn't supposed to be there.

She prided herself on being a rule-breaker, but feeling out of place at a red carpet for a men's achievement awards ceremony was only natural. Strutting along the stretch of scarlet fabric, she acted as if she owned the place.

The late summer night whispered against her bare knees, which were unabashedly exposed by her artfully ripped jeans. Gossipy breaths and greedy camera clicks bombarded the air. Images coasted along her eyeline like kaleidoscopic clouds. Nonetheless, her vision was narrowed down like binoculars, seeking one person in particular, and exhilaration coated her tongue.

Life after the Maldives had been constructive, healing and...*boring*. She'd done the right thing by going back home, keeping a low profile and scheduling an appointment with her therapist.

She had expected to receive a figurative pat on the back from the psychological professional. But just the reverse. The sixty-minute session had triggered a deeper dialogue about what she'd like to do now that she was no longer working in entertainment. The Maldives getaway had been a great starting point, but there was still work to be done concerning the reconstruction of her identity.

Who was Damica Foye?

Damica still didn't have an answer. She was learning to accept that finding herself was a lifelong process, and that in order to unlock new dimensions of her personality she would have to try different things.

She'd dabbled in gardening, online history classes and archery—all of which she'd sucked at. But when it came to knitting and sewing, she'd displayed some promise. Designing and making a winter hat for Jalen had been a rewarding project.

Being in a stable, loving relationship was another experience she had been willing to try. And now Damica was feeling the fear and doing it anyway. At the twelve-month mark she had got in contact with Dorian again and they'd taken up a slow correspondence. Nothing had been on the table—they were just two people emailing back and forth.

And now, knowing Dorian as well as she did, Damica was prepared to initiate what they both wanted so badly.

At last, she spotted him.

Dorian—all the way at the other end of the carpet.

Their eyes met in a sustained hold, through the haze of people darting everywhere.

Damica watched him excuse himself from the interview he was taking part in with a contrite bow of his head. Her stride quickened in conjunction with her pulse—for a good reason this time. On the Étoile Privée beach Dorian had boldly proclaimed that she and Jalen were his, but she'd shied away from being publicly associated with him. Now it was her turn to proudly—and spontaneously—assert her love for him.

Narrowly avoiding a collision with an event usher guiding a boy band through the throng, Damica limboed and shimmied her way to the midpoint of the red carpet. Dorian had slowed to a stop, tuning out the assistant who was buzzing over his shoulder.

Their nervous smiles and absorbed eyes did most of the talking as they stood together for the first time since their torturous parting in the Maldives. She soaked in the rakish spin of his dapper suit: the undone buttons, loose tie, the single earring dangling from one lobe and the chunky rings adorning his fingers. And she knew he was admiring the springy curls of her natural hair all the way down to her sneakers.

'A-are you sure this is what you want?' he checked, breaking their embargo on speech.

Tears of happiness sprang to her eyes as she gave him a small nod.

She understood now that being in control wasn't a guarantee that she would always feel confident. Nonetheless, she was here as the main character in her own destiny. Whether

her happily-ever-after with Dorian lasted for six months or six decades, she was choosing to do this with him.

They came together with a cathartic kiss. Dorian's affectionate hands cradled the back of her neck whilst their lips made love. She quivered under the thorough caress of his mouth and the lick of his tongue. Her own touch raked feverishly through his long hair, hanging on to his body for sustenance.

Every watchful eye and camera lens zoomed in on them, and a sea of flashing lights rose up...

The name Étoile Privée LA had a better ring to it, but the bedsheets were just as crisp there as in the Maldives location.

Having already abandoned her shoes at the door of the hotel suite where Dorian was staying, Damica tugged down the zipper of her jeans.

'Are you sure you're not going to get in trouble for skipping the ceremony?'

'They can send me the award by post.'

Dorian wormed the final button of his dress shirt out of its hole and flung his clothing onto the bedroom's Persian-style rug. Sitting on the edge of the awaiting California king-size bed, he snaked an arm around Damica's hips. Once she was standing between his open knees, he hooked his thumbs around both Damica's denim waistline and the lace of her underwear, then pushed the garments down.

Whilst undressing her, Dorian joked, 'Since when did you care about being well behaved?'

'Since being a fully-fledged adult with hobbies now, remember?'

Damica held on to his shoulders for balance as she stepped out of the jeans and kicked away the pesky material restraining her ankles. Dorian lifted the hem of her T-shirt and kissed his way up her abdomen in a line to her navel. Taking off her T-shirt and bralette, Damica giggled at his impatience.

Dorian put his mouth on pause to look up adoringly at her nakedness. 'Your fashion ventures? Yes… I think this is your best design so far, actually.'

She struck a playful pose. 'The Birthday Suit?'

'Yes…' Dorian gazed at her breasts, as if reliving their sensual massage session in the Maldives.

Damica bent down to trap him in another searing embrace.

Regaining awareness, and reciprocating the passion of her lips, Dorian hauled her onto the bed. Damica squeaked, bouncing into the mattress upon impact. They laughed together as he crawled on top of her and accepted the invitation between her spread thighs.

History was repeating itself, but Dorian was more confident this time around and there was no Ravi to hide from.

With his mouth and his tongue he relayed his devotion, leaving no area of Damica's body unappreciated. Bothered by his own state of half-dress, he stopped briefly to get rid of his dress trousers and boxers.

He kissed the crook of her neck. Around her navel. The backs of her knees. Up the span of her trembling thighs in pursuit of her core.

Every moan from her lips was well earned, and each stroke brought them closer together in ecstasy. The most intimate parts of her were on display, in a way that was new and invigorating for them both, but Dorian sank into the finer details and messy intensities. He held her open and applied an enticing pressure with his fingers until she shattered.

Afterwards, Damica lay in his arms, catching her breath whilst tracing patterns into his skin. She peered around the bedroom, through the extravagant drapes curtaining the large bed. 'I could get used to this…'

Dorian cringed at the sight of clothes and jewellery littering the floor like puddles. 'If I'd known you were coming tonight I would have prepared something special.' Keeping an arm curled firmly around her, he reached blindly for the phone on the bedside table. 'I'll order a room service meal for us. What are you in the mood for?'

Damica fiddled idly with a strand of his chest hair and smiled softly at the embarrassment tinging his cheeks. 'I like you like this.'

Dorian's reach fell dramatically short of the telephone. 'Mmm?'

'More relaxed. Ordinary. Normal.'

'I don't think we'll ever be normal, no matter how hard we try,' he admitted.

They shared a knowing gaze, ready for the consequences that waited for them in the outside world following their red carpet kiss.

A retired popstar and an ex-prince would always attract coverage—it was the natural way of things. The threat to her privacy would exist with or without Dorian, so she might as well tolerate the plague of locusts *with* him.

'We're as close as we can get, which is still a win.'

Damica remained optimistic, challenging her own negative thoughts and accepting that her lifelong struggles would not disappear overnight.

'I know that we agreed to take our time with things, but I need you to know that I don't want to do *this* with anyone else. I get that we don't have all the answers right now...about how to handle the headlines tomorrow or the best way for us to have kids. But I want us to figure it out together. Day by day, or much later down the line. I love you, Dorian.'

Dorian gave up his fumbling for the phone, his eyes alight with affection. 'The food can wait.'

'I told you I love you and *that's* what you have to say?'

'We've exchanged over twenty years' worth of words...'

Dorian rolled their bodies over, so that their legs were intertwined. Damica lay below him, gasping at the attack of kisses launched at her face.

Pecks rained down on her cheeks. He singled out her forehead next. 'Saying "I love you" back isn't enough…' Then her mouth. 'I have to show you.'

And he did.

* * * * *

MILLS & BOON®

Coming next month

COPENHAGEN ESCAPE WITH THE BILLIONAIRE
Sophie Pembroke

Jesper was a stronger man than she suspected he'd ever give himself credit for. And it stirred up all sorts of feelings inside her chest that she really wasn't ready for.

She swallowed and looked away. 'So, tomorrow's a new dawn - what will that bring? What have you got planned for us next? Another message I assume?'

'Of course,' he replied. 'But I can't tell you what just yet.'

She jerked her head up to meet his gaze, only to discover that he was closer than ever. So close that, if she wanted, she could bring her lips to his without only the slightest movement.

If she wanted to.

Oh God, she wanted to.

Her throat dry, she tried to swallow before she spoke. 'You can't tell me?'

He shook his head, bringing his face ever closer to hers, the last of the sunlight shimmering off the silver in his beard. 'But I promise you it's magical.'

Magical.

That kiss at New Year had been magical - unexpected, with literal fireworks going off in the sky behind them. A gentle, but all-encompassing kiss that had suddenly opened up a world or a future she hadn't even contemplated before. That kiss had been her sunken church finding a new lease of life, her oceans meeting and crashing, her sunset before the sunrise.

And she could have it again, if she just leant in one iota.

She couldn't breathe with wanting it.

Continue reading

COPENHAGEN ESCAPE WITH THE BILLIONAIRE
Sophie Pembroke

Available next month
millsandboon.co.uk

COMING SOON!

We really hope you enjoyed reading this book.
If you're looking for more romance
be sure to head to the shops when
new books are available on

Thursday 16th January

To see which titles are coming soon, please visit

millsandboon.co.uk/nextmonth

MILLS & BOON

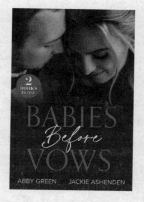
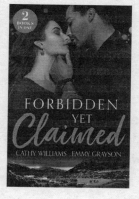

afterglow BOOKS

Afterglow Books is a trend-led, trope-filled list of books with diverse, authentic and relatable characters, a wide array of voices and representations, plus real world trials and tribulations. Featuring all the tropes you could possibly want (think small-town settings, fake relationships, grumpy vs sunshine, enemies to lovers) and all with a generous dose of spice in every story.

♪ @millsandboonuk
◎ @millsandboonuk
afterglowbooks.co.uk
#AfterglowBooks

For all the latest book news, exclusive content and giveaways scan the QR code below to sign up to the Afterglow newsletter:

SCAN ME

afterglow BOOKS

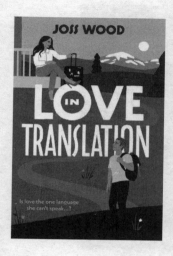

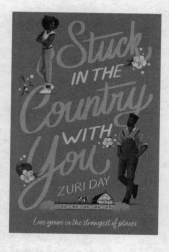

🌓 Opposites attract

💻 Workplace romance

📡 Forced proximity

📡 Forced proximity

🏠 Small-town romance

🖤 Second chance

OUT NOW

Two stories published every month. Discover more at:
Afterglowbooks.co.uk

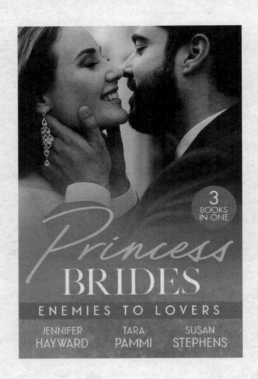

LET'S TALK
Romance

For exclusive extracts, competitions and special offers, find us online:

- **f** MillsandBoon
- **X** @MillsandBoon
- **⌾** @MillsandBoonUK
- **♪** @MillsandBoonUK

Get in touch on 01413 063 232